LO

VOLUME 2: BEFORE THE DAWN BURNS US

IMAGE COMICS, INC.

Robert Kirkman - Chief Operating Officer
Erik Larsen - Chief Financial Officer
Todd McFarlane - President
Marc Silvestri - Chief Executive Officer
Jim Valentino - Vice-President

Eric Stephenson - Publisher
Corey Murphy - Director of Sales
Jeff Boison - Director of Publishing
Planning & Book Trade Sales
Jeremy Sullivan - Director of Digital Sales
Kat Salazar - Director of PR & Marketing
Emily Miller - Director of Operations

Branwyn Bigglestone - Senior Accounts Manager
Sarah Mello - Accounts Manager
Drew Gill - Art Director
Jonathan Chan - Production Manager
Meredith Wallace - Print Manager
Briah Skelly - Publicity Assistant
Randy Okamura - Marketing Production Designer
David Brothers - Branding Manager
Ally Power - Content Manager
Addison Duke - Production Artist
Vincent Kukua - Production Artist
Sasha Head - Production Artist
Tricia Ramos - Production Artist
Jeff Stang - Direct Market Sales Representative
Emilio Bautista - Digital Sales Associate
Chloe Ramos-Peterson - Administrative Assistant

IMAGECOMICS.COM

JEFF POWELL
Book Design

ISBN 978-1-63215-469-9

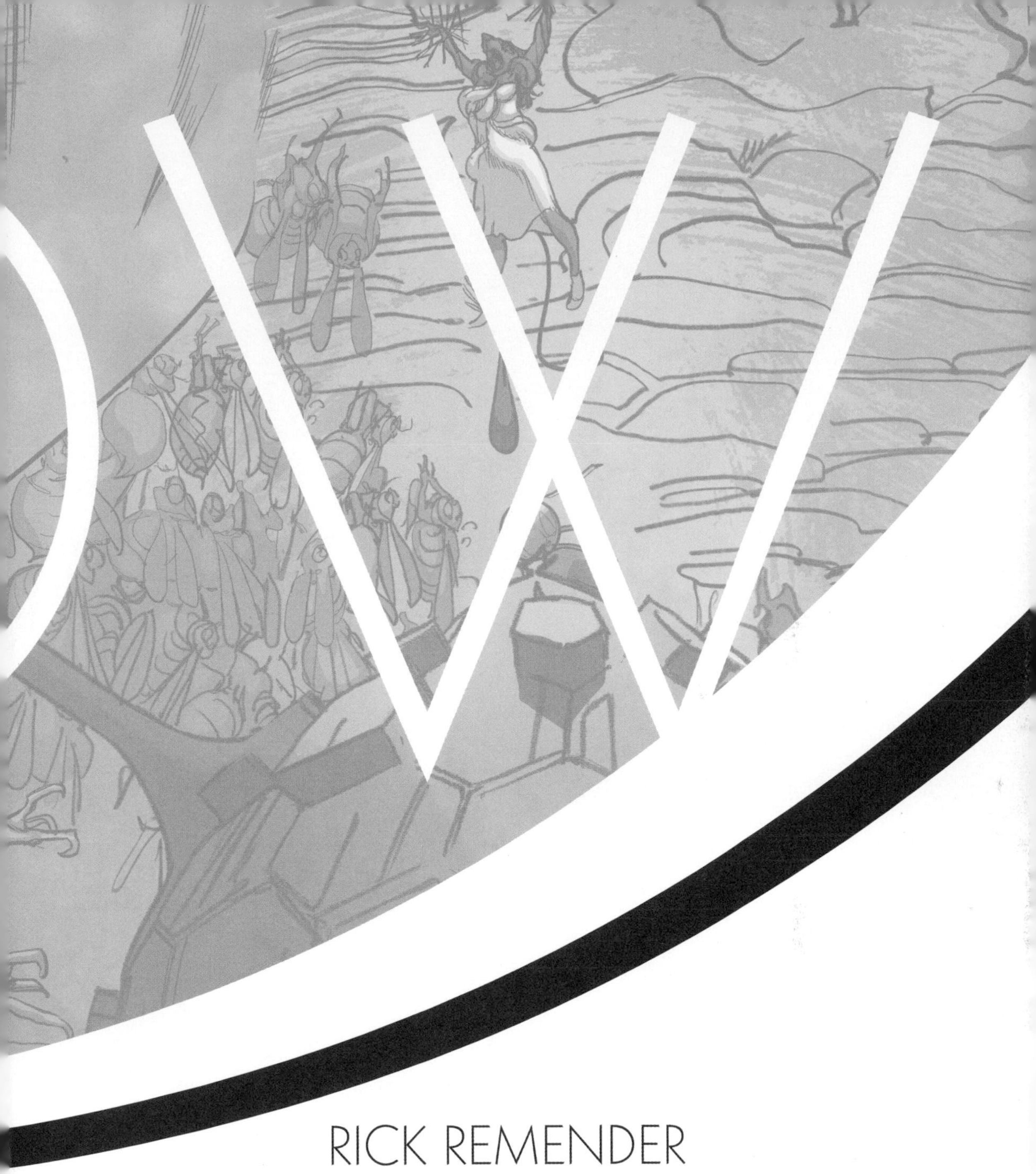

RICK REMENDER
writer

GREG TOCCHINI
artist, colors (#7), cover art

DAVE McCAIG
colors (#8-10)

RUS WOOTON
letterer

SEBASTIAN GIRNER
editor

Created by Rick Remender & Greg Tocchini

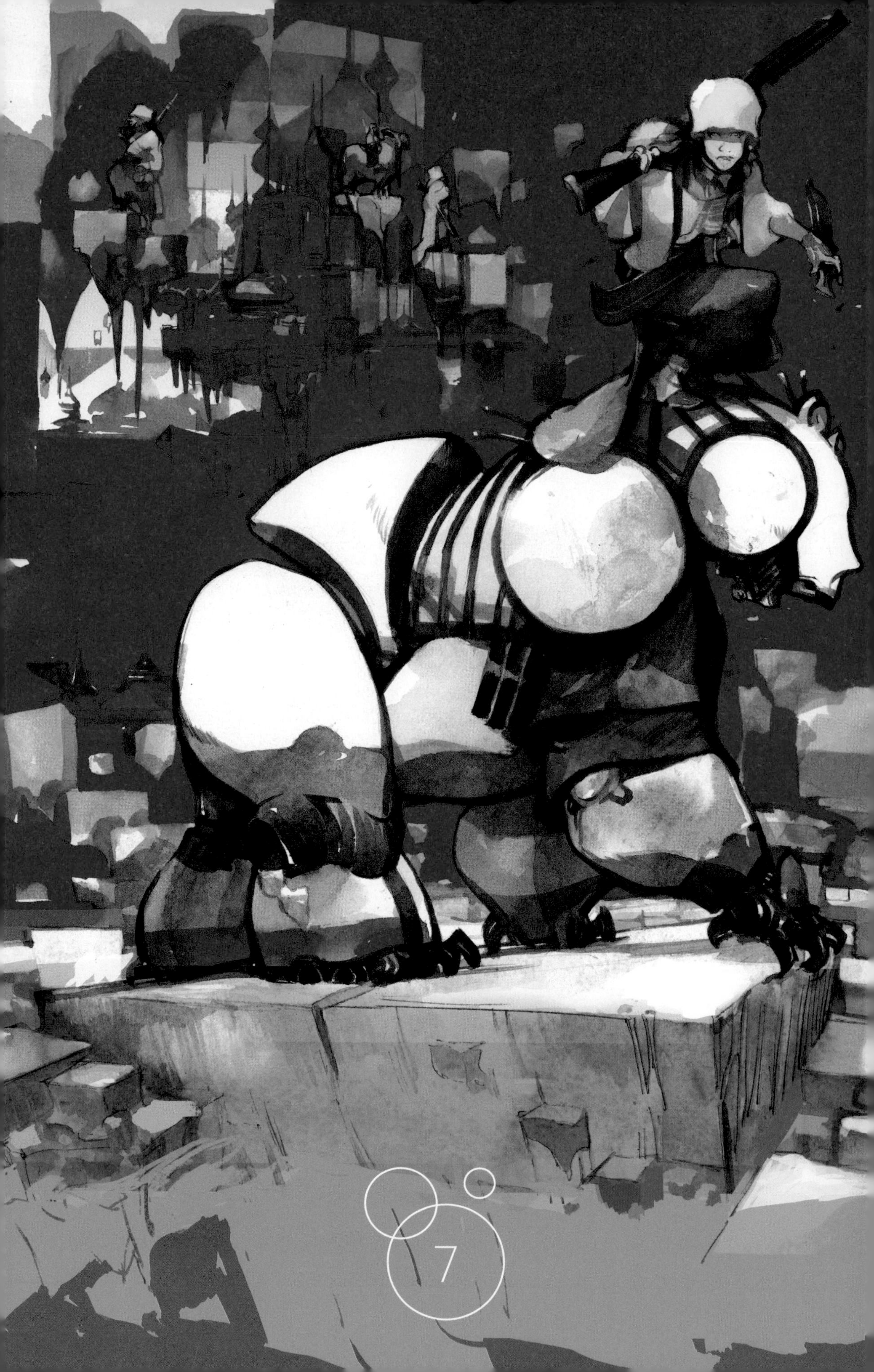

7

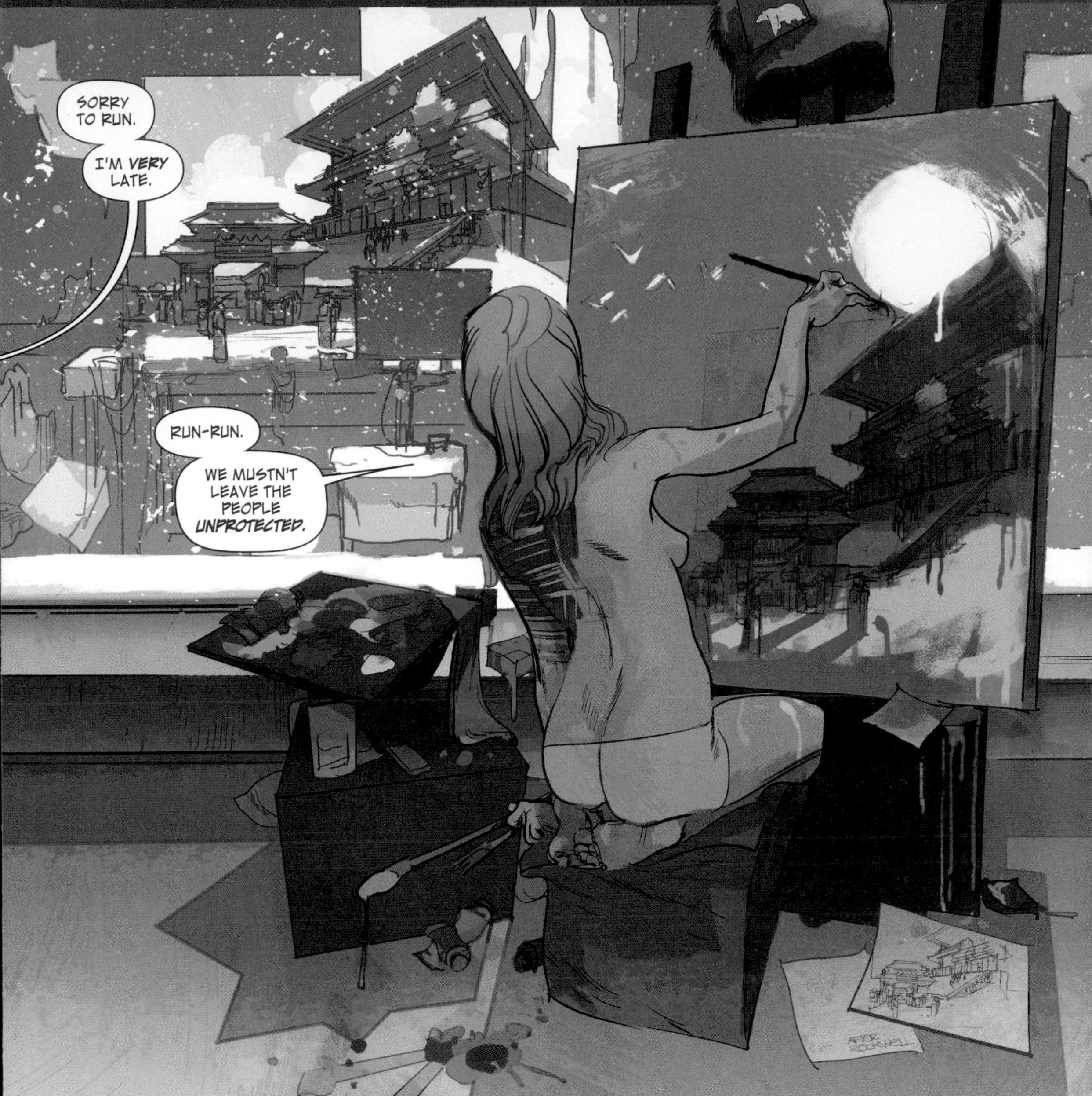
SORRY TO RUN.
I'M VERY LATE.
RUN-RUN.
WE MUSTN'T LEAVE THE PEOPLE UNPROTECTED.

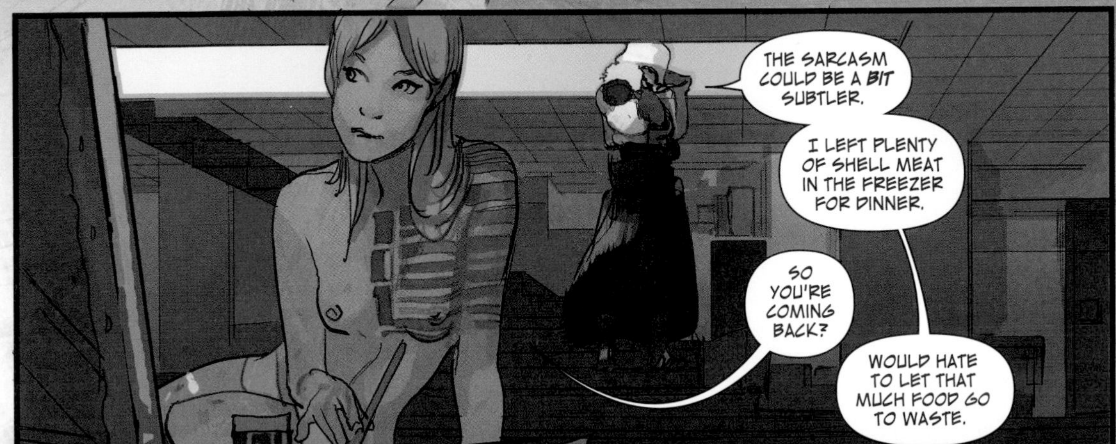
THE SARCASM COULD BE A BIT SUBTLER.
I LEFT PLENTY OF SHELL MEAT IN THE FREEZER FOR DINNER.
SO YOU'RE COMING BACK?
WOULD HATE TO LET THAT MUCH FOOD GO TO WASTE.

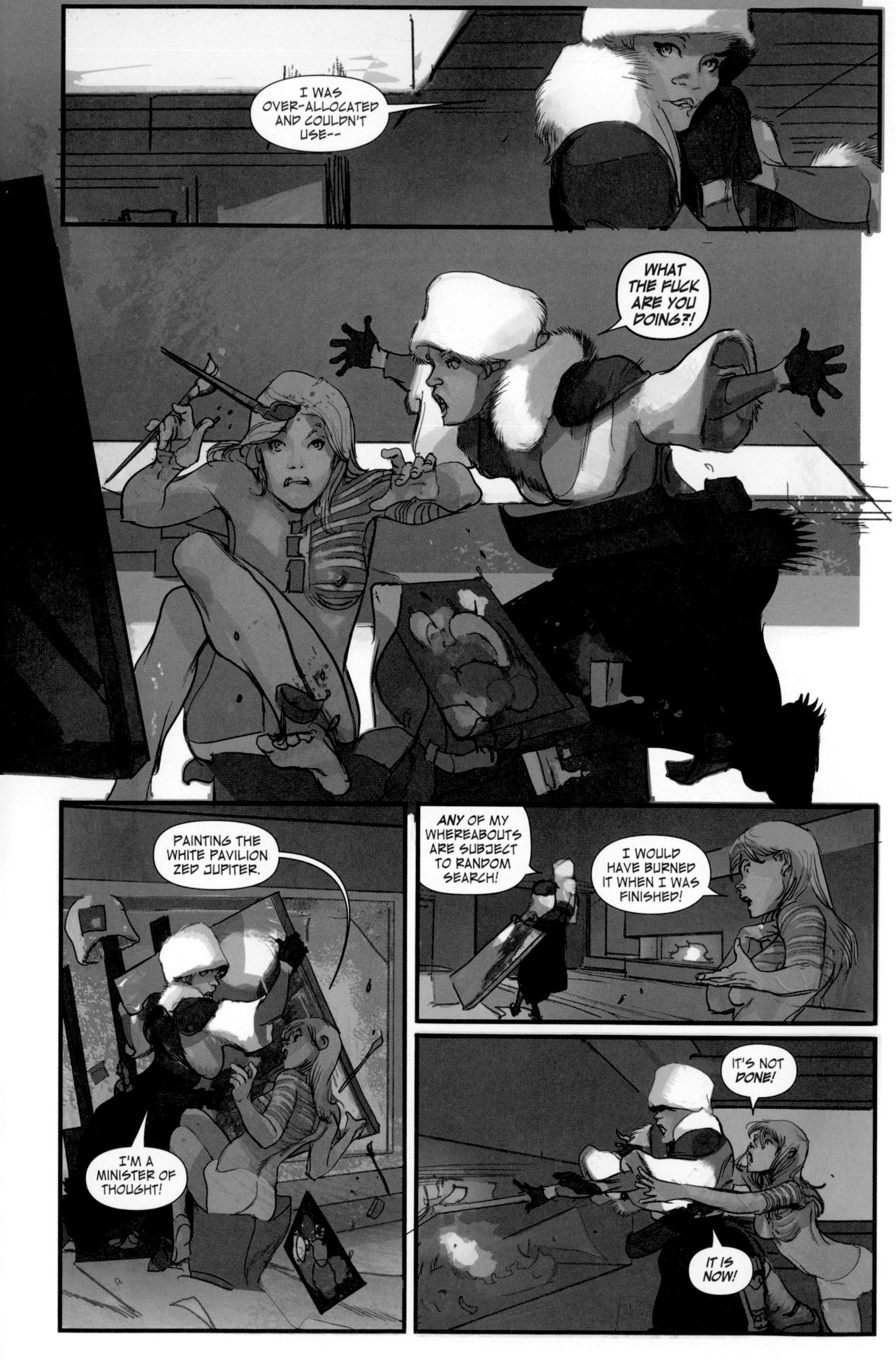
I WAS OVER-ALLOCATED AND COULDN'T USE--
WHAT THE FUCK ARE YOU DOING?!
PAINTING THE WHITE PAVILION ZED JUPITER.
I'M A MINISTER OF THOUGHT!
ANY OF MY WHEREABOUTS ARE SUBJECT TO RANDOM SEARCH!
I WOULD HAVE BURNED IT WHEN I WAS FINISHED!
IT'S NOT DONE!
IT IS NOW!

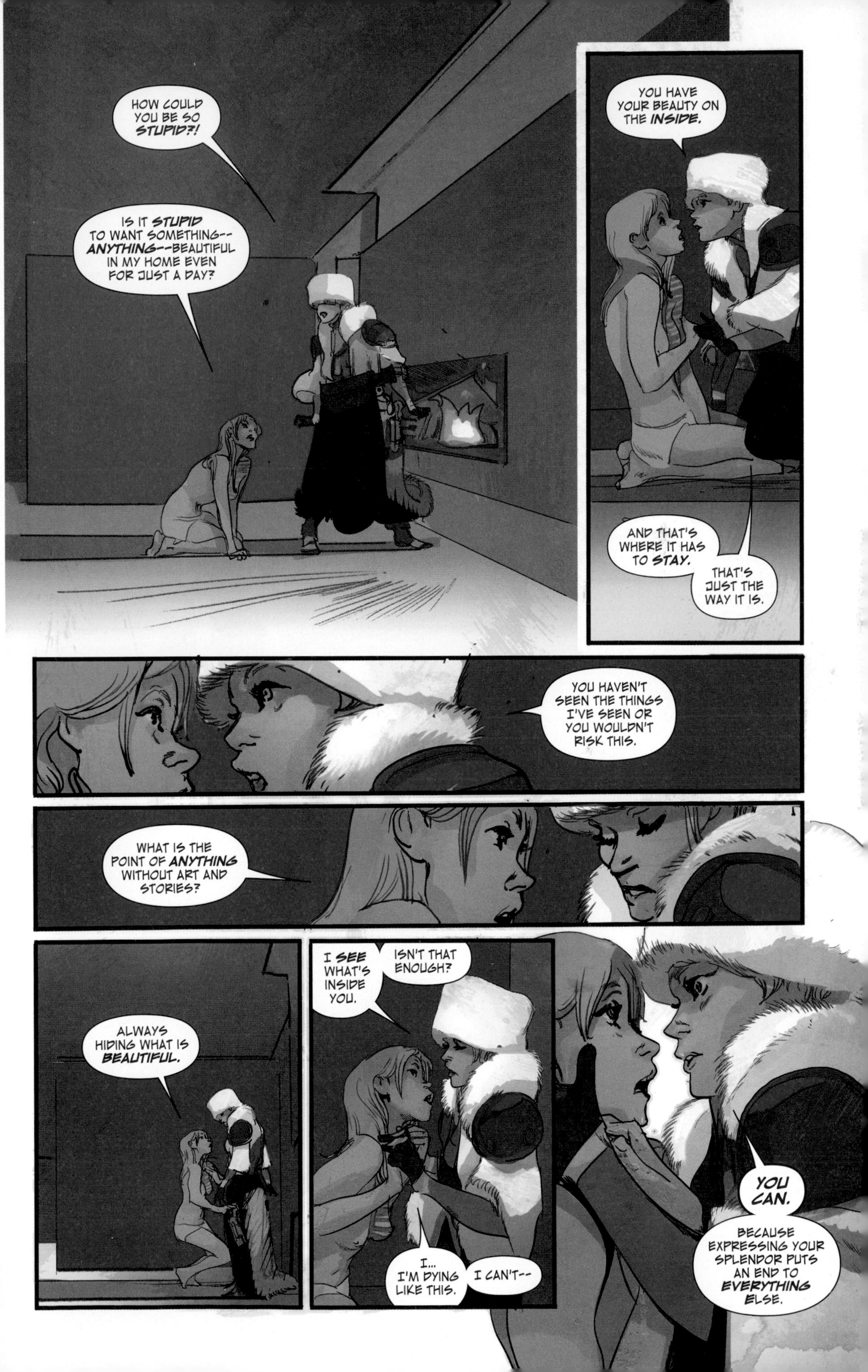
HOW COULD YOU BE SO STUPID?!
IS IT STUPID TO WANT SOMETHING-- ANYTHING--BEAUTIFUL IN MY HOME EVEN FOR JUST A DAY?
YOU HAVE YOUR BEAUTY ON THE INSIDE.
AND THAT'S WHERE IT HAS TO STAY.
THAT'S JUST THE WAY IT IS.
YOU HAVEN'T SEEN THE THINGS I'VE SEEN OR YOU WOULDN'T RISK THIS.
WHAT IS THE POINT OF ANYTHING WITHOUT ART AND STORIES?
ALWAYS HIDING WHAT IS BEAUTIFUL.
I SEE WHAT'S INSIDE YOU.
ISN'T THAT ENOUGH?
I... I'M DYING LIKE THIS.
I CAN'T--
YOU CAN.
BECAUSE EXPRESSING YOUR SPLENDOR PUTS AN END TO EVERYTHING ELSE.

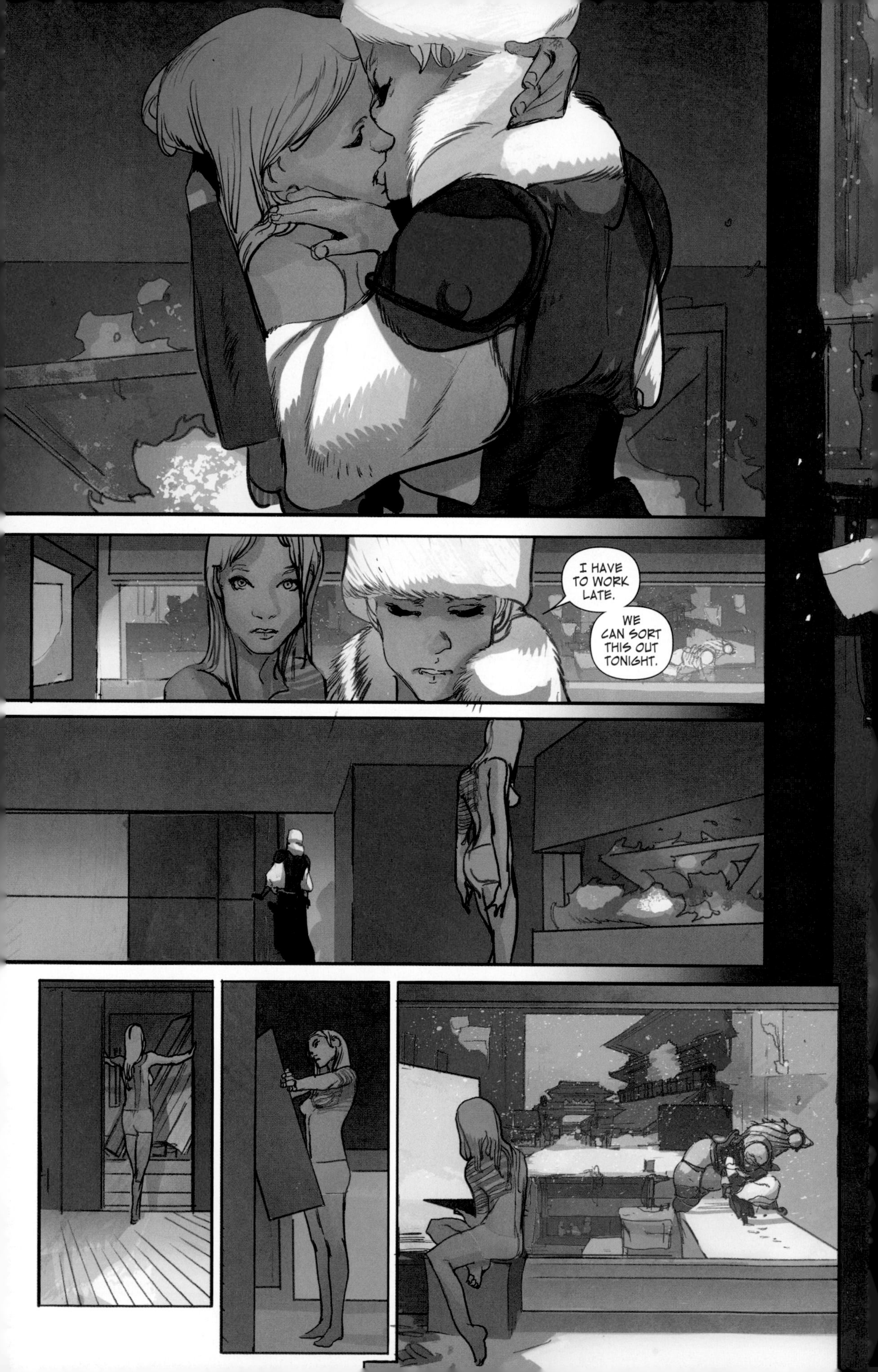
I HAVE TO WORK LATE.
WE CAN SORT THIS OUT TONIGHT.

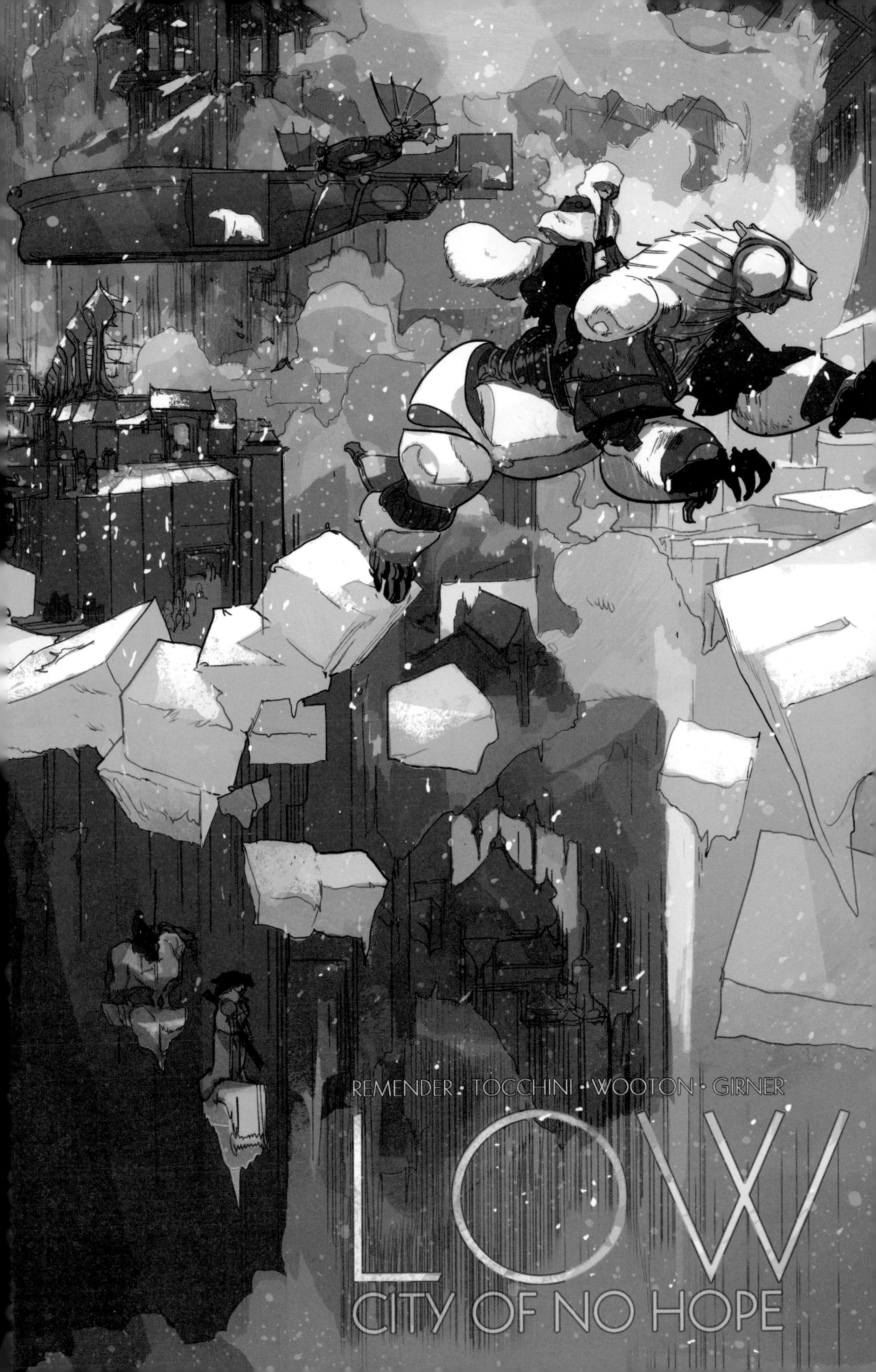
REMENDER · TOCCHINI · WOOTON · GIRNER
LOW
CITY OF NO HOPE

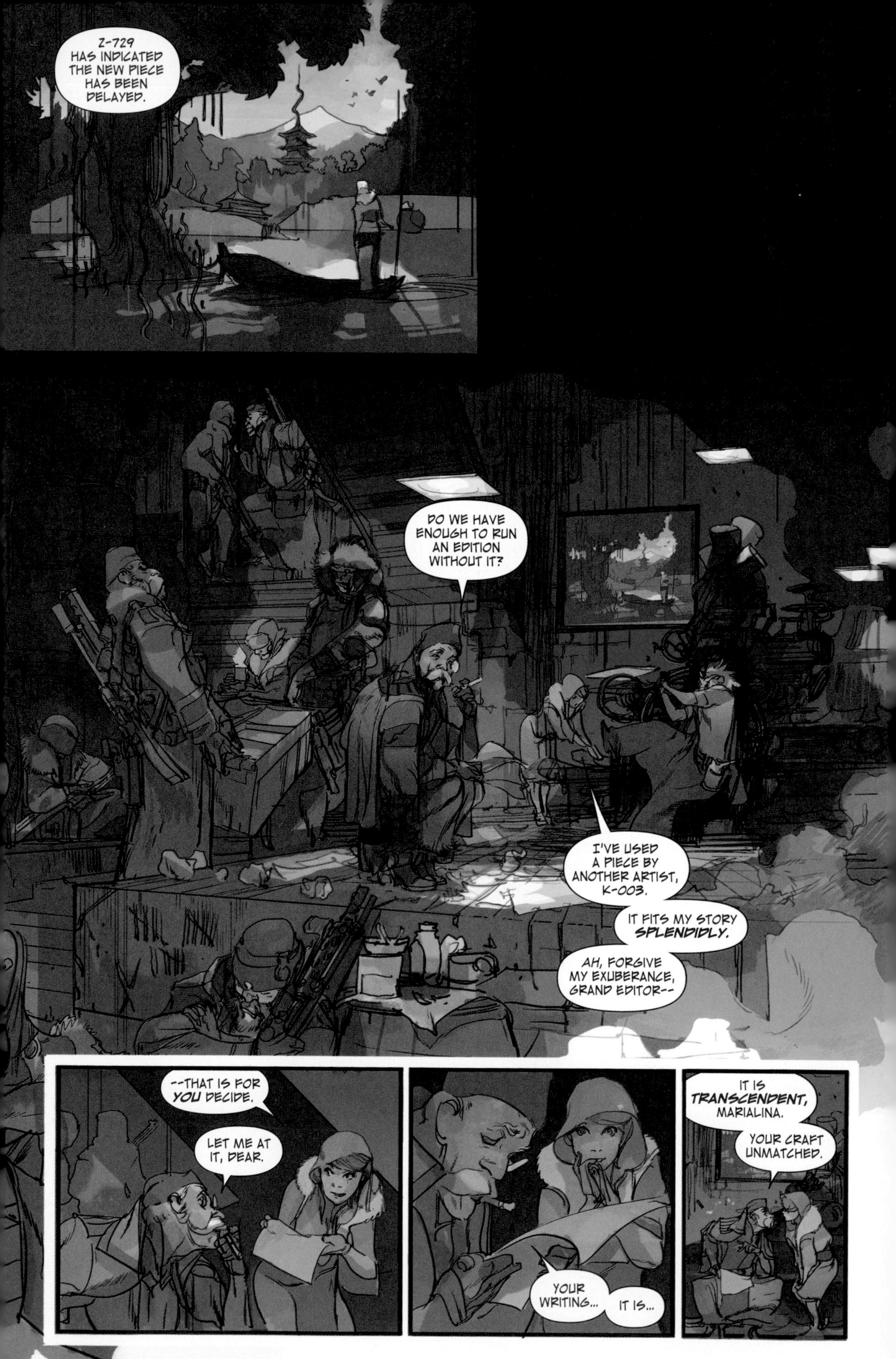
Z-729 HAS INDICATED THE NEW PIECE HAS BEEN DELAYED.
DO WE HAVE ENOUGH TO RUN AN EDITION WITHOUT IT?
I'VE USED A PIECE BY ANOTHER ARTIST, K-003.
IT FITS MY STORY SPLENDIDLY.
AH, FORGIVE MY EXUBERANCE, GRAND EDITOR--
--THAT IS FOR YOU DECIDE.
LET ME AT IT, DEAR.
YOUR WRITING...
IT IS...
IT IS TRANSCENDENT, MARIALINA.
YOUR CRAFT UNMATCHED.

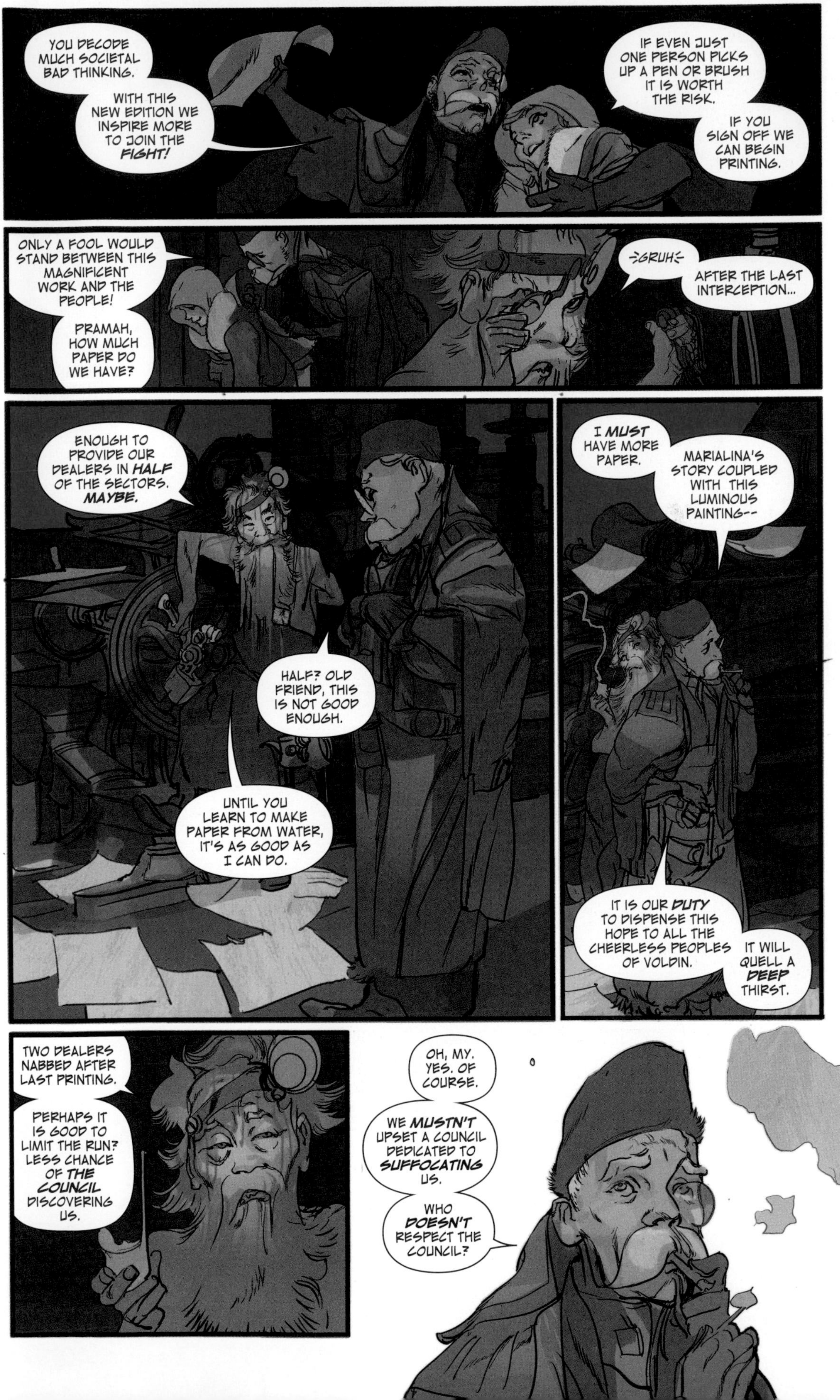
YOU DECODE MUCH SOCIETAL BAD THINKING.
WITH THIS NEW EDITION WE INSPIRE MORE TO JOIN THE FIGHT!
IF EVEN JUST ONE PERSON PICKS UP A PEN OR BRUSH IT IS WORTH THE RISK.
IF YOU SIGN OFF WE CAN BEGIN PRINTING.
ONLY A FOOL WOULD STAND BETWEEN THIS MAGNIFICENT WORK AND THE PEOPLE!
PRAMAH, HOW MUCH PAPER DO WE HAVE?
GRUH
AFTER THE LAST INTERCEPTION...
ENOUGH TO PROVIDE OUR DEALERS IN HALF OF THE SECTORS. MAYBE.
HALF? OLD FRIEND, THIS IS NOT GOOD ENOUGH.
UNTIL YOU LEARN TO MAKE PAPER FROM WATER, IT'S AS GOOD AS I CAN DO.
I MUST HAVE MORE PAPER.
MARIALINA'S STORY COUPLED WITH THIS LUMINOUS PAINTING--
IT IS OUR DUTY TO DISPENSE THIS HOPE TO ALL THE CHEERLESS PEOPLES OF VOLDIN.
IT WILL QUELL A DEEP THIRST.
TWO DEALERS NABBED AFTER LAST PRINTING.
PERHAPS IT IS GOOD TO LIMIT THE RUN? LESS CHANCE OF THE COUNCIL DISCOVERING US.
OH, MY. YES. OF COURSE.
WE MUSTN'T UPSET A COUNCIL DEDICATED TO SUFFOCATING US.
WHO DOESN'T RESPECT THE COUNCIL?

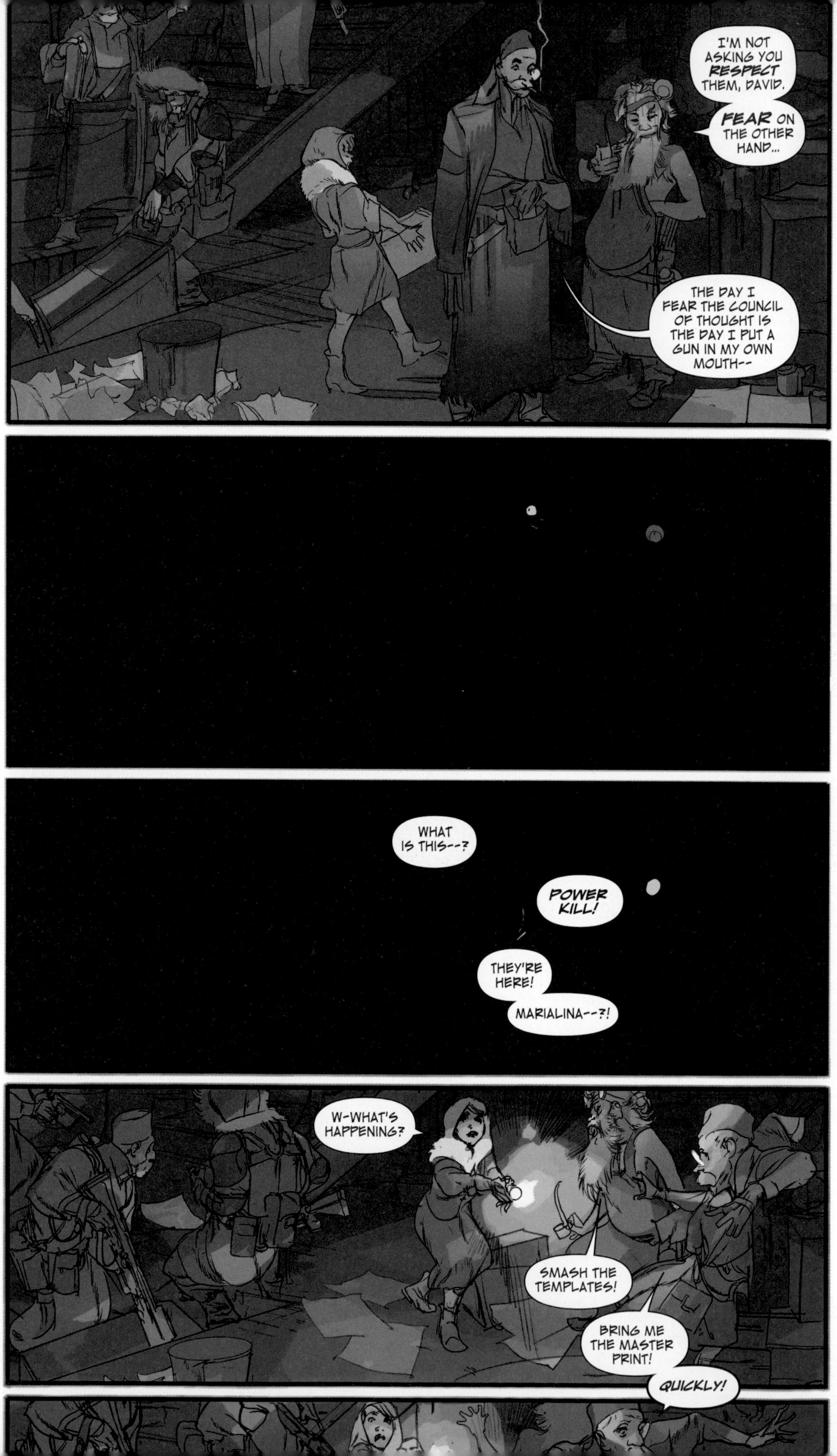

I'M NOT ASKING YOU RESPECT THEM, DAVID.
FEAR ON THE OTHER HAND...
THE DAY I FEAR THE COUNCIL OF THOUGHT IS THE DAY I PUT A GUN IN MY OWN MOUTH--
WHAT IS THIS--?
POWER KILL!
THEY'RE HERE!
MARIALINA--?!
W-WHAT'S HAPPENING?
SMASH THE TEMPLATES!
BRING ME THE MASTER PRINT!
QUICKLY!

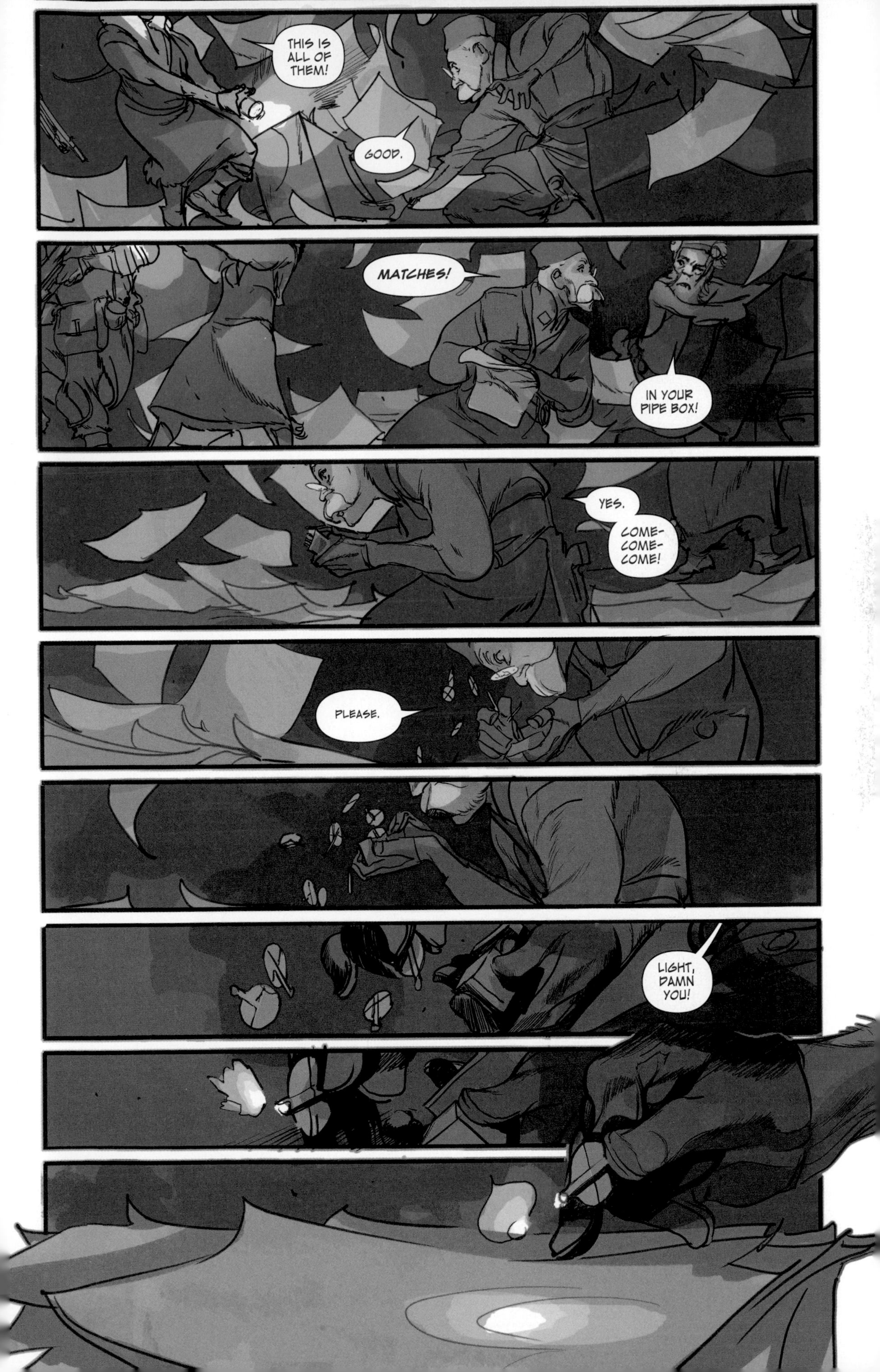
THIS IS ALL OF THEM!
GOOD.
MATCHES!
IN YOUR PIPE BOX!
YES.
COME-COME-COME!
PLEASE.
LIGHT, DAMN YOU!

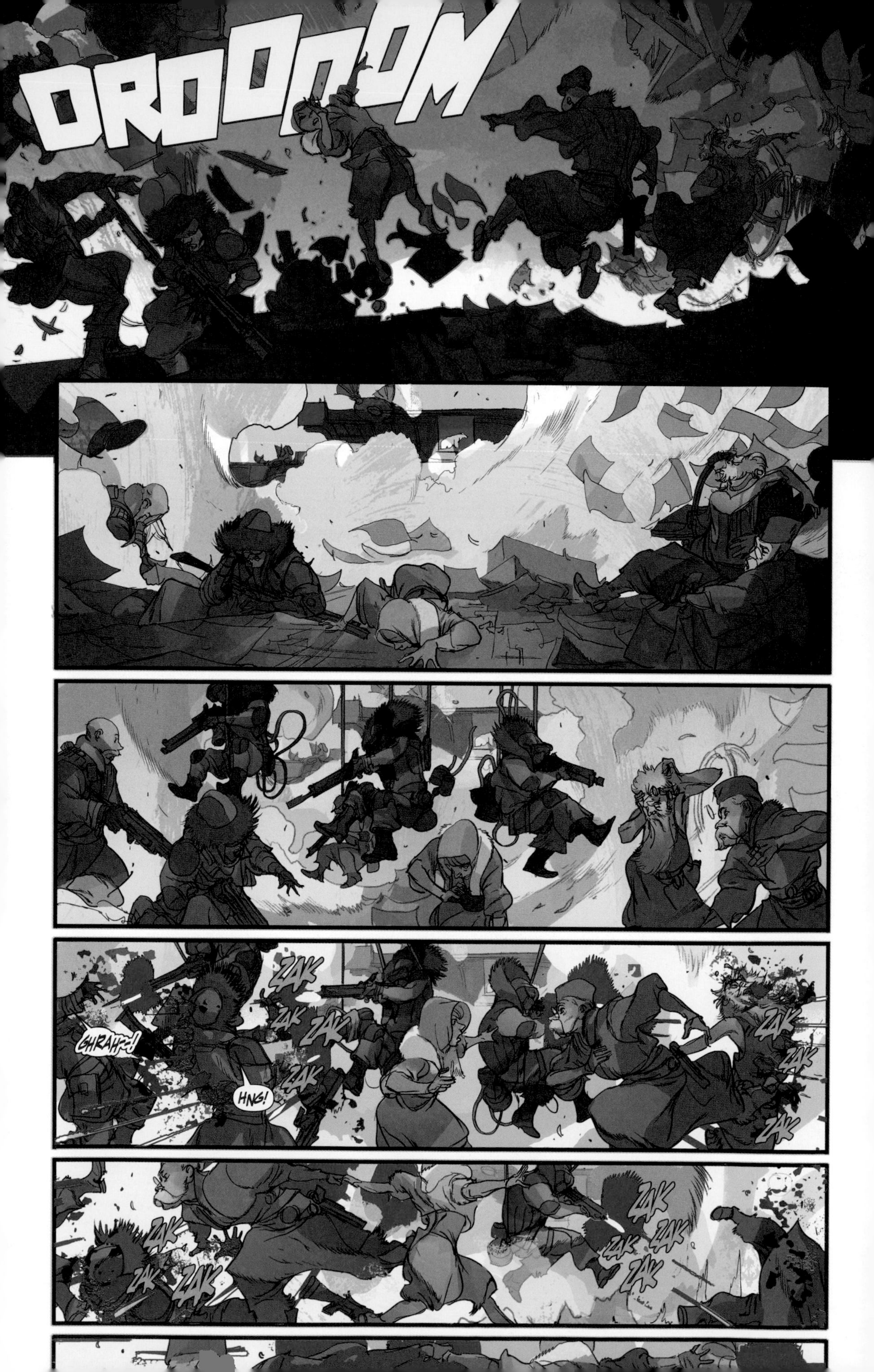
DROOOOOM
ZAK
ZAK
ZAK
GHRAHH!
ZAK
HNG!
ZAK
ZAK
ZAK
ZAK
ZAK
ZAK
ZAK
ZAK
ZAK
ZAK
ZAK

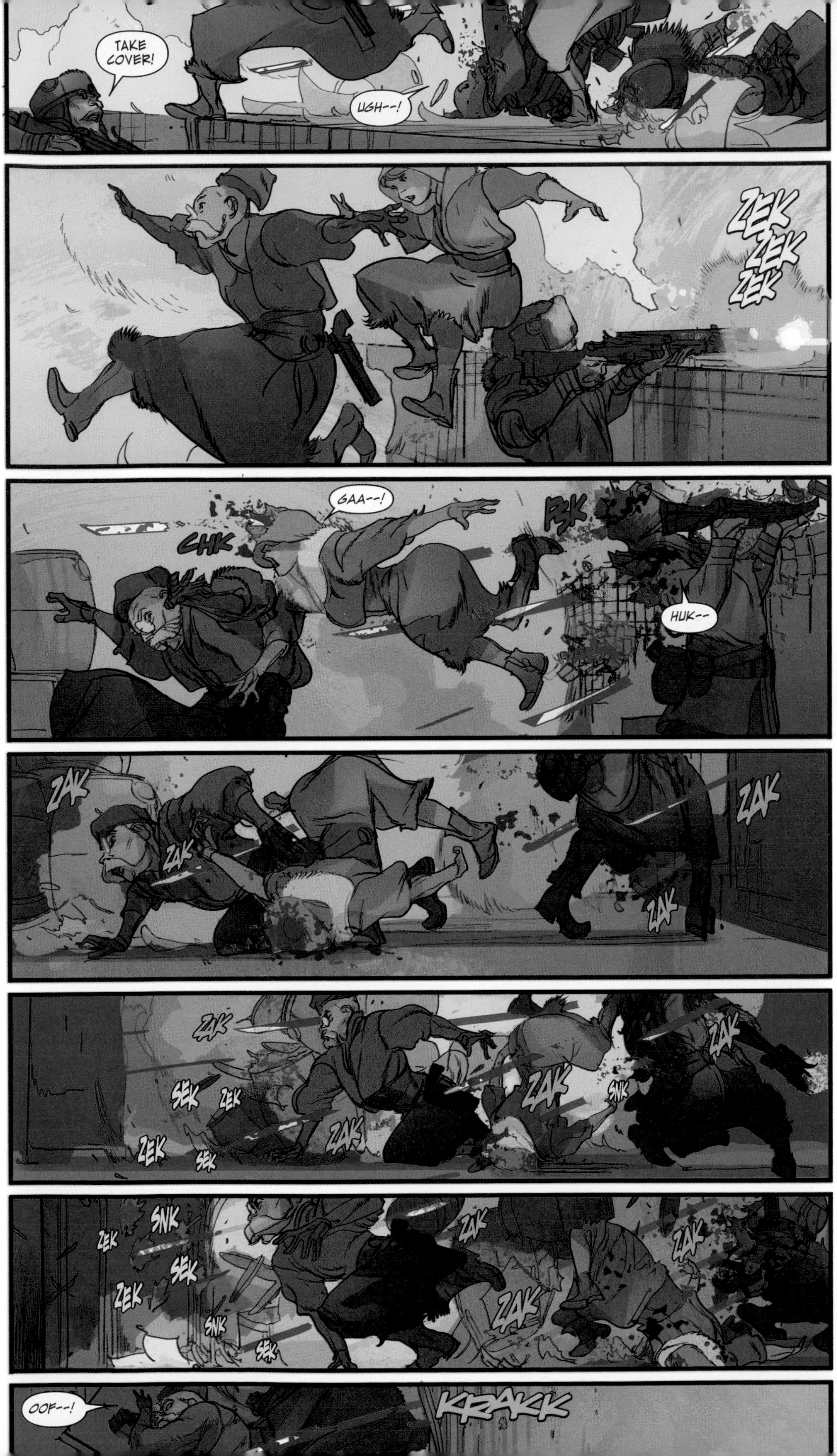
TAKE COVER!
UGH--!
ZEK
ZEK
ZEK
GAA--!
CHK
PSK
HUK--
ZAK
ZAK
ZAK
ZAK
ZAK
SEK
ZEK
ZEK
SEK
ZAK
ZAK
SNK
ZAK
ZEK
SNK
ZEK
SEK
SNK
SEK
ZAK
ZAK
ZAK
OOF--!
KRAKK

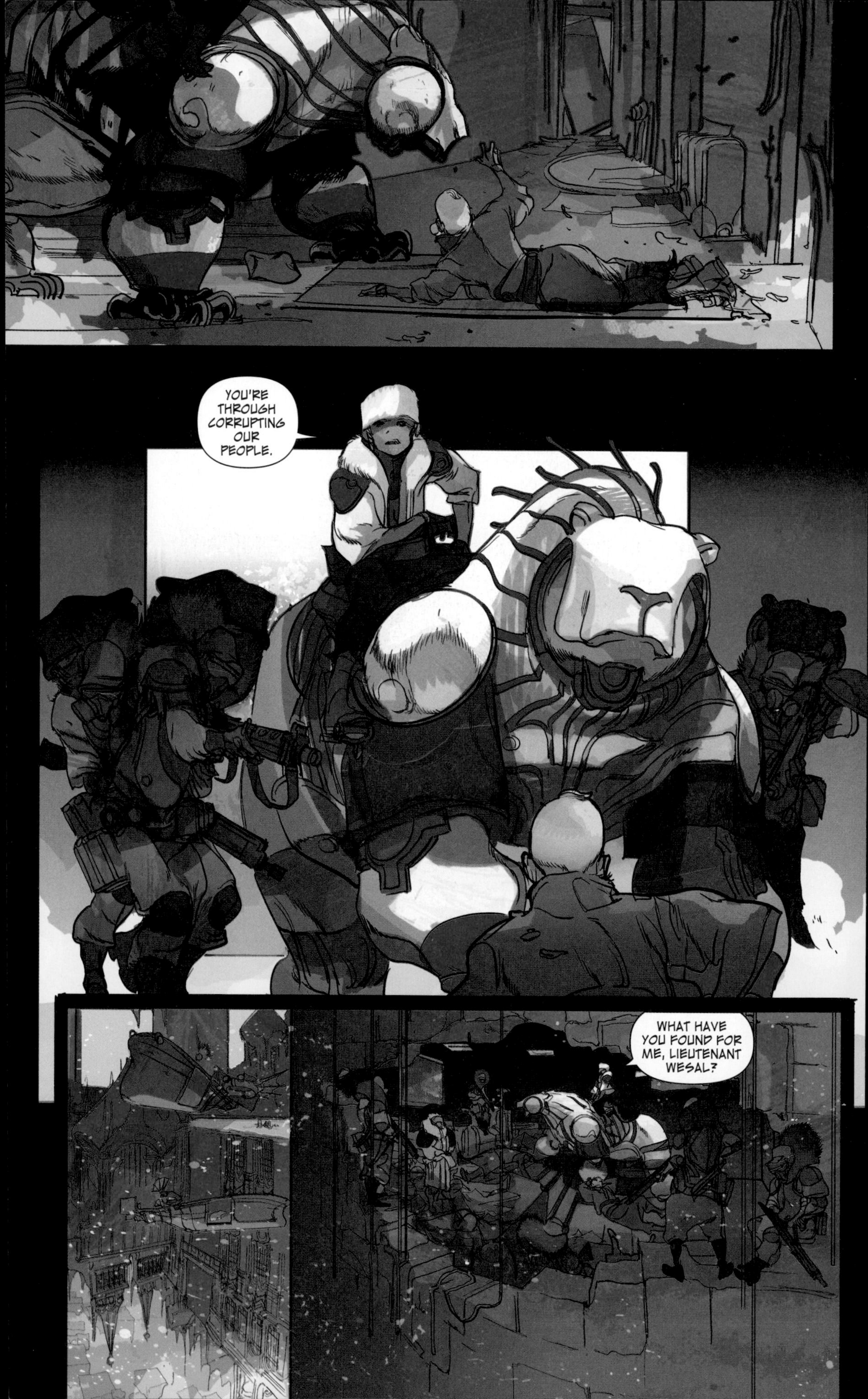
YOU'RE THROUGH CORRUPTING OUR PEOPLE.
WHAT HAVE YOU FOUND FOR ME, LIEUTENANT WESAL?

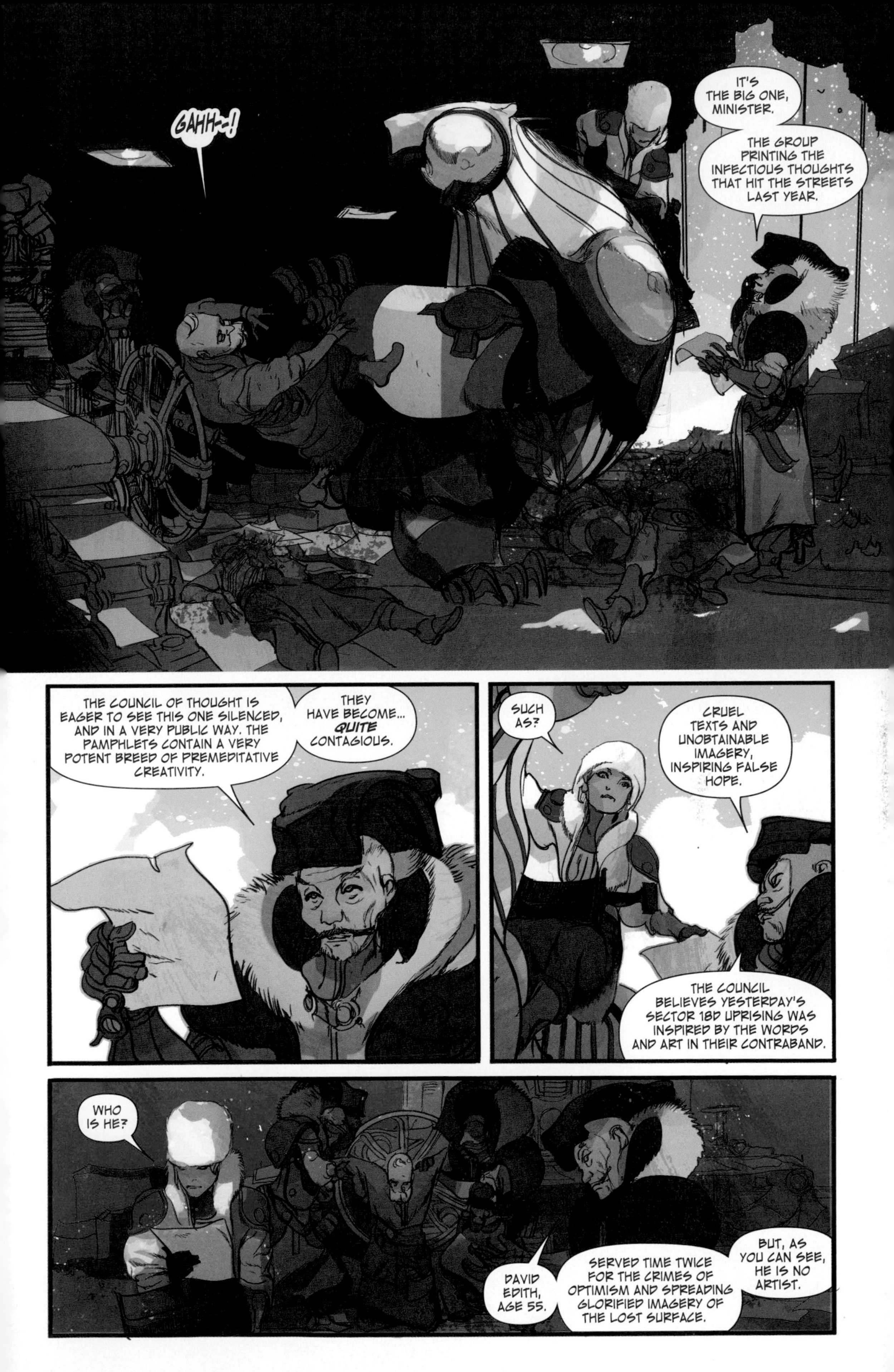
GAHH--!
IT'S THE BIG ONE, MINISTER.
THE GROUP PRINTING THE INFECTIOUS THOUGHTS THAT HIT THE STREETS LAST YEAR.
THE COUNCIL OF THOUGHT IS EAGER TO SEE THIS ONE SILENCED, AND IN A VERY PUBLIC WAY. THE PAMPHLETS CONTAIN A VERY POTENT BREED OF PREMEDITATIVE CREATIVITY.
THEY HAVE BECOME... QUITE CONTAGIOUS.
SUCH AS?
CRUEL TEXTS AND UNOBTAINABLE IMAGERY, INSPIRING FALSE HOPE.
THE COUNCIL BELIEVES YESTERDAY'S SECTOR 18D UPRISING WAS INSPIRED BY THE WORDS AND ART IN THEIR CONTRABAND.
WHO IS HE?
DAVID EDITH, AGE 55.
SERVED TIME TWICE FOR THE CRIMES OF OPTIMISM AND SPREADING GLORIFIED IMAGERY OF THE LOST SURFACE.
BUT, AS YOU CAN SEE, HE IS NO ARTIST.

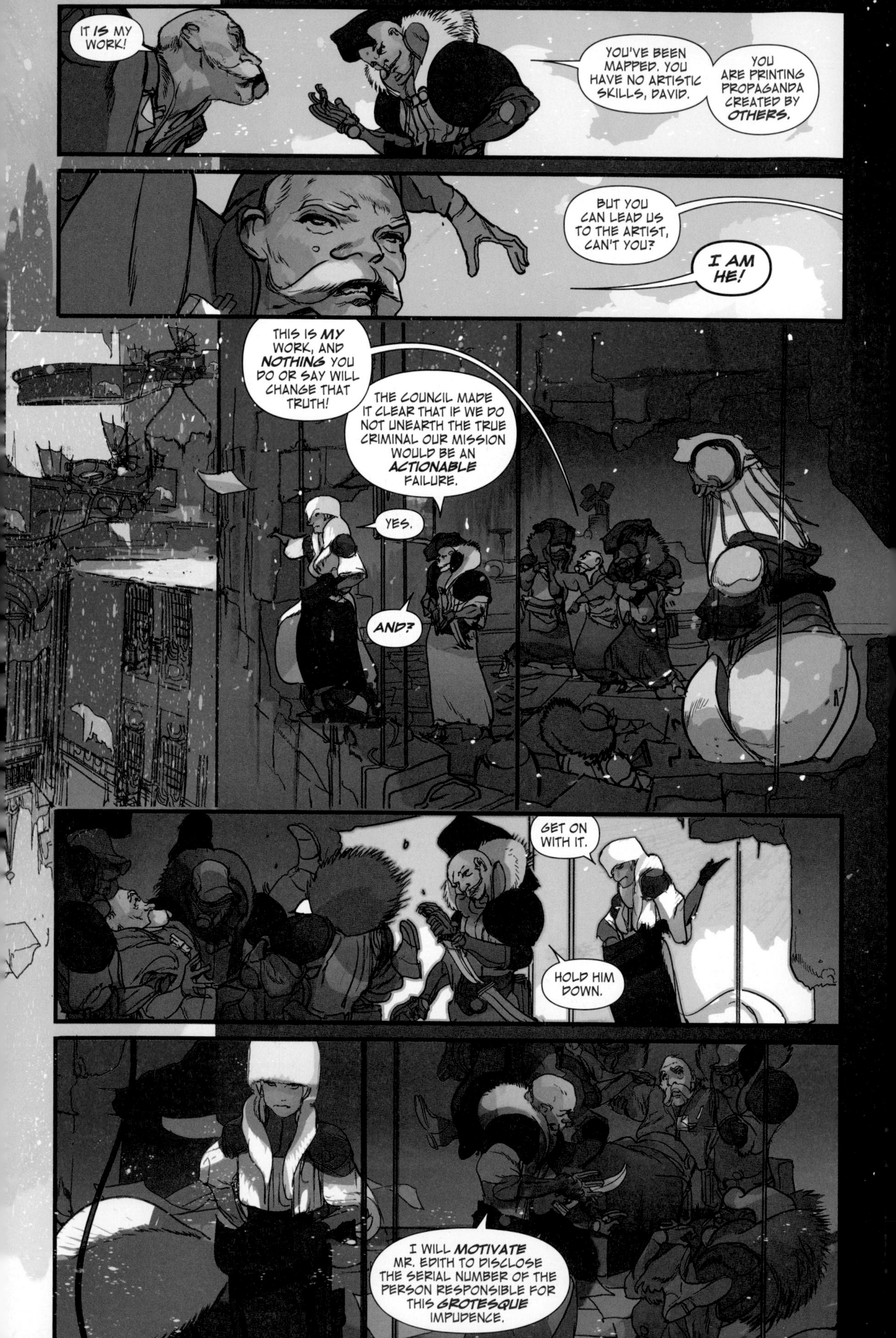
IT IS MY WORK!
YOU'VE BEEN MAPPED. YOU HAVE NO ARTISTIC SKILLS, DAVID.
YOU ARE PRINTING PROPAGANDA CREATED BY OTHERS.
BUT YOU CAN LEAD US TO THE ARTIST, CAN'T YOU?
I AM HE!
THIS IS MY WORK, AND NOTHING YOU DO OR SAY WILL CHANGE THAT TRUTH!
THE COUNCIL MADE IT CLEAR THAT IF WE DO NOT UNEARTH THE TRUE CRIMINAL OUR MISSION WOULD BE AN ACTIONABLE FAILURE.
YES.
AND?
GET ON WITH IT.
HOLD HIM DOWN.
I WILL MOTIVATE MR. EDITH TO DISCLOSE THE SERIAL NUMBER OF THE PERSON RESPONSIBLE FOR THIS GROTESQUE IMPUDENCE.

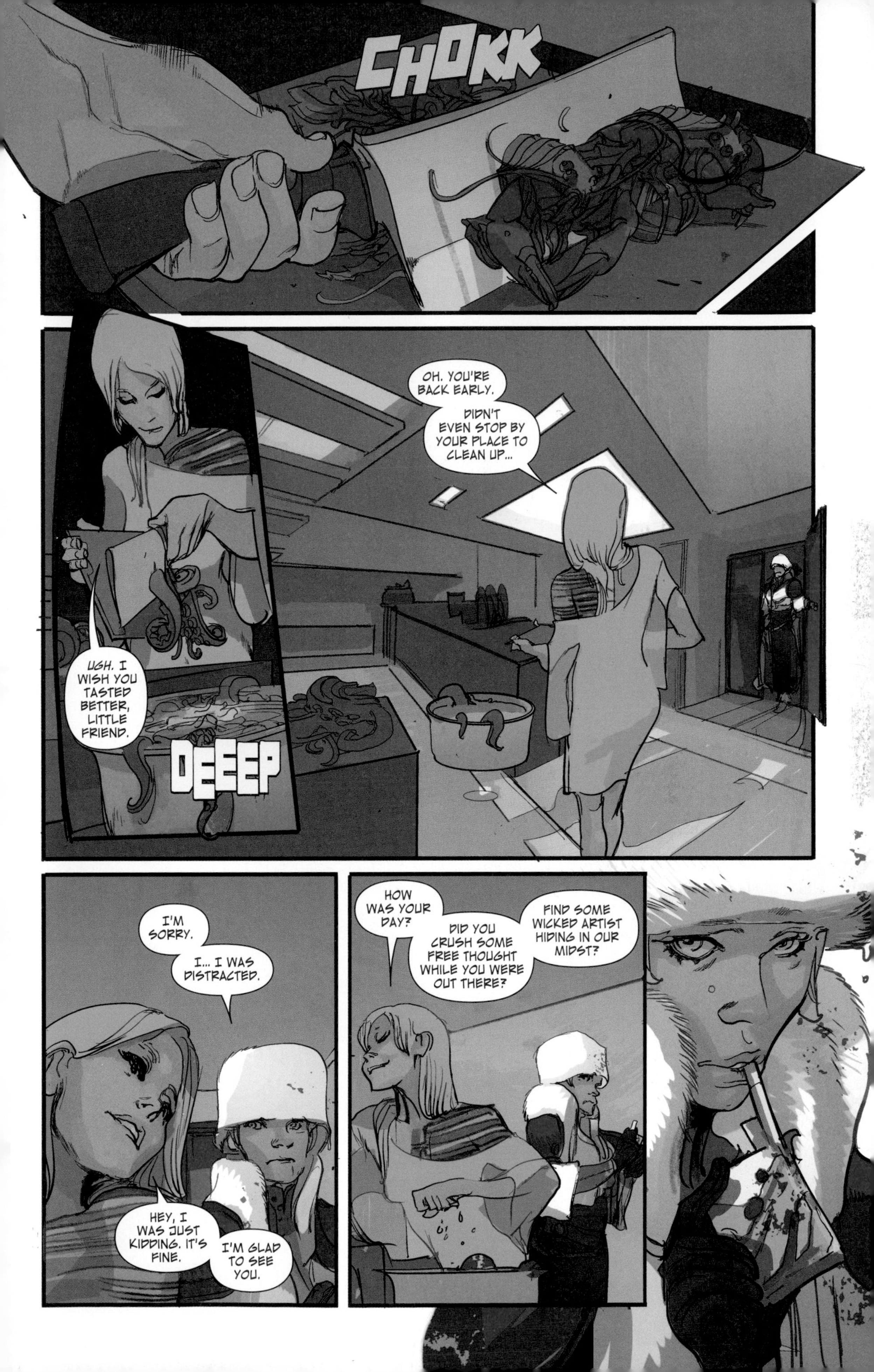
CHOKK
OH. YOU'RE BACK EARLY.
DIDN'T EVEN STOP BY YOUR PLACE TO CLEAN UP...
UGH. I WISH YOU TASTED BETTER, LITTLE FRIEND.
DEEEP
I'M SORRY.
I... I WAS DISTRACTED.
HEY, I WAS JUST KIDDING. IT'S FINE.
I'M GLAD TO SEE YOU.
HOW WAS YOUR DAY?
DID YOU CRUSH SOME FREE THOUGHT WHILE YOU WERE OUT THERE?
FIND SOME WICKED ARTIST HIDING IN OUR MIDST?

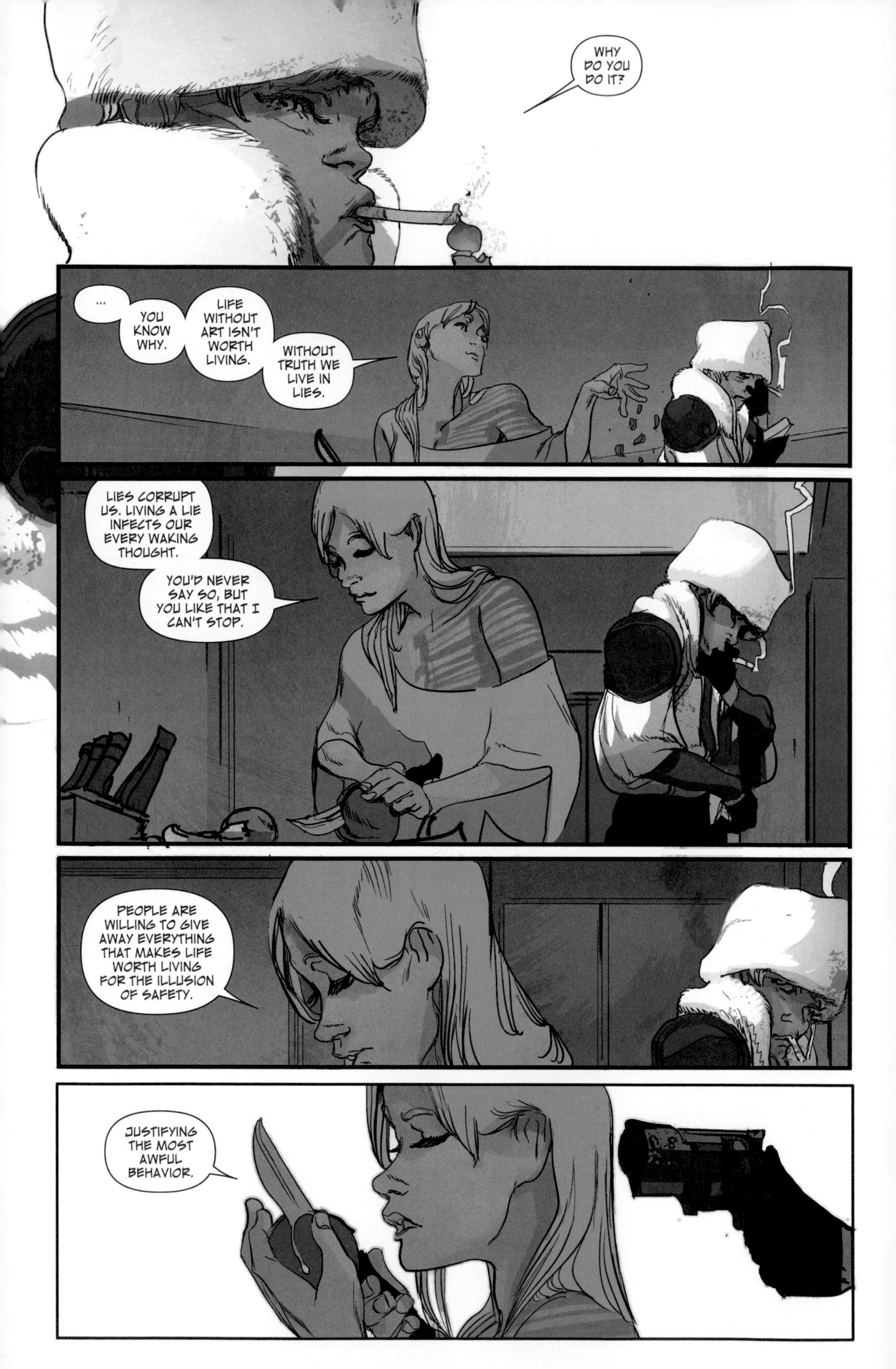
WHY DO YOU DO IT?
...
YOU KNOW WHY.
LIFE WITHOUT ART ISN'T WORTH LIVING.
WITHOUT TRUTH WE LIVE IN LIES.
LIES CORRUPT US. LIVING A LIE INFECTS OUR EVERY WAKING THOUGHT.
YOU'D NEVER SAY SO, BUT YOU LIKE THAT I CAN'T STOP.
PEOPLE ARE WILLING TO GIVE AWAY EVERYTHING THAT MAKES LIFE WORTH LIVING FOR THE ILLUSION OF SAFETY.
JUSTIFYING THE MOST AWFUL BEHAVIOR.

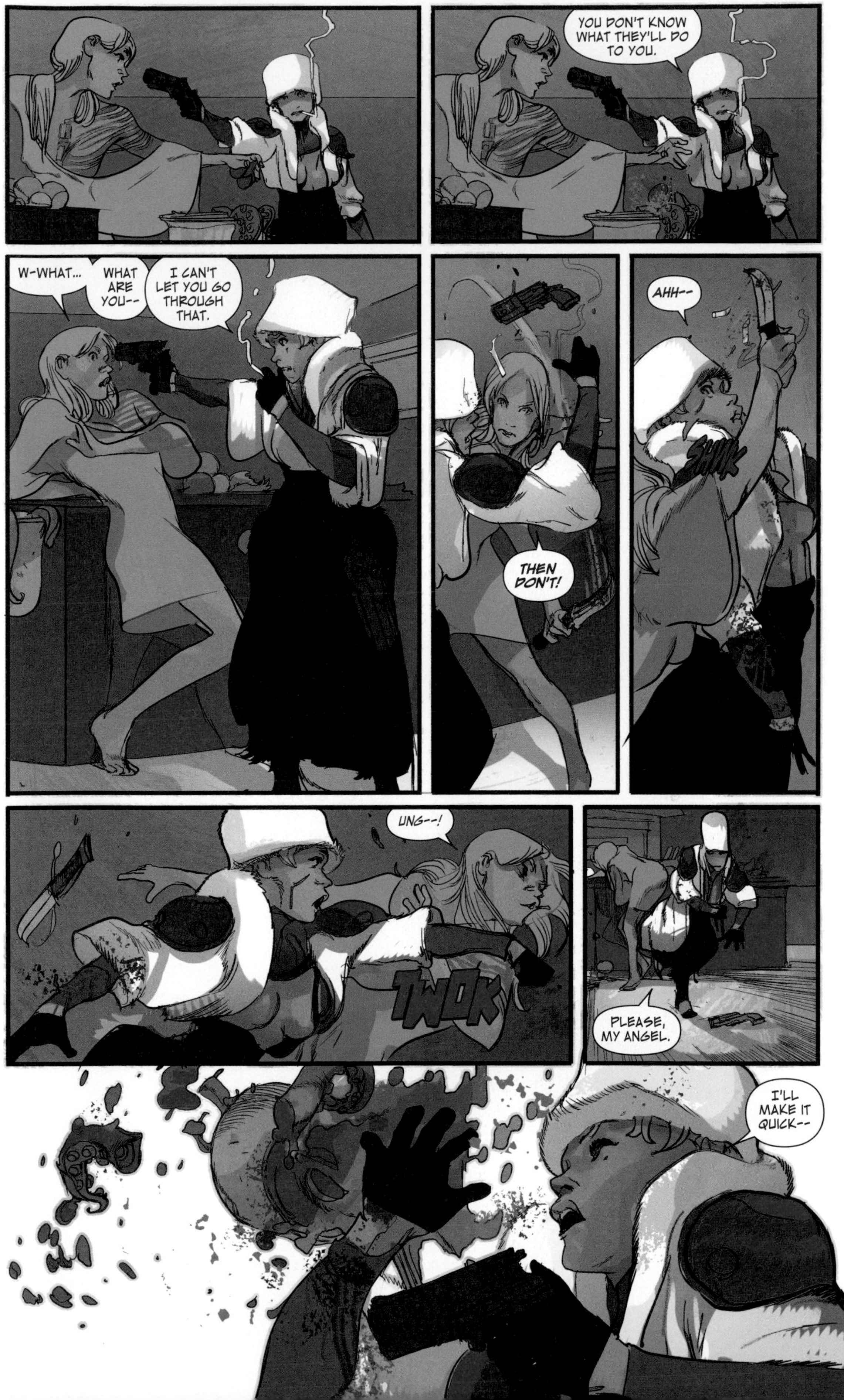
YOU DON'T KNOW WHAT THEY'LL DO TO YOU.
W-WHAT...
WHAT ARE YOU--
I CAN'T LET YOU GO THROUGH THAT.
THEN DON'T!
AHH--
SHNK
UNG--!
TWOK
PLEASE, MY ANGEL.
I'LL MAKE IT QUICK--

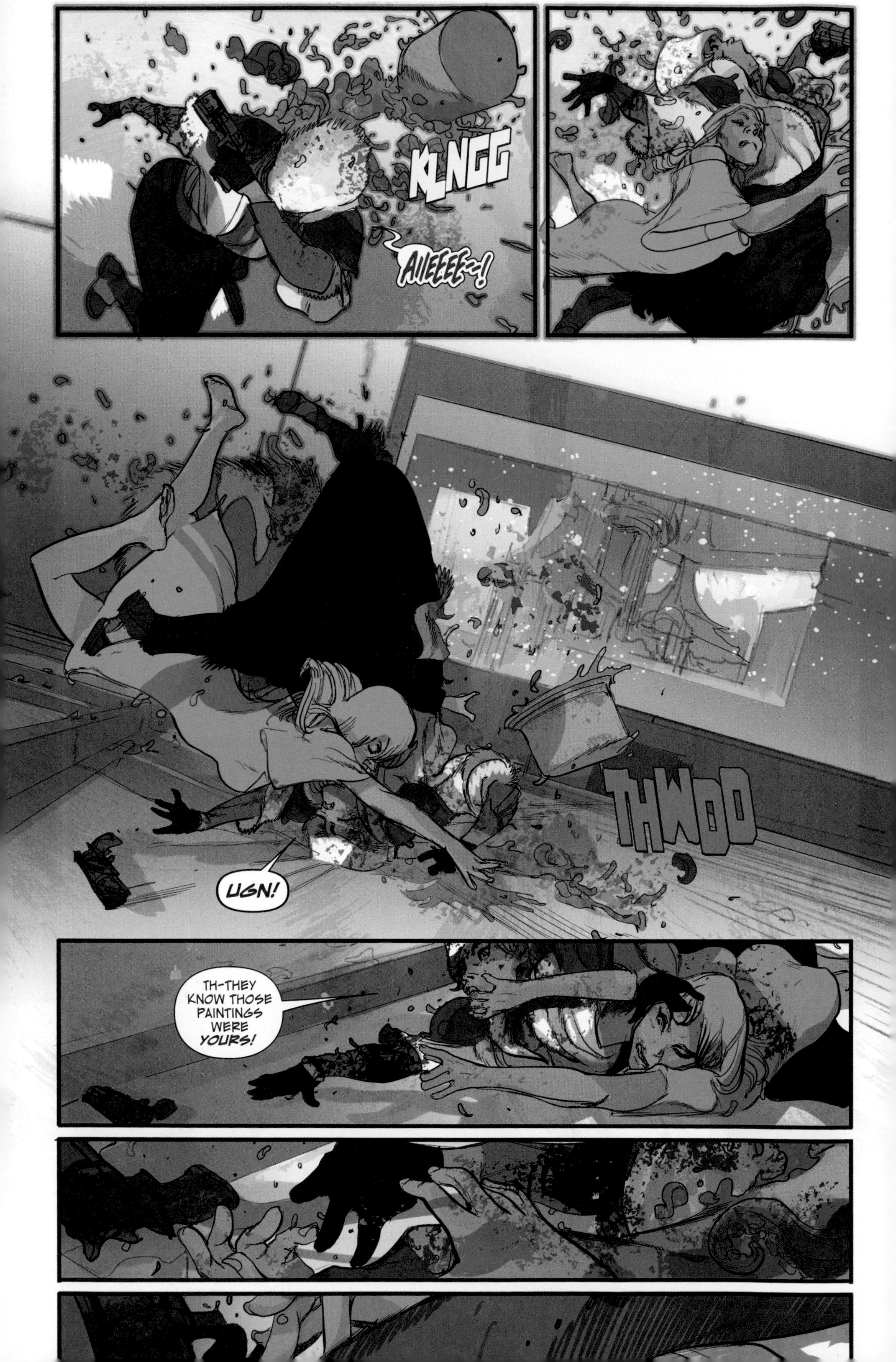
KLNGG
AIEEEE--!
THWOO
UGN!
TH-THEY KNOW THOSE PAINTINGS WERE *YOURS!*

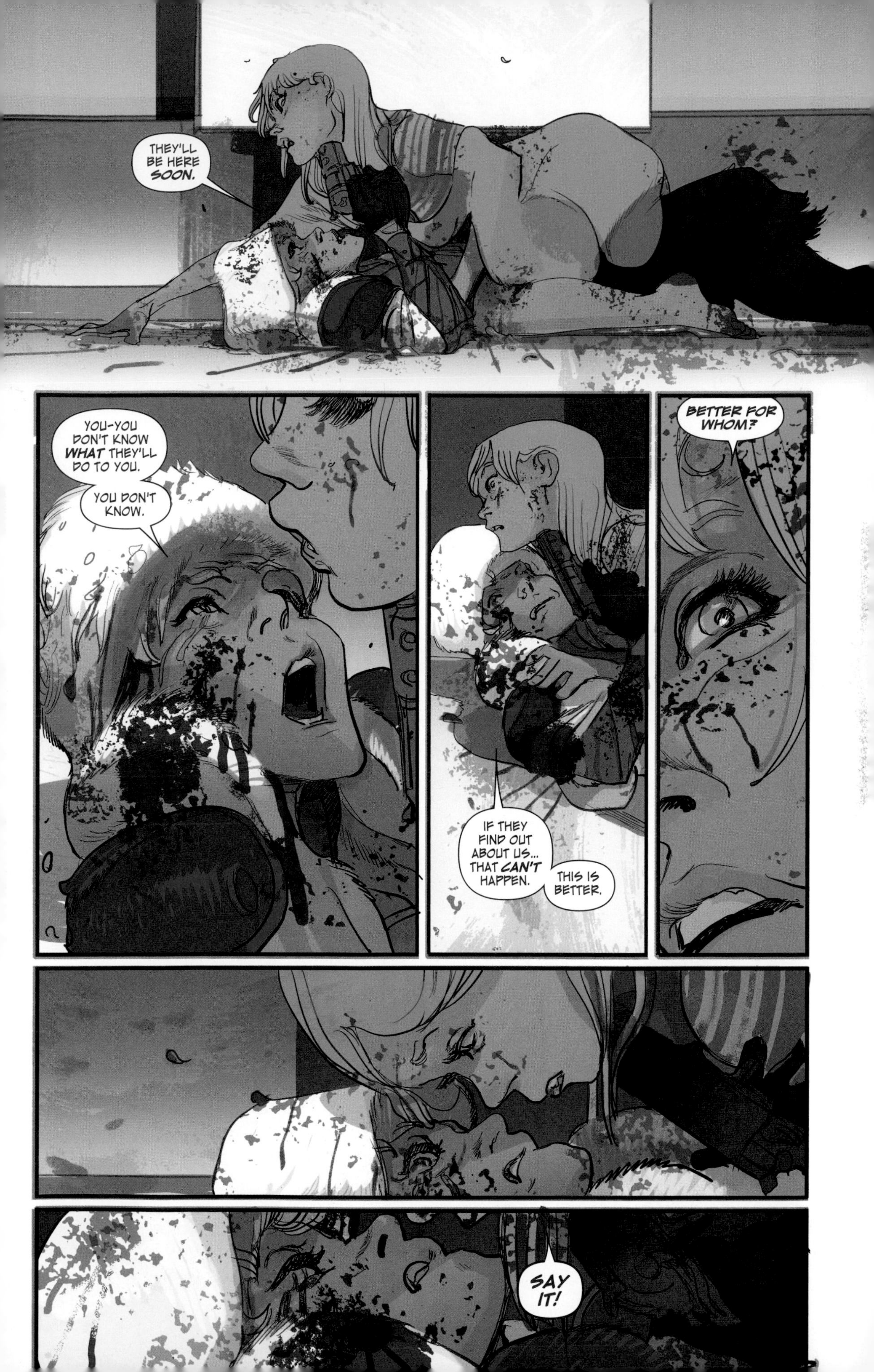
THEY'LL BE HERE SOON.
YOU-YOU DON'T KNOW WHAT THEY'LL DO TO YOU.
YOU DON'T KNOW.
IF THEY FIND OUT ABOUT US... THAT CAN'T HAPPEN.
THIS IS BETTER.
BETTER FOR WHOM?
SAY IT!

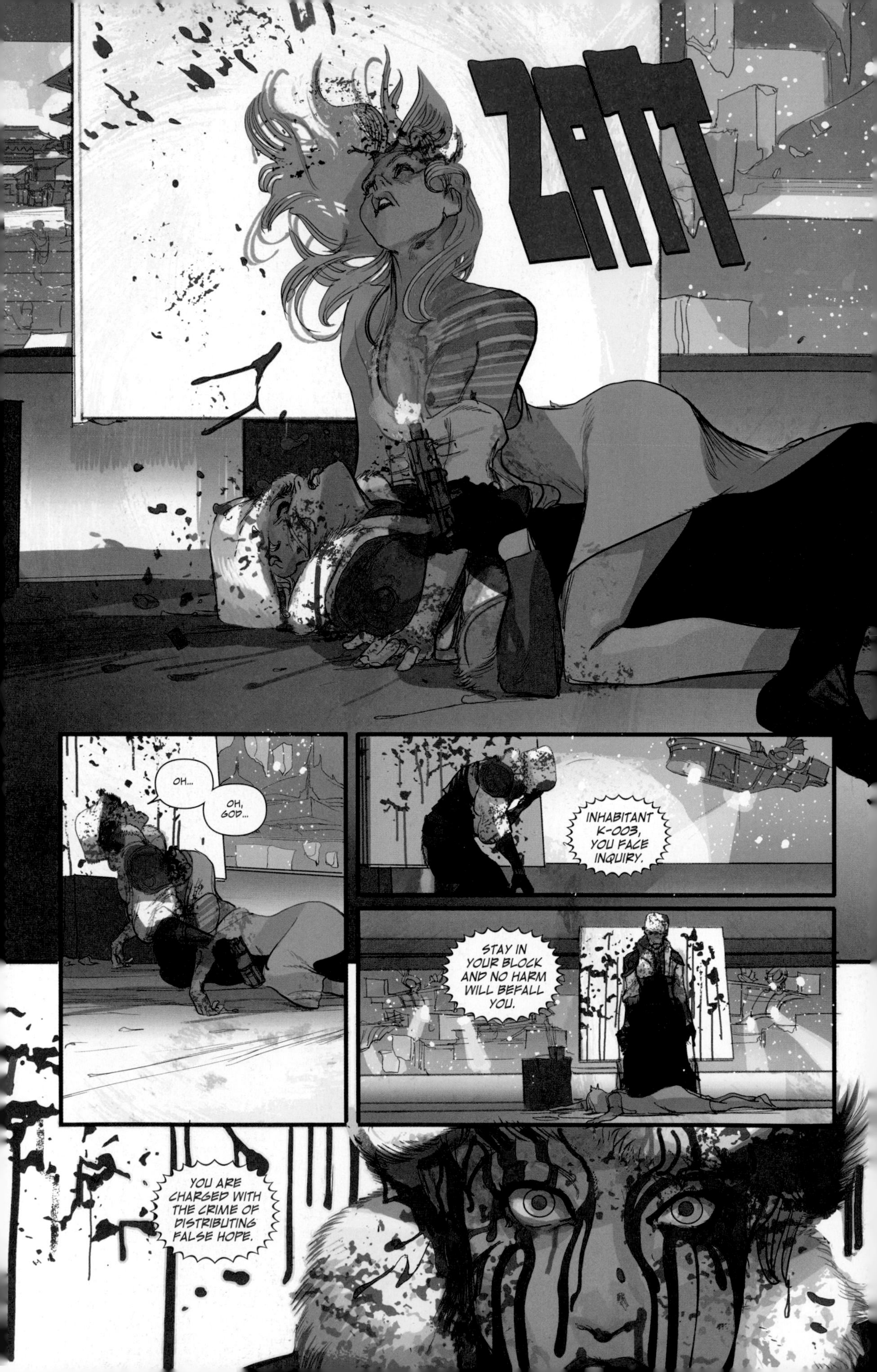
ZATT
OH...
OH, GOD...
INHABITANT K-003, YOU FACE INQUIRY.
STAY IN YOUR BLOCK AND NO HARM WILL BEFALL YOU.
YOU ARE CHARGED WITH THE CRIME OF DISTRIBUTING FALSE HOPE.

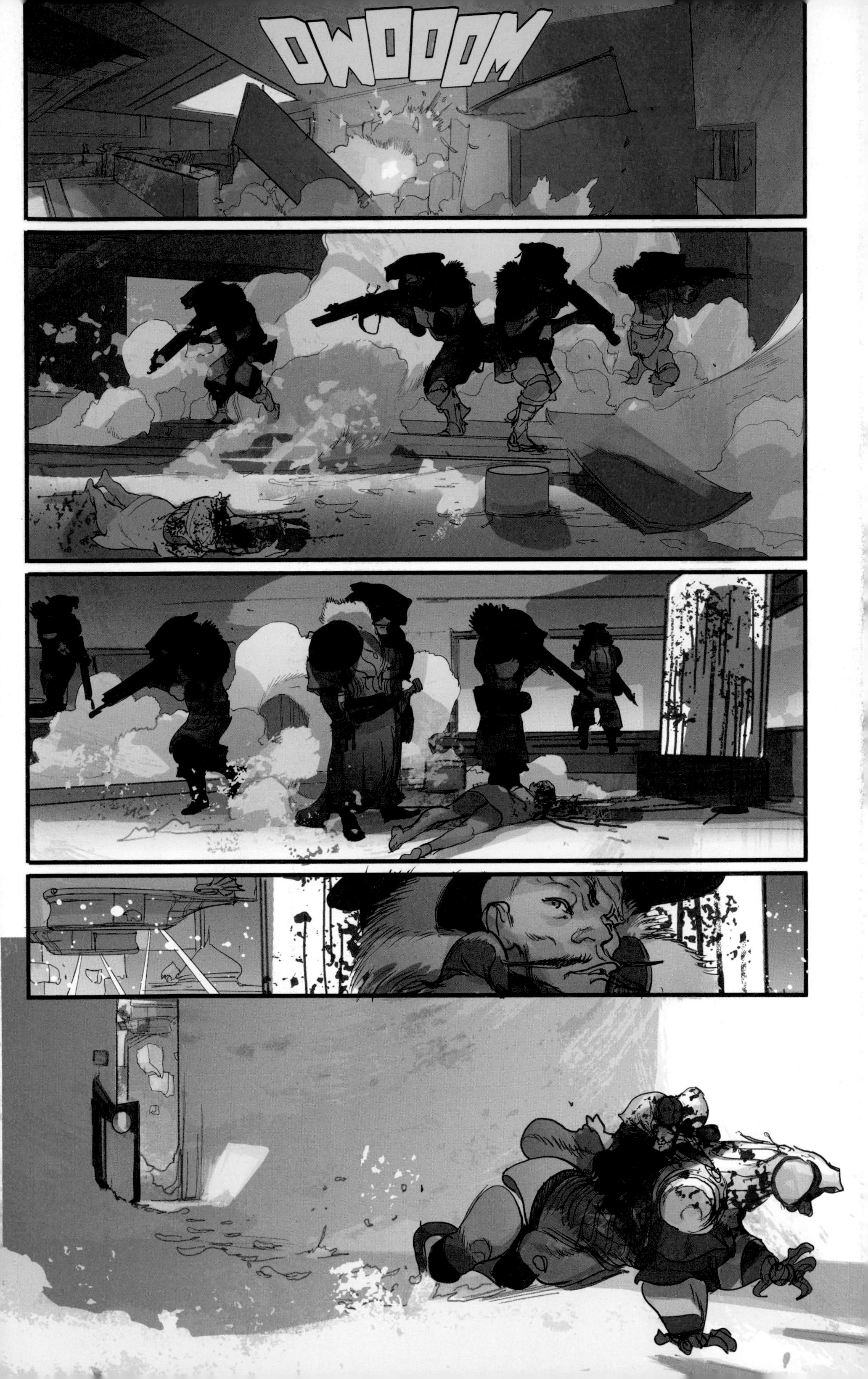
DWOOOM

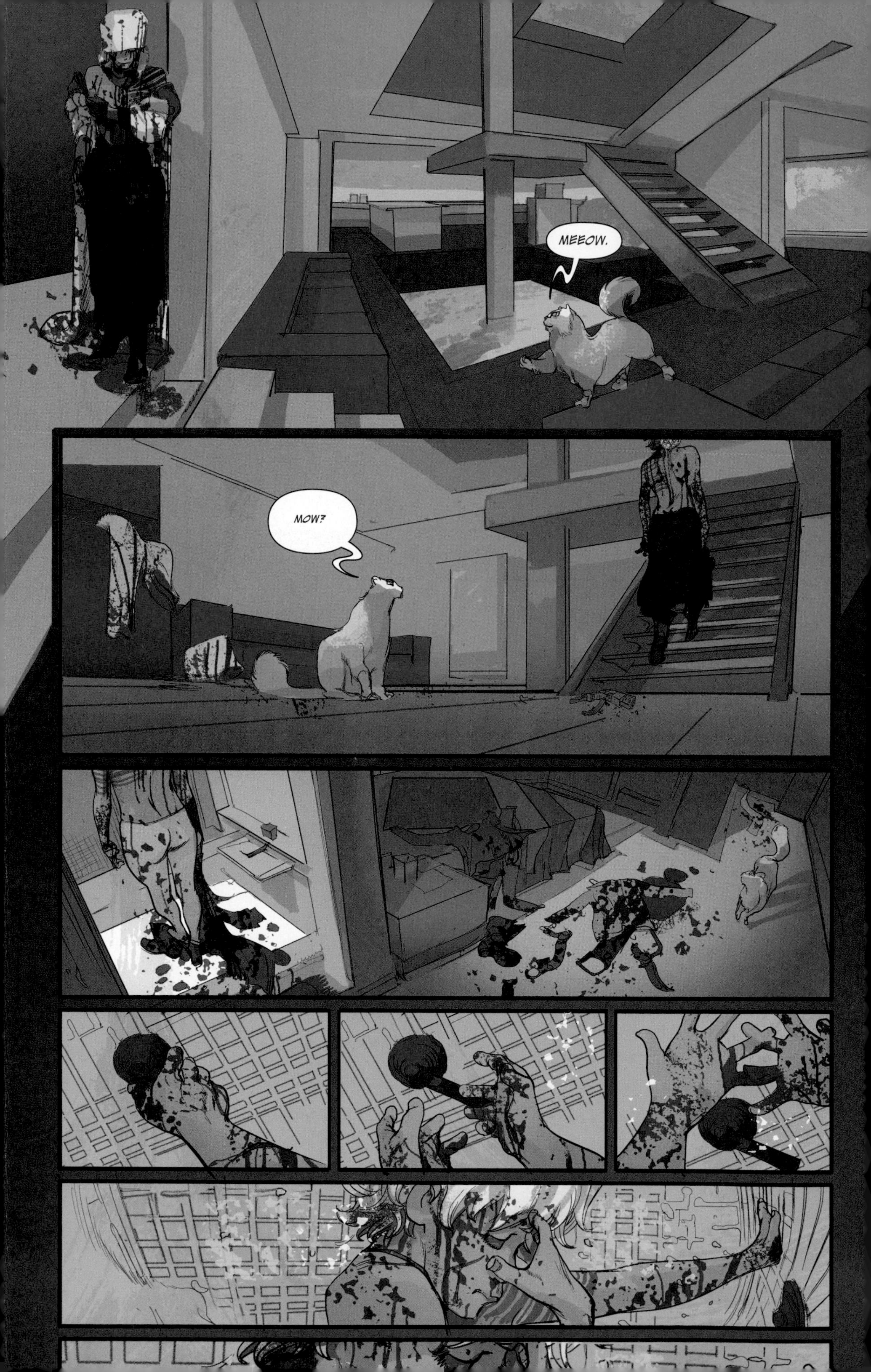
MEEOW.
MOW?

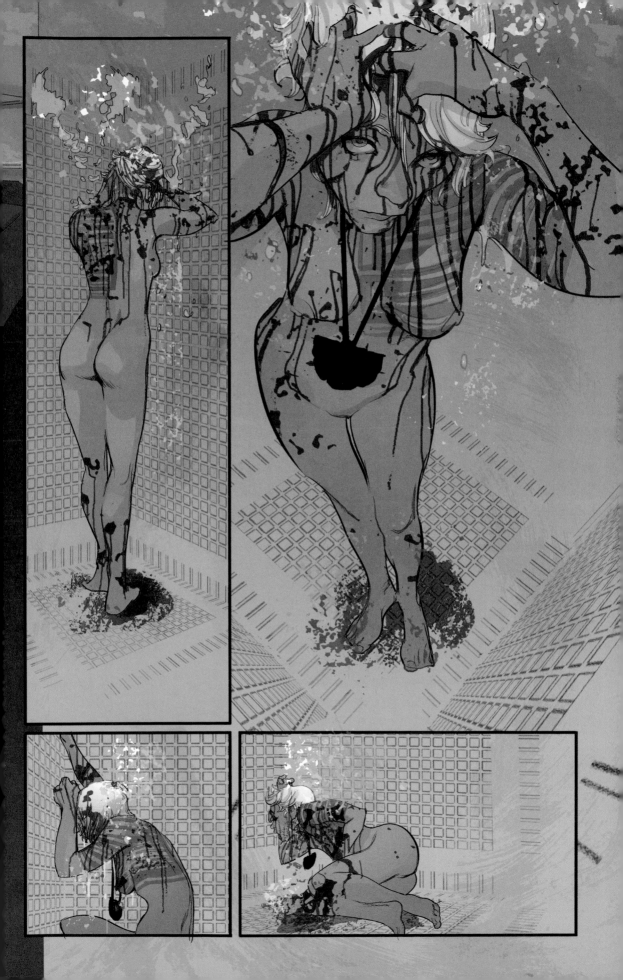

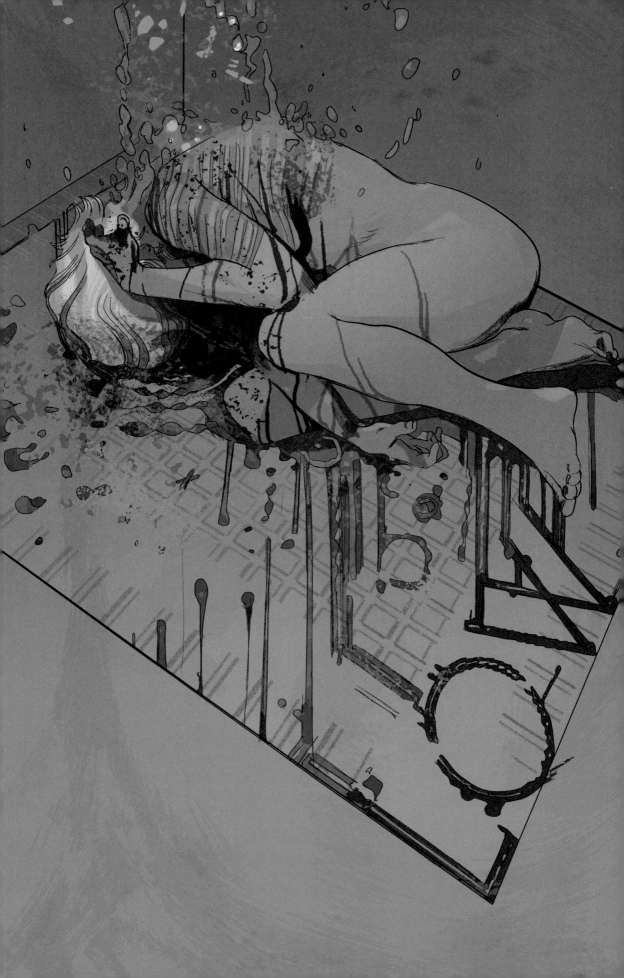

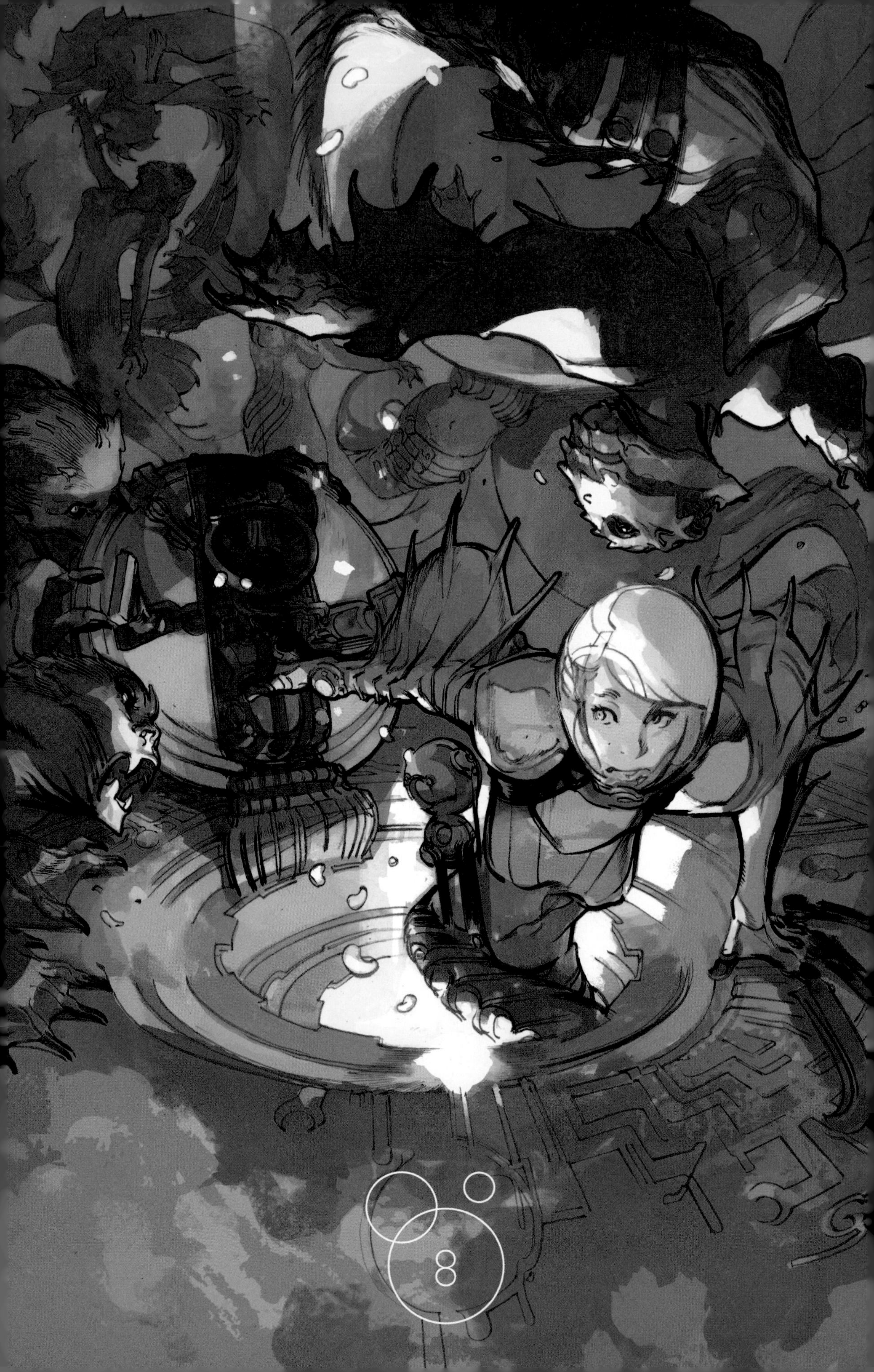
8

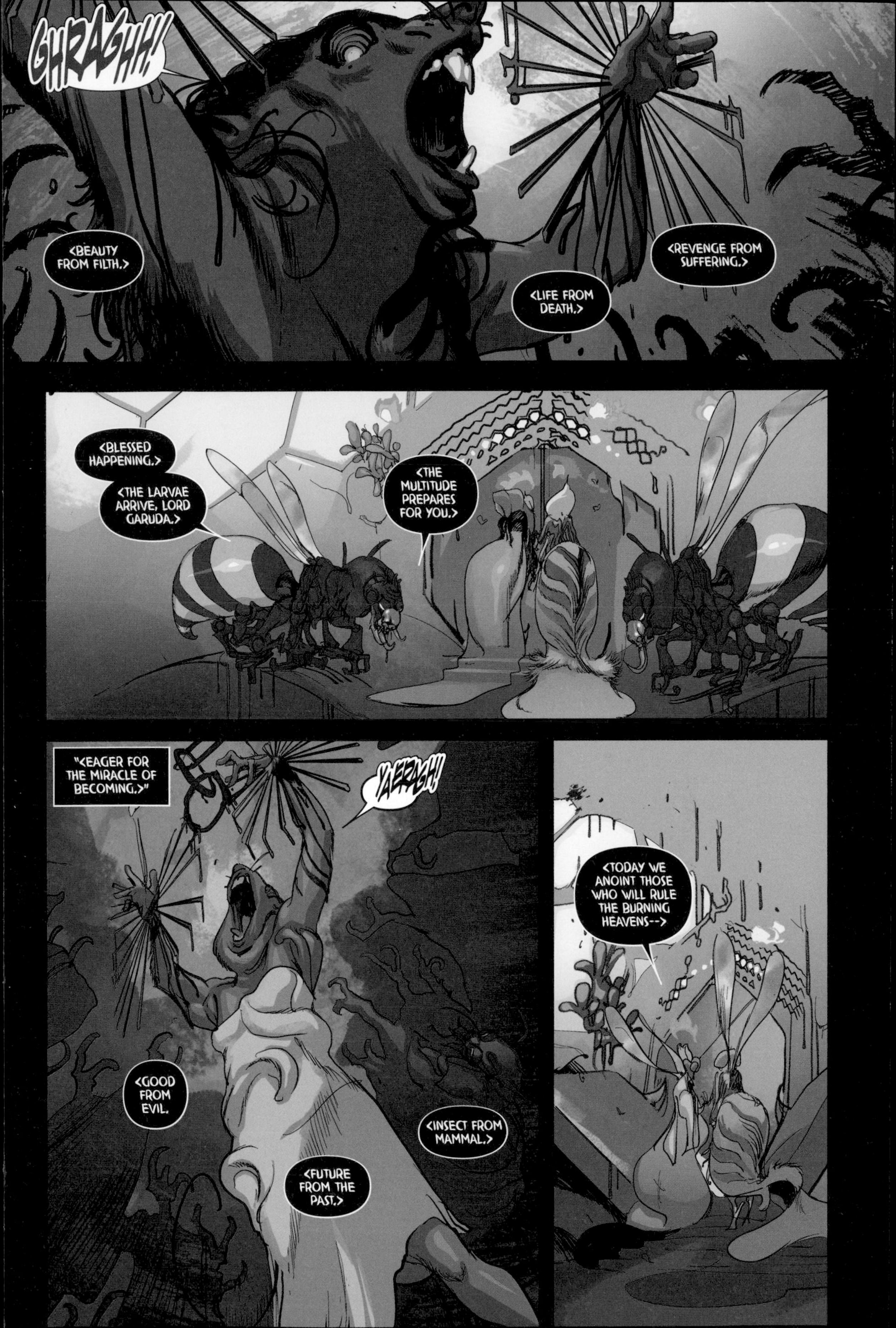
GHRAGHH!
<BEAUTY FROM FILTH.>
<LIFE FROM DEATH.>
<REVENGE FROM SUFFERING.>
<BLESSED HAPPENING.>
<THE LARVAE ARRIVE, LORD GARUDA.>
<THE MULTITUDE PREPARES FOR YOU.>
"<EAGER FOR THE MIRACLE OF BECOMING.>"
YAERAGH!
<GOOD FROM EVIL.
<FUTURE FROM THE PAST.>
<INSECT FROM MAMMAL.>
<TODAY WE ANOINT THOSE WHO WILL RULE THE BURNING HEAVENS-->

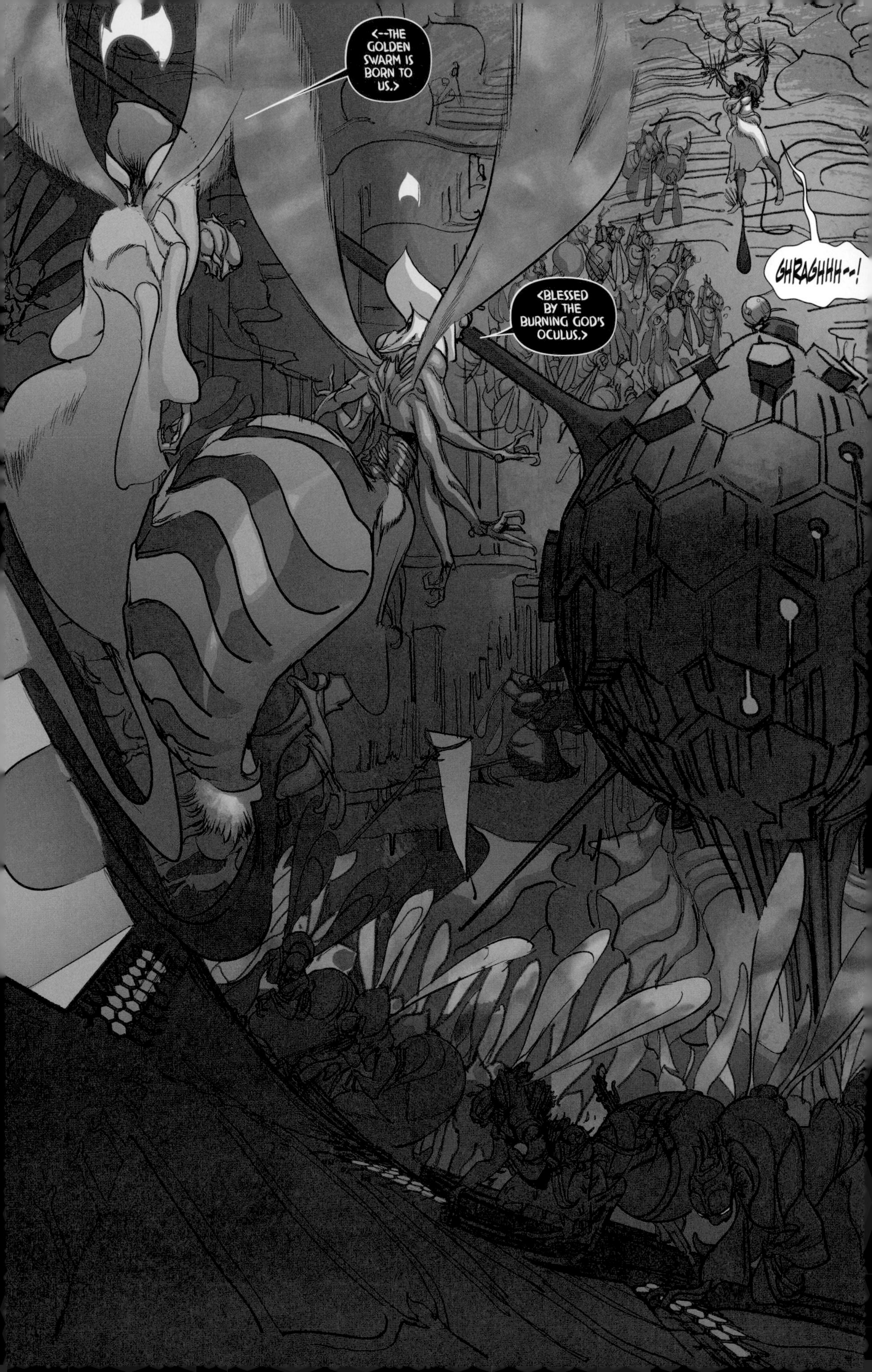
<--THE GOLDEN SWARM IS BORN TO US.>
<BLESSED BY THE BURNING GOD'S OCULUS.>
GHRAGHHH--!

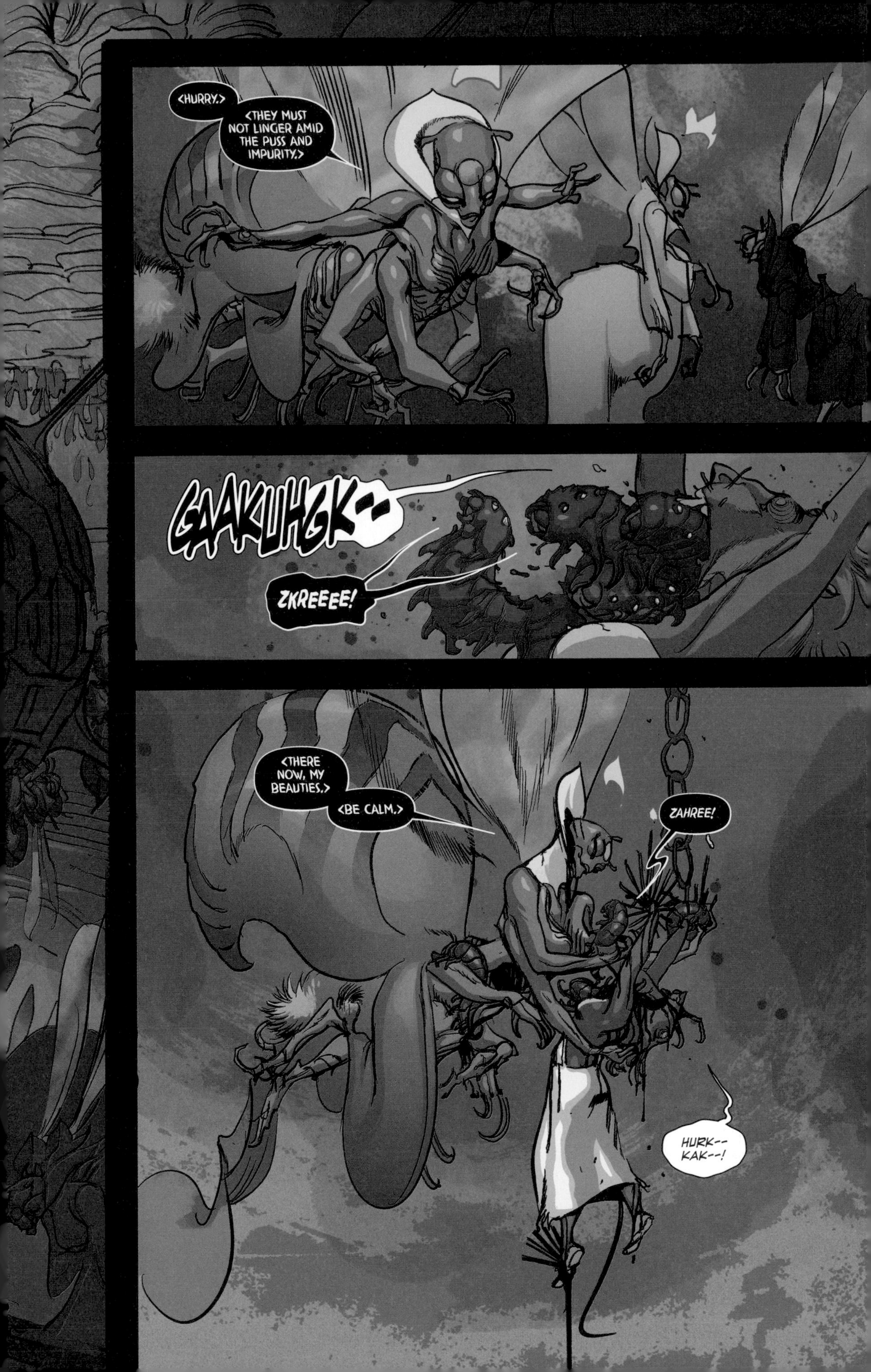
<HURRY.>
<THEY MUST NOT LINGER AMID THE PUSS AND IMPURITY.>
GAAKUHGK--
ZKREEEE!
<THERE NOW, MY BEAUTIES.>
<BE CALM.>
ZAHREE!
HURK-- KAK--!

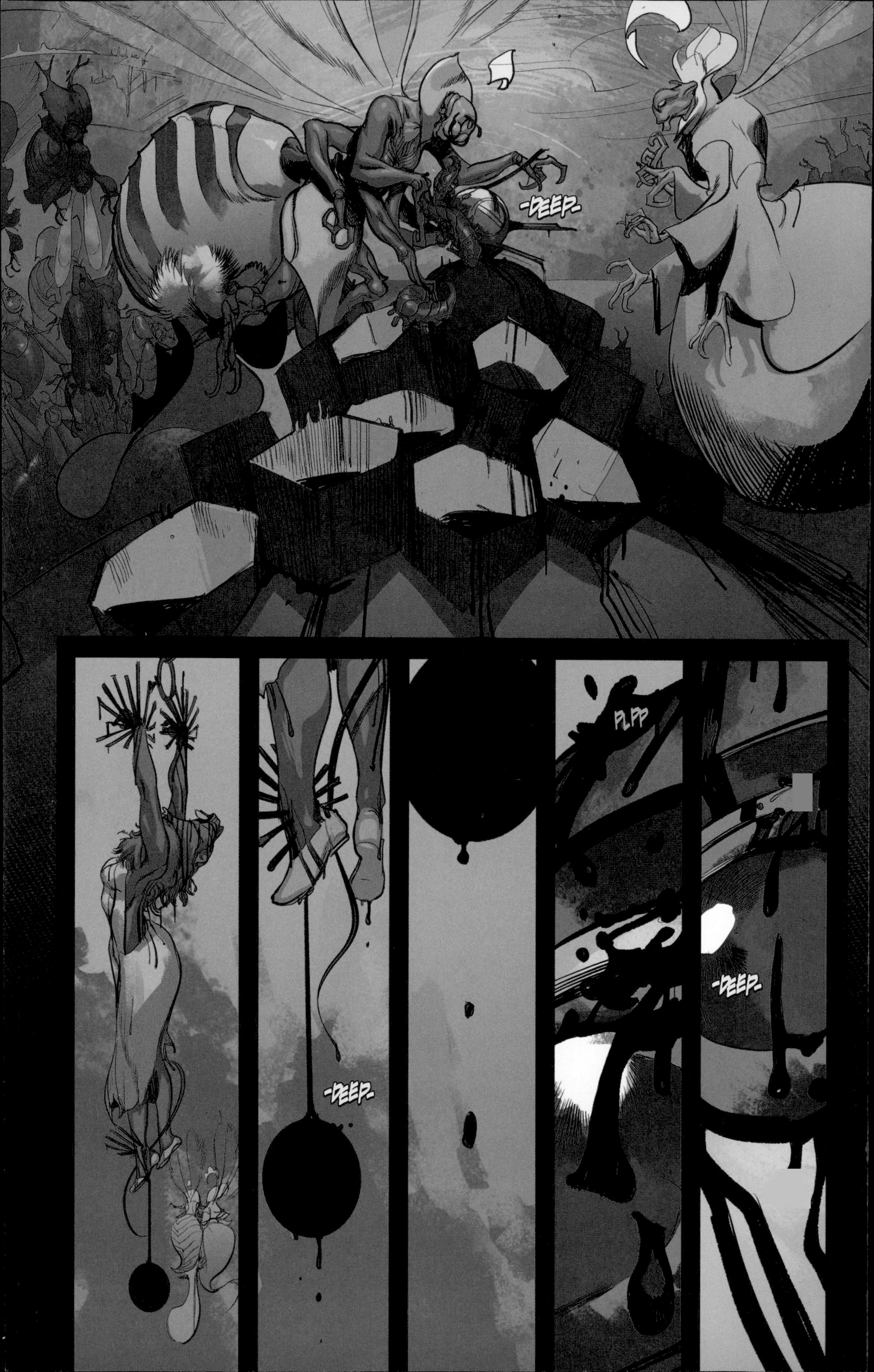

-DEEP-
-DEEP-
PLPP
-DEEP-

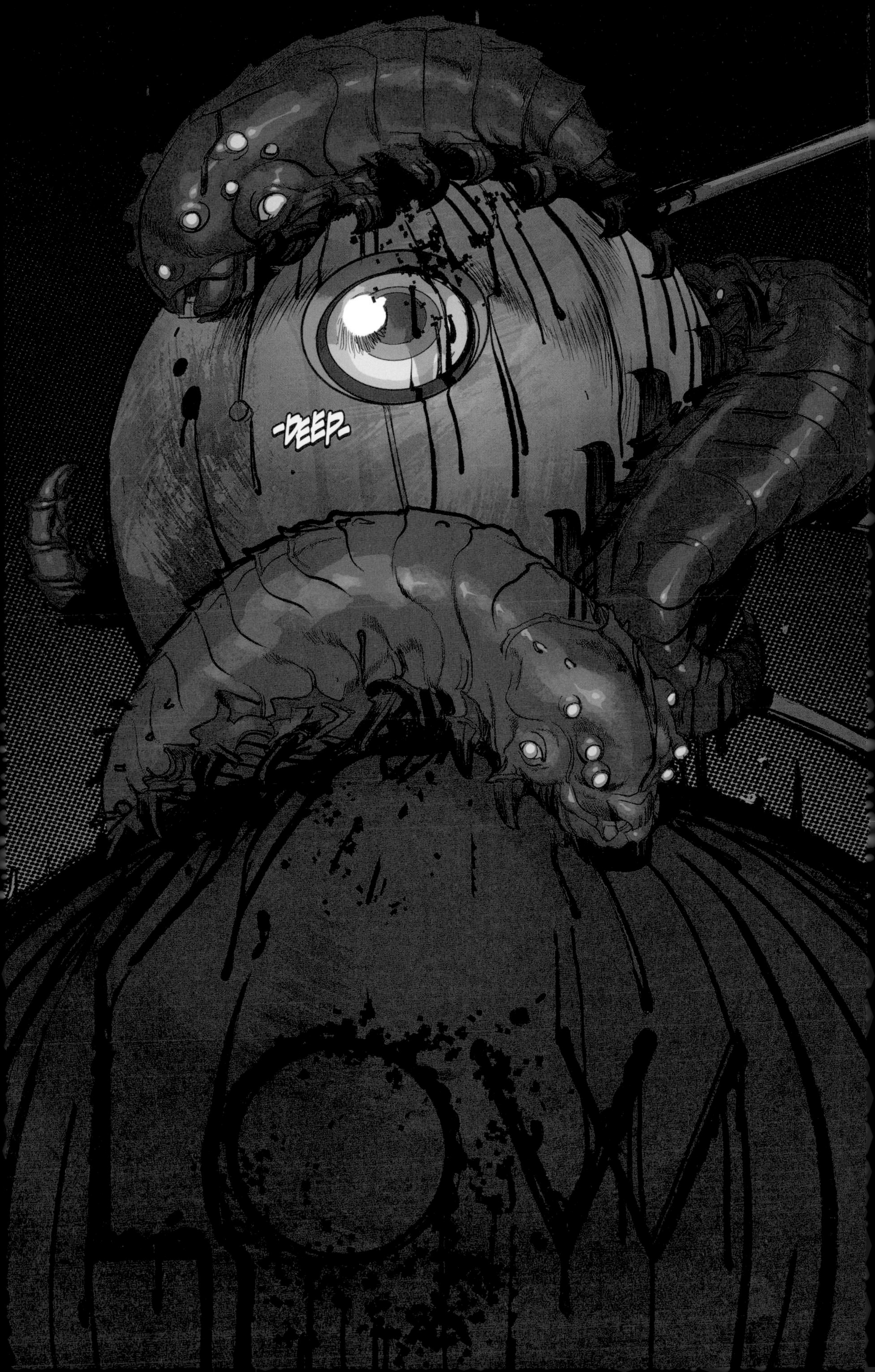
-DEEP-

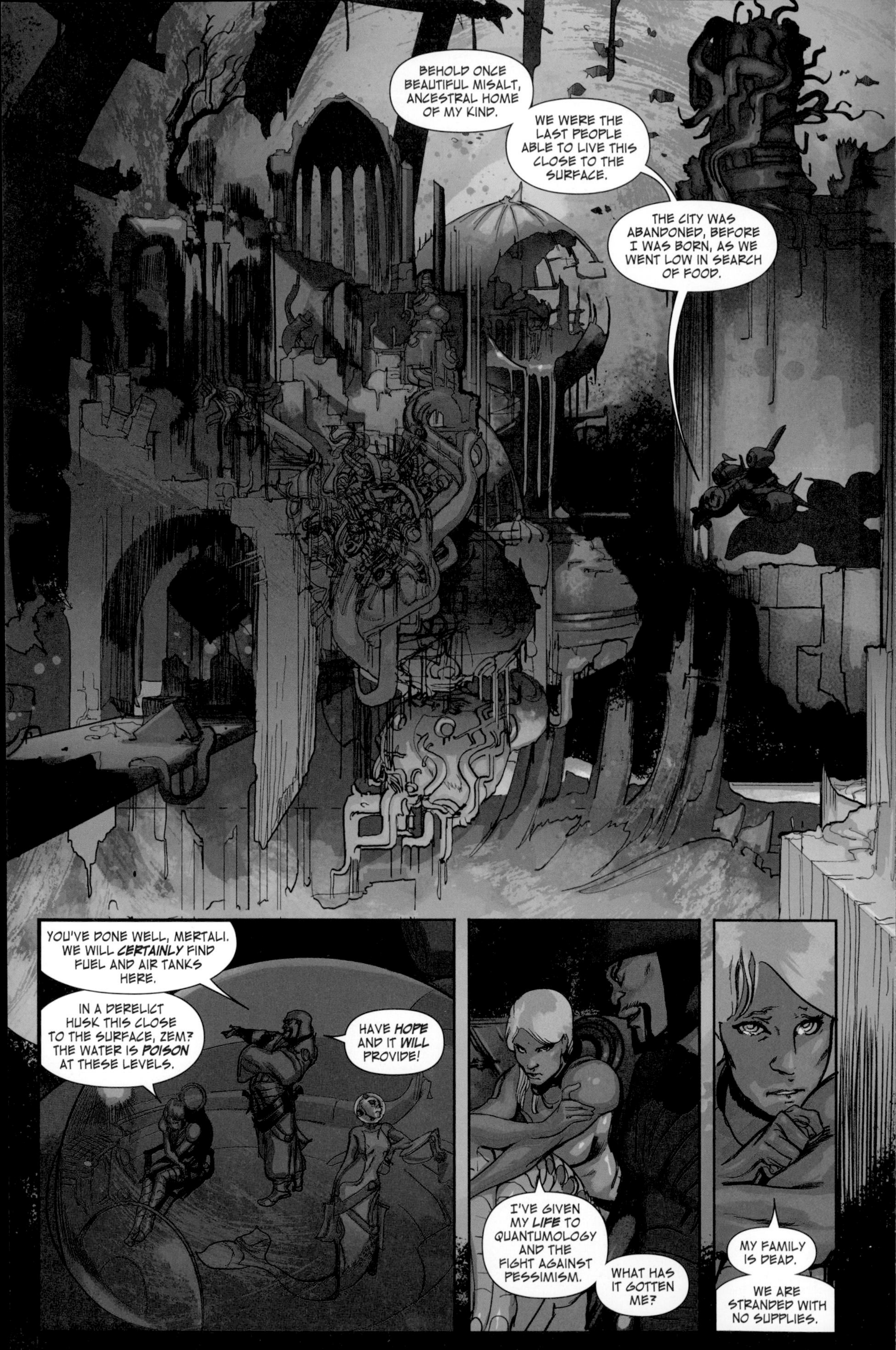
BEHOLD ONCE BEAUTIFUL MISALT, ANCESTRAL HOME OF MY KIND.
WE WERE THE LAST PEOPLE ABLE TO LIVE THIS CLOSE TO THE SURFACE.
THE CITY WAS ABANDONED, BEFORE I WAS BORN, AS WE WENT LOW IN SEARCH OF FOOD.
YOU'VE DONE WELL, MERTALI. WE WILL *CERTAINLY* FIND FUEL AND AIR TANKS HERE.
IN A DERELICT HUSK THIS CLOSE TO THE SURFACE, ZEM? THE WATER IS *POISON* AT THESE LEVELS.
HAVE *HOPE* AND IT *WILL* PROVIDE!
I'VE GIVEN MY *LIFE* TO QUANTUMOLOGY AND THE FIGHT AGAINST PESSIMISM.
WHAT HAS IT GOTTEN ME?
MY FAMILY IS DEAD.
WE ARE STRANDED WITH NO SUPPLIES.

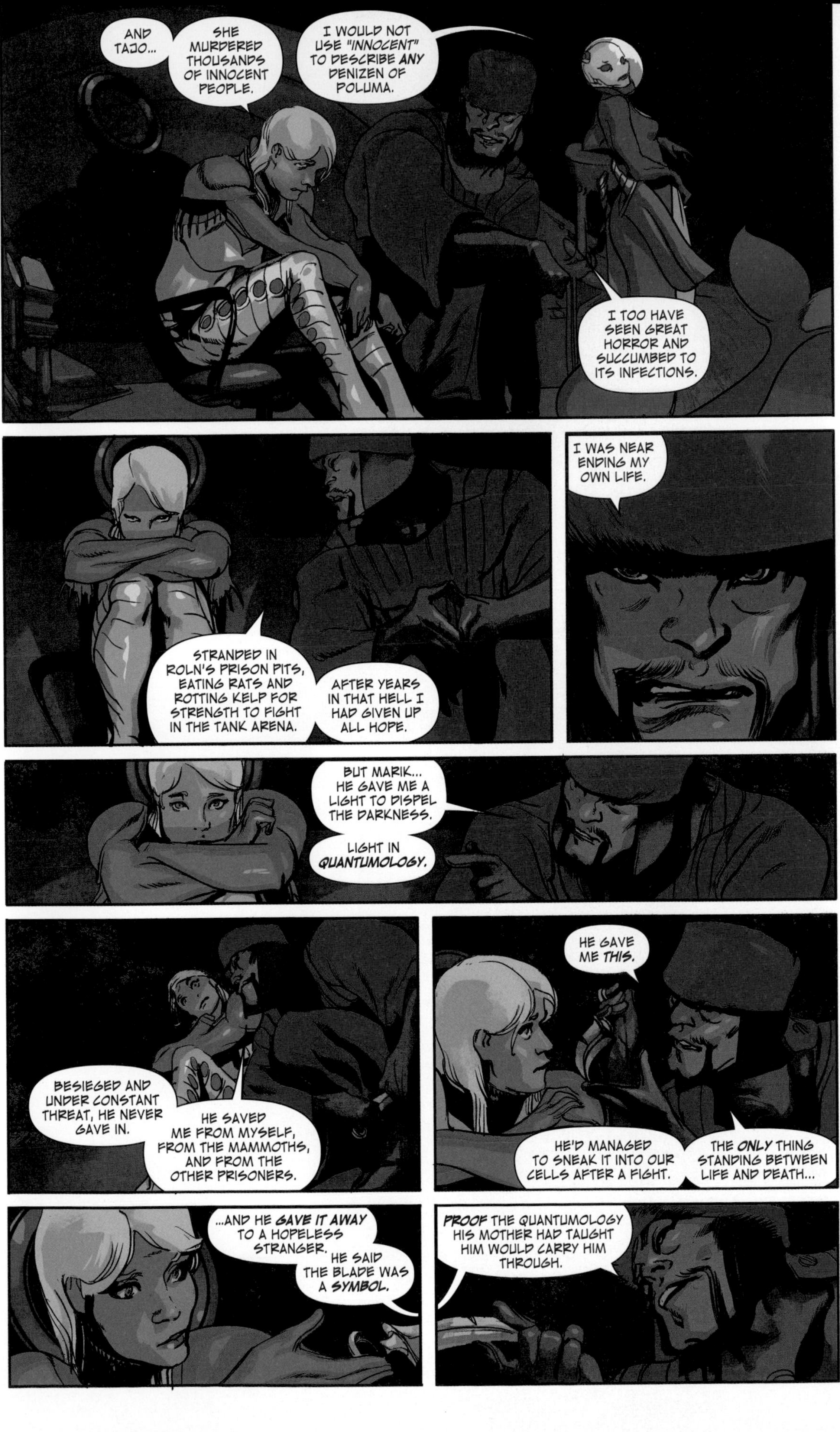
AND TAJO...
SHE MURDERED THOUSANDS OF INNOCENT PEOPLE.
I WOULD NOT USE "INNOCENT" TO DESCRIBE ANY DENIZEN OF POLUMA.
I TOO HAVE SEEN GREAT HORROR AND SUCCUMBED TO ITS INFECTIONS.
STRANDED IN ROLN'S PRISON PITS, EATING RATS AND ROTTING KELP FOR STRENGTH TO FIGHT IN THE TANK ARENA.
AFTER YEARS IN THAT HELL I HAD GIVEN UP ALL HOPE.
I WAS NEAR ENDING MY OWN LIFE.
BUT MARIK... HE GAVE ME A LIGHT TO DISPEL THE DARKNESS.
LIGHT IN QUANTUMOLOGY.
BESIEGED AND UNDER CONSTANT THREAT, HE NEVER GAVE IN.
HE SAVED ME FROM MYSELF, FROM THE MAMMOTHS, AND FROM THE OTHER PRISONERS.
HE GAVE ME THIS.
HE'D MANAGED TO SNEAK IT INTO OUR CELLS AFTER A FIGHT.
THE ONLY THING STANDING BETWEEN LIFE AND DEATH...
...AND HE GAVE IT AWAY TO A HOPELESS STRANGER.
HE SAID THE BLADE WAS A SYMBOL.
PROOF THE QUANTUMOLOGY HIS MOTHER HAD TAUGHT HIM WOULD CARRY HIM THROUGH.

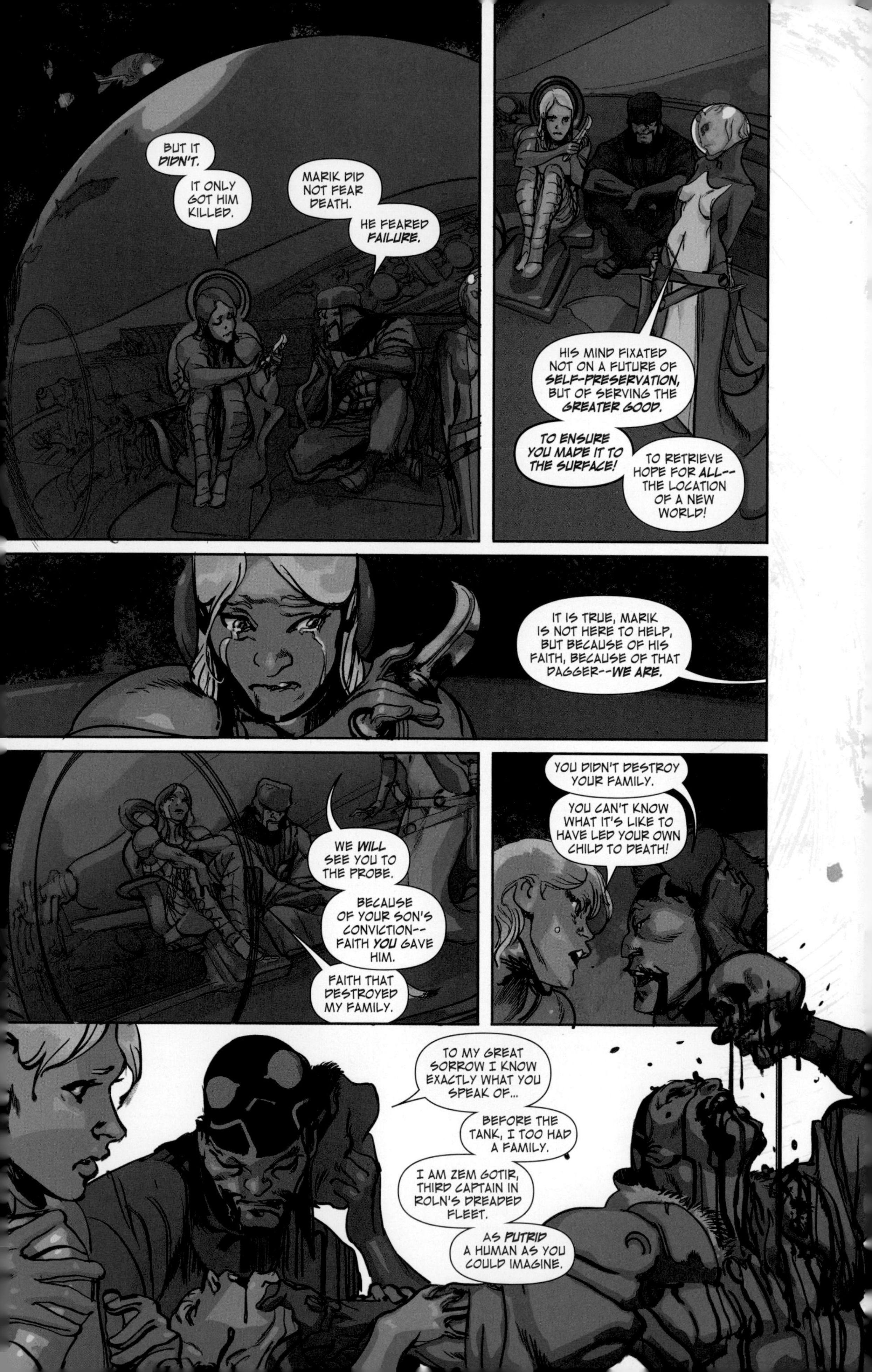
BUT IT DIDN'T.
IT ONLY GOT HIM KILLED.
MARIK DID NOT FEAR DEATH.
HE FEARED FAILURE.
HIS MIND FIXATED NOT ON A FUTURE OF SELF-PRESERVATION, BUT OF SERVING THE GREATER GOOD.
TO ENSURE YOU MADE IT TO THE SURFACE!
TO RETRIEVE HOPE FOR ALL-- THE LOCATION OF A NEW WORLD!
IT IS TRUE, MARIK IS NOT HERE TO HELP, BUT BECAUSE OF HIS FAITH, BECAUSE OF THAT DAGGER--WE ARE.
WE WILL SEE YOU TO THE PROBE.
BECAUSE OF YOUR SON'S CONVICTION-- FAITH YOU GAVE HIM.
FAITH THAT DESTROYED MY FAMILY.
YOU DIDN'T DESTROY YOUR FAMILY.
YOU CAN'T KNOW WHAT IT'S LIKE TO HAVE LED YOUR OWN CHILD TO DEATH!
TO MY GREAT SORROW I KNOW EXACTLY WHAT YOU SPEAK OF...
BEFORE THE TANK, I TOO HAD A FAMILY.
I AM ZEM GOTIR, THIRD CAPTAIN IN ROLN'S DREADED FLEET.
AS PUTRID A HUMAN AS YOU COULD IMAGINE.

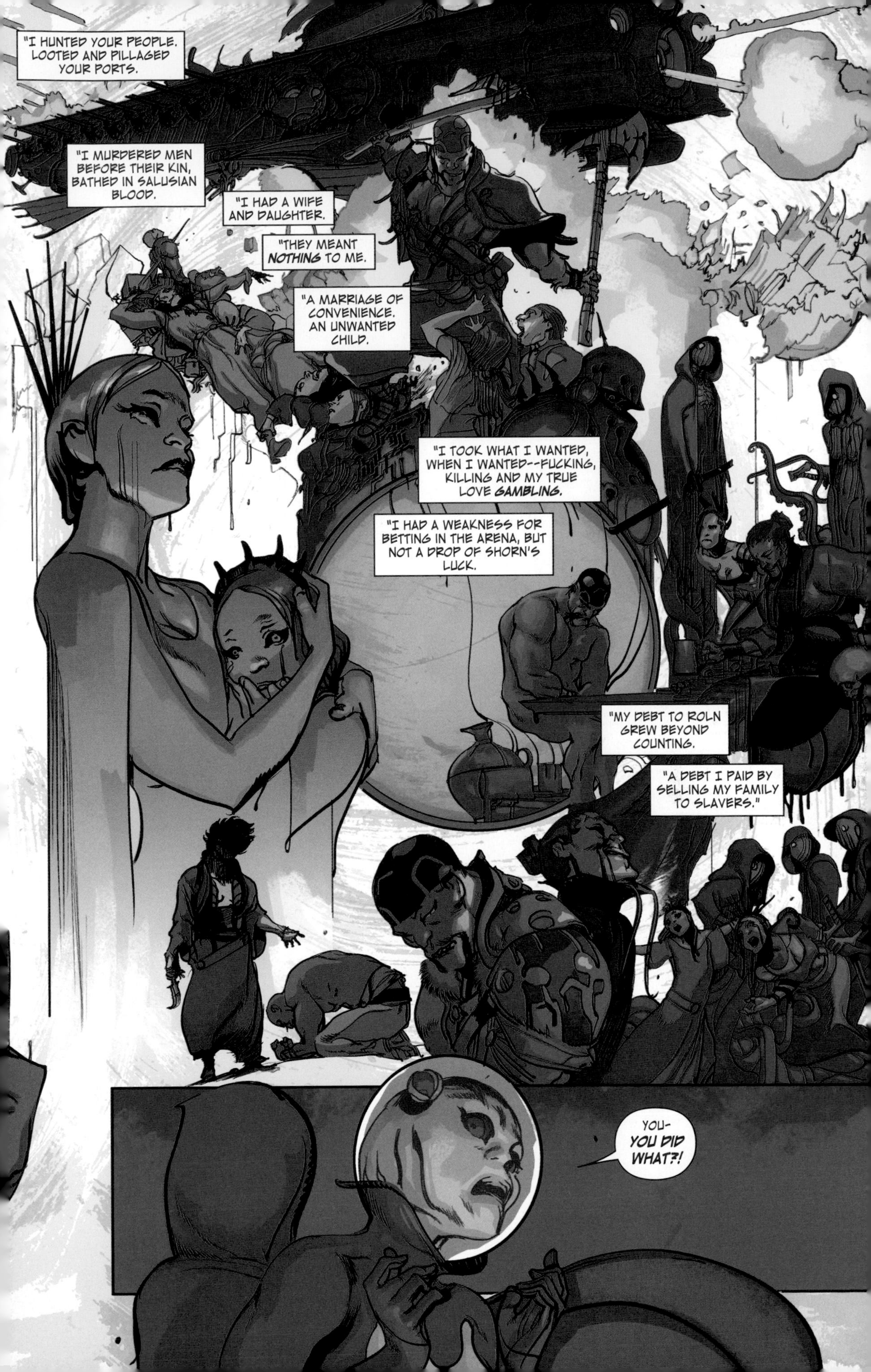
"I HUNTED YOUR PEOPLE. LOOTED AND PILLAGED YOUR PORTS.
"I MURDERED MEN BEFORE THEIR KIN, BATHED IN SALUSIAN BLOOD.
"I HAD A WIFE AND DAUGHTER.
"THEY MEANT NOTHING TO ME.
"A MARRIAGE OF CONVENIENCE. AN UNWANTED CHILD.
"I TOOK WHAT I WANTED, WHEN I WANTED--FUCKING, KILLING AND MY TRUE LOVE GAMBLING.
"I HAD A WEAKNESS FOR BETTING IN THE ARENA, BUT NOT A DROP OF SHORN'S LUCK.
"MY DEBT TO ROLN GREW BEYOND COUNTING.
"A DEBT I PAID BY SELLING MY FAMILY TO SLAVERS."
YOU- YOU DID WHAT?!

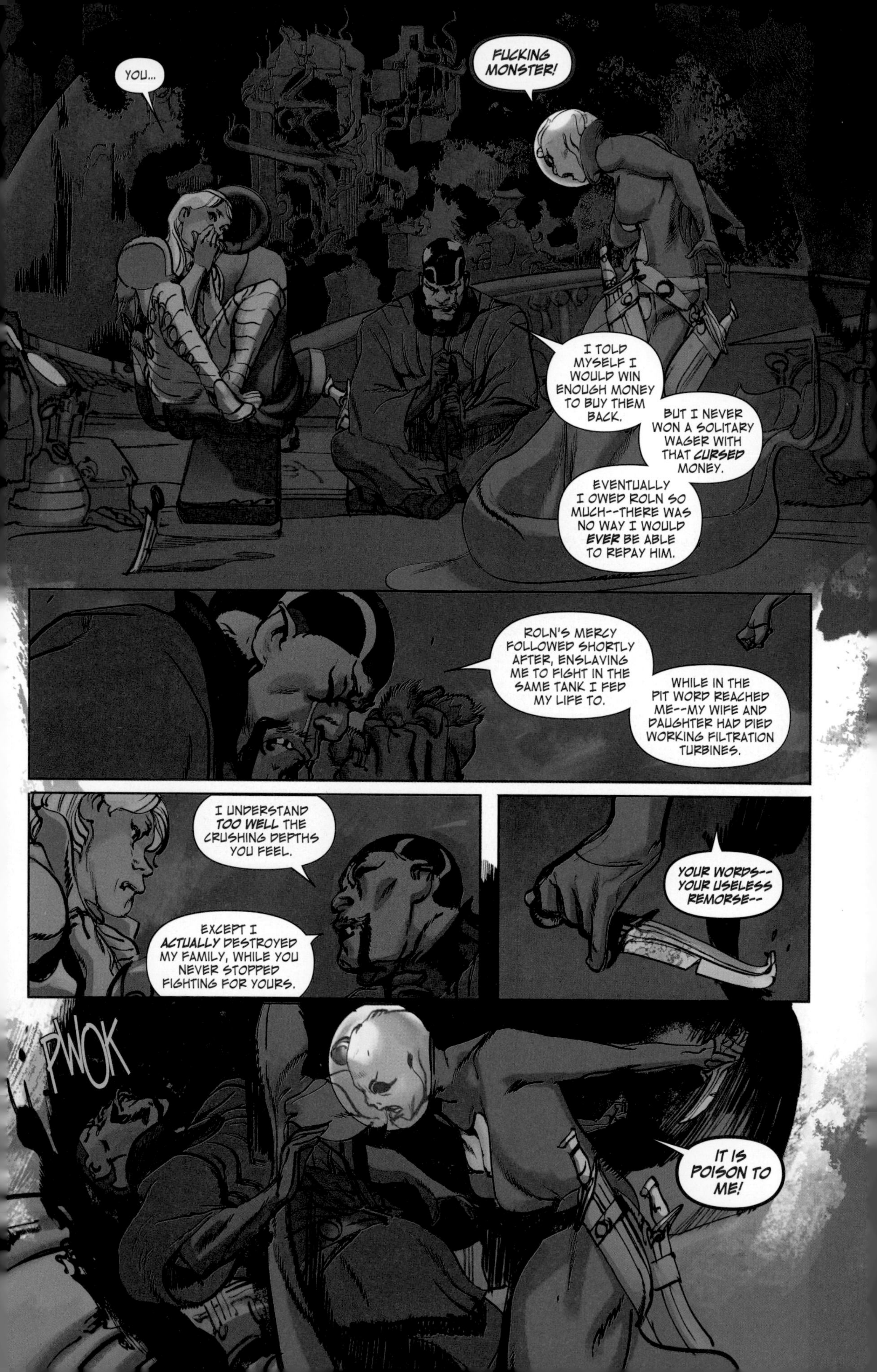
YOU...
FUCKING MONSTER!
I TOLD MYSELF I WOULD WIN ENOUGH MONEY TO BUY THEM BACK.
BUT I NEVER WON A SOLITARY WAGER WITH THAT CURSED MONEY.
EVENTUALLY I OWED ROLN SO MUCH--THERE WAS NO WAY I WOULD EVER BE ABLE TO REPAY HIM.
ROLN'S MERCY FOLLOWED SHORTLY AFTER, ENSLAVING ME TO FIGHT IN THE SAME TANK I FED MY LIFE TO.
WHILE IN THE PIT WORD REACHED ME--MY WIFE AND DAUGHTER HAD DIED WORKING FILTRATION TURBINES.
I UNDERSTAND TOO WELL THE CRUSHING DEPTHS YOU FEEL.
EXCEPT I ACTUALLY DESTROYED MY FAMILY, WHILE YOU NEVER STOPPED FIGHTING FOR YOURS.
YOUR WORDS--YOUR USELESS REMORSE--
PWOK
IT IS POISON TO ME!

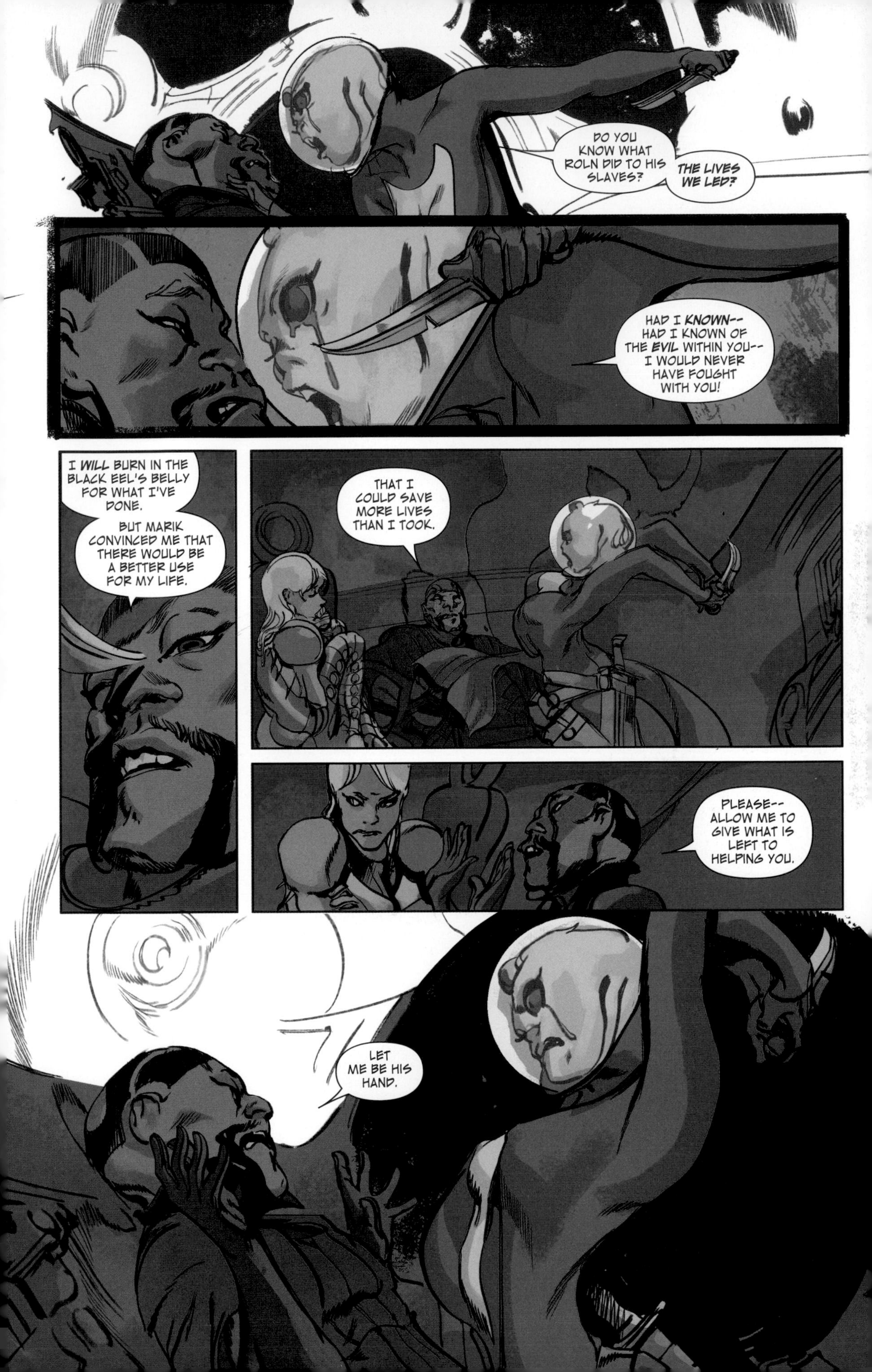
DO YOU KNOW WHAT ROLN DID TO HIS SLAVES?
THE LIVES WE LED?
HAD I KNOWN-- HAD I KNOWN OF THE EVIL WITHIN YOU-- I WOULD NEVER HAVE FOUGHT WITH YOU!
I WILL BURN IN THE BLACK EEL'S BELLY FOR WHAT I'VE DONE.
BUT MARIK CONVINCED ME THAT THERE WOULD BE A BETTER USE FOR MY LIFE.
THAT I COULD SAVE MORE LIVES THAN I TOOK.
PLEASE-- ALLOW ME TO GIVE WHAT IS LEFT TO HELPING YOU.
LET ME BE HIS HAND.

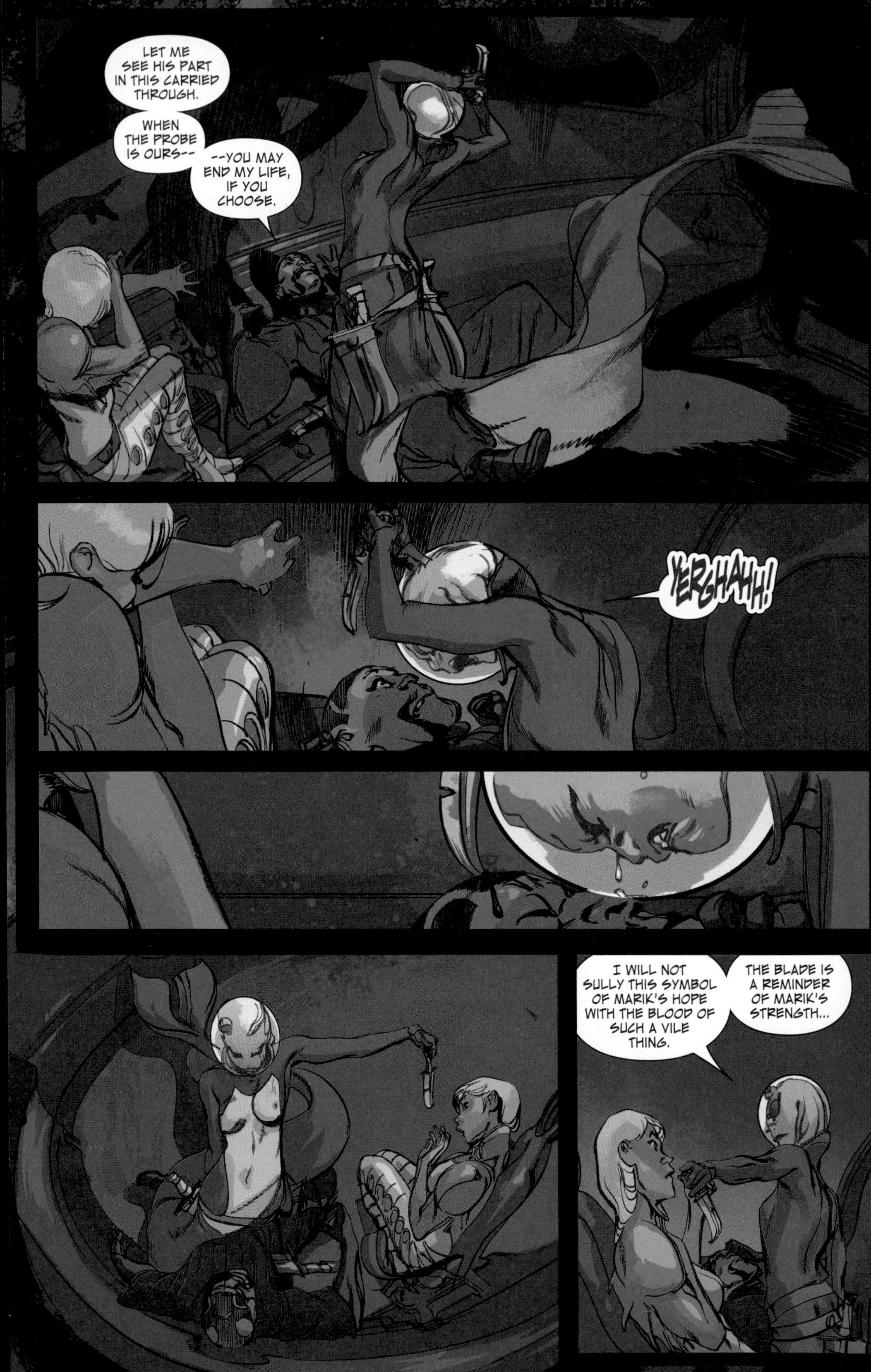
LET ME SEE HIS PART IN THIS CARRIED THROUGH.
WHEN THE PROBE IS OURS--
--YOU MAY END MY LIFE, IF YOU CHOOSE.
YERGHAHH!
I WILL NOT SULLY THIS SYMBOL OF MARIK'S HOPE WITH THE BLOOD OF SUCH A VILE THING.
THE BLADE IS A REMINDER OF MARIK'S STRENGTH...

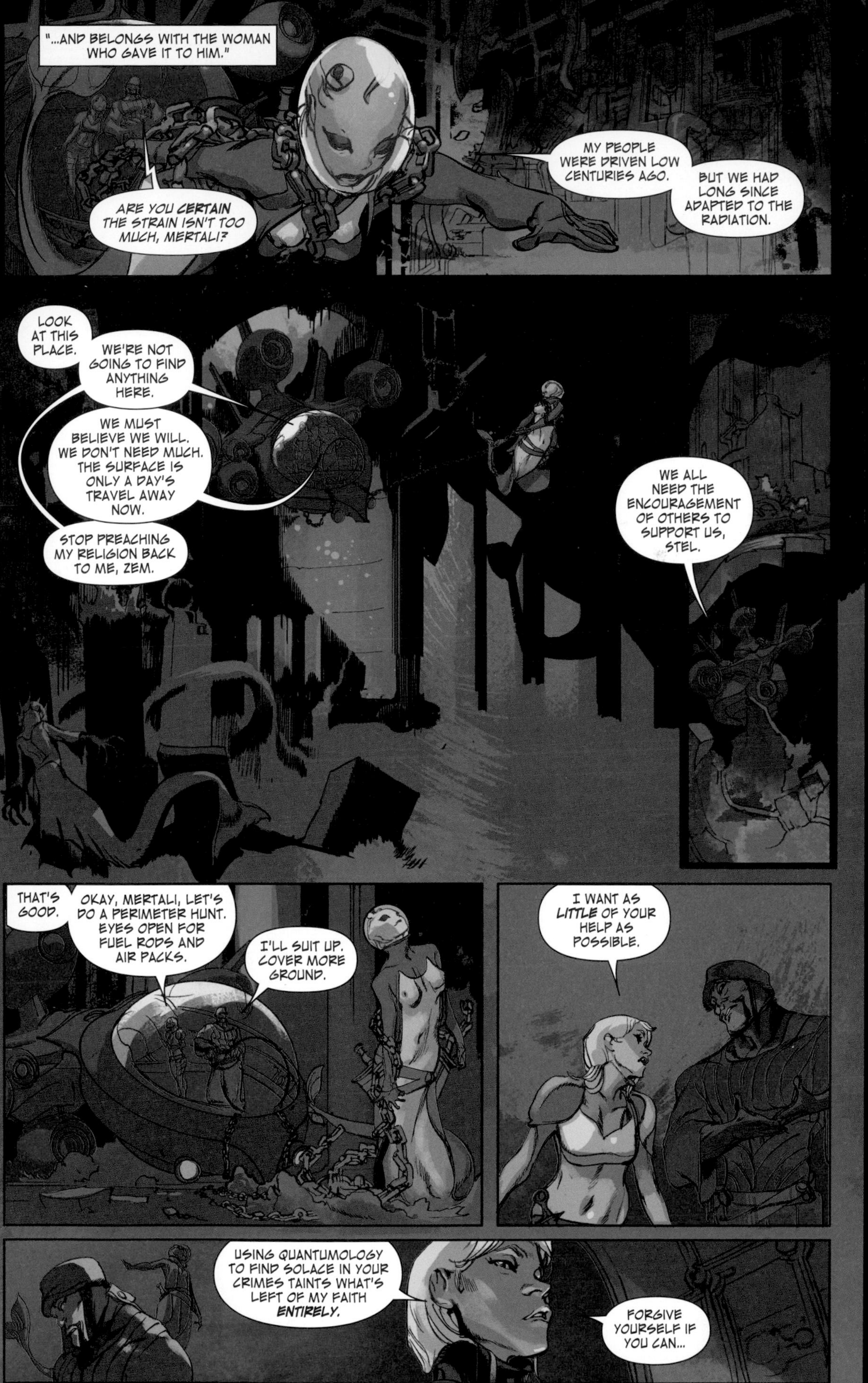
"...AND BELONGS WITH THE WOMAN WHO GAVE IT TO HIM."
ARE YOU CERTAIN THE STRAIN ISN'T TOO MUCH, MERTALI?
MY PEOPLE WERE DRIVEN LOW CENTURIES AGO.
BUT WE HAD LONG SINCE ADAPTED TO THE RADIATION.
LOOK AT THIS PLACE.
WE'RE NOT GOING TO FIND ANYTHING HERE.
WE MUST BELIEVE WE WILL. WE DON'T NEED MUCH. THE SURFACE IS ONLY A DAY'S TRAVEL AWAY NOW.
STOP PREACHING MY RELIGION BACK TO ME, ZEM.
WE ALL NEED THE ENCOURAGEMENT OF OTHERS TO SUPPORT US, STEL.
THAT'S GOOD.
OKAY, MERTALI, LET'S DO A PERIMETER HUNT. EYES OPEN FOR FUEL RODS AND AIR PACKS.
I'LL SUIT UP. COVER MORE GROUND.
I WANT AS LITTLE OF YOUR HELP AS POSSIBLE.
USING QUANTUMOLOGY TO FIND SOLACE IN YOUR CRIMES TAINTS WHAT'S LEFT OF MY FAITH ENTIRELY.
FORGIVE YOURSELF IF YOU CAN...

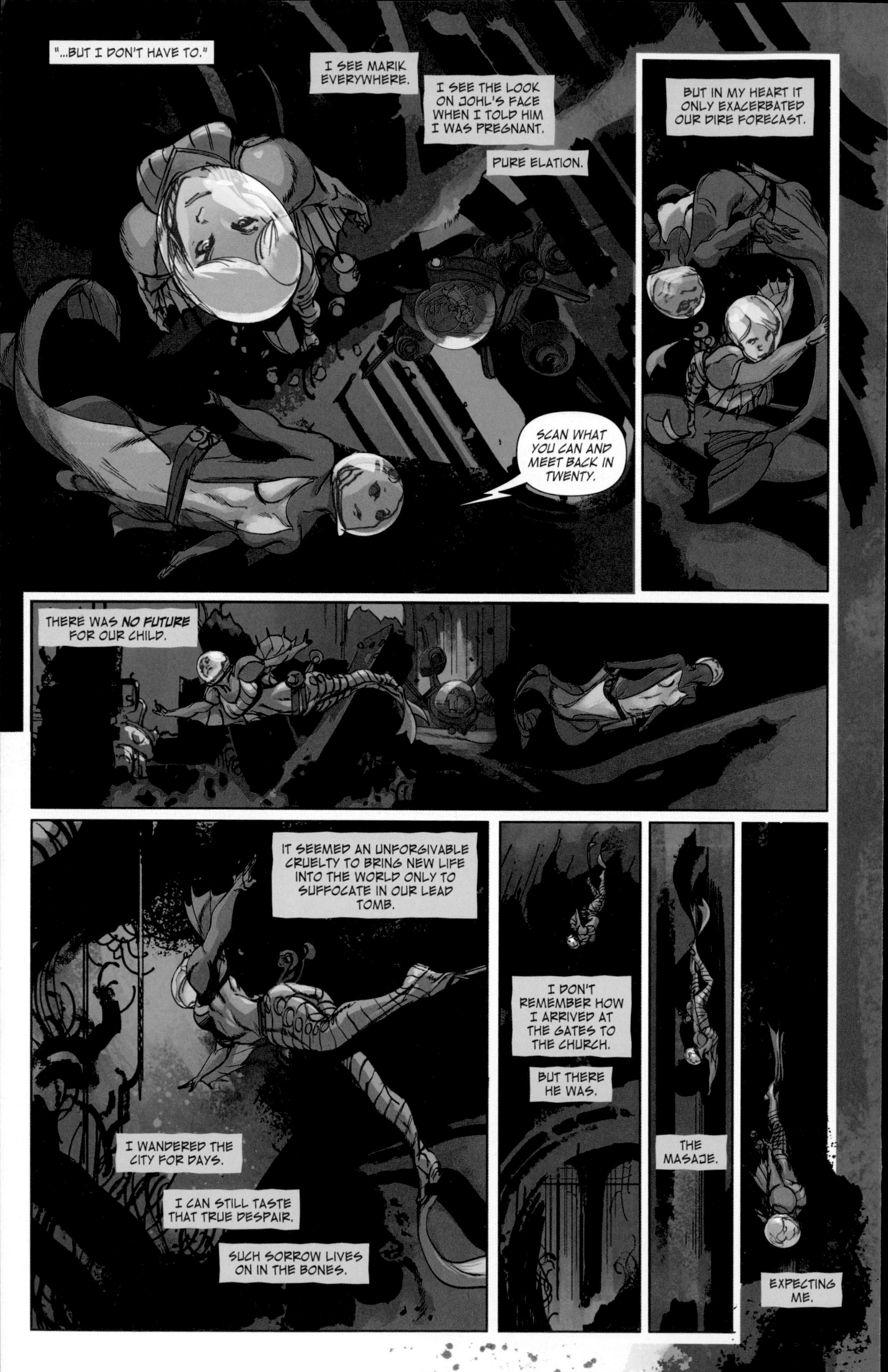
"...BUT I DON'T HAVE TO."
I SEE MARIK EVERYWHERE.
I SEE THE LOOK ON JOHL'S FACE WHEN I TOLD HIM I WAS PREGNANT.
PURE ELATION.
SCAN WHAT YOU CAN AND MEET BACK IN TWENTY.
BUT IN MY HEART IT ONLY EXACERBATED OUR DIRE FORECAST.
THERE WAS *NO FUTURE* FOR OUR CHILD.
IT SEEMED AN UNFORGIVABLE CRUELTY TO BRING NEW LIFE INTO THE WORLD ONLY TO SUFFOCATE IN OUR LEAD TOMB.
I WANDERED THE CITY FOR DAYS.
I CAN STILL TASTE THAT TRUE DESPAIR.
SUCH SORROW LIVES ON IN THE BONES.
I DON'T REMEMBER HOW I ARRIVED AT THE GATES TO THE CHURCH.
BUT THERE HE WAS.
THE MASAJE.
EXPECTING ME.

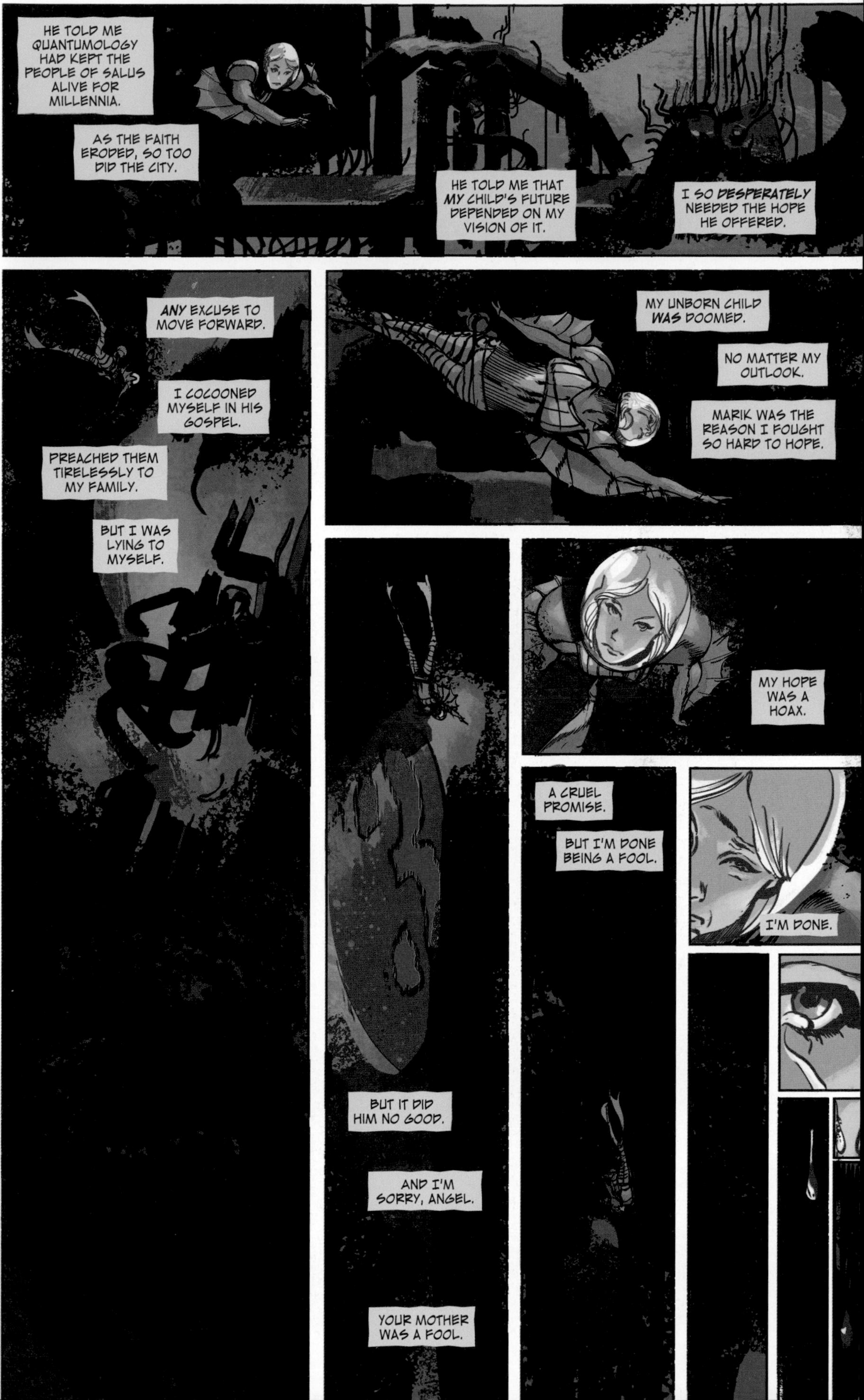
HE TOLD ME QUANTUMOLOGY HAD KEPT THE PEOPLE OF SALUS ALIVE FOR MILLENNIA.
AS THE FAITH ERODED, SO TOO DID THE CITY.
HE TOLD ME THAT MY CHILD'S FUTURE DEPENDED ON MY VISION OF IT.
I SO DESPERATELY NEEDED THE HOPE HE OFFERED.
ANY EXCUSE TO MOVE FORWARD.
I COCOONED MYSELF IN HIS GOSPEL.
PREACHED THEM TIRELESSLY TO MY FAMILY.
BUT I WAS LYING TO MYSELF.
MY UNBORN CHILD WAS DOOMED.
NO MATTER MY OUTLOOK.
MARIK WAS THE REASON I FOUGHT SO HARD TO HOPE.
BUT IT DID HIM NO GOOD.
AND I'M SORRY, ANGEL.
YOUR MOTHER WAS A FOOL.
MY HOPE WAS A HOAX.
A CRUEL PROMISE.
BUT I'M DONE BEING A FOOL.
I'M DONE.

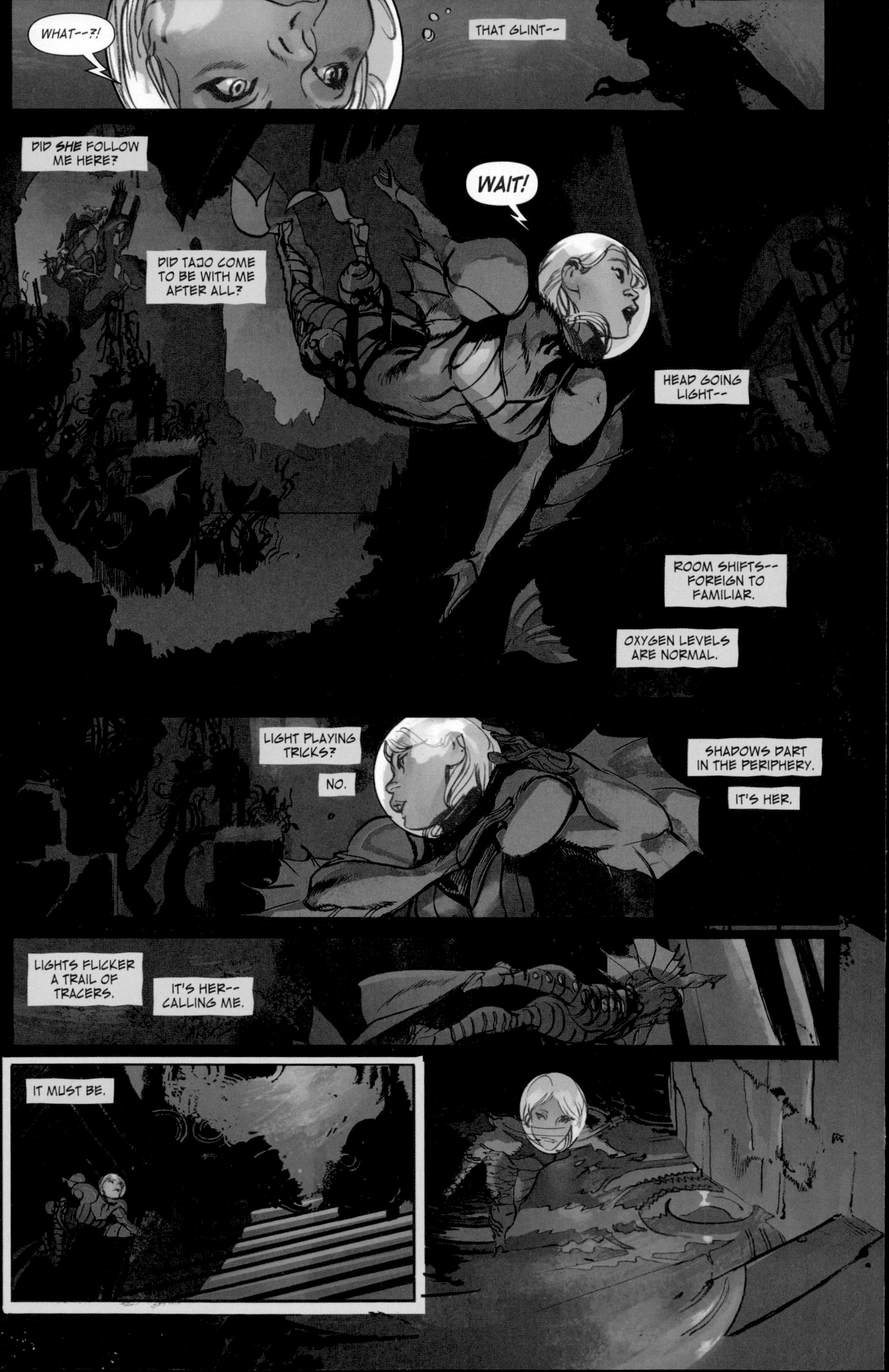
WHAT--?!
THAT GLINT--
DID SHE FOLLOW ME HERE?
WAIT!
DID TAJO COME TO BE WITH ME AFTER ALL?
HEAD GOING LIGHT--
ROOM SHIFTS-- FOREIGN TO FAMILIAR.
OXYGEN LEVELS ARE NORMAL.
LIGHT PLAYING TRICKS?
NO.
SHADOWS DART IN THE PERIPHERY.
IT'S HER.
LIGHTS FLICKER A TRAIL OF TRACERS.
IT'S HER-- CALLING ME.
IT MUST BE.

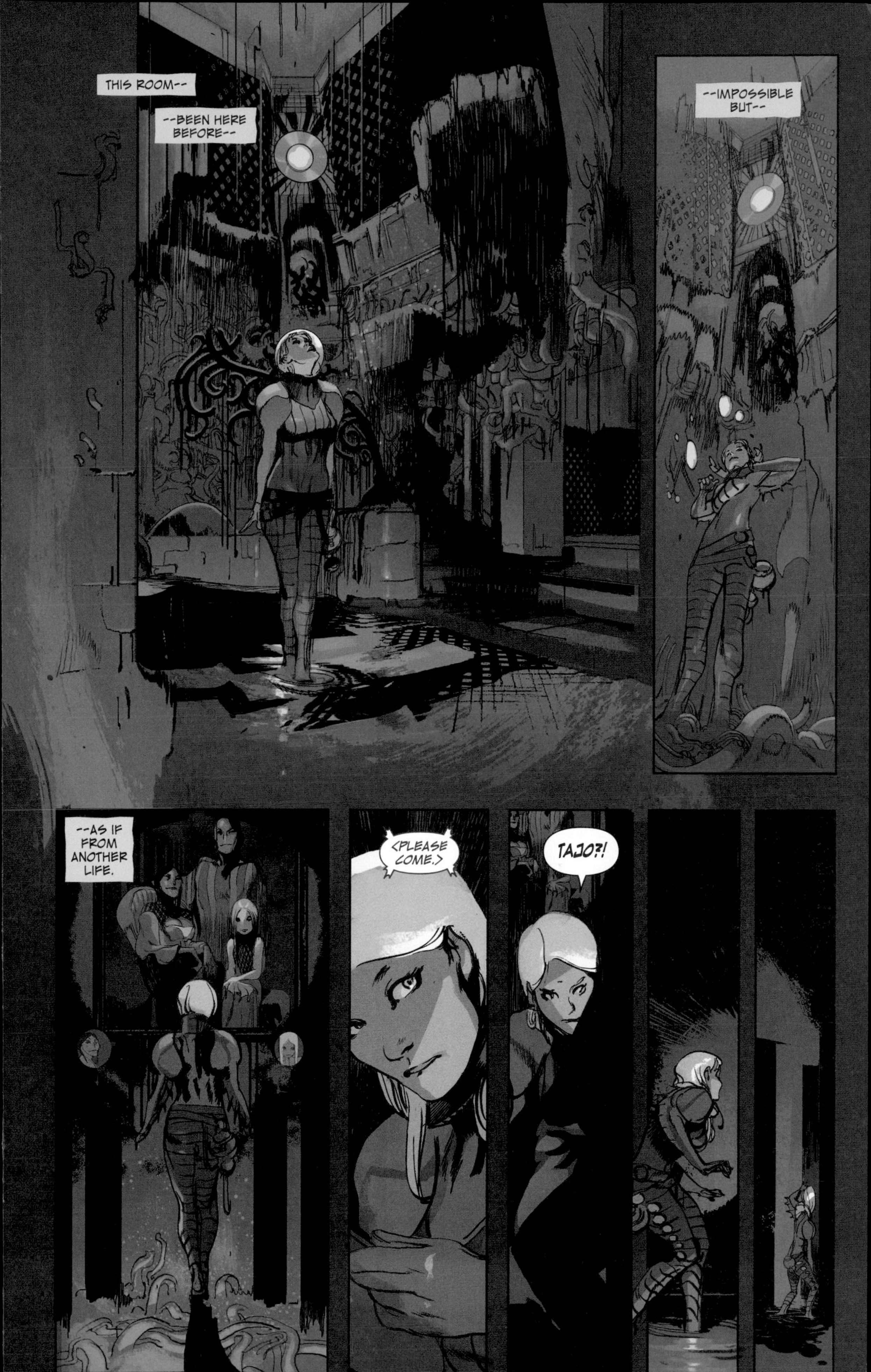
THIS ROOM--
--BEEN HERE BEFORE--
--IMPOSSIBLE BUT--
--AS IF FROM ANOTHER LIFE.
<PLEASE COME.>
TAJO?!

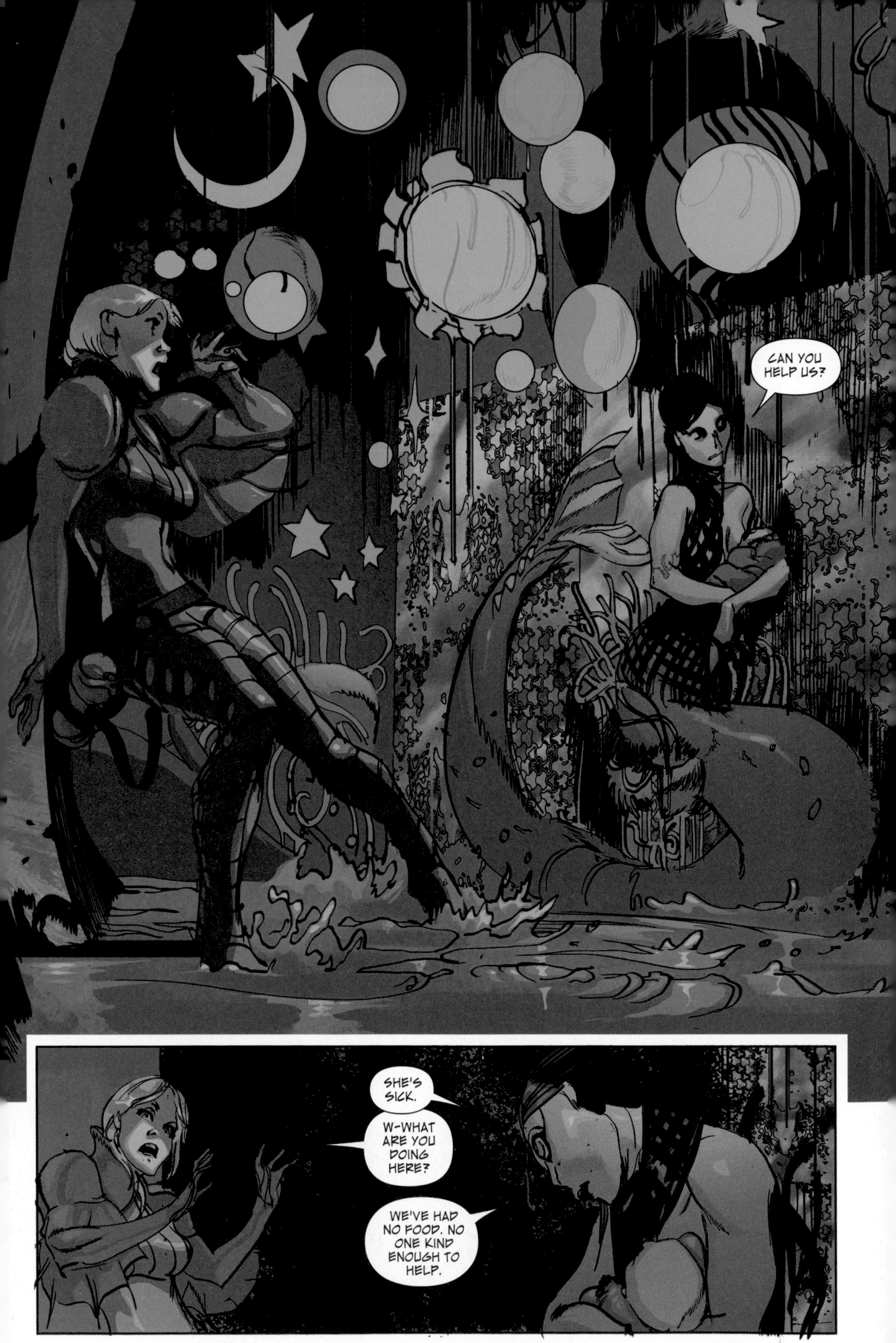
CAN YOU HELP US?
SHE'S SICK.
W-WHAT ARE YOU DOING HERE?
WE'VE HAD NO FOOD. NO ONE KIND ENOUGH TO HELP.

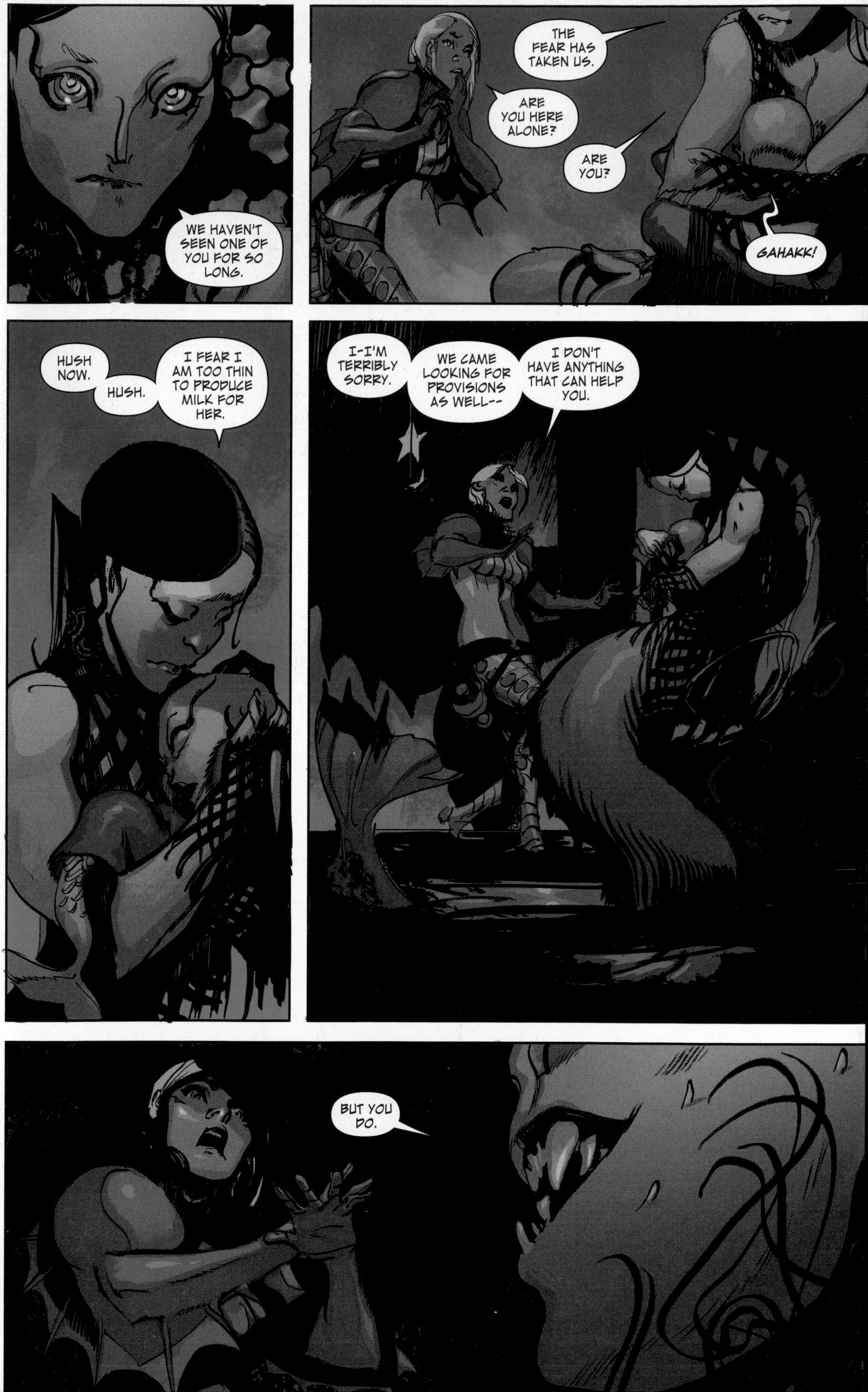
WE HAVEN'T SEEN ONE OF YOU FOR SO LONG.
THE FEAR HAS TAKEN US.
ARE YOU HERE ALONE?
ARE YOU?
GAHAKK!
HUSH NOW.
HUSH.
I FEAR I AM TOO THIN TO PRODUCE MILK FOR HER.
I-I'M TERRIBLY SORRY.
WE CAME LOOKING FOR PROVISIONS AS WELL--
I DON'T HAVE ANYTHING THAT CAN HELP YOU.
BUT YOU DO.

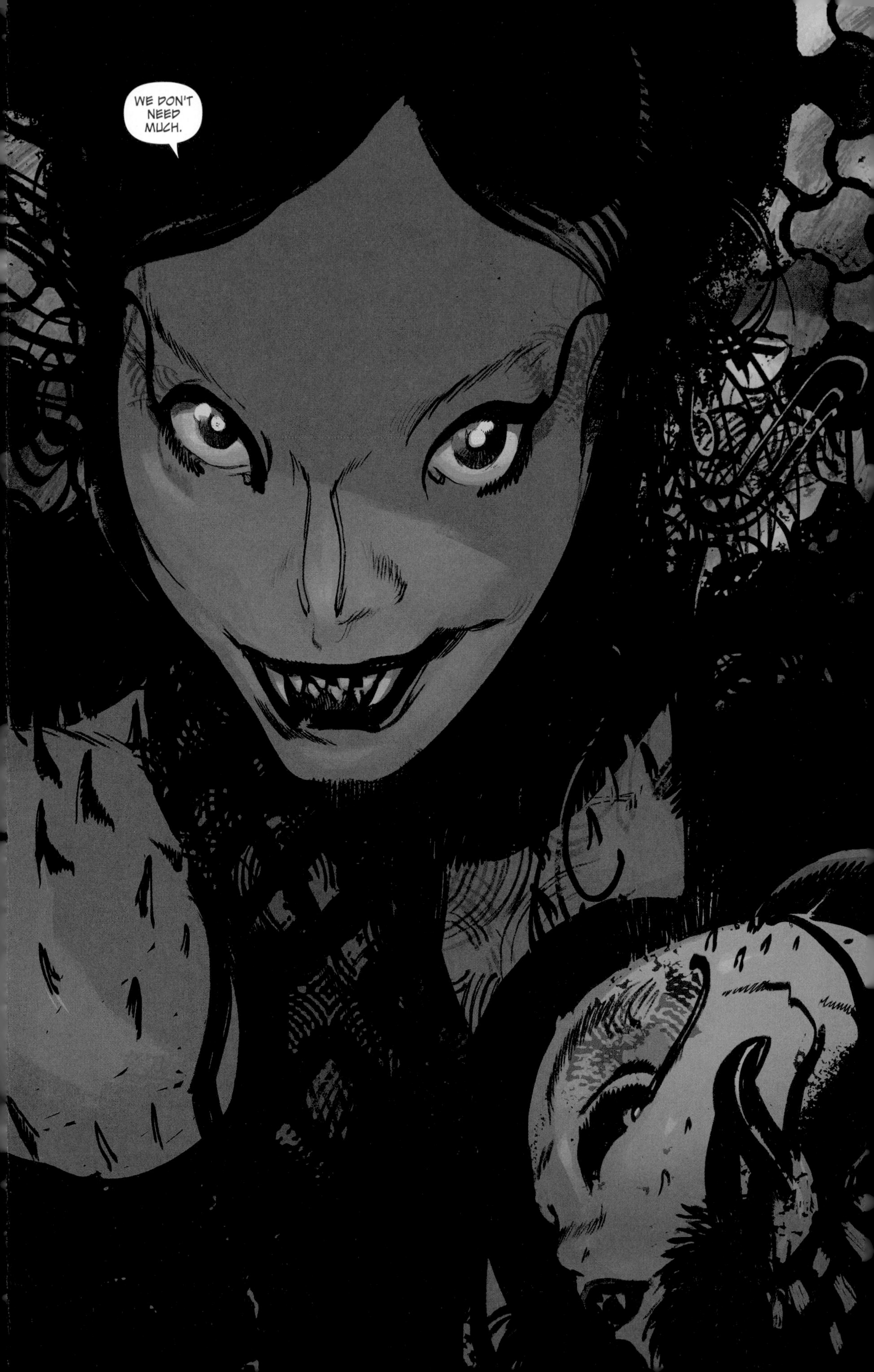
WE DON'T NEED MUCH.

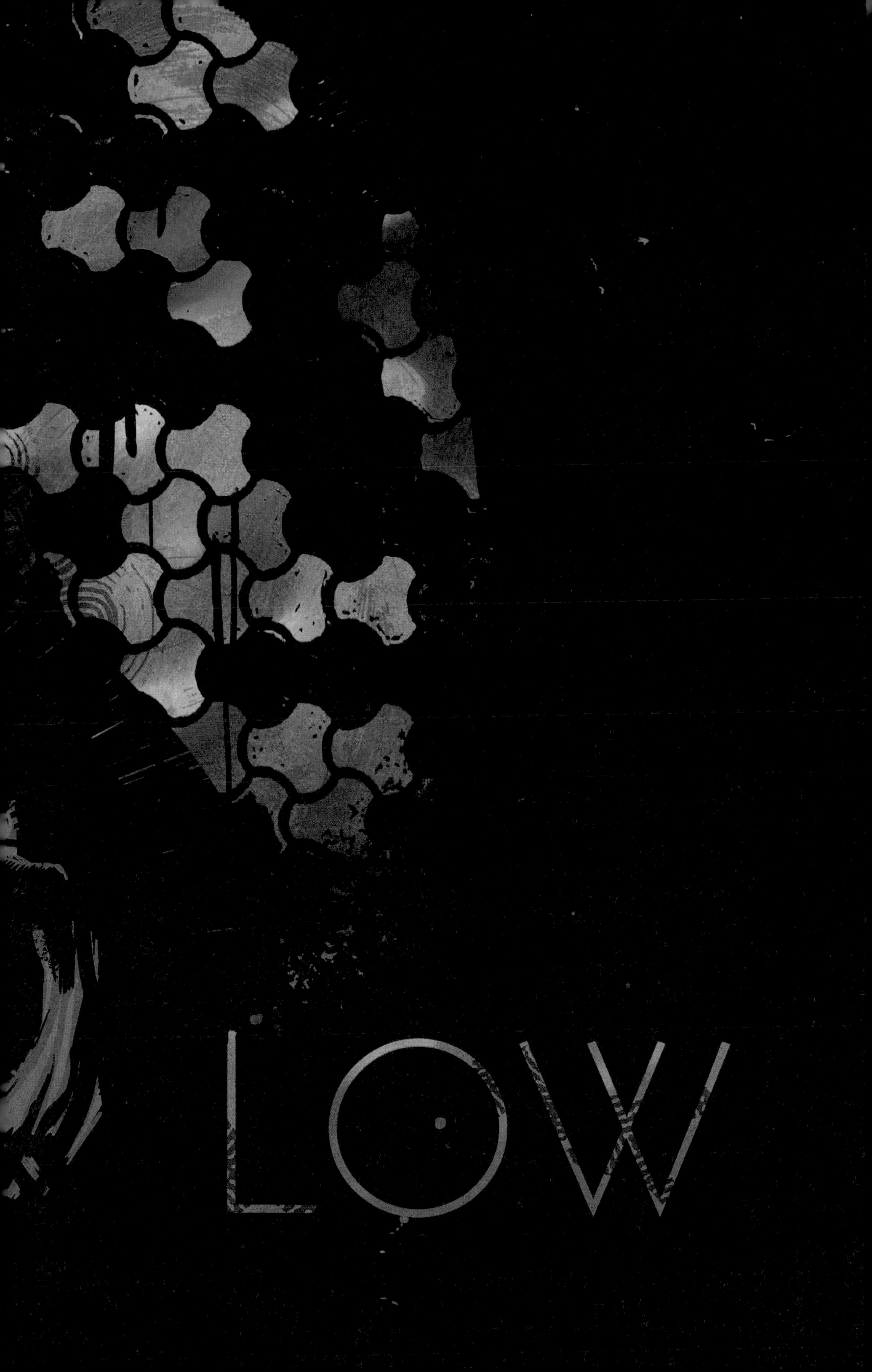
LOW

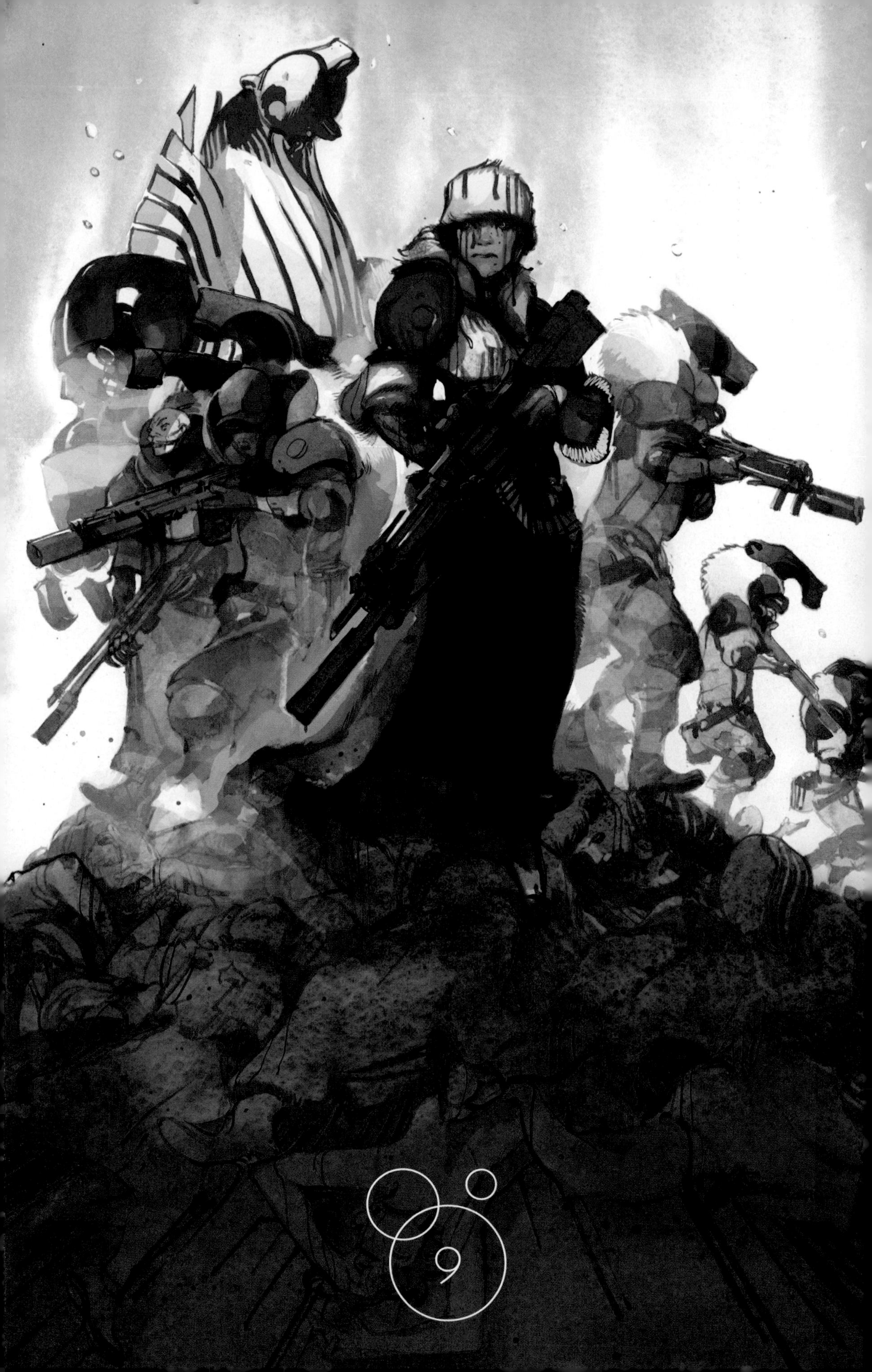
9

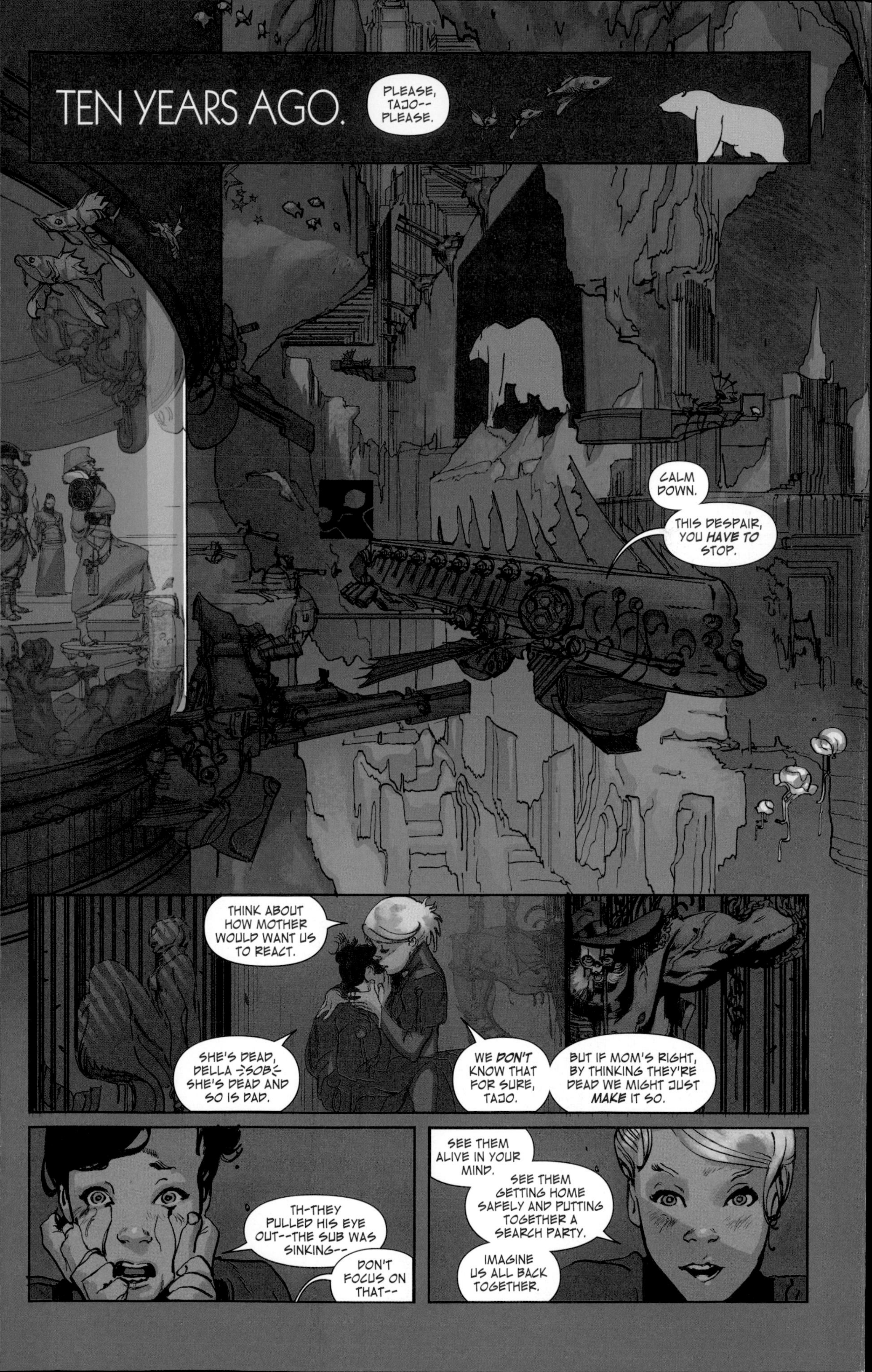
TEN YEARS AGO.
PLEASE, TAJO-- PLEASE.
CALM DOWN.
THIS DESPAIR, YOU HAVE TO STOP.
THINK ABOUT HOW MOTHER WOULD WANT US TO REACT.
SHE'S DEAD, DELLA -SOB- SHE'S DEAD AND SO IS DAD.
WE DON'T KNOW THAT FOR SURE, TAJO.
BUT IF MOM'S RIGHT, BY THINKING THEY'RE DEAD WE MIGHT JUST MAKE IT SO.
TH-THEY PULLED HIS EYE OUT--THE SUB WAS SINKING--
DON'T FOCUS ON THAT--
SEE THEM ALIVE IN YOUR MIND.
SEE THEM GETTING HOME SAFELY AND PUTTING TOGETHER A SEARCH PARTY.
IMAGINE US ALL BACK TOGETHER.

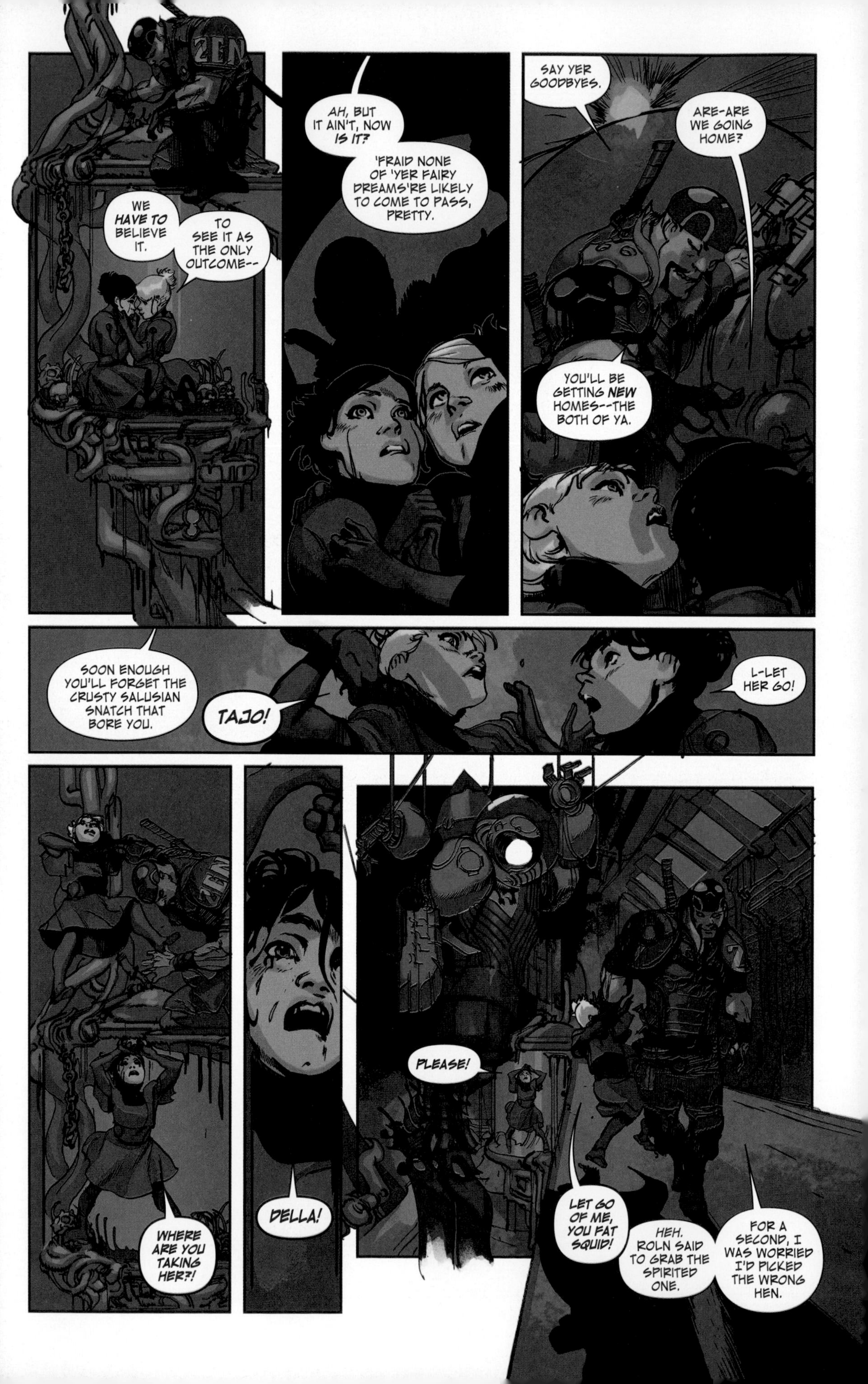

WE HAVE TO BELIEVE IT.
TO SEE IT AS THE ONLY OUTCOME--
AH, BUT IT AIN'T, NOW IS IT?
'FRAID NONE OF 'YER FAIRY DREAMS'RE LIKELY TO COME TO PASS, PRETTY.
SAY YER GOODBYES.
ARE-ARE WE GOING HOME?
YOU'LL BE GETTING NEW HOMES--THE BOTH OF YA.
SOON ENOUGH YOU'LL FORGET THE CRUSTY SALUSIAN SNATCH THAT BORE YOU.
TAJO!
L-LET HER GO!
WHERE ARE YOU TAKING HER?!
DELLA!
PLEASE!
LET GO OF ME, YOU FAT SQUID!
HEH. ROLN SAID TO GRAB THE SPIRITED ONE.
FOR A SECOND, I WAS WORRIED I'D PICKED THE WRONG HEN.

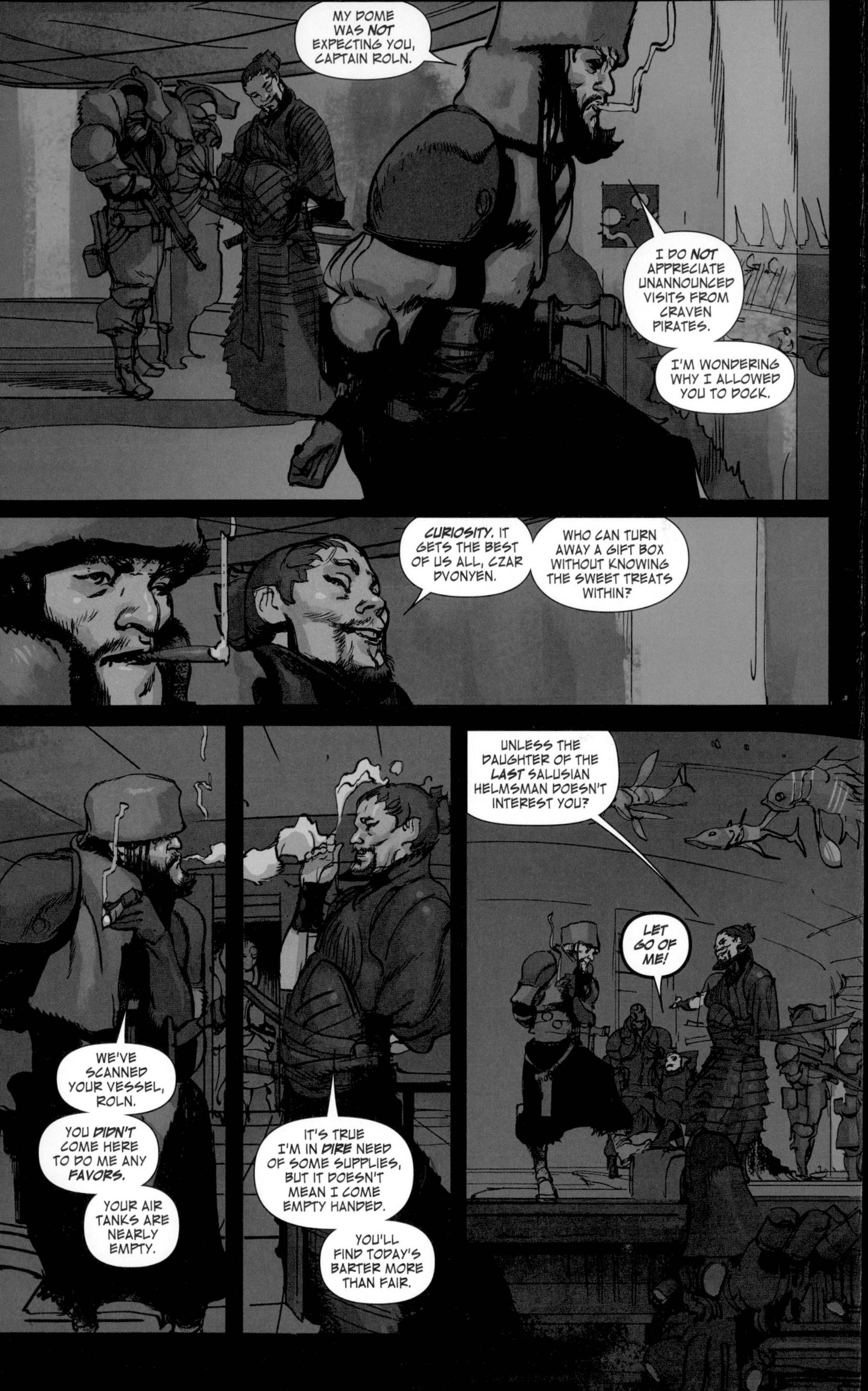
MY DOME WAS NOT EXPECTING YOU, CAPTAIN ROLN.
I DO NOT APPRECIATE UNANNOUNCED VISITS FROM CRAVEN PIRATES.
I'M WONDERING WHY I ALLOWED YOU TO DOCK.
CURIOSITY. IT GETS THE BEST OF US ALL, CZAR DVONYEN.
WHO CAN TURN AWAY A GIFT BOX WITHOUT KNOWING THE SWEET TREATS WITHIN?
WE'VE SCANNED YOUR VESSEL, ROLN.
YOU DIDN'T COME HERE TO DO ME ANY FAVORS.
YOUR AIR TANKS ARE NEARLY EMPTY.
IT'S TRUE I'M IN DIRE NEED OF SOME SUPPLIES, BUT IT DOESN'T MEAN I COME EMPTY HANDED.
YOU'LL FIND TODAY'S BARTER MORE THAN FAIR.
UNLESS THE DAUGHTER OF THE LAST SALUSIAN HELMSMAN DOESN'T INTEREST YOU?
LET GO OF ME!

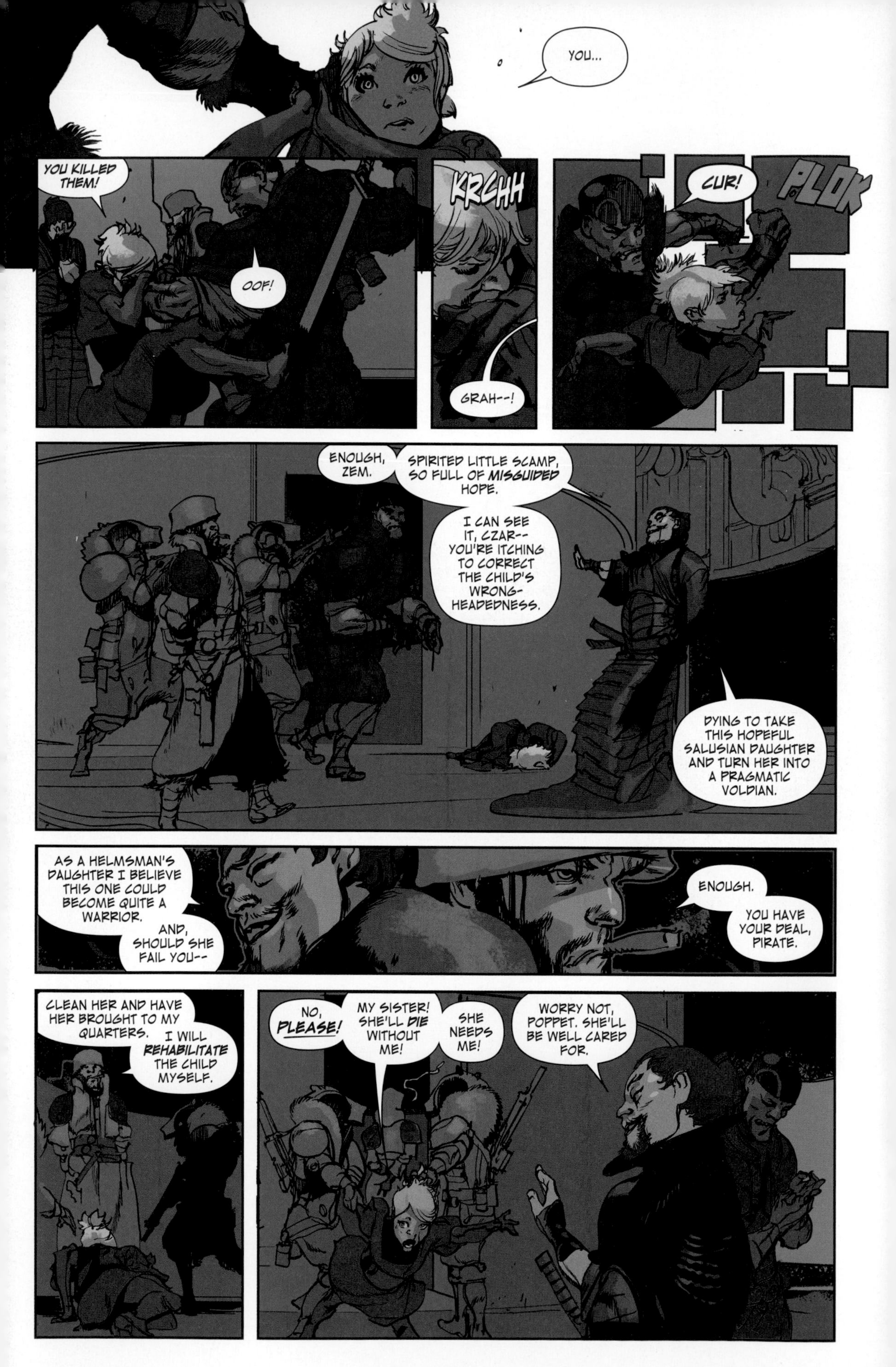
YOU...
YOU KILLED THEM!
OOF!
KRCHH
GRAH--!
CUR!
PLOK
ENOUGH, ZEM.
SPIRITED LITTLE SCAMP, SO FULL OF MISGUIDED HOPE.
I CAN SEE IT, CZAR-- YOU'RE ITCHING TO CORRECT THE CHILD'S WRONG-HEADEDNESS.
DYING TO TAKE THIS HOPEFUL SALUSIAN DAUGHTER AND TURN HER INTO A PRAGMATIC VOLDIAN.
AS A HELMSMAN'S DAUGHTER I BELIEVE THIS ONE COULD BECOME QUITE A WARRIOR.
AND, SHOULD SHE FAIL YOU--
ENOUGH.
YOU HAVE YOUR DEAL, PIRATE.
CLEAN HER AND HAVE HER BROUGHT TO MY QUARTERS.
I WILL REHABILITATE THE CHILD MYSELF.
NO, PLEASE!
MY SISTER! SHE'LL DIE WITHOUT ME!
SHE NEEDS ME!
WORRY NOT, POPPET. SHE'LL BE WELL CARED FOR.

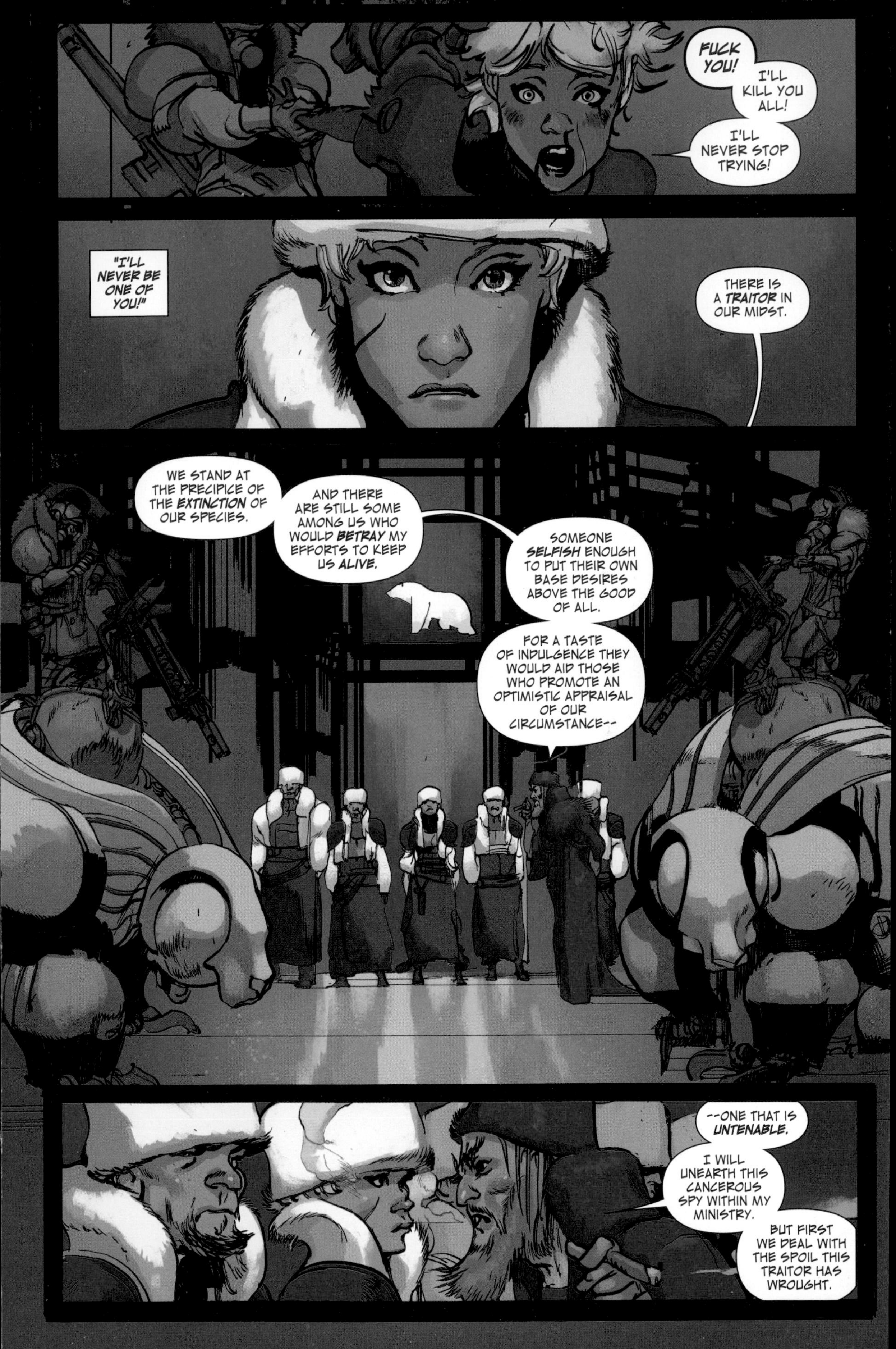
FUCK YOU!
I'LL KILL YOU ALL!
I'LL NEVER STOP TRYING!
"I'LL NEVER BE ONE OF YOU!"
THERE IS A TRAITOR IN OUR MIDST.
WE STAND AT THE PRECIPICE OF THE EXTINCTION OF OUR SPECIES.
AND THERE ARE STILL SOME AMONG US WHO WOULD BETRAY MY EFFORTS TO KEEP US ALIVE.
SOMEONE SELFISH ENOUGH TO PUT THEIR OWN BASE DESIRES ABOVE THE GOOD OF ALL.
FOR A TASTE OF INDULGENCE THEY WOULD AID THOSE WHO PROMOTE AN OPTIMISTIC APPRAISAL OF OUR CIRCUMSTANCE--
--ONE THAT IS UNTENABLE.
I WILL UNEARTH THIS CANCEROUS SPY WITHIN MY MINISTRY.
BUT FIRST WE DEAL WITH THE SPOIL THIS TRAITOR HAS WROUGHT.

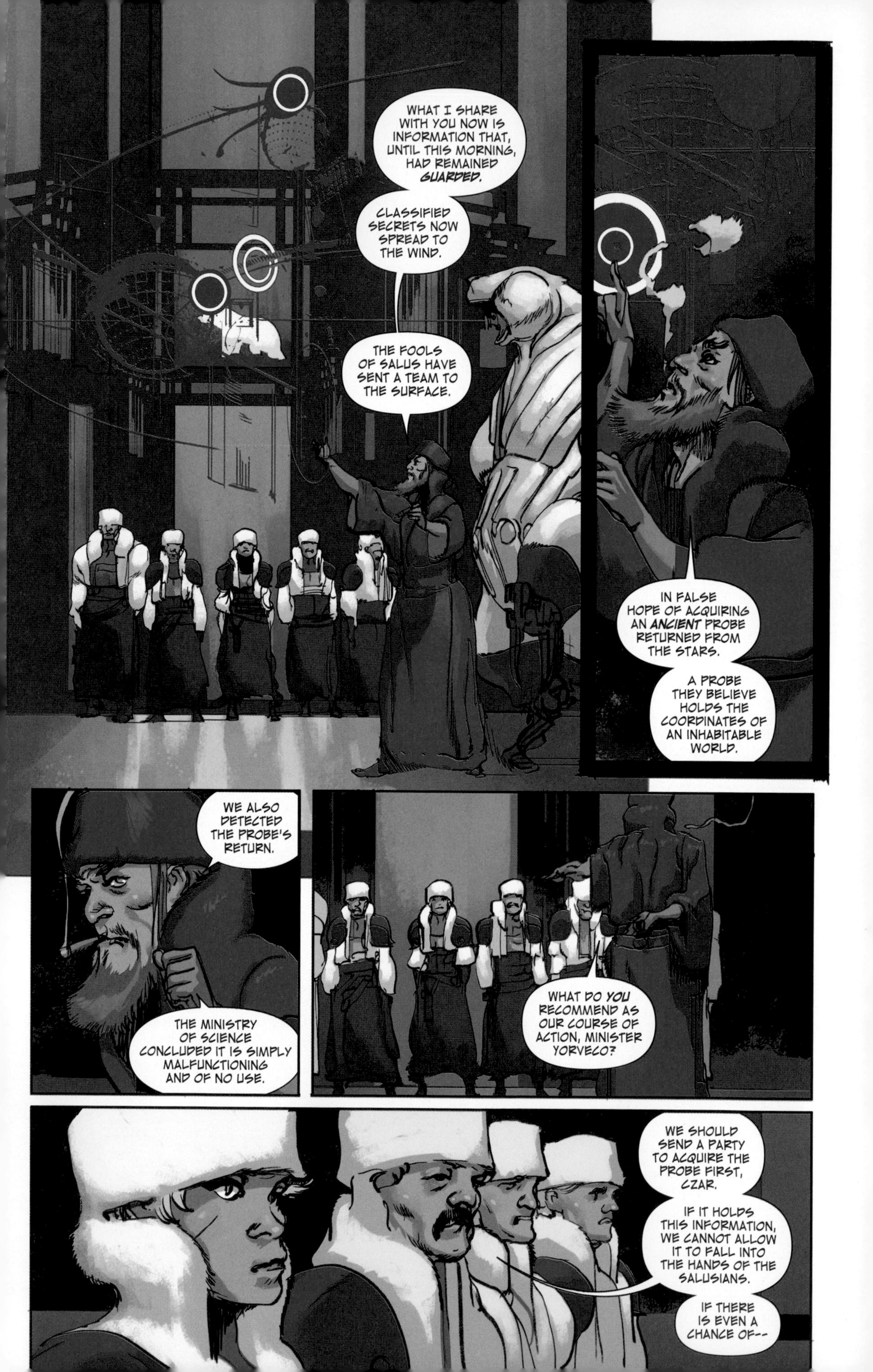

WHAT I SHARE WITH YOU NOW IS INFORMATION THAT, UNTIL THIS MORNING, HAD REMAINED *GUARDED.*
CLASSIFIED SECRETS NOW SPREAD TO THE WIND.
THE FOOLS OF SALUS HAVE SENT A TEAM TO THE SURFACE.
IN FALSE HOPE OF ACQUIRING AN *ANCIENT* PROBE RETURNED FROM THE STARS.
A PROBE THEY BELIEVE HOLDS THE COORDINATES OF AN INHABITABLE WORLD.
WE ALSO DETECTED THE PROBE'S RETURN.
THE MINISTRY OF SCIENCE CONCLUDED IT IS SIMPLY MALFUNCTIONING AND OF NO USE.
WHAT DO *YOU* RECOMMEND AS OUR COURSE OF ACTION, MINISTER YORVECO?
WE SHOULD SEND A PARTY TO ACQUIRE THE PROBE FIRST, CZAR.
IF IT HOLDS THIS INFORMATION, WE CANNOT ALLOW IT TO FALL INTO THE HANDS OF THE SALUSIANS.
IF THERE IS EVEN A CHANCE OF--

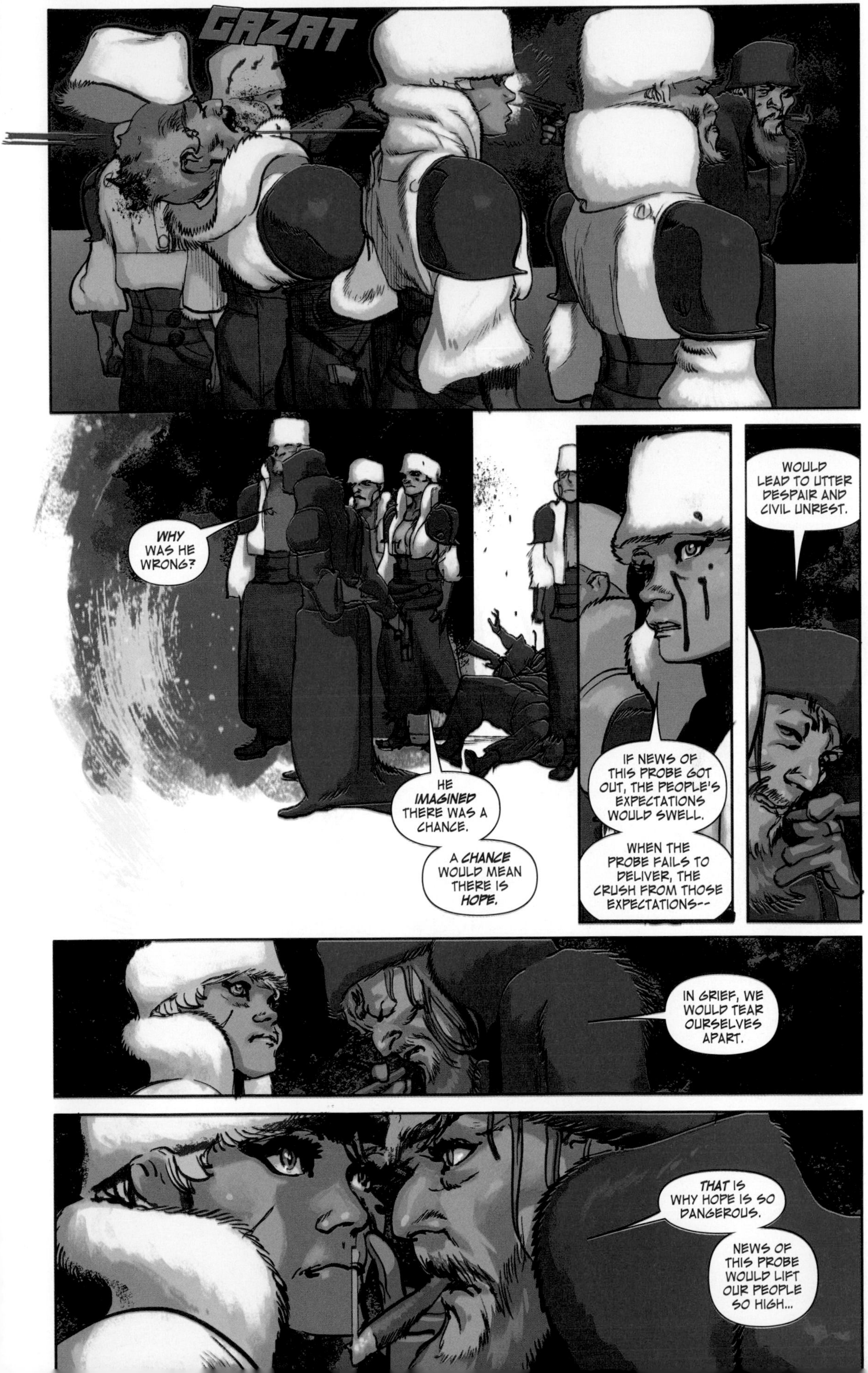
GAZAT
WHY WAS HE WRONG?
HE IMAGINED THERE WAS A CHANCE.
A CHANCE WOULD MEAN THERE IS HOPE.
IF NEWS OF THIS PROBE GOT OUT, THE PEOPLE'S EXPECTATIONS WOULD SWELL.
WHEN THE PROBE FAILS TO DELIVER, THE CRUSH FROM THOSE EXPECTATIONS--
WOULD LEAD TO UTTER DESPAIR AND CIVIL UNREST.
IN GRIEF, WE WOULD TEAR OURSELVES APART.
THAT IS WHY HOPE IS SO DANGEROUS.
NEWS OF THIS PROBE WOULD LIFT OUR PEOPLE SO HIGH...

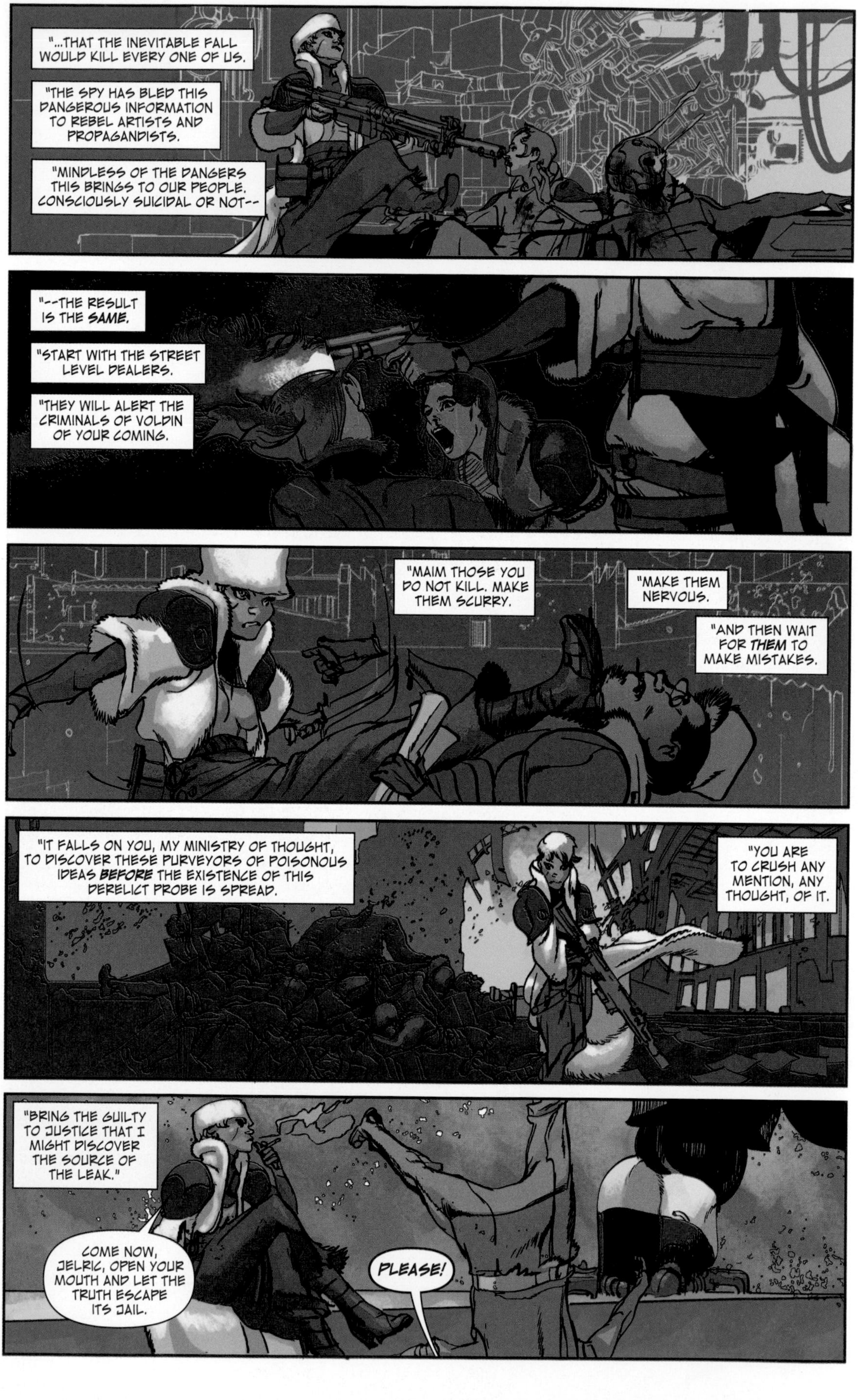
"...THAT THE INEVITABLE FALL WOULD KILL EVERY ONE OF US.
"THE SPY HAS BLED THIS DANGEROUS INFORMATION TO REBEL ARTISTS AND PROPAGANDISTS.
"MINDLESS OF THE DANGERS THIS BRINGS TO OUR PEOPLE. CONSCIOUSLY SUICIDAL OR NOT--
"--THE RESULT IS THE ***SAME.***
"START WITH THE STREET LEVEL DEALERS.
"THEY WILL ALERT THE CRIMINALS OF VOLDIN OF YOUR COMING.
"MAIM THOSE YOU DO NOT KILL. MAKE THEM SCURRY.
"MAKE THEM NERVOUS.
"AND THEN WAIT FOR ***THEM*** TO MAKE MISTAKES.
"IT FALLS ON YOU, MY MINISTRY OF THOUGHT, TO DISCOVER THESE PURVEYORS OF POISONOUS IDEAS ***BEFORE*** THE EXISTENCE OF THIS DERELICT PROBE IS SPREAD.
"YOU ARE TO CRUSH ANY MENTION, ANY THOUGHT, OF IT.
"BRING THE GUILTY TO JUSTICE THAT I MIGHT DISCOVER THE SOURCE OF THE LEAK."
COME NOW, JELRIC, OPEN YOUR MOUTH AND LET THE TRUTH ESCAPE ITS JAIL.
PLEASE!

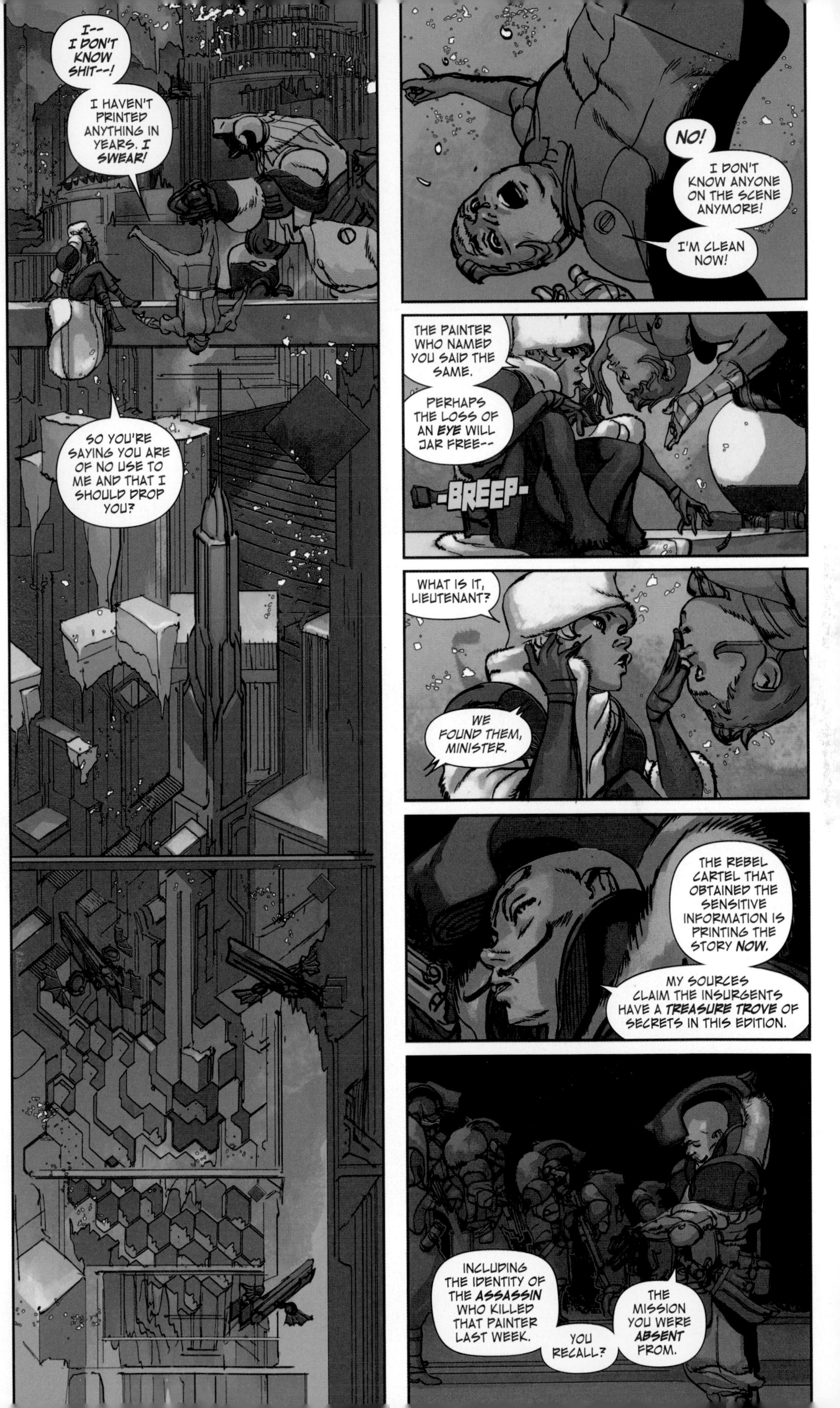
I-- I DON'T KNOW SHIT--!
I HAVEN'T PRINTED ANYTHING IN YEARS. I SWEAR!
SO YOU'RE SAYING YOU ARE OF NO USE TO ME AND THAT I SHOULD DROP YOU?
NO!
I DON'T KNOW ANYONE ON THE SCENE ANYMORE!
I'M CLEAN NOW!
THE PAINTER WHO NAMED YOU SAID THE SAME.
PERHAPS THE LOSS OF AN EYE WILL JAR FREE--
-BREEP-
WHAT IS IT, LIEUTENANT?
WE FOUND THEM, MINISTER.
THE REBEL CARTEL THAT OBTAINED THE SENSITIVE INFORMATION IS PRINTING THE STORY NOW.
MY SOURCES CLAIM THE INSURGENTS HAVE A TREASURE TROVE OF SECRETS IN THIS EDITION.
INCLUDING THE IDENTITY OF THE ASSASSIN WHO KILLED THAT PAINTER LAST WEEK.
YOU RECALL?
THE MISSION YOU WERE ABSENT FROM.

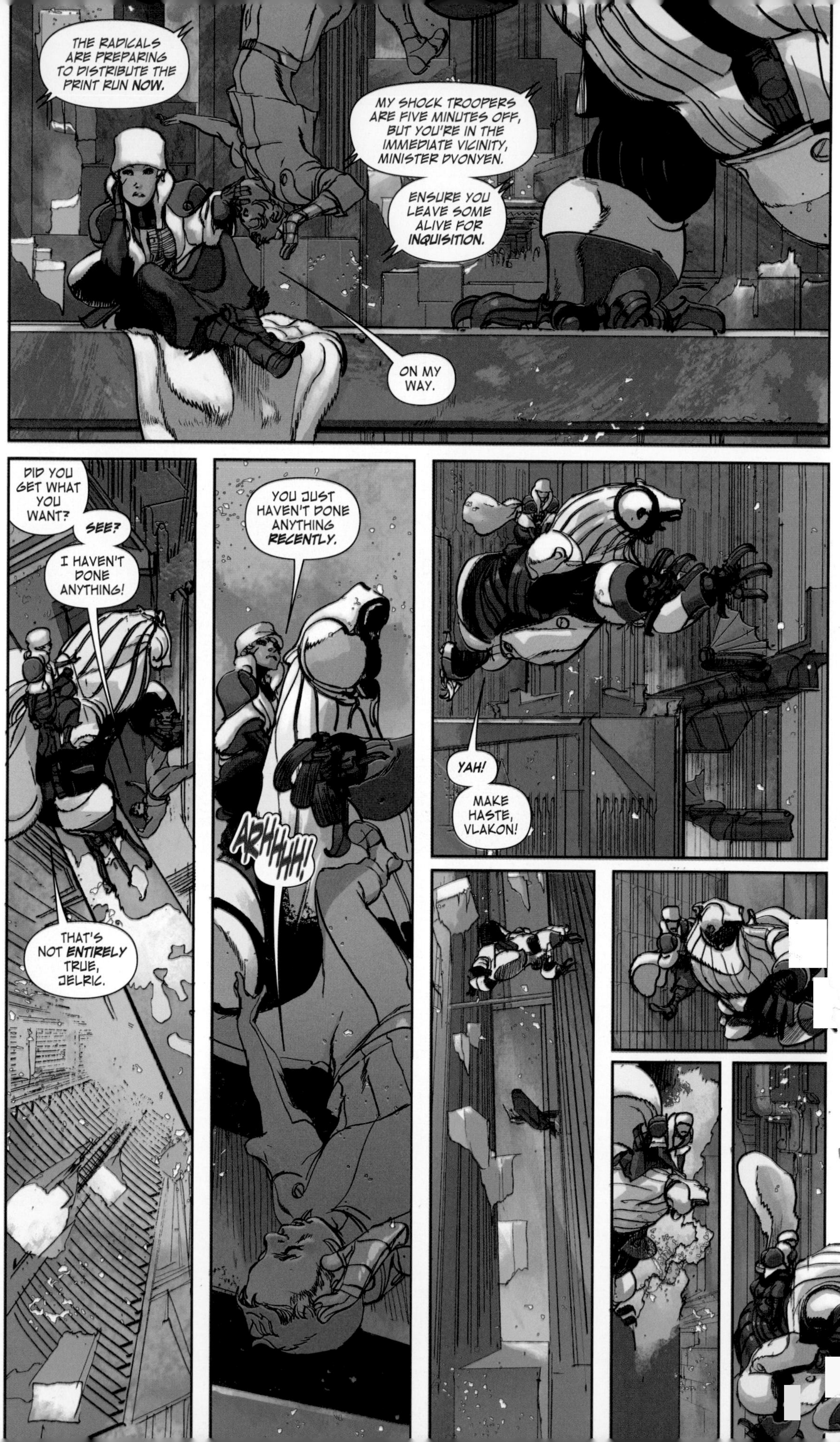
THE RADICALS ARE PREPARING TO DISTRIBUTE THE PRINT RUN NOW.
MY SHOCK TROOPERS ARE FIVE MINUTES OFF, BUT YOU'RE IN THE IMMEDIATE VICINITY, MINISTER DVONYEN.
ENSURE YOU LEAVE SOME ALIVE FOR INQUISITION.
ON MY WAY.
DID YOU GET WHAT YOU WANT?
SEE?
I HAVEN'T DONE ANYTHING!
THAT'S NOT ENTIRELY TRUE, JELRIC.
YOU JUST HAVEN'T DONE ANYTHING RECENTLY.
ARHHHH!
YAH!
MAKE HASTE, VLAKON!

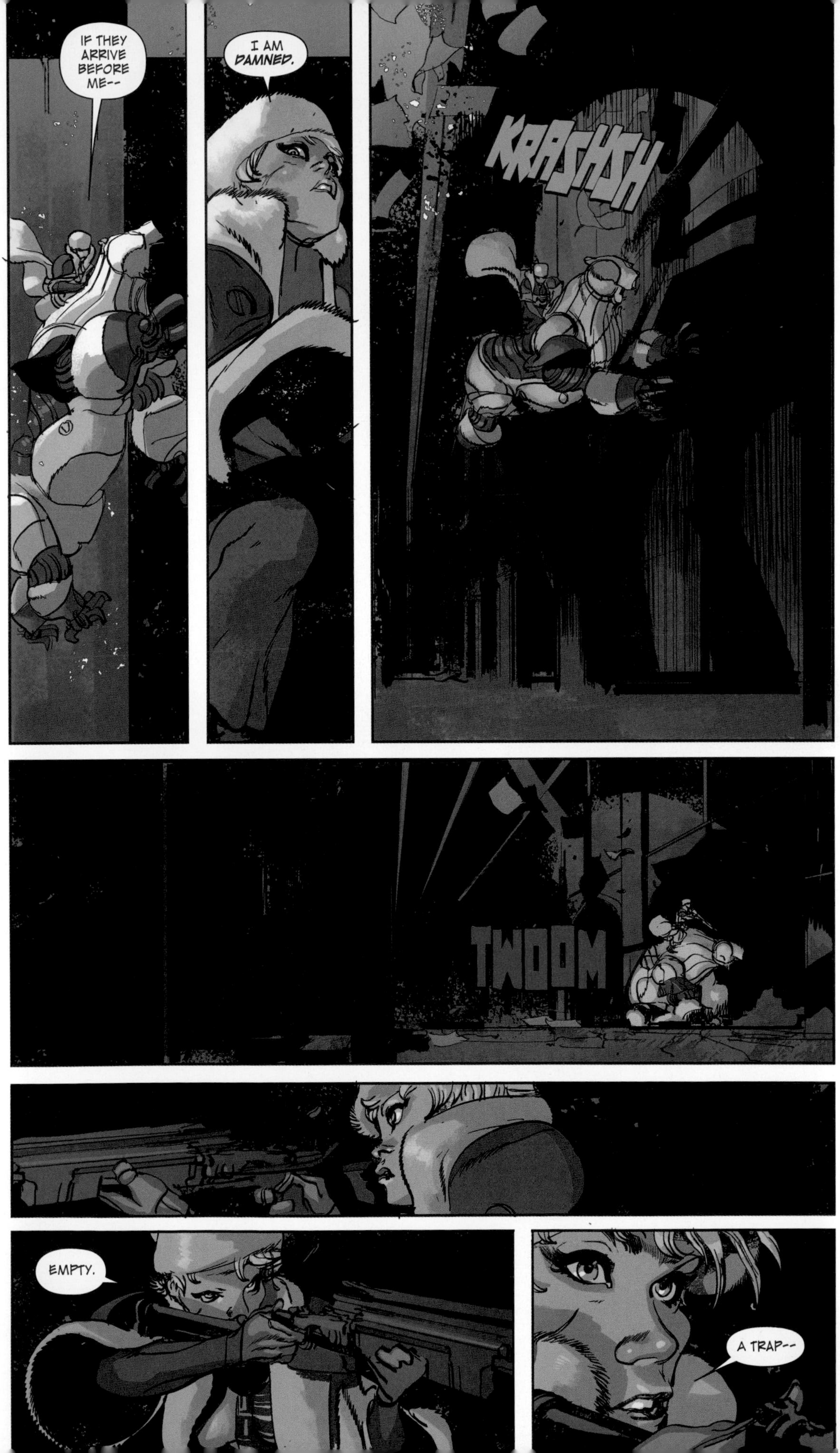
IF THEY ARRIVE BEFORE ME--
I AM DAMNED.
KRASHSH
TWOOM
EMPTY.
A TRAP--

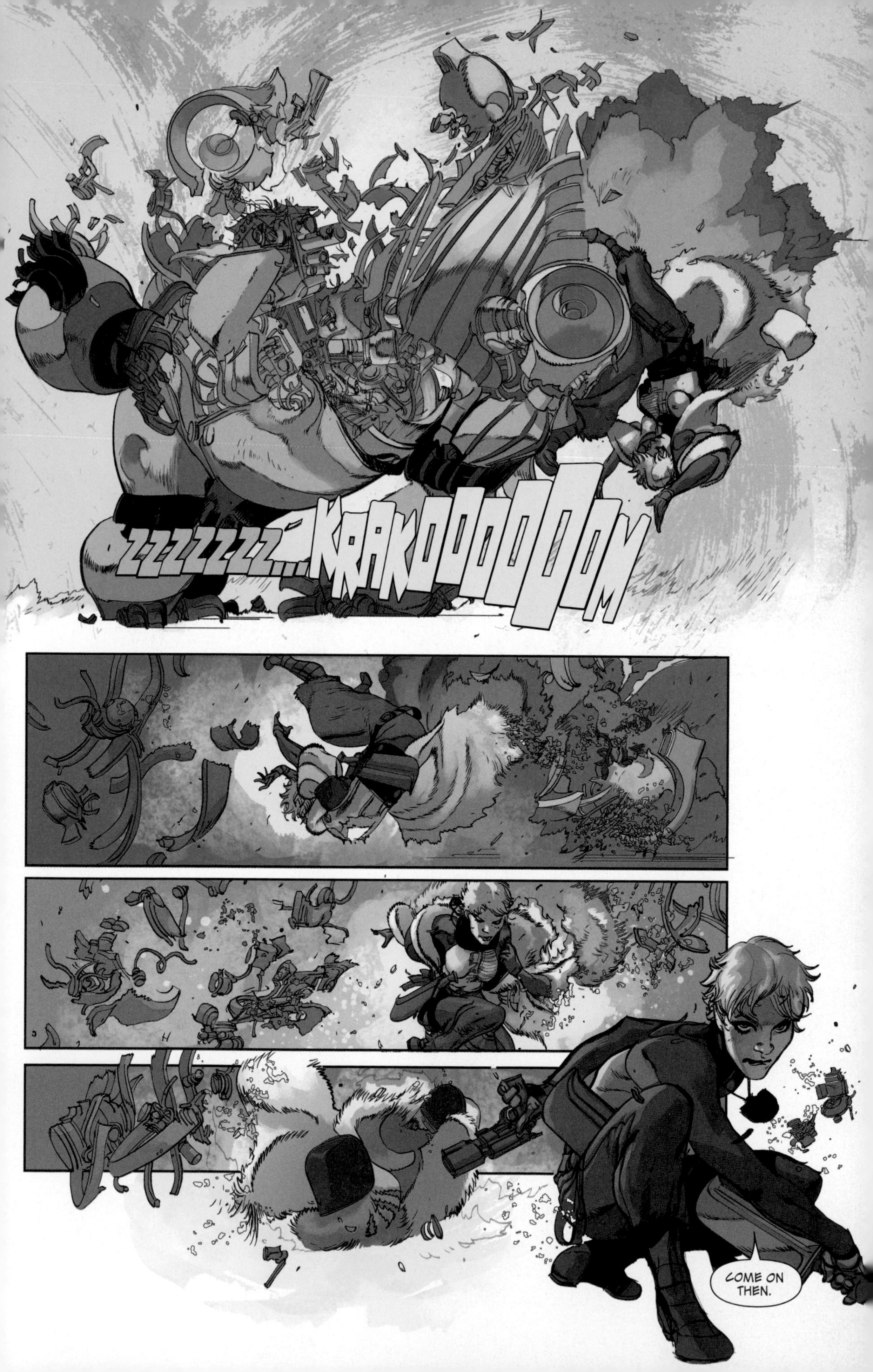

ZZZZZZZ...KRAKOOOOOOOM
COME ON THEN.

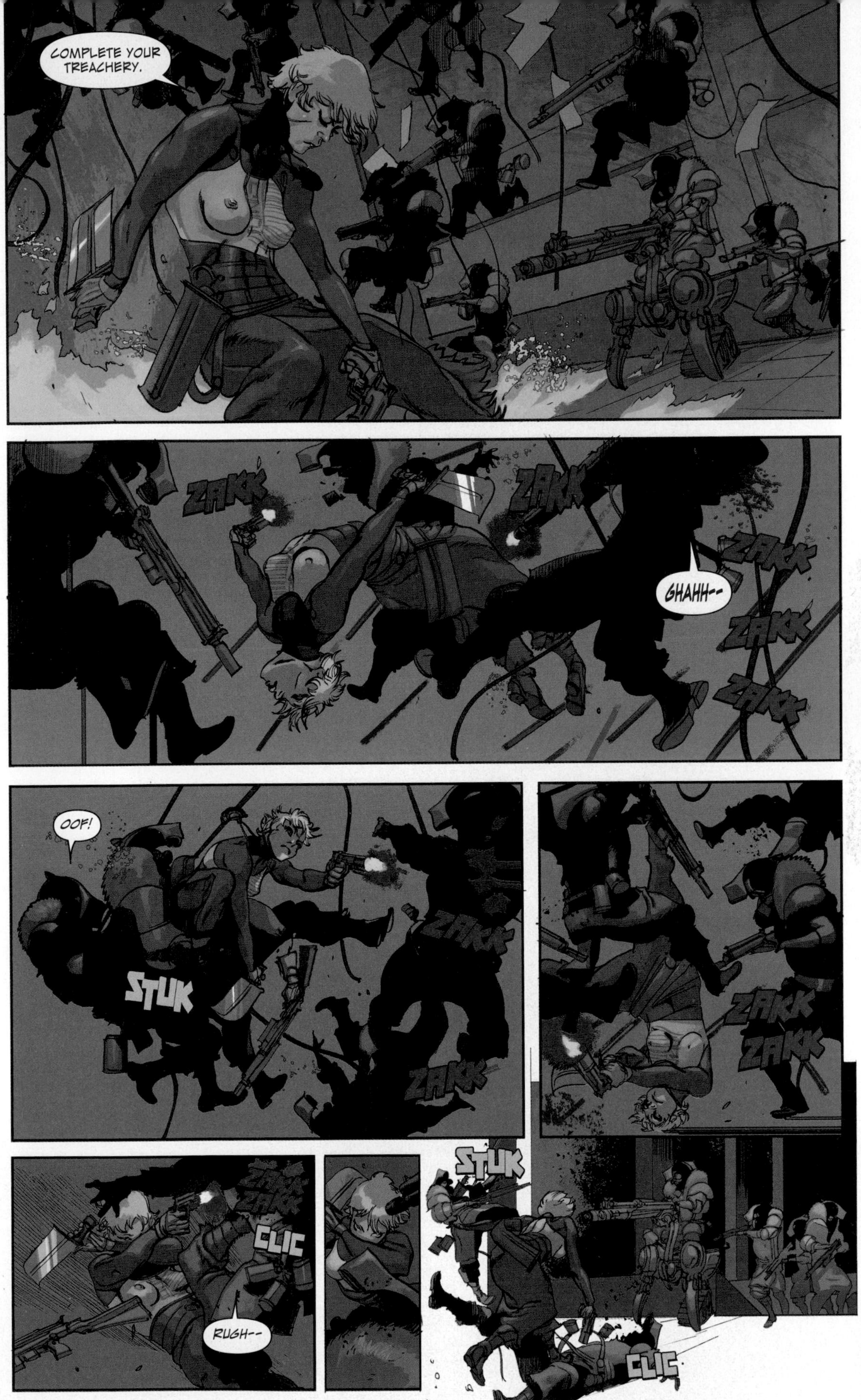
COMPLETE YOUR TREACHERY.
ZAKK
ZAKK
GHAHH--
ZAKK
ZAKK
ZAKK
OOF!
STUK
ZAKK
ZAKK
ZAKK
ZAKK
ZAKK
ZAKK
CLIC
RUGH--
STUK
CLIC

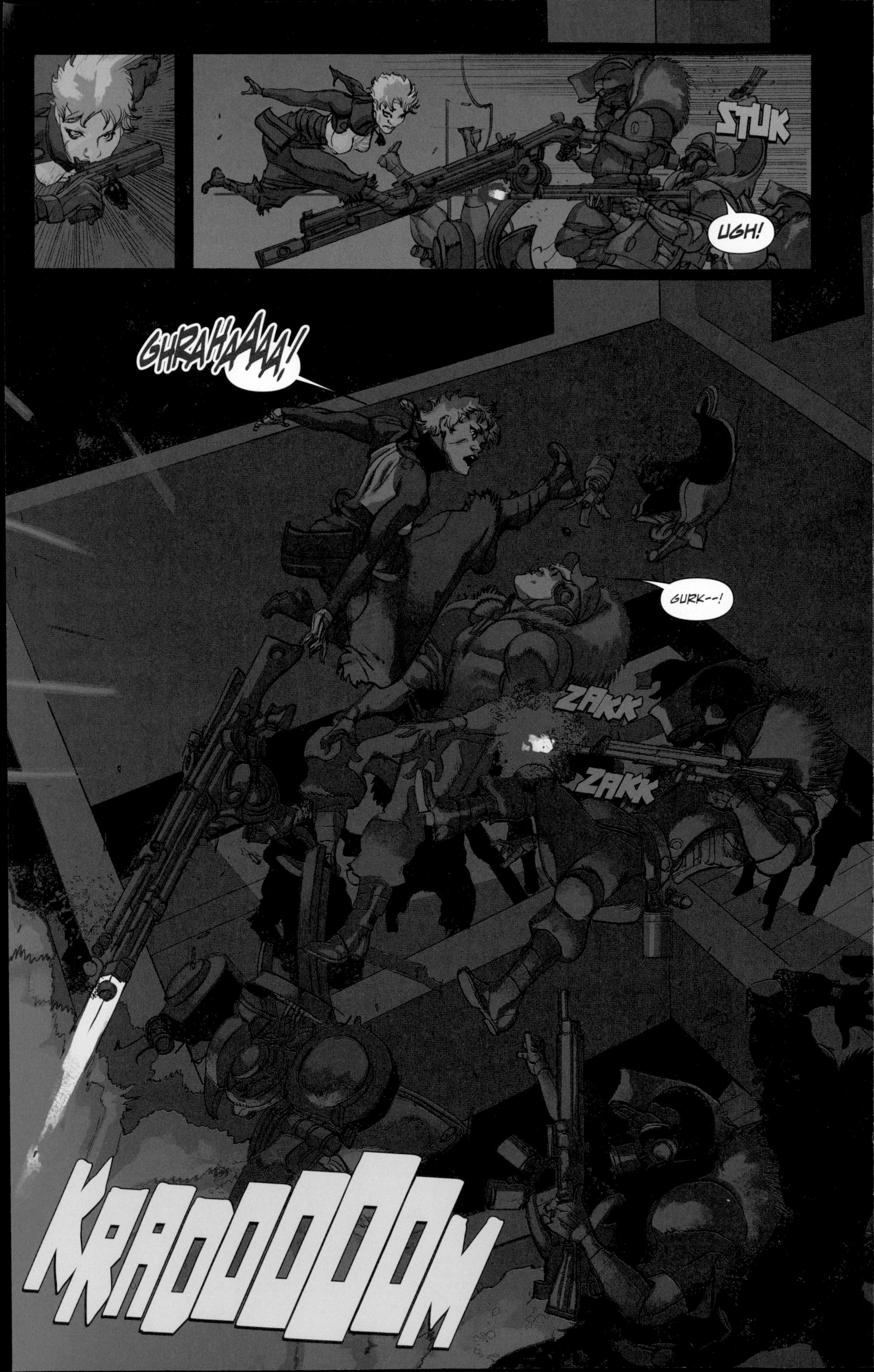
STUK
UGH!
GHRAHAAAA!
GURK--!
ZAKK
ZAKK
KRAOOOOOOM

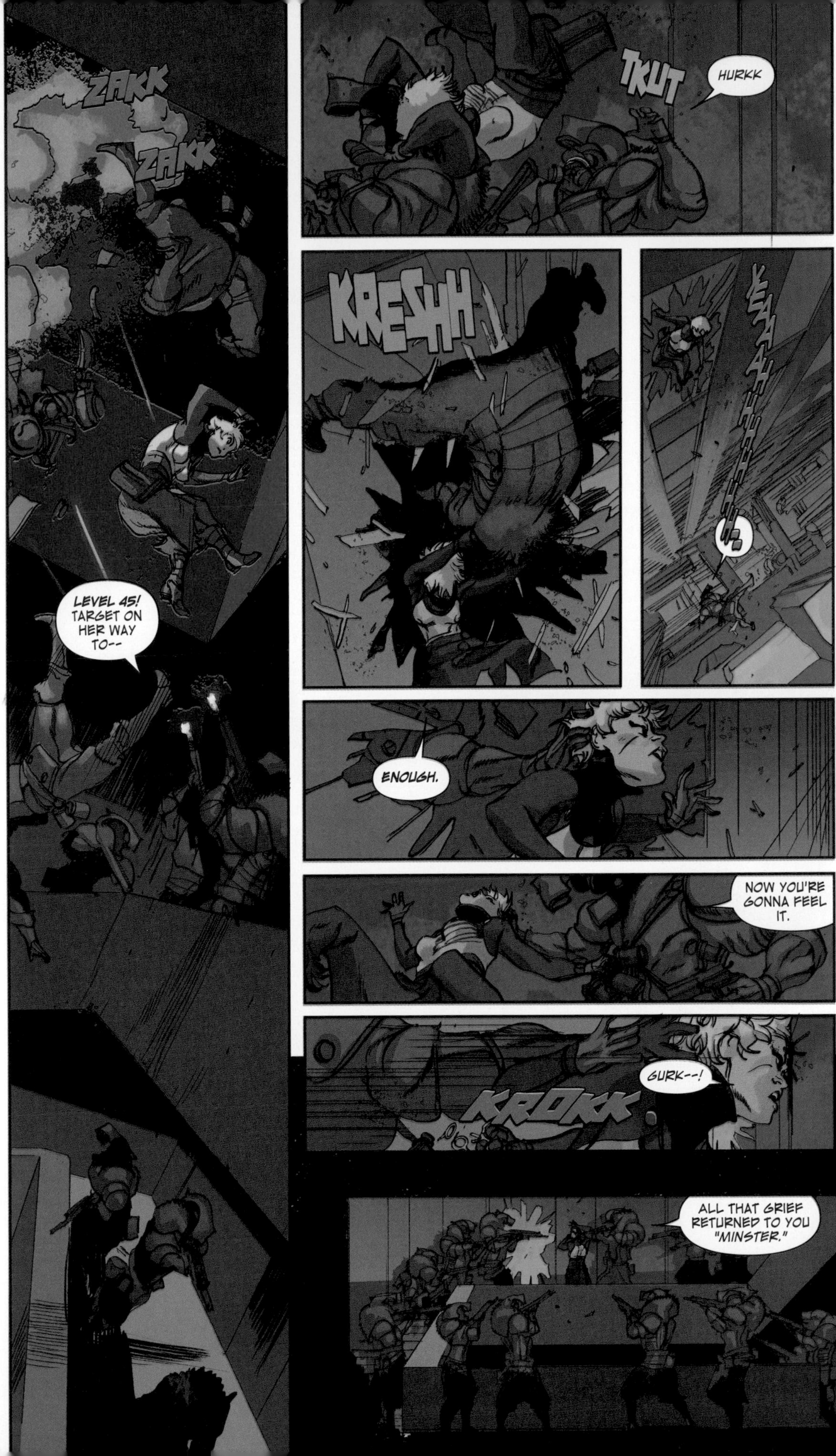
ZAKK
ZAKK
LEVEL 45! TARGET ON HER WAY TO--
TKUT
HURKK
KRESHH
YEAAAAHHHH
ENOUGH.
NOW YOU'RE GONNA FEEL IT.
GURK--!
KROKK
ALL THAT GRIEF RETURNED TO YOU "MINSTER."

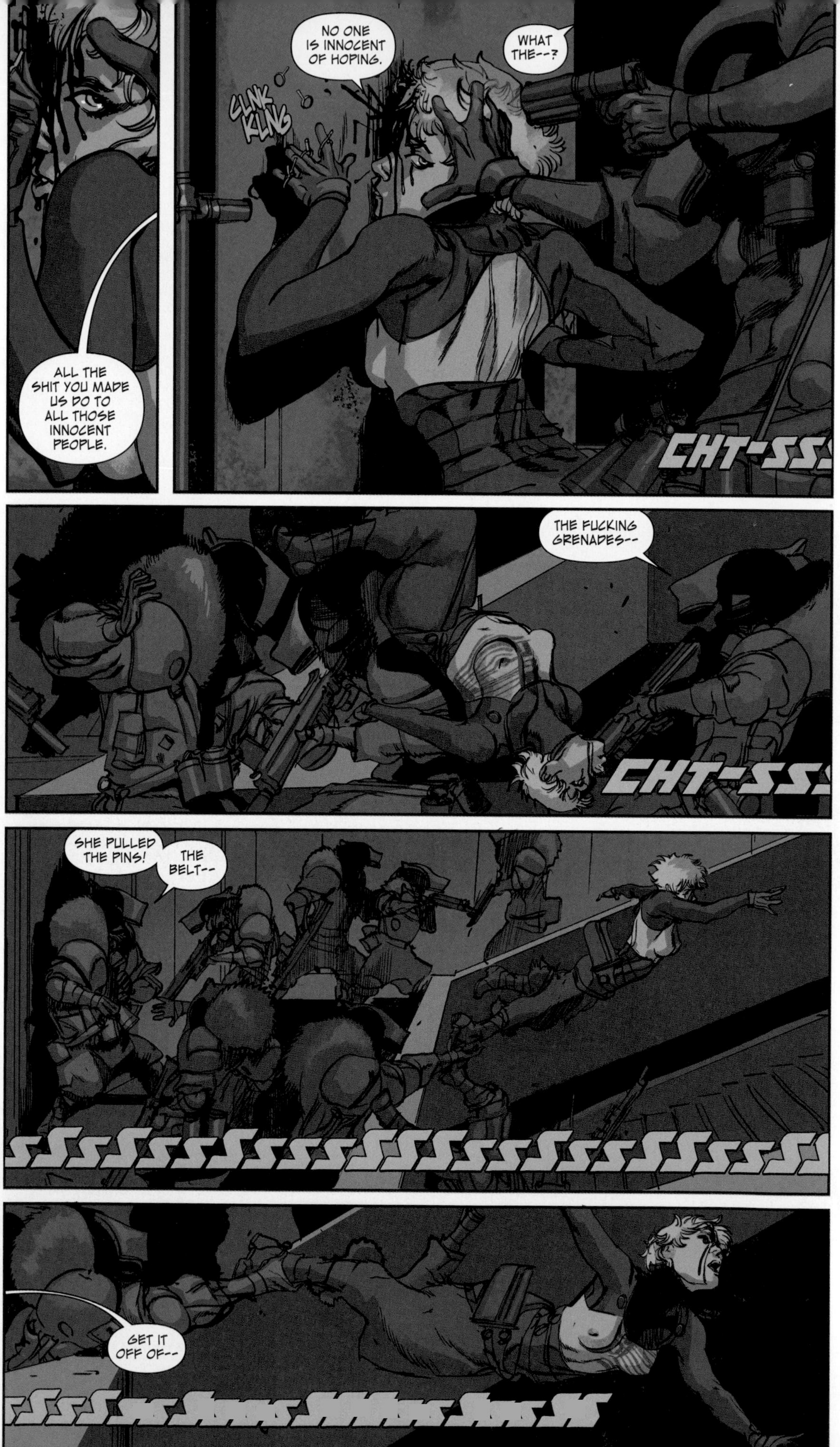

NO ONE IS INNOCENT OF HOPING.
CLNK KLNG
WHAT THE--?
ALL THE SHIT YOU MADE US DO TO ALL THOSE INNOCENT PEOPLE.
CHT-SSS
THE FUCKING GRENADES--
CHT-SSS
SHE PULLED THE PINS!
THE BELT--
GET IT OFF OF--

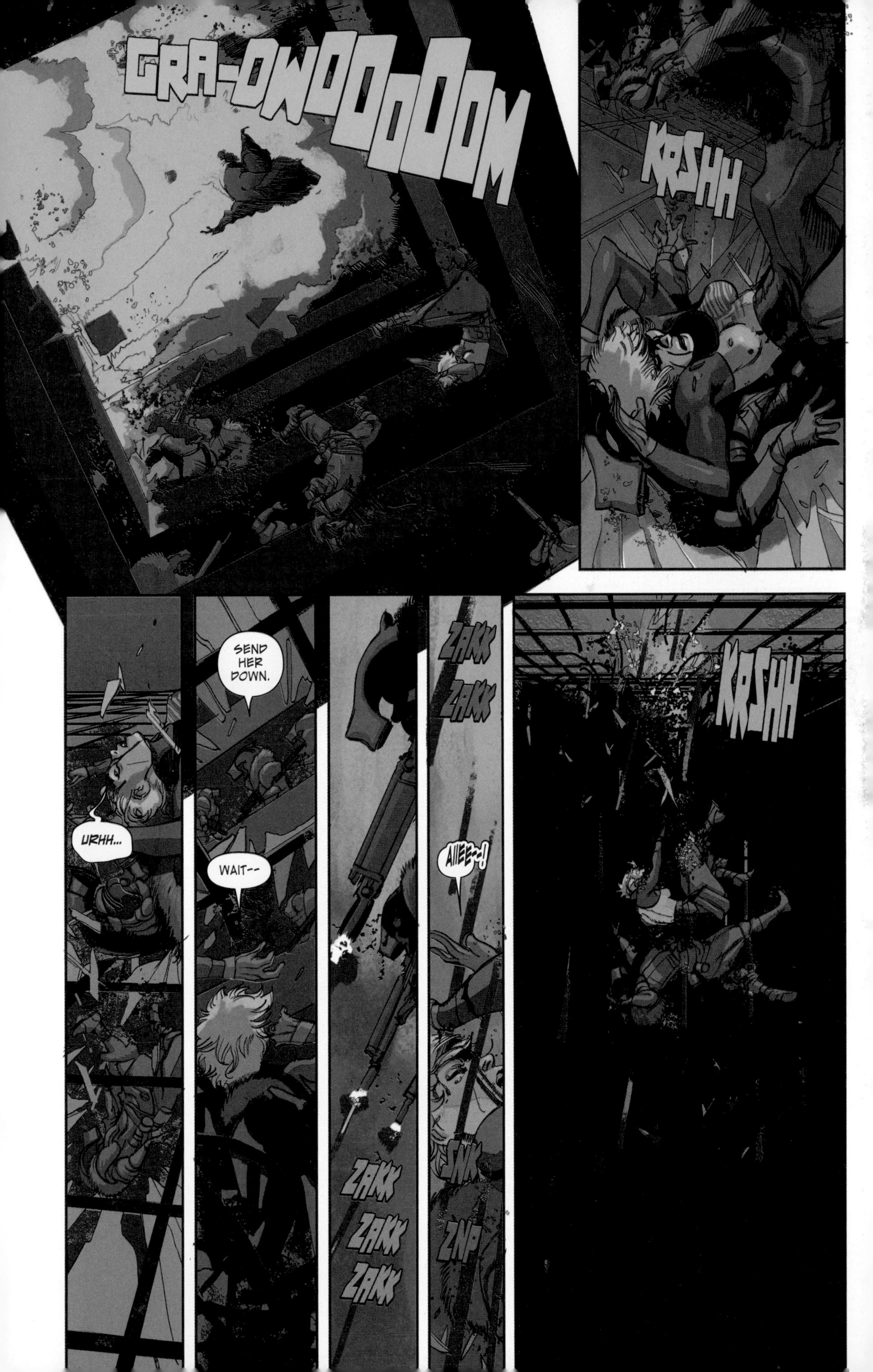
GRA-OWOOOOOOM
KRSHH
URHH...
SEND HER DOWN.
WAIT--
ZAKK
ZAKK
ZAKK
ZAKK
ZAKK
AIIEEE--!
ZAKK
ZAKK
SNK
ZNP
KRSHH

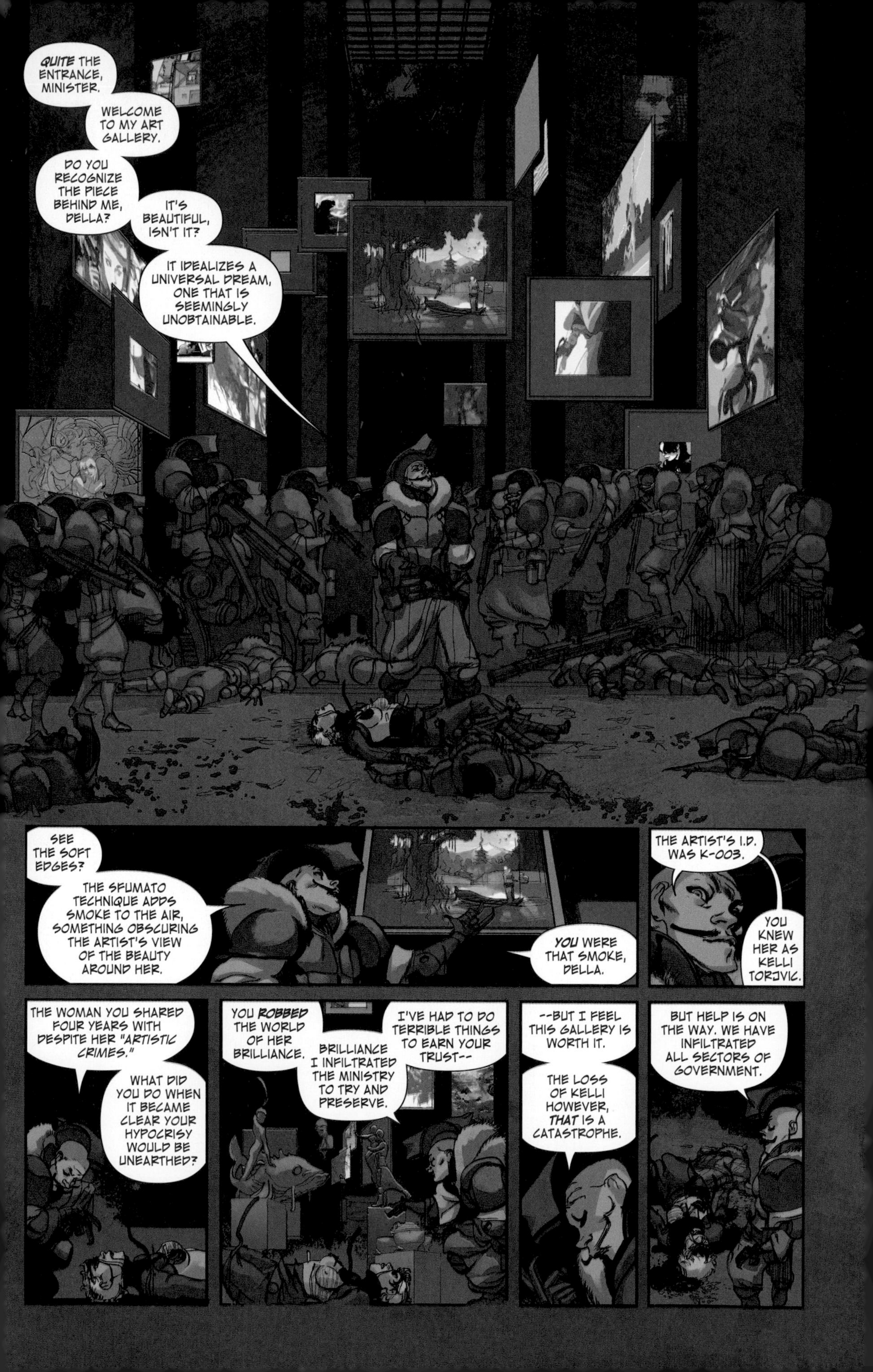

QUITE THE ENTRANCE, MINISTER.
WELCOME TO MY ART GALLERY.
DO YOU RECOGNIZE THE PIECE BEHIND ME, DELLA?
IT'S BEAUTIFUL, ISN'T IT?
IT IDEALIZES A UNIVERSAL DREAM, ONE THAT IS SEEMINGLY UNOBTAINABLE.
SEE THE SOFT EDGES?
THE SFUMATO TECHNIQUE ADDS SMOKE TO THE AIR, SOMETHING OBSCURING THE ARTIST'S VIEW OF THE BEAUTY AROUND HER.
YOU WERE THAT SMOKE, DELLA.
THE ARTIST'S I.D. WAS K-003.
YOU KNEW HER AS KELLI TORJVIC.
THE WOMAN YOU SHARED FOUR YEARS WITH DESPITE HER "ARTISTIC CRIMES."
WHAT DID YOU DO WHEN IT BECAME CLEAR YOUR HYPOCRISY WOULD BE UNEARTHED?
YOU ROBBED THE WORLD OF HER BRILLIANCE.
BRILLIANCE I INFILTRATED THE MINISTRY TO TRY AND PRESERVE.
I'VE HAD TO DO TERRIBLE THINGS TO EARN YOUR TRUST--
--BUT I FEEL THIS GALLERY IS WORTH IT.
THE LOSS OF KELLI HOWEVER, THAT IS A CATASTROPHE.
BUT HELP IS ON THE WAY. WE HAVE INFILTRATED ALL SECTORS OF GOVERNMENT.

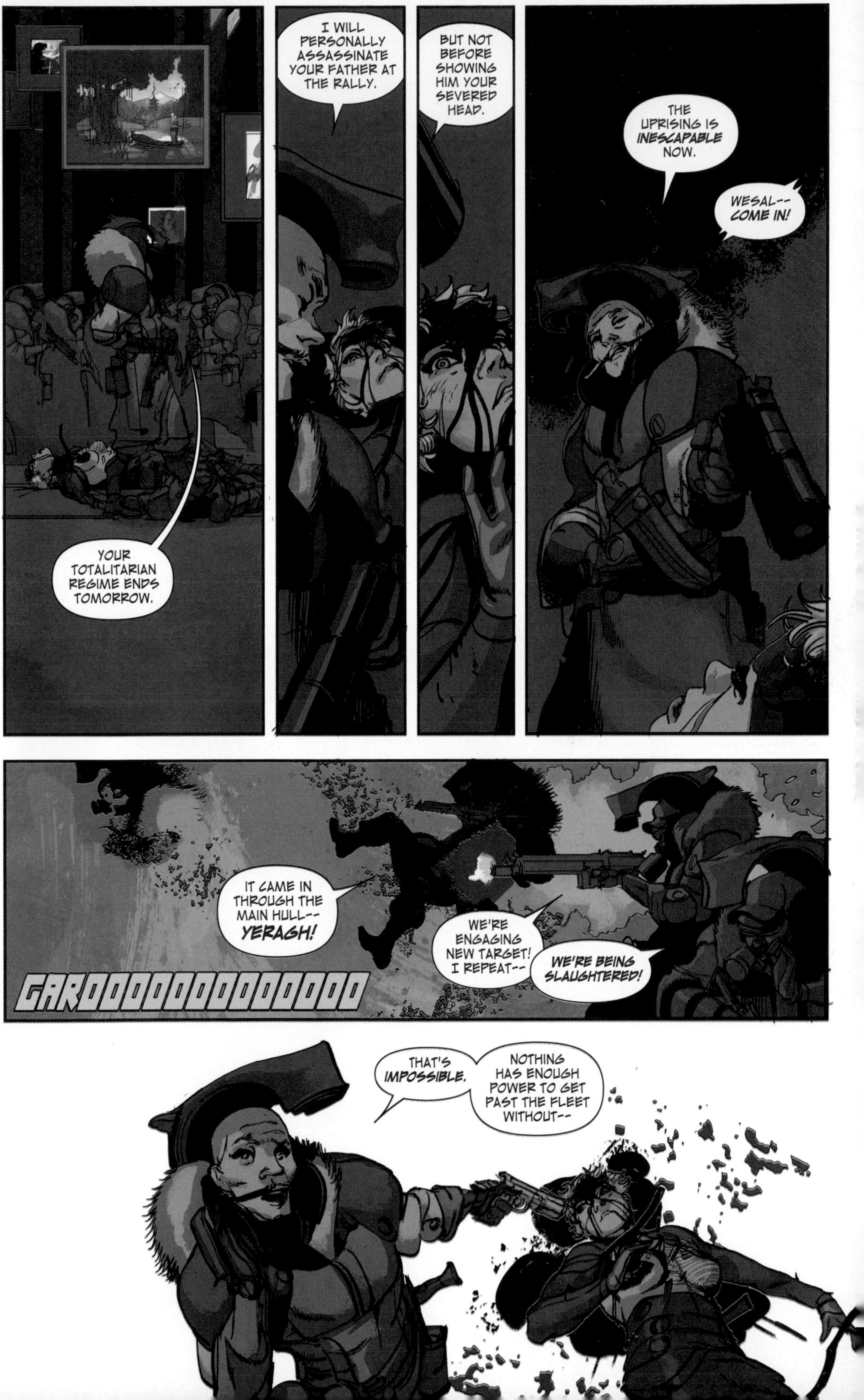
YOUR TOTALITARIAN REGIME ENDS TOMORROW.
I WILL PERSONALLY ASSASSINATE YOUR FATHER AT THE RALLY.
BUT NOT BEFORE SHOWING HIM YOUR SEVERED HEAD.
THE UPRISING IS INESCAPABLE NOW.
WESAL-- COME IN!
IT CAME IN THROUGH THE MAIN HULL-- YERAGH!
WE'RE ENGAGING NEW TARGET! I REPEAT--
WE'RE BEING SLAUGHTERED!
GAROOOOOOOOOOOOO
THAT'S IMPOSSIBLE.
NOTHING HAS ENOUGH POWER TO GET PAST THE FLEET WITHOUT--

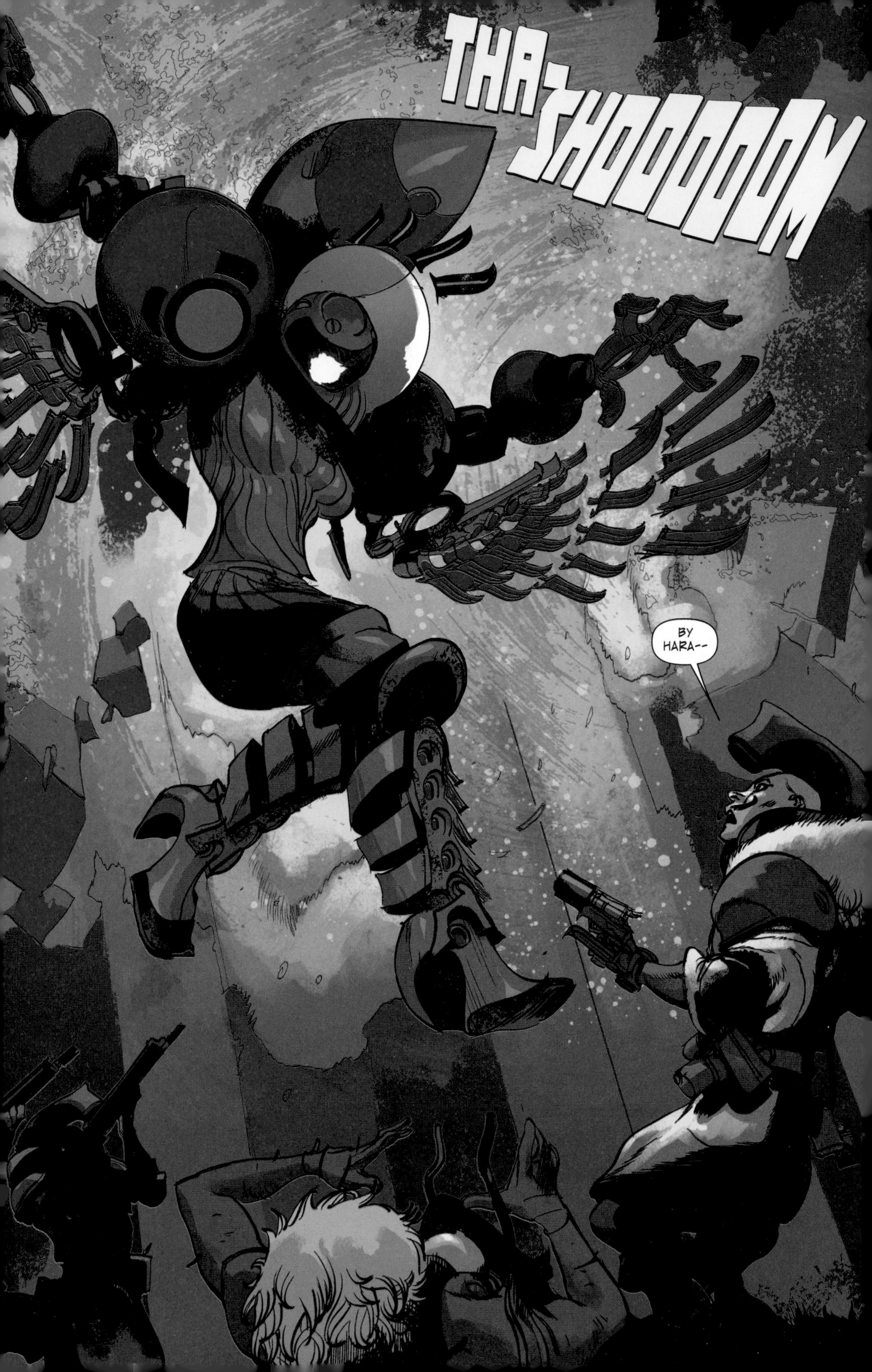
THA-SHOOOOOM
BY HARA--

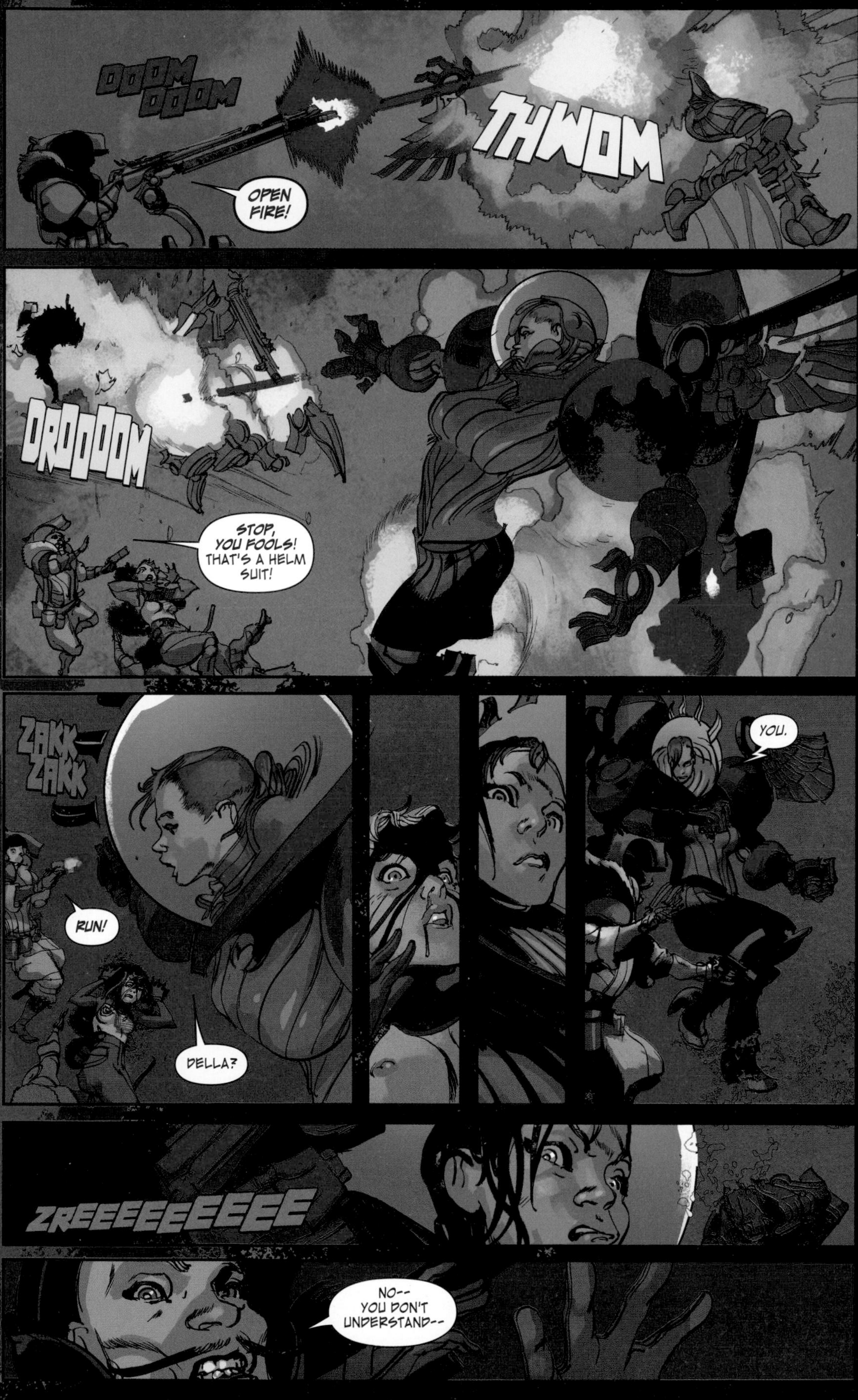
DOOM DOOM
THWOM
OPEN FIRE!
DROOOOM
STOP, YOU FOOLS! THAT'S A HELM SUIT!
ZAKK ZAKK
RUN!
DELLA?
YOU.
ZREEEEEEEEEE
NO-- YOU DON'T UNDERSTAND--

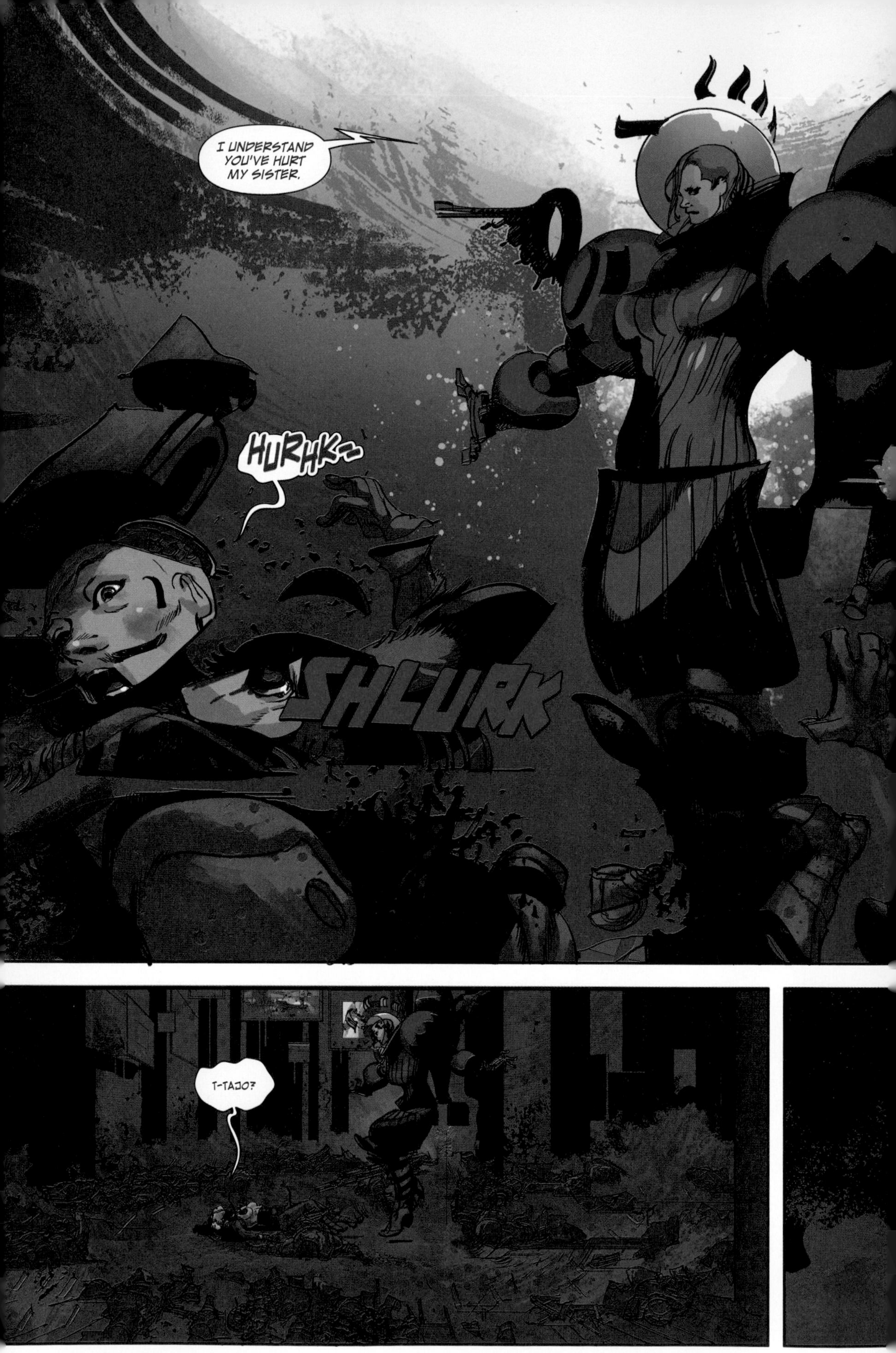
I UNDERSTAND YOU'VE HURT MY SISTER.
HURHK--
SHLURK
T-TAJO?

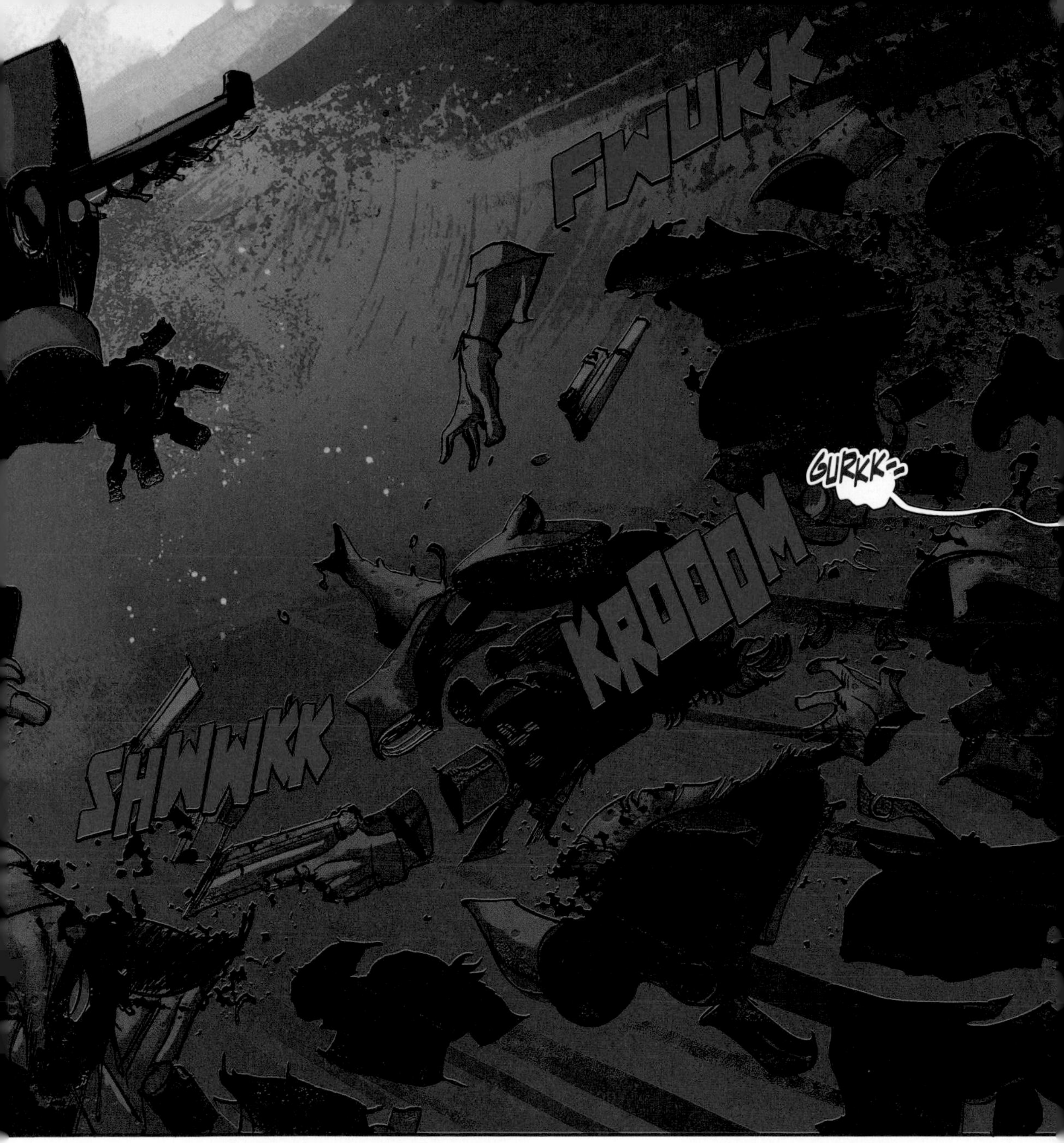
FWUKK
GURKK--
KROOOM
SHWWKK
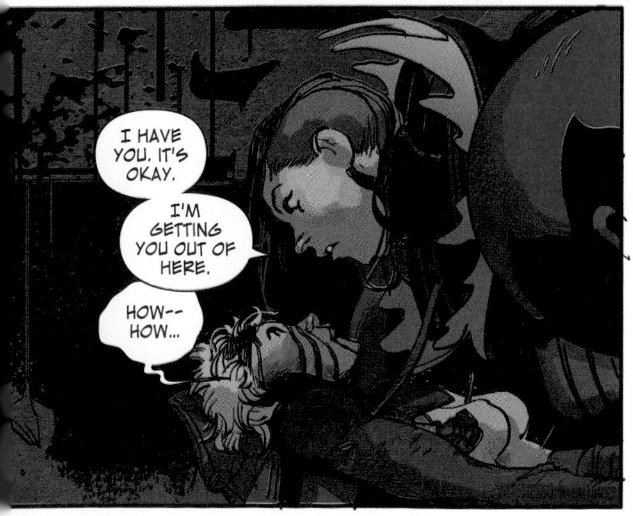
I HAVE YOU. IT'S OKAY.
I'M GETTING YOU OUT OF HERE.
HOW-- HOW...
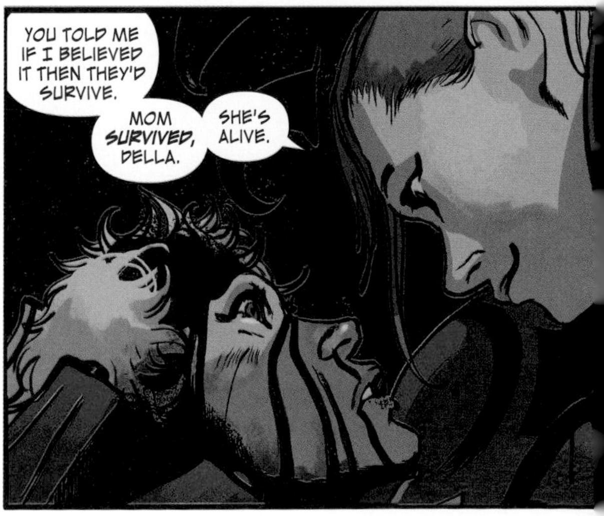
YOU TOLD ME IF I BELIEVED IT THEN THEY'D SURVIVE.
MOM SURVIVED, DELLA.
SHE'S ALIVE.

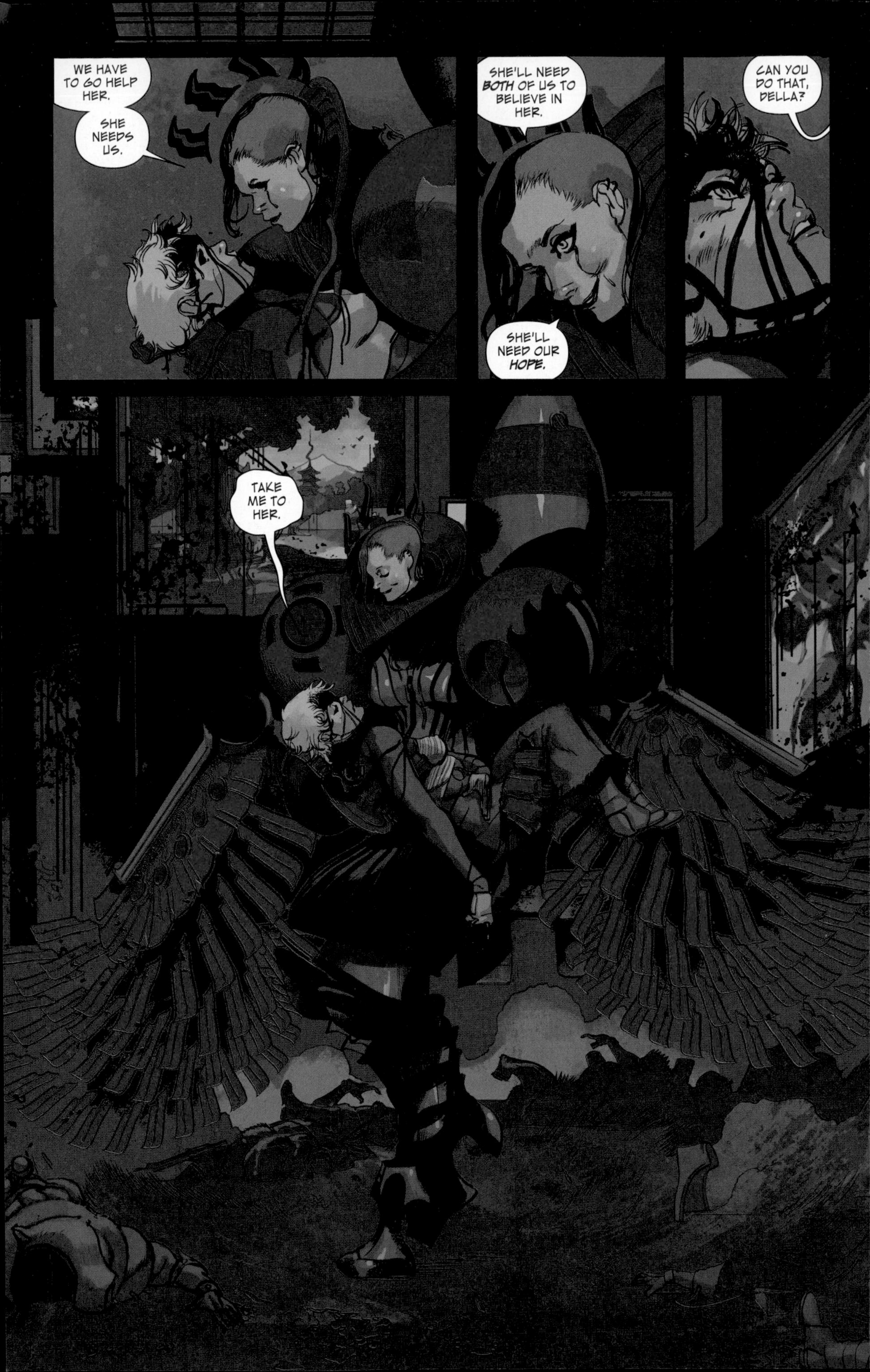
WE HAVE TO GO HELP HER.
SHE NEEDS US.
SHE'LL NEED BOTH OF US TO BELIEVE IN HER.
SHE'LL NEED OUR HOPE.
CAN YOU DO THAT, DELLA?
TAKE ME TO HER.

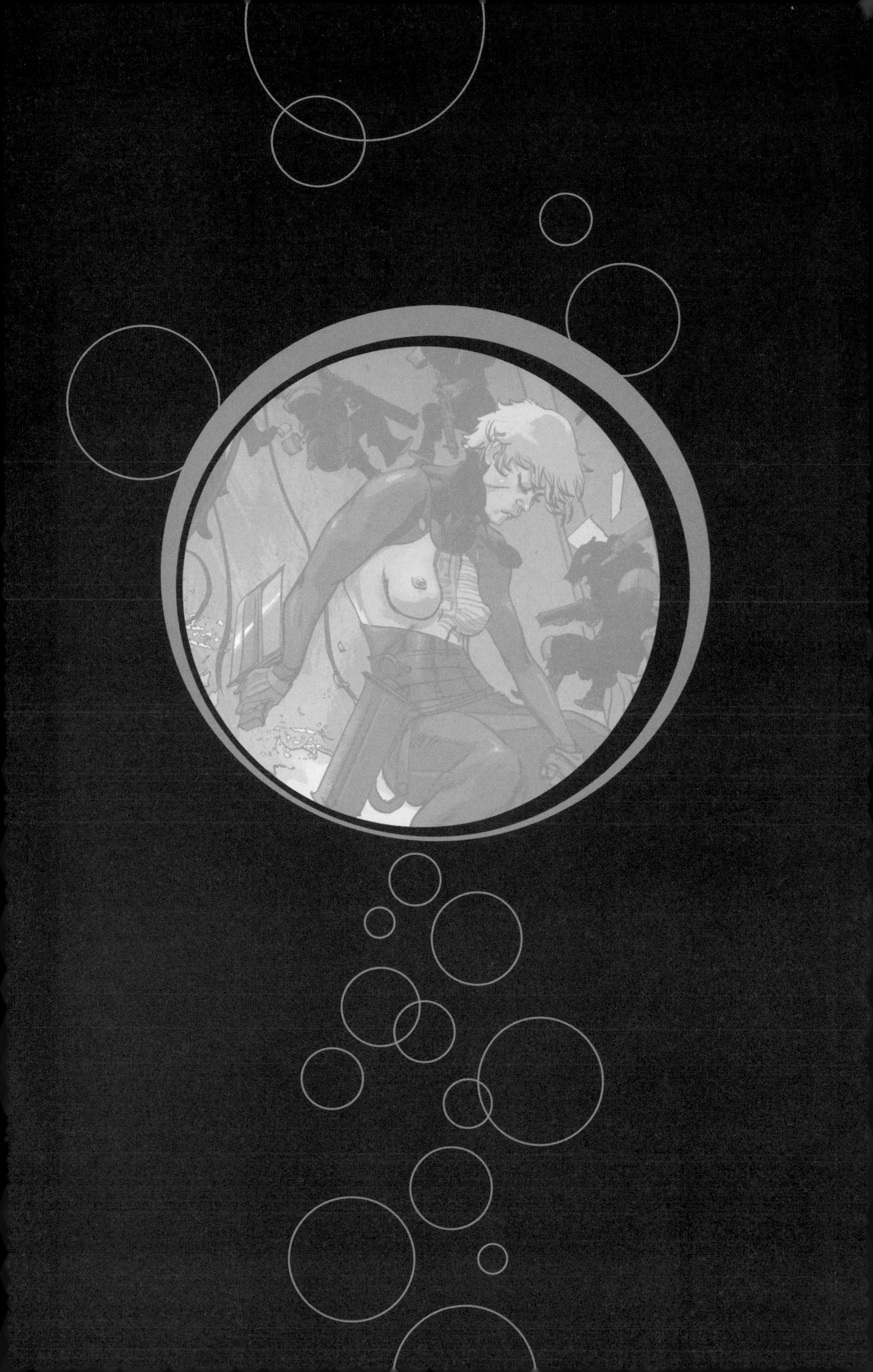

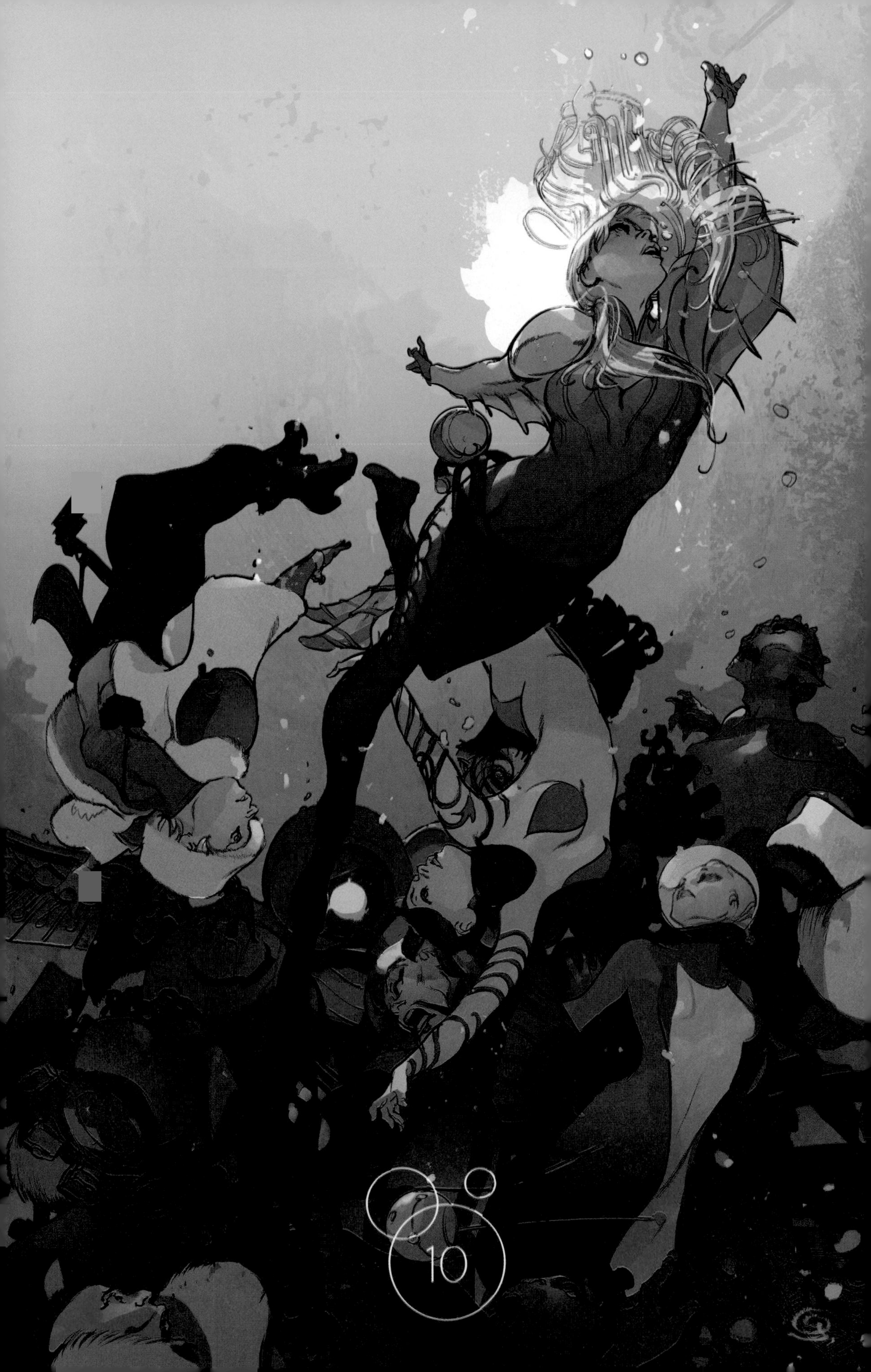
10

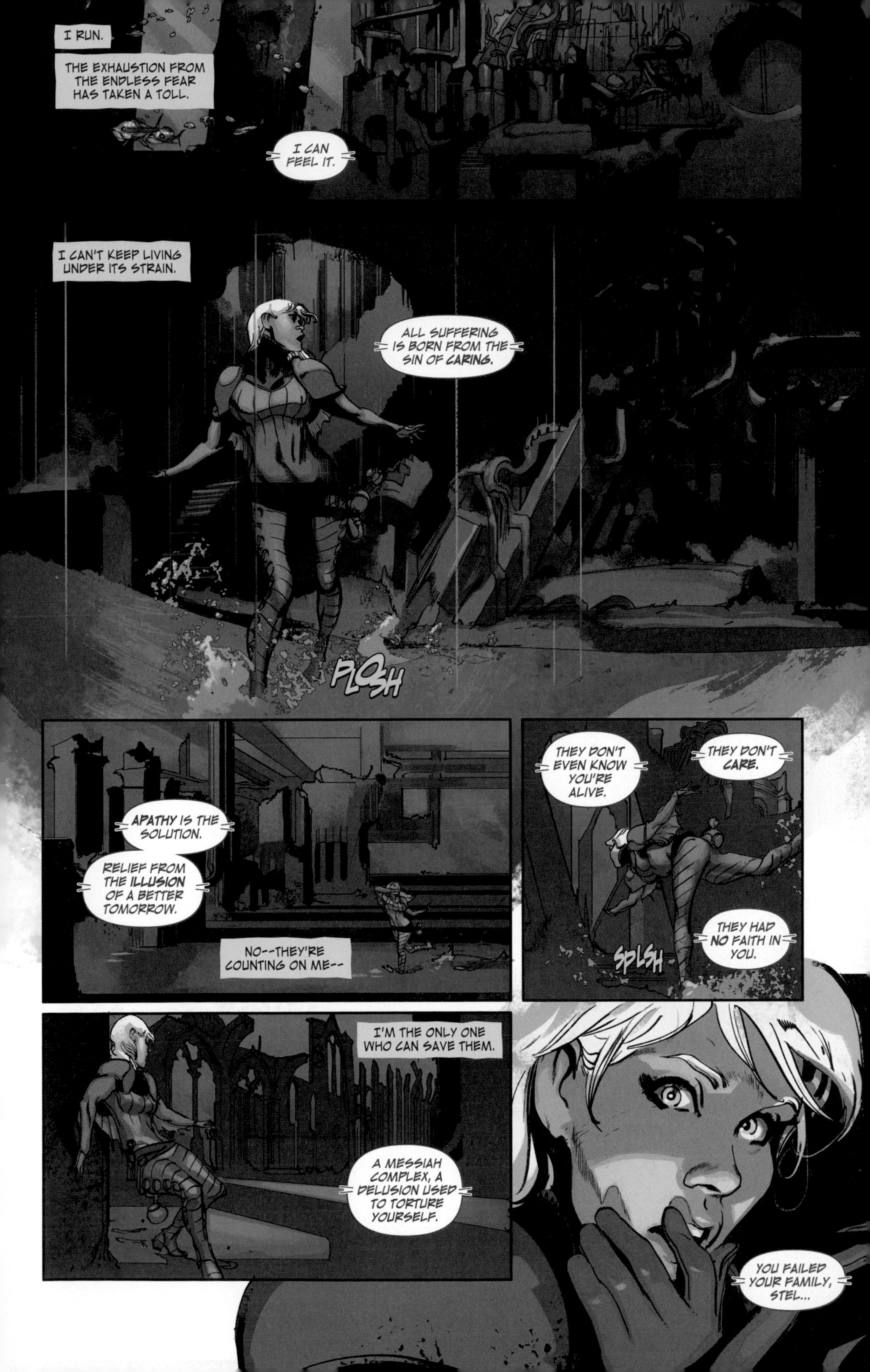
I RUN.
THE EXHAUSTION FROM THE ENDLESS FEAR HAS TAKEN A TOLL.
I CAN FEEL IT.
I CAN'T KEEP LIVING UNDER ITS STRAIN.
ALL SUFFERING IS BORN FROM THE SIN OF CARING.
PLOSH
APATHY IS THE SOLUTION.
RELIEF FROM THE ILLUSION OF A BETTER TOMORROW.
NO--THEY'RE COUNTING ON ME--
THEY DON'T EVEN KNOW YOU'RE ALIVE.
THEY DON'T CARE.
THEY HAD NO FAITH IN YOU.
SPLSH
I'M THE ONLY ONE WHO CAN SAVE THEM.
A MESSIAH COMPLEX, A DELUSION USED TO TORTURE YOURSELF.
YOU FAILED YOUR FAMILY, STEL...

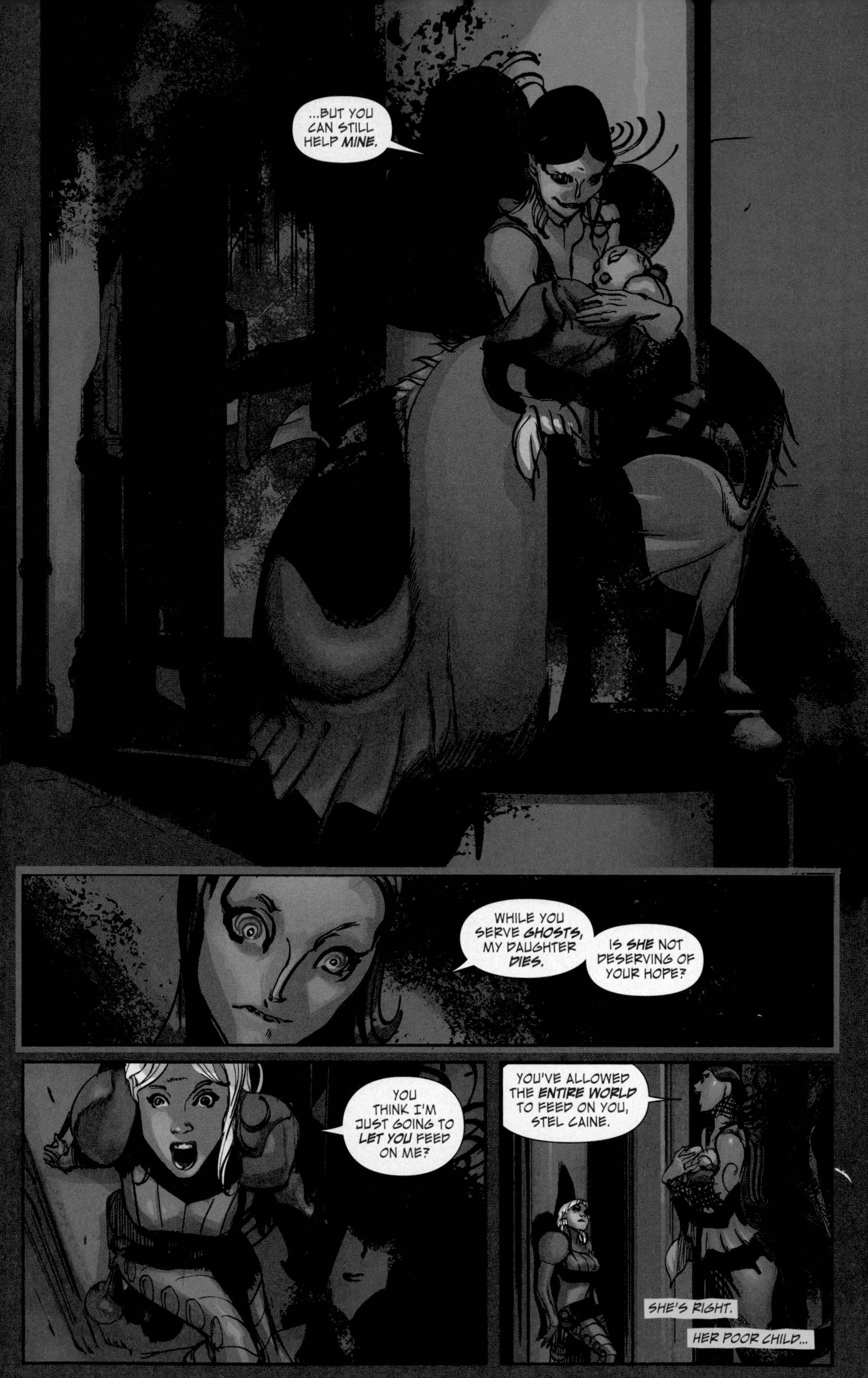
...BUT YOU CAN STILL HELP MINE.
WHILE YOU SERVE GHOSTS, MY DAUGHTER DIES.
IS SHE NOT DESERVING OF YOUR HOPE?
YOU THINK I'M JUST GOING TO LET YOU FEED ON ME?
YOU'VE ALLOWED THE ENTIRE WORLD TO FEED ON YOU, STEL CAINE.
SHE'S RIGHT.
HER POOR CHILD...

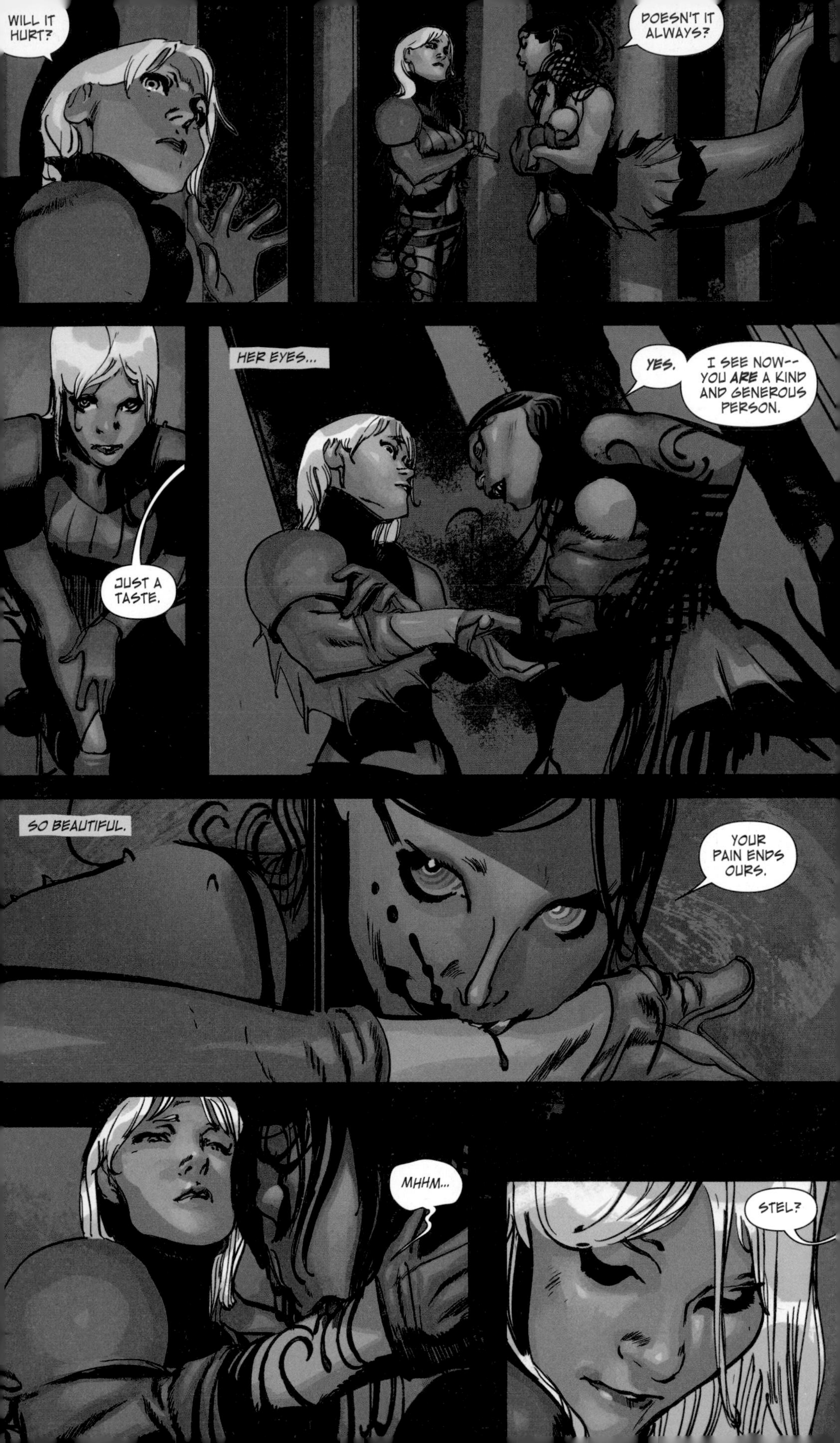
WILL IT HURT?
DOESN'T IT ALWAYS?
JUST A TASTE.
HER EYES...
YES.
I SEE NOW-- YOU ARE A KIND AND GENEROUS PERSON.
SO BEAUTIFUL.
YOUR PAIN ENDS OURS.
MHHM...
STEL?

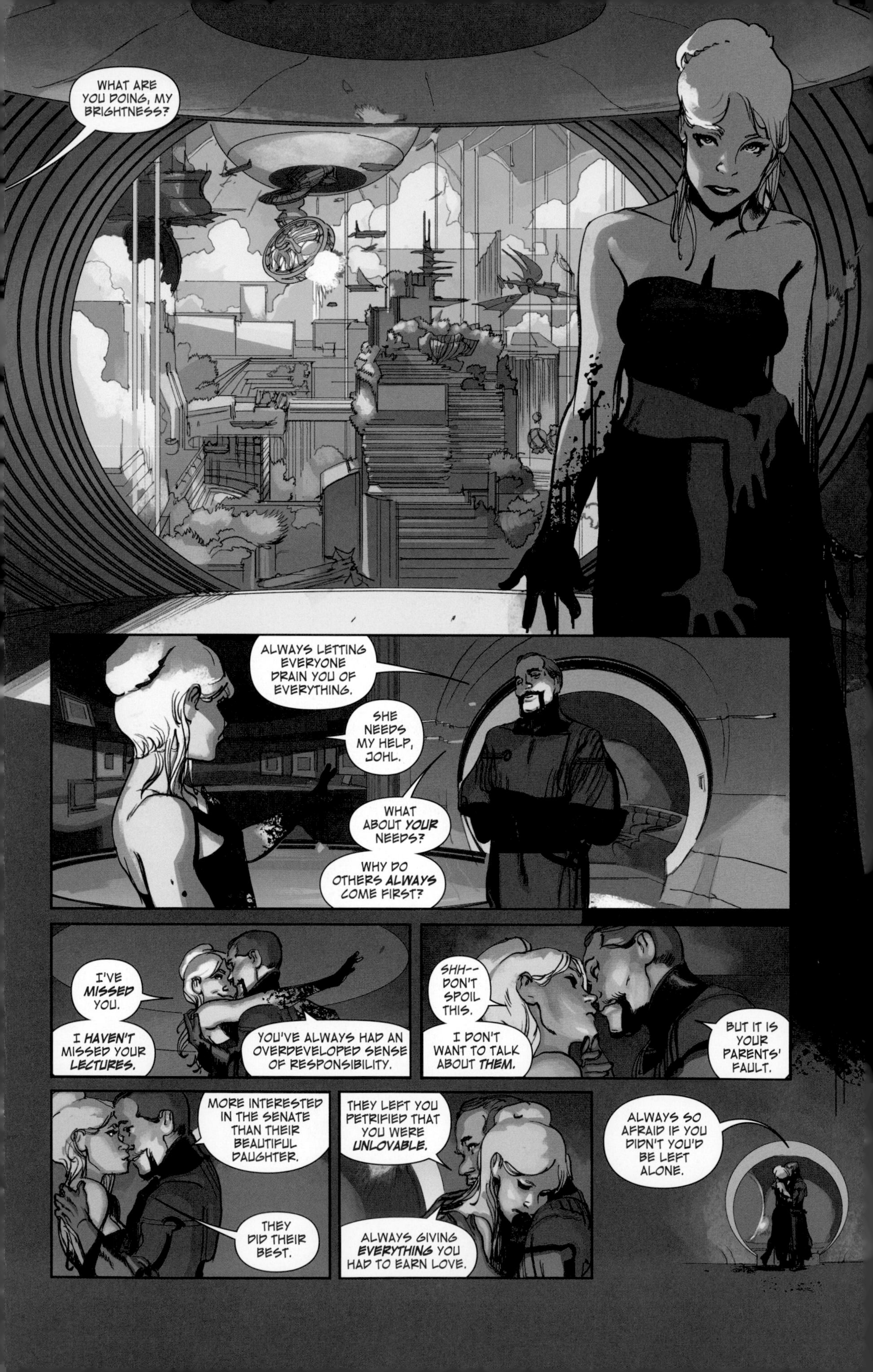
WHAT ARE YOU DOING, MY BRIGHTNESS?
ALWAYS LETTING EVERYONE DRAIN YOU OF EVERYTHING.
SHE NEEDS MY HELP, JOHL.
WHAT ABOUT YOUR NEEDS?
WHY DO OTHERS ALWAYS COME FIRST?
I'VE MISSED YOU.
I HAVEN'T MISSED YOUR LECTURES.
YOU'VE ALWAYS HAD AN OVERDEVELOPED SENSE OF RESPONSIBILITY.
SHH-- DON'T SPOIL THIS.
I DON'T WANT TO TALK ABOUT THEM.
BUT IT IS YOUR PARENTS' FAULT.
MORE INTERESTED IN THE SENATE THAN THEIR BEAUTIFUL DAUGHTER.
THEY DID THEIR BEST.
THEY LEFT YOU PETRIFIED THAT YOU WERE UNLOVABLE.
ALWAYS GIVING EVERYTHING YOU HAD TO EARN LOVE.
ALWAYS SO AFRAID IF YOU DIDN'T YOU'D BE LEFT ALONE.

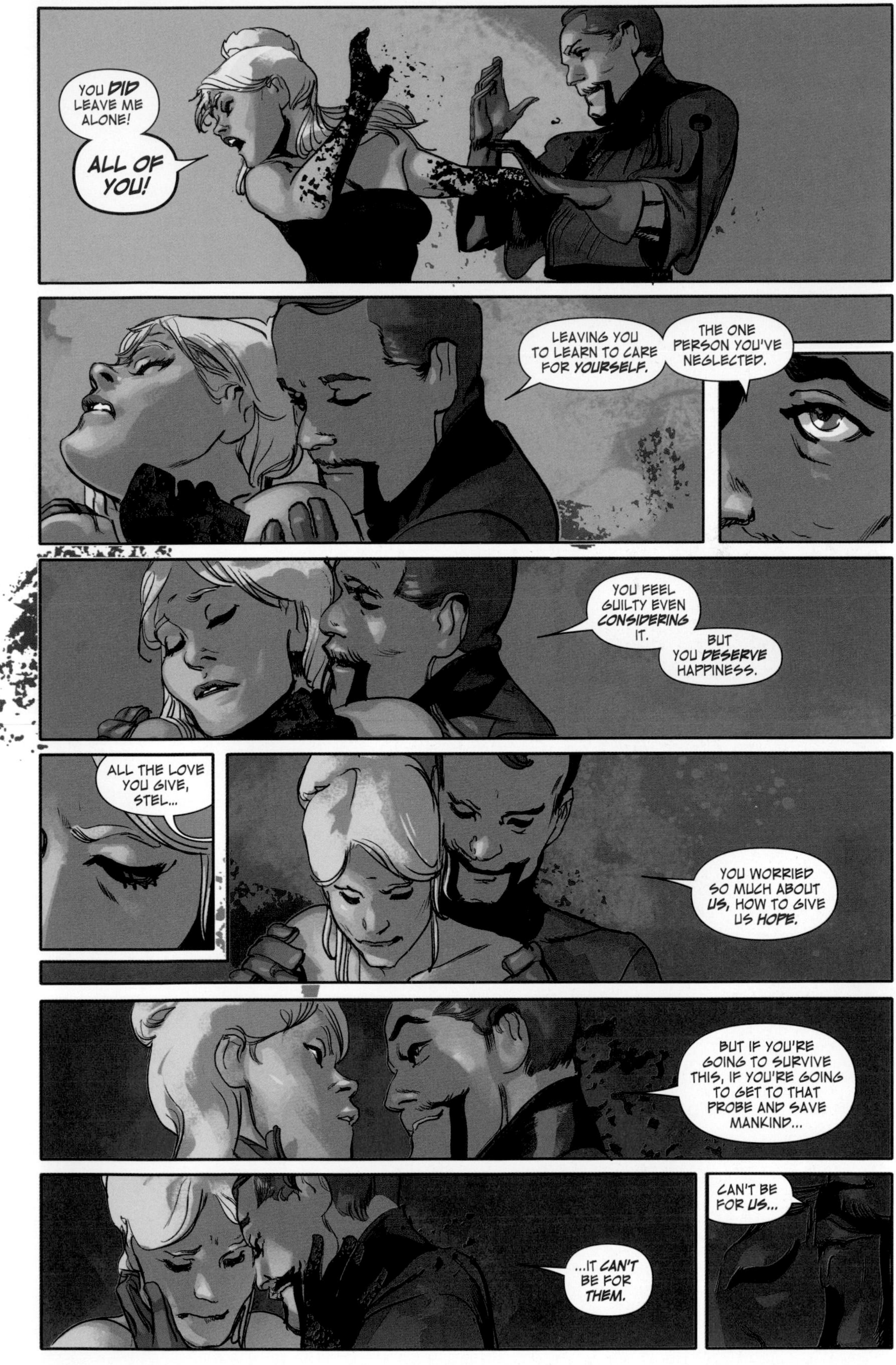
YOU DID LEAVE ME ALONE!
ALL OF YOU!
LEAVING YOU TO LEARN TO CARE FOR YOURSELF.
THE ONE PERSON YOU'VE NEGLECTED.
YOU FEEL GUILTY EVEN CONSIDERING IT.
BUT YOU DESERVE HAPPINESS.
ALL THE LOVE YOU GIVE, STEL...
YOU WORRIED SO MUCH ABOUT US, HOW TO GIVE US HOPE.
BUT IF YOU'RE GOING TO SURVIVE THIS, IF YOU'RE GOING TO GET TO THAT PROBE AND SAVE MANKIND...
...IT CAN'T BE FOR THEM.
CAN'T BE FOR US...

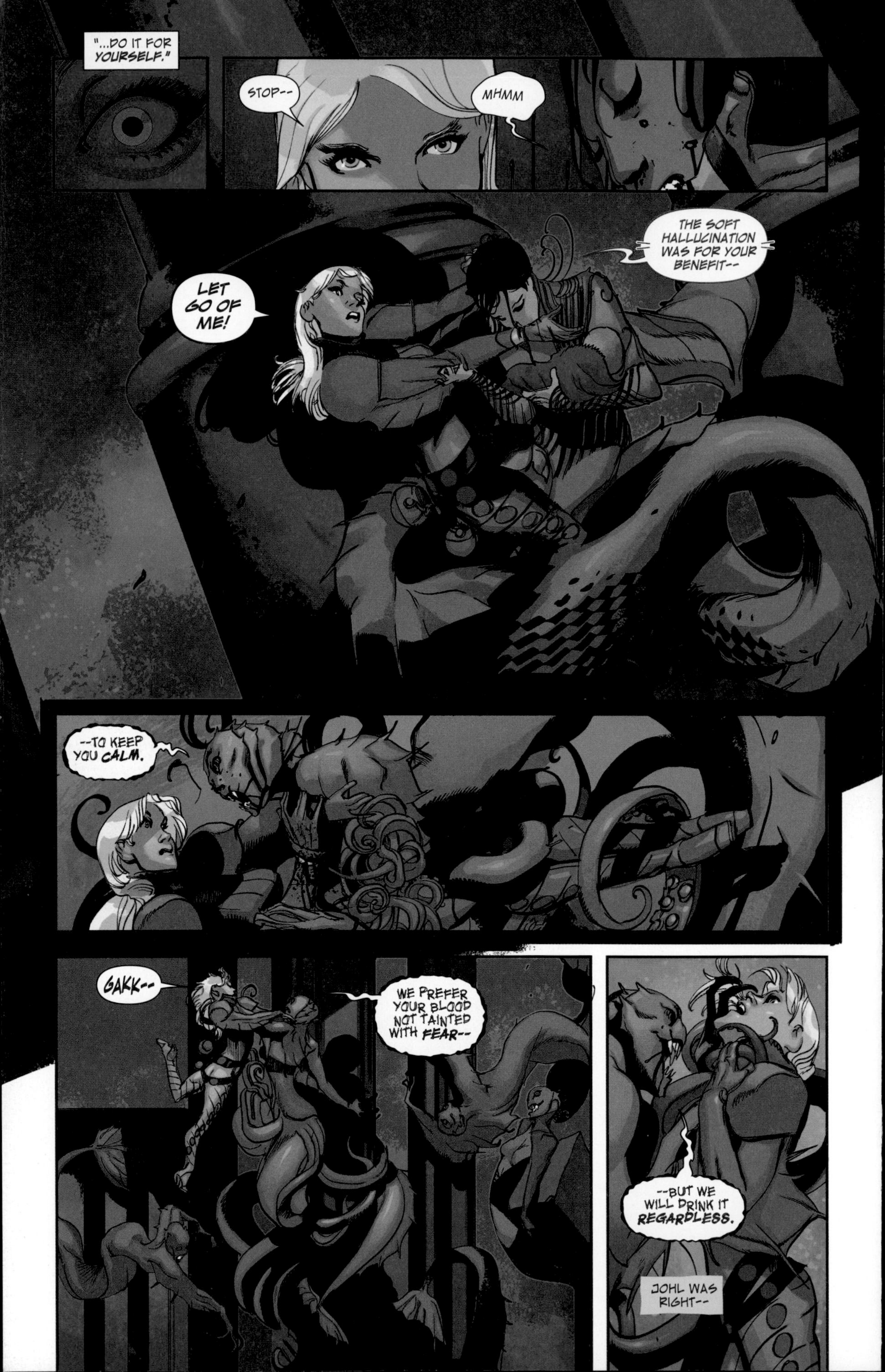
"...DO IT FOR YOURSELF."
STOP--
MHMM
THE SOFT HALLUCINATION WAS FOR YOUR BENEFIT--
LET GO OF ME!
--TO KEEP YOU CALM.
GAKK--
WE PREFER YOUR BLOOD NOT TAINTED WITH FEAR--
--BUT WE WILL DRINK IT REGARDLESS.
JOHL WAS RIGHT--

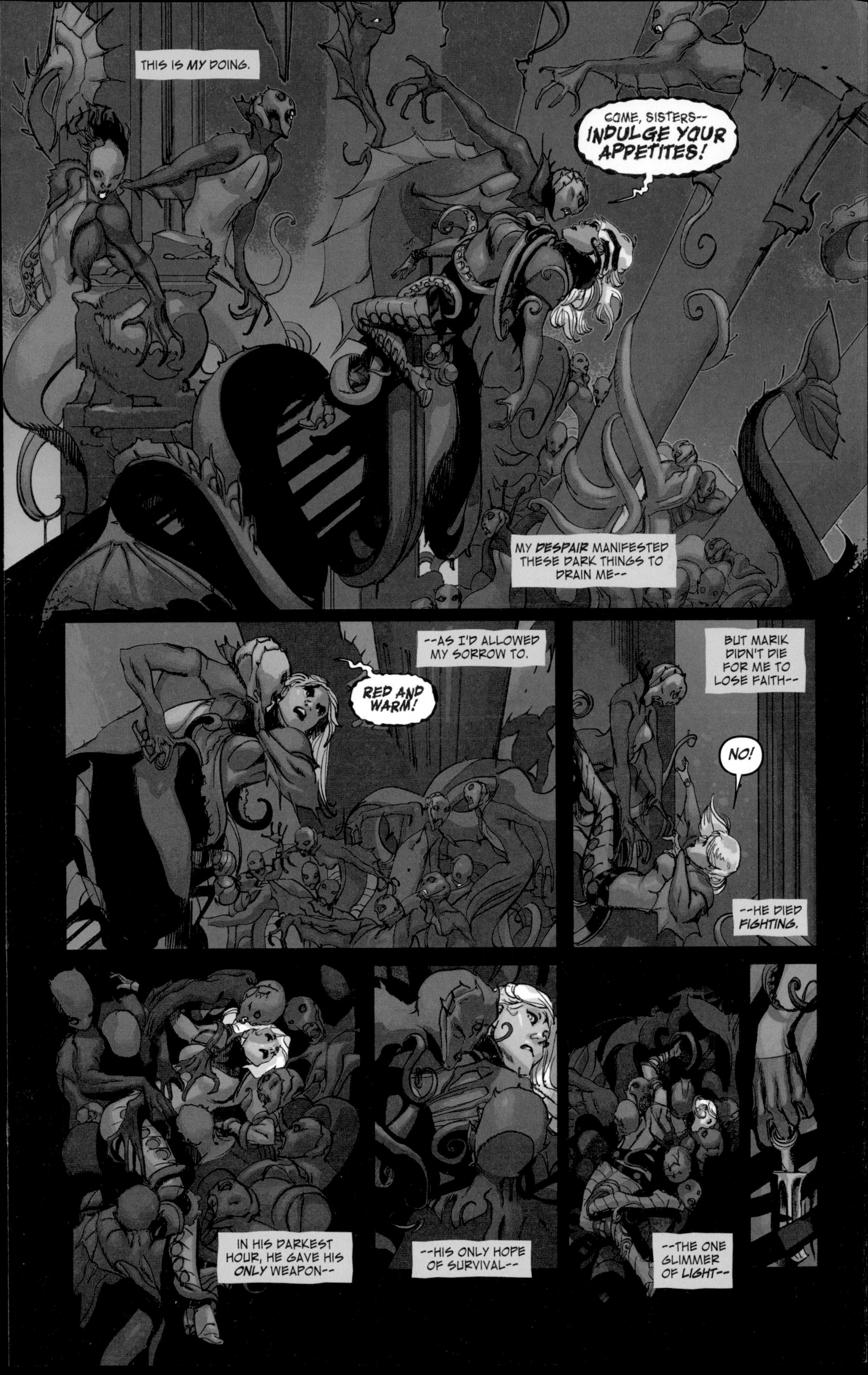

THIS IS MY DOING.
COME, SISTERS-- INDULGE YOUR APPETITES!
MY DESPAIR MANIFESTED THESE DARK THINGS TO DRAIN ME--
--AS I'D ALLOWED MY SORROW TO.
RED AND WARM!
BUT MARIK DIDN'T DIE FOR ME TO LOSE FAITH--
NO!
--HE DIED FIGHTING.
IN HIS DARKEST HOUR, HE GAVE HIS ONLY WEAPON--
--HIS ONLY HOPE OF SURVIVAL--
--THE ONE GLIMMER OF LIGHT--

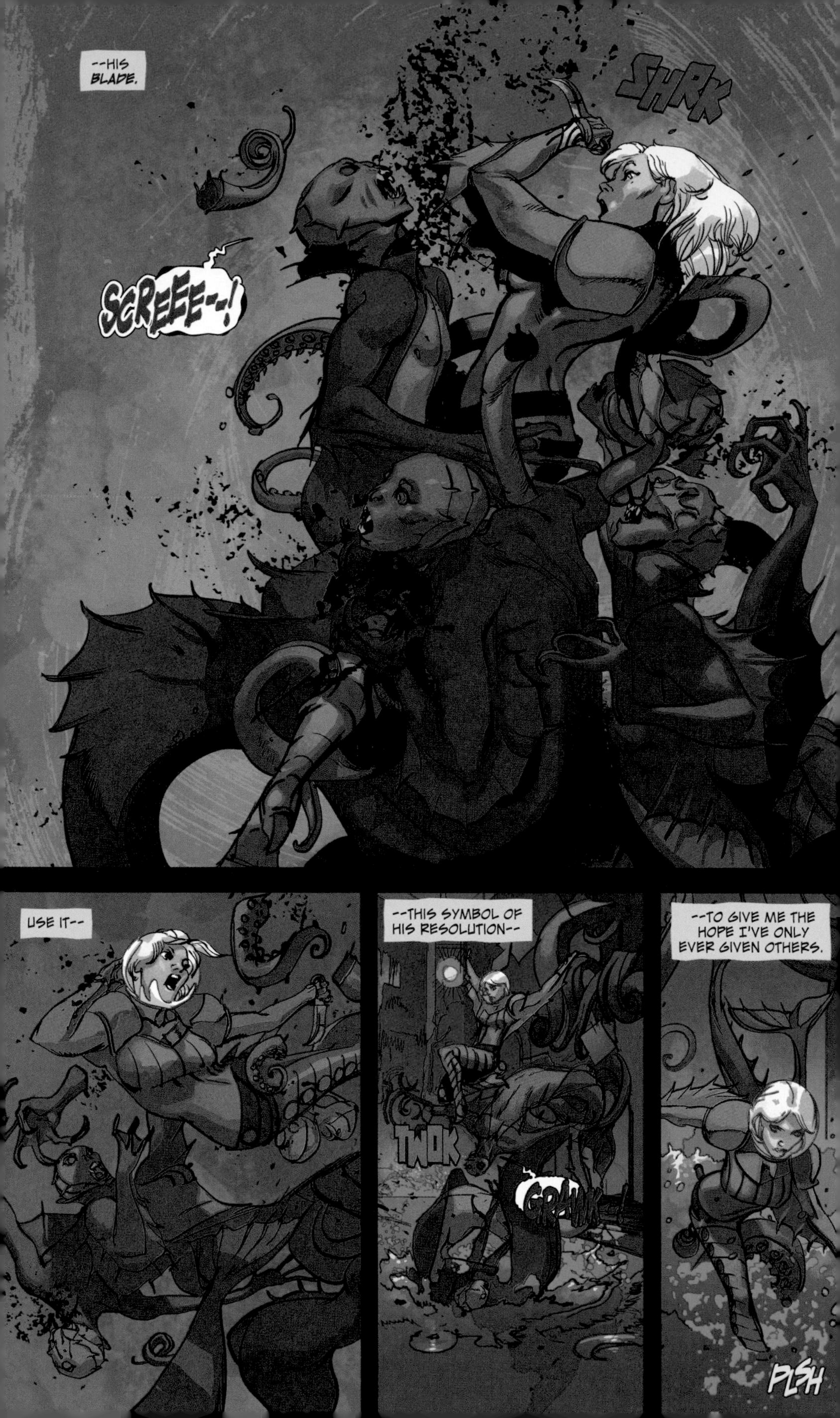
--HIS BLADE.
SHRK
SCREEE--!
USE IT--
--THIS SYMBOL OF HIS RESOLUTION--
TWOK
GRAHK
--TO GIVE ME THE HOPE I'VE ONLY EVER GIVEN OTHERS.
PLSH

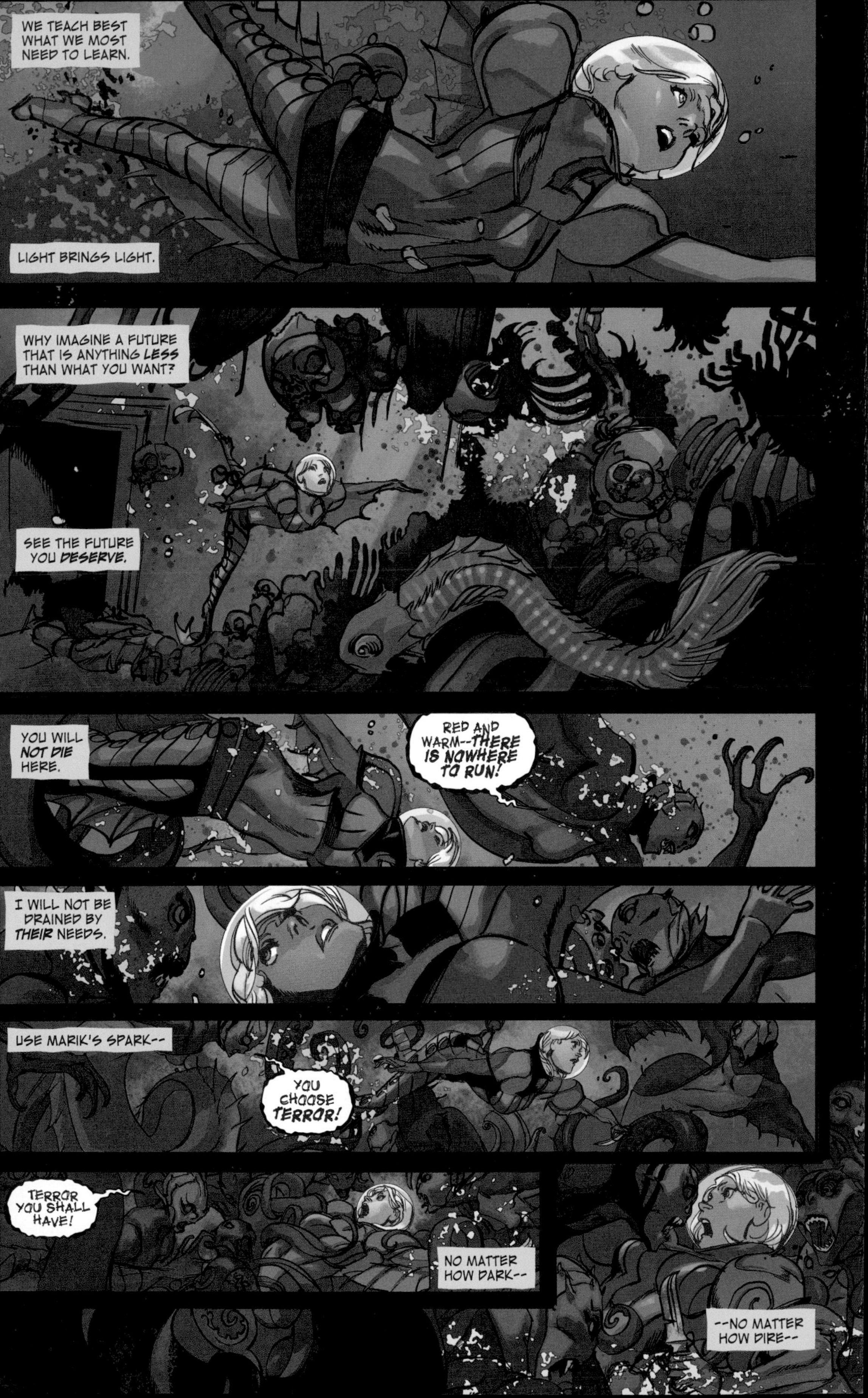
WE TEACH BEST WHAT WE MOST NEED TO LEARN.
LIGHT BRINGS LIGHT.
WHY IMAGINE A FUTURE THAT IS ANYTHING LESS THAN WHAT YOU WANT?
SEE THE FUTURE YOU DESERVE.
YOU WILL NOT DIE HERE.
RED AND WARM--THERE IS NOWHERE TO RUN!
I WILL NOT BE DRAINED BY THEIR NEEDS.
USE MARIK'S SPARK--
YOU CHOOSE TERROR!
TERROR YOU SHALL HAVE!
NO MATTER HOW DARK--
--NO MATTER HOW DIRE--

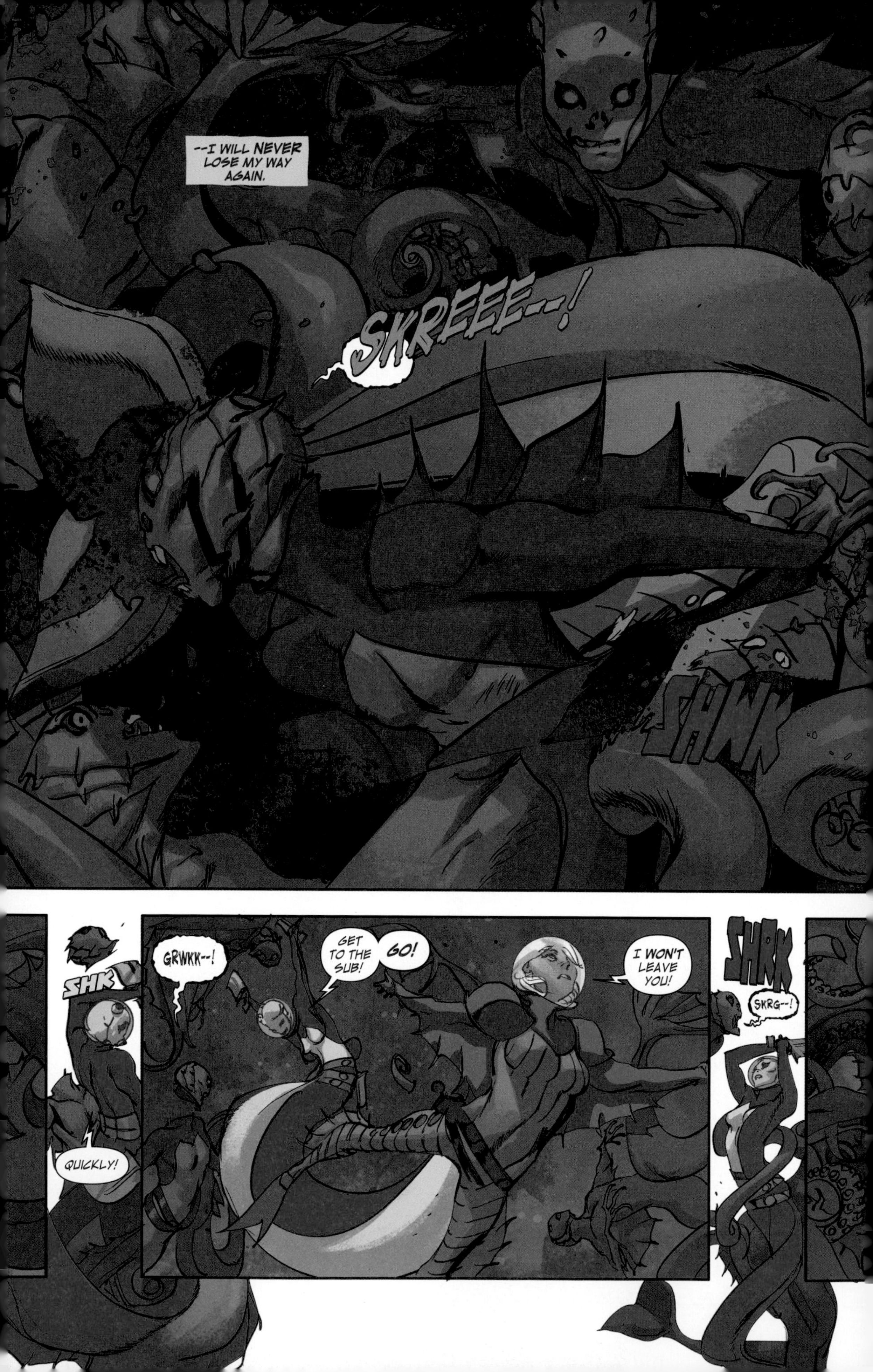
--I WILL NEVER LOSE MY WAY AGAIN.
SKREEE--!
SHNK
SHK
QUICKLY!
GRWKK--!
GET TO THE SUB!
GO!
I WON'T LEAVE YOU!
SHRK
SKRG--!

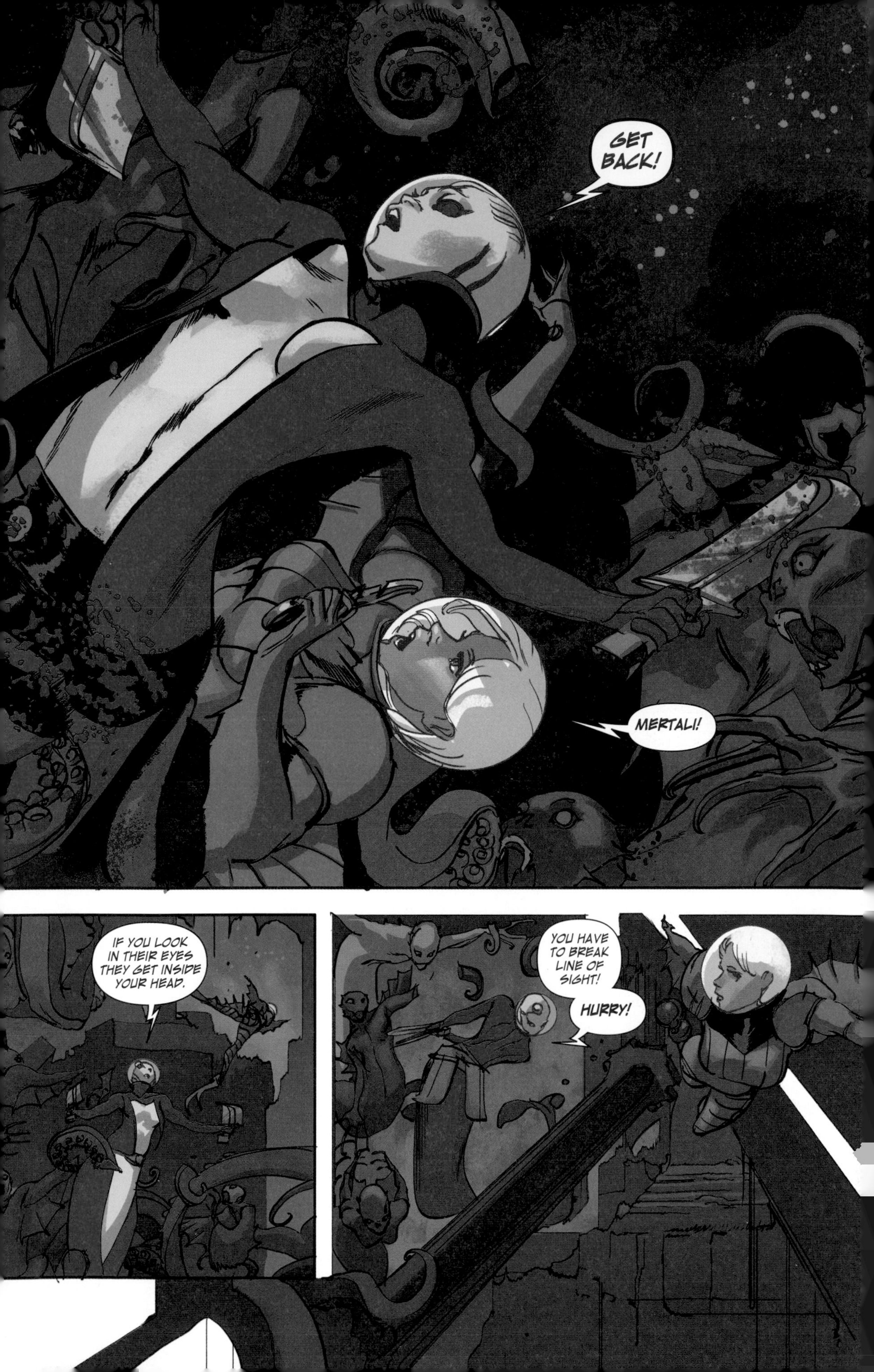
GET BACK!
MERTALI!
IF YOU LOOK IN THEIR EYES THEY GET INSIDE YOUR HEAD.
YOU HAVE TO BREAK LINE OF SIGHT!
HURRY!

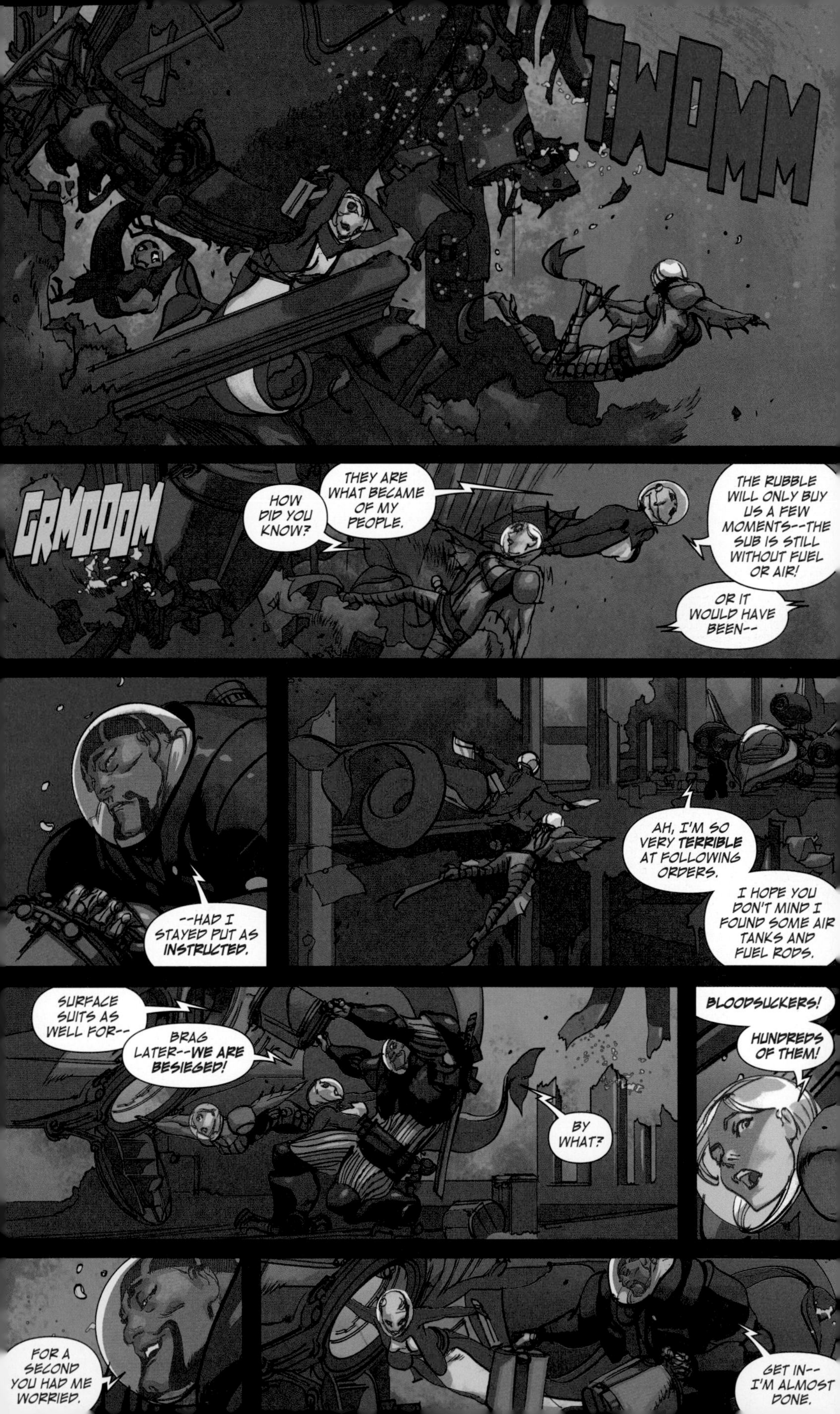
TWOMM
GRMOOOM
HOW DID YOU KNOW?
THEY ARE WHAT BECAME OF MY PEOPLE.
THE RUBBLE WILL ONLY BUY US A FEW MOMENTS--THE SUB IS STILL WITHOUT FUEL OR AIR!
OR IT WOULD HAVE BEEN--
--HAD I STAYED PUT AS INSTRUCTED.
AH, I'M SO VERY TERRIBLE AT FOLLOWING ORDERS.
I HOPE YOU DON'T MIND I FOUND SOME AIR TANKS AND FUEL RODS.
SURFACE SUITS AS WELL FOR--
BRAG LATER--WE ARE BESIEGED!
BY WHAT?
BLOODSUCKERS!
HUNDREDS OF THEM!
FOR A SECOND YOU HAD ME WORRIED.
GET IN-- I'M ALMOST DONE.

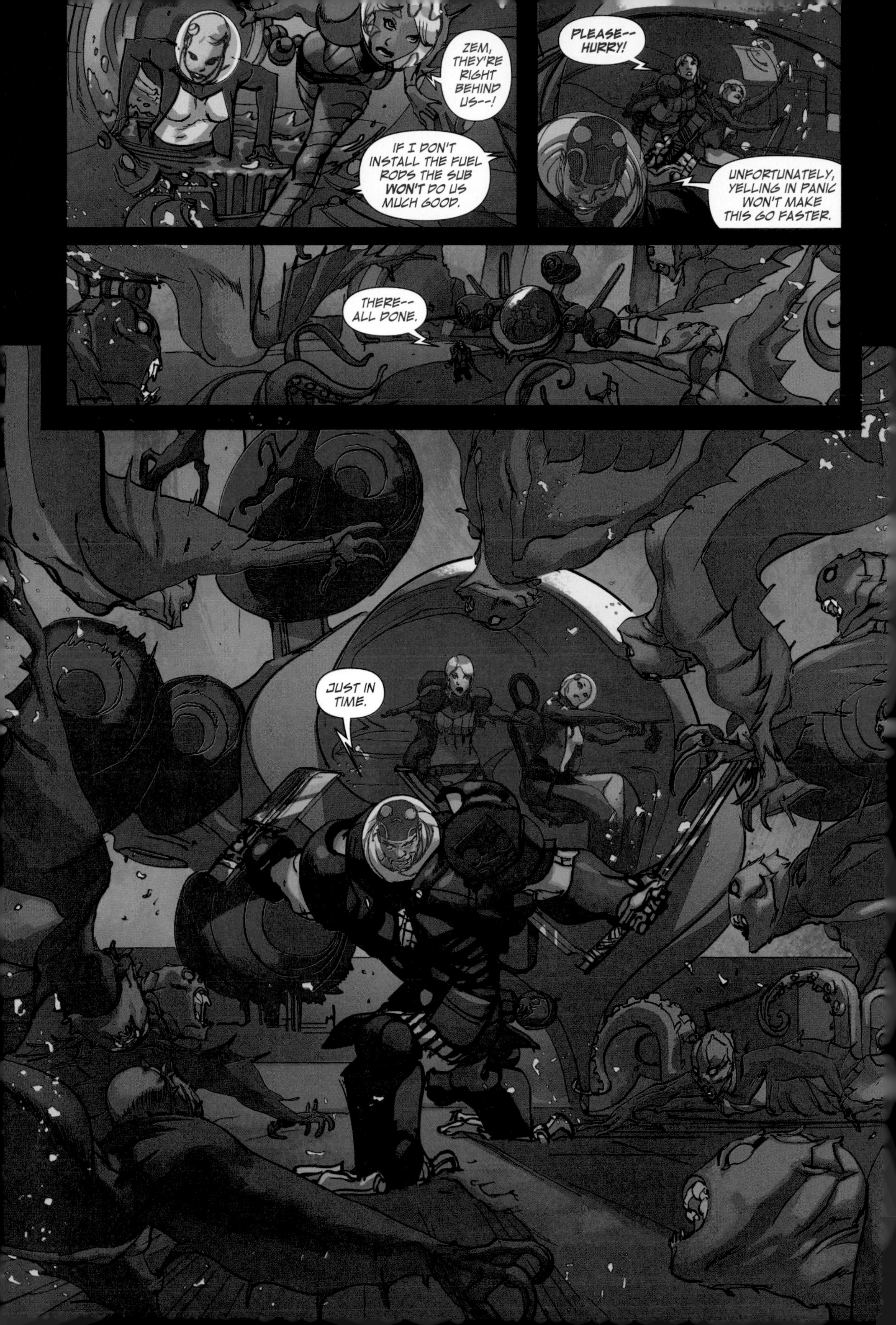
ZEM, THEY'RE RIGHT BEHIND US--!
IF I DON'T INSTALL THE FUEL RODS THE SUB **WON'T** DO US MUCH GOOD.
PLEASE--HURRY!
UNFORTUNATELY, YELLING IN PANIC WON'T MAKE THIS GO FASTER.
THERE--ALL DONE.
JUST IN TIME.

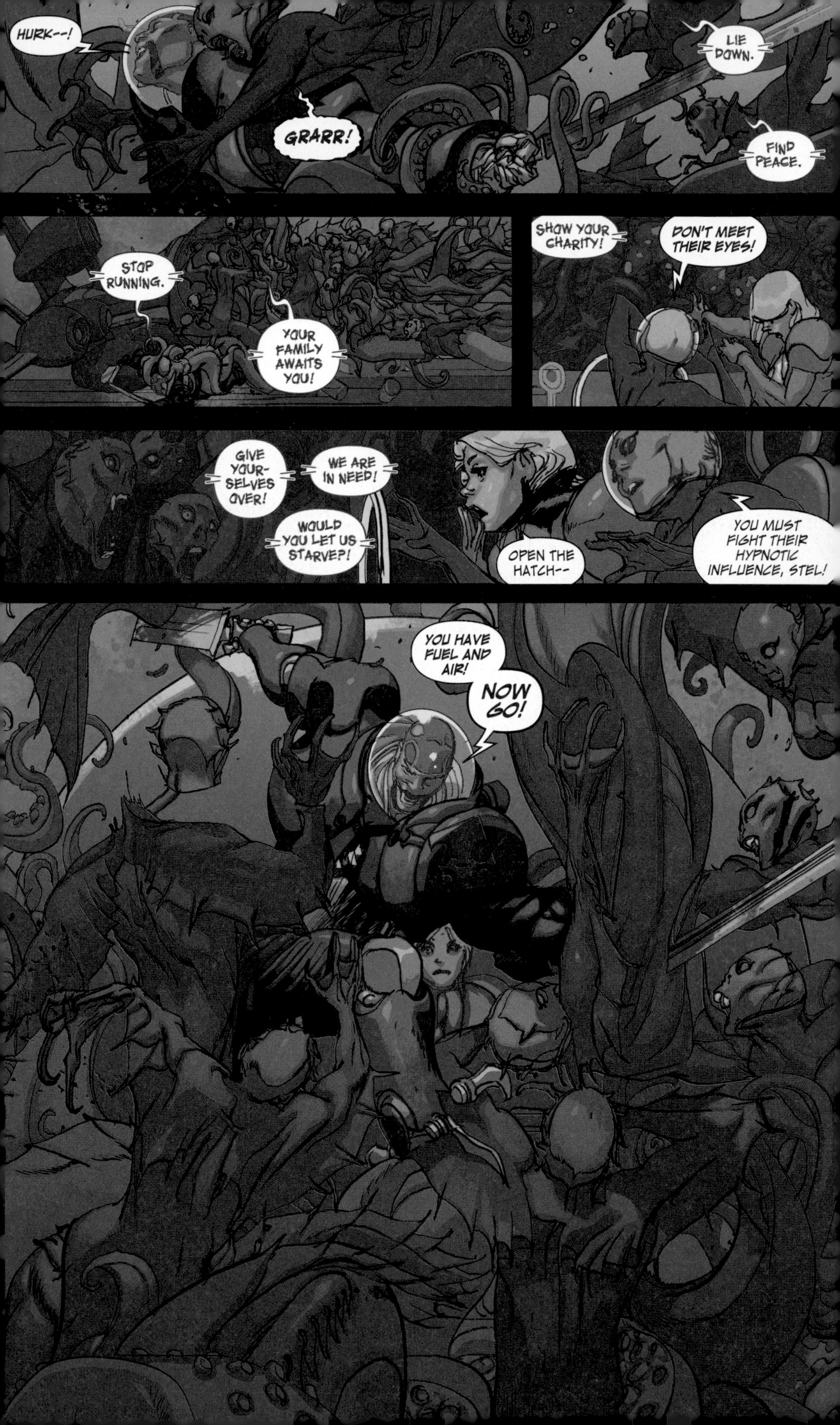
HURK--!
GRARR!
LIE DOWN.
FIND PEACE.
STOP RUNNING.
YOUR FAMILY AWAITS YOU!
SHOW YOUR CHARITY!
DON'T MEET THEIR EYES!
GIVE YOUR-SELVES OVER!
WE ARE IN NEED!
WOULD YOU LET US STARVE?!
OPEN THE HATCH--
YOU MUST FIGHT THEIR HYPNOTIC INFLUENCE, STEL!
YOU HAVE FUEL AND AIR!
NOW GO!

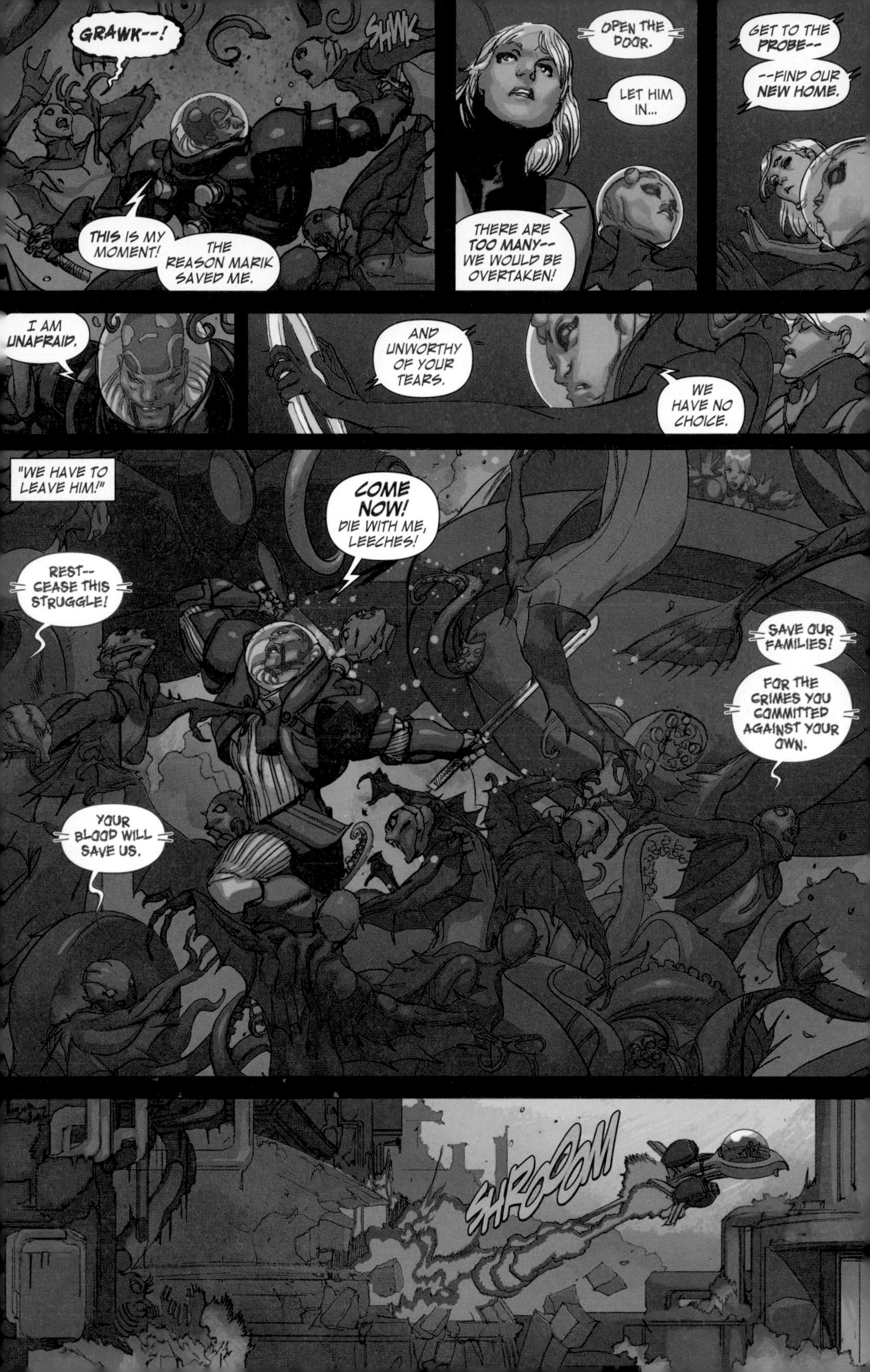
GRAWK--!
SHNK
THIS IS MY MOMENT!
THE REASON MARIK SAVED ME.
OPEN THE DOOR.
LET HIM IN...
THERE ARE TOO MANY-- WE WOULD BE OVERTAKEN!
GET TO THE PROBE--
--FIND OUR NEW HOME.
I AM UNAFRAID.
AND UNWORTHY OF YOUR TEARS.
WE HAVE NO CHOICE.
"WE HAVE TO LEAVE HIM!"
COME NOW! DIE WITH ME, LEECHES!
REST-- CEASE THIS STRUGGLE!
SAVE OUR FAMILIES!
FOR THE CRIMES YOU COMMITTED AGAINST YOUR OWN.
YOUR BLOOD WILL SAVE US.
SHROOOM

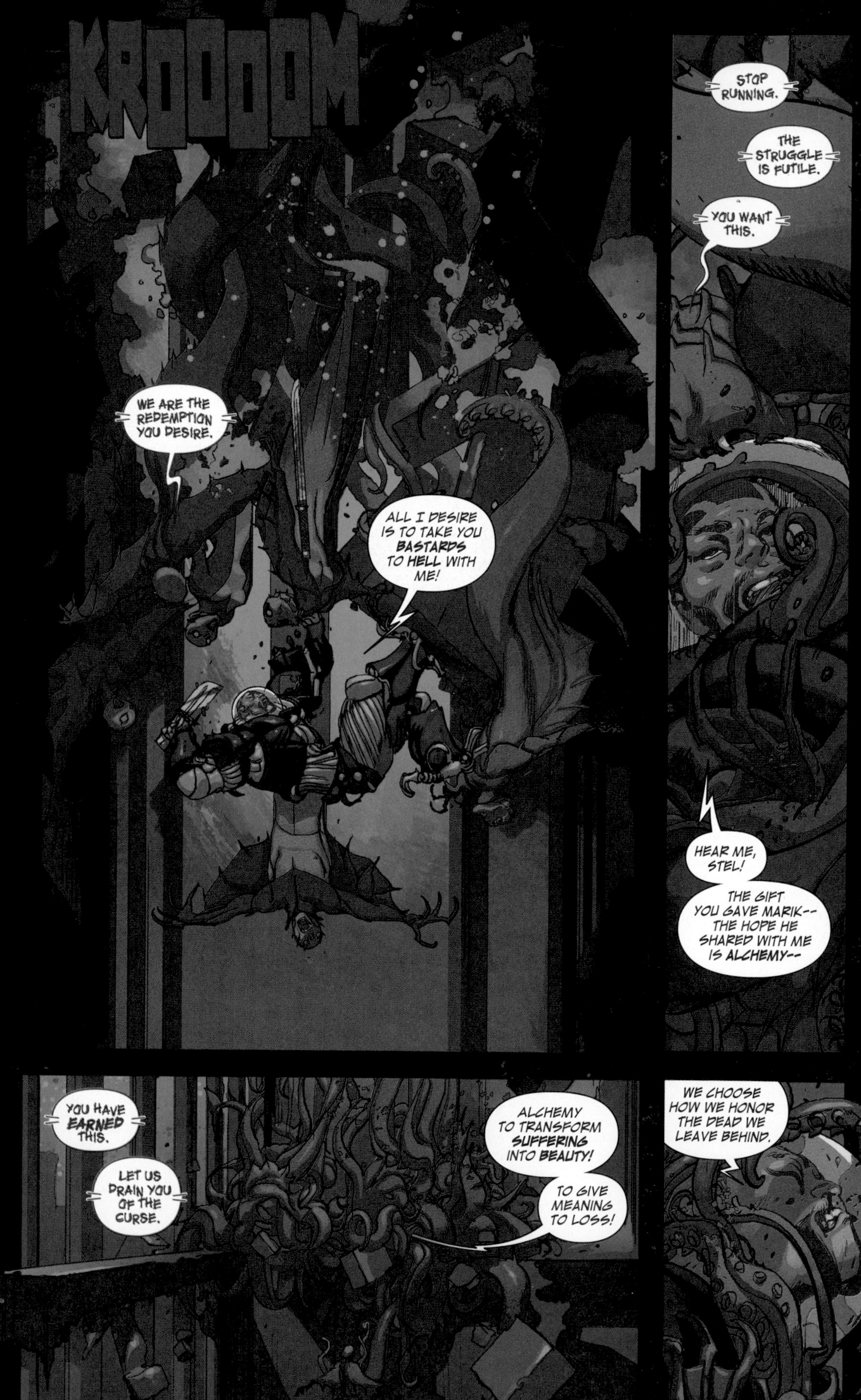
KROOOOM
WE ARE THE REDEMPTION YOU DESIRE.
ALL I DESIRE IS TO TAKE YOU BASTARDS TO HELL WITH ME!
STOP RUNNING.
THE STRUGGLE IS FUTILE.
YOU WANT THIS.
HEAR ME, STEL!
THE GIFT YOU GAVE MARIK-- THE HOPE HE SHARED WITH ME IS ALCHEMY--
YOU HAVE EARNED THIS.
LET US DRAIN YOU OF THE CURSE.
ALCHEMY TO TRANSFORM SUFFERING INTO BEAUTY!
TO GIVE MEANING TO LOSS!
WE CHOOSE HOW WE HONOR THE DEAD WE LEAVE BEHIND.

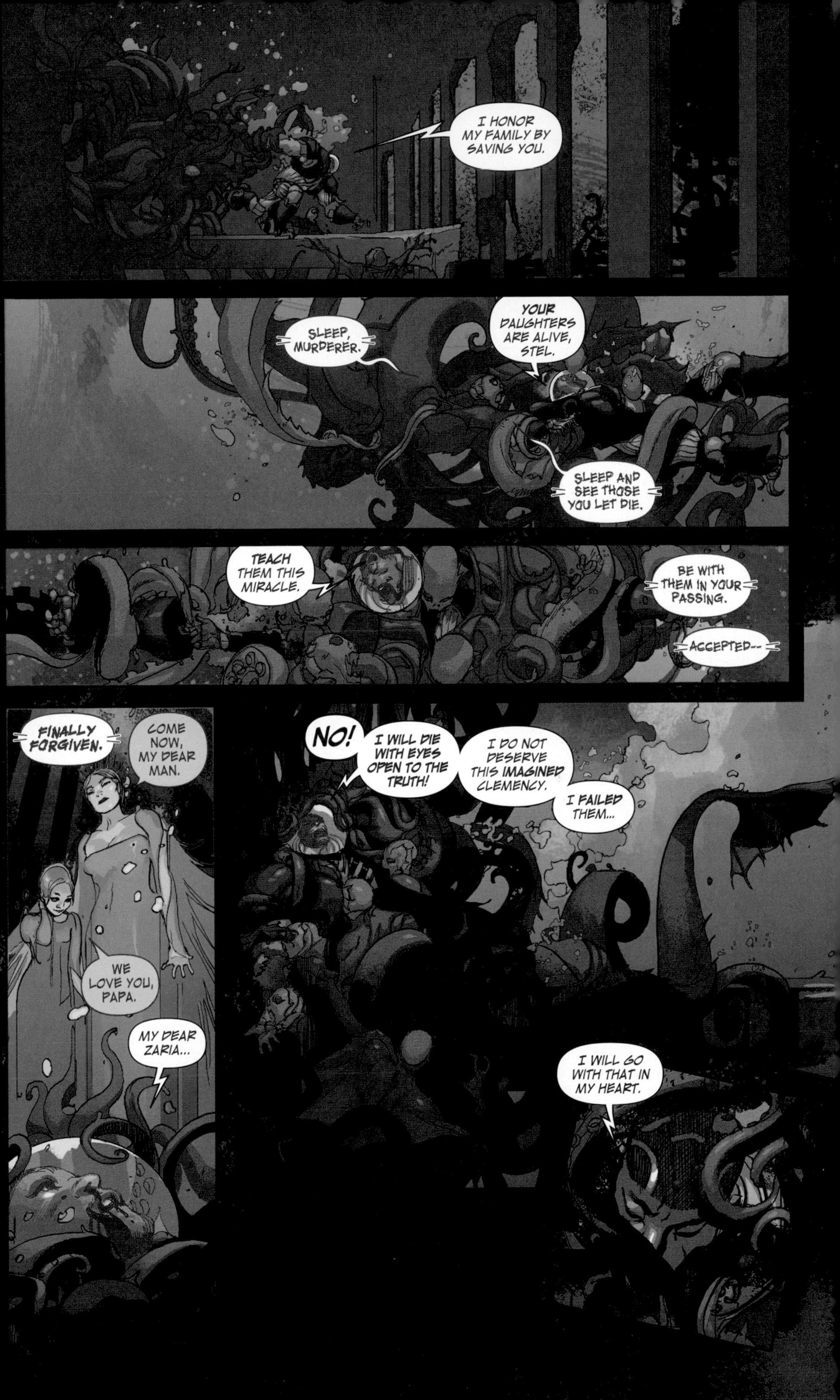
I HONOR MY FAMILY BY SAVING YOU.
SLEEP, MURDERER.
YOUR DAUGHTERS ARE ALIVE, STEL.
SLEEP AND SEE THOSE YOU LET DIE.
TEACH THEM THIS MIRACLE.
BE WITH THEM IN YOUR PASSING.
ACCEPTED--
FINALLY FORGIVEN.
COME NOW, MY DEAR MAN.
WE LOVE YOU, PAPA.
MY DEAR ZARIA...
NO!
I WILL DIE WITH EYES OPEN TO THE TRUTH!
I DO NOT DESERVE THIS IMAGINED CLEMENCY.
I FAILED THEM...
I WILL GO WITH THAT IN MY HEART.

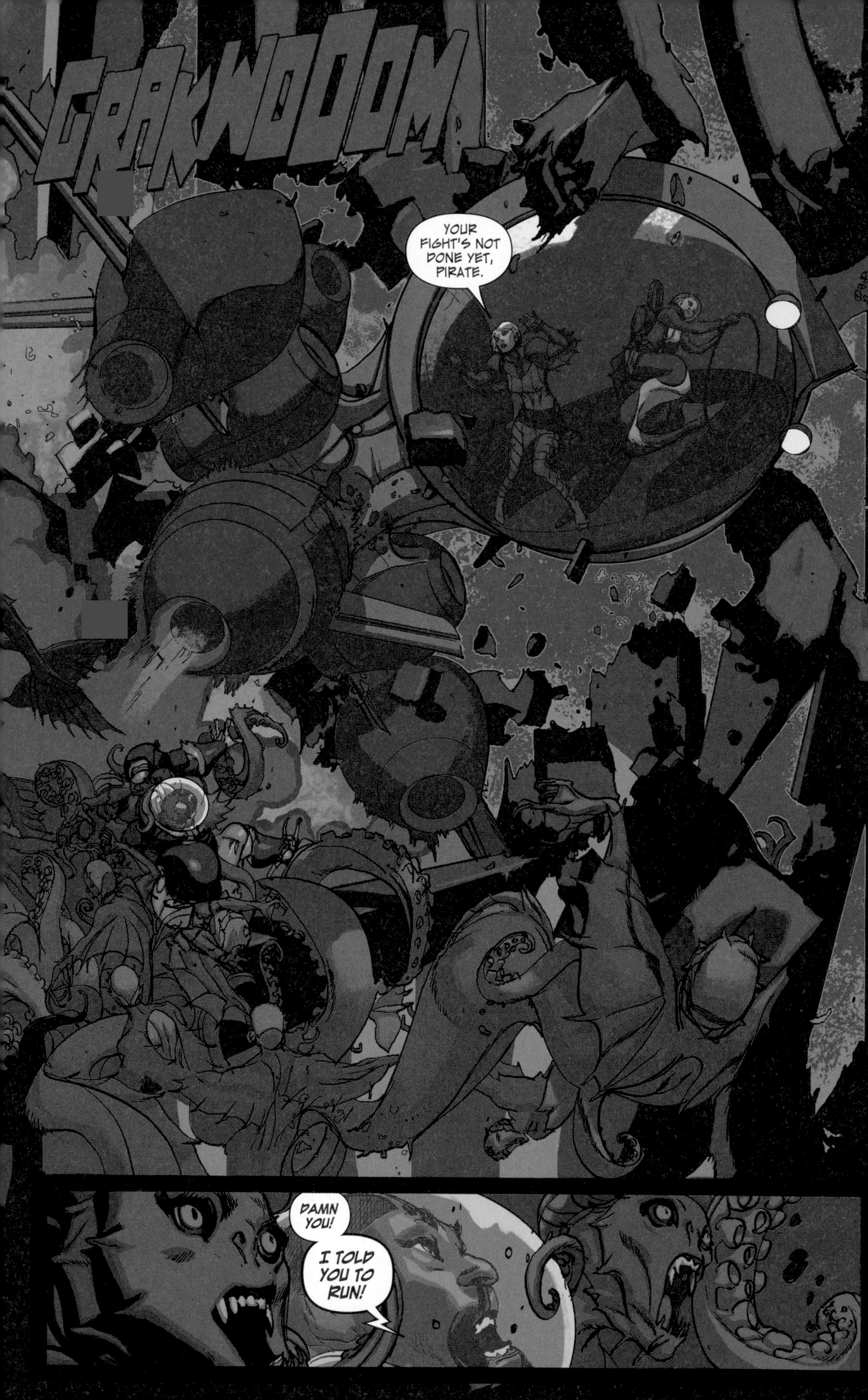
CRAKWOOOM
YOUR FIGHT'S NOT DONE YET, PIRATE.
DAMN YOU!
I TOLD YOU TO RUN!

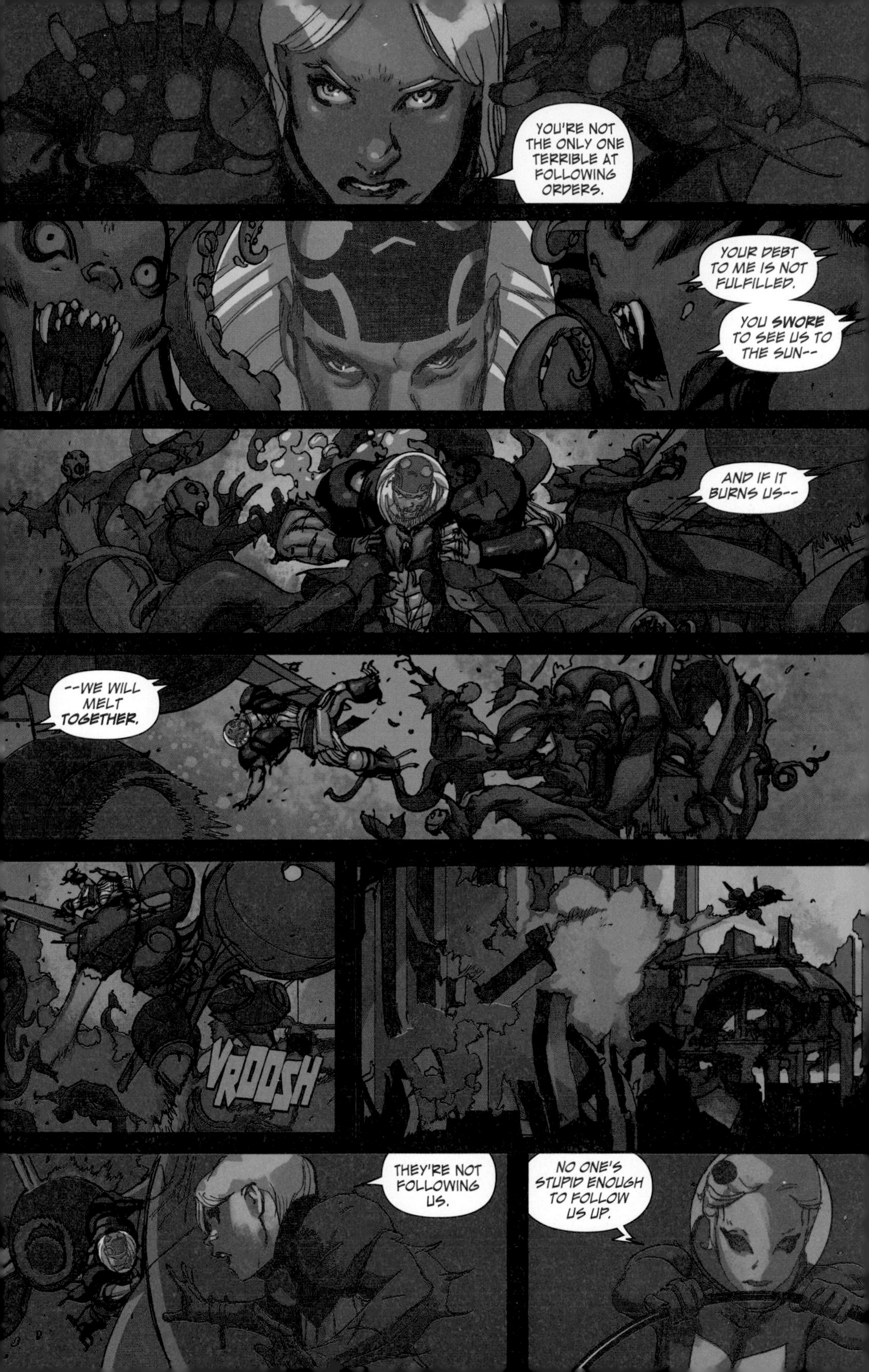
YOU'RE NOT THE ONLY ONE TERRIBLE AT FOLLOWING ORDERS.
YOUR DEBT TO ME IS NOT FULFILLED.
YOU SWORE TO SEE US TO THE SUN--
AND IF IT BURNS US--
--WE WILL MELT TOGETHER.
VROOSH
THEY'RE NOT FOLLOWING US.
NO ONE'S STUPID ENOUGH TO FOLLOW US UP.

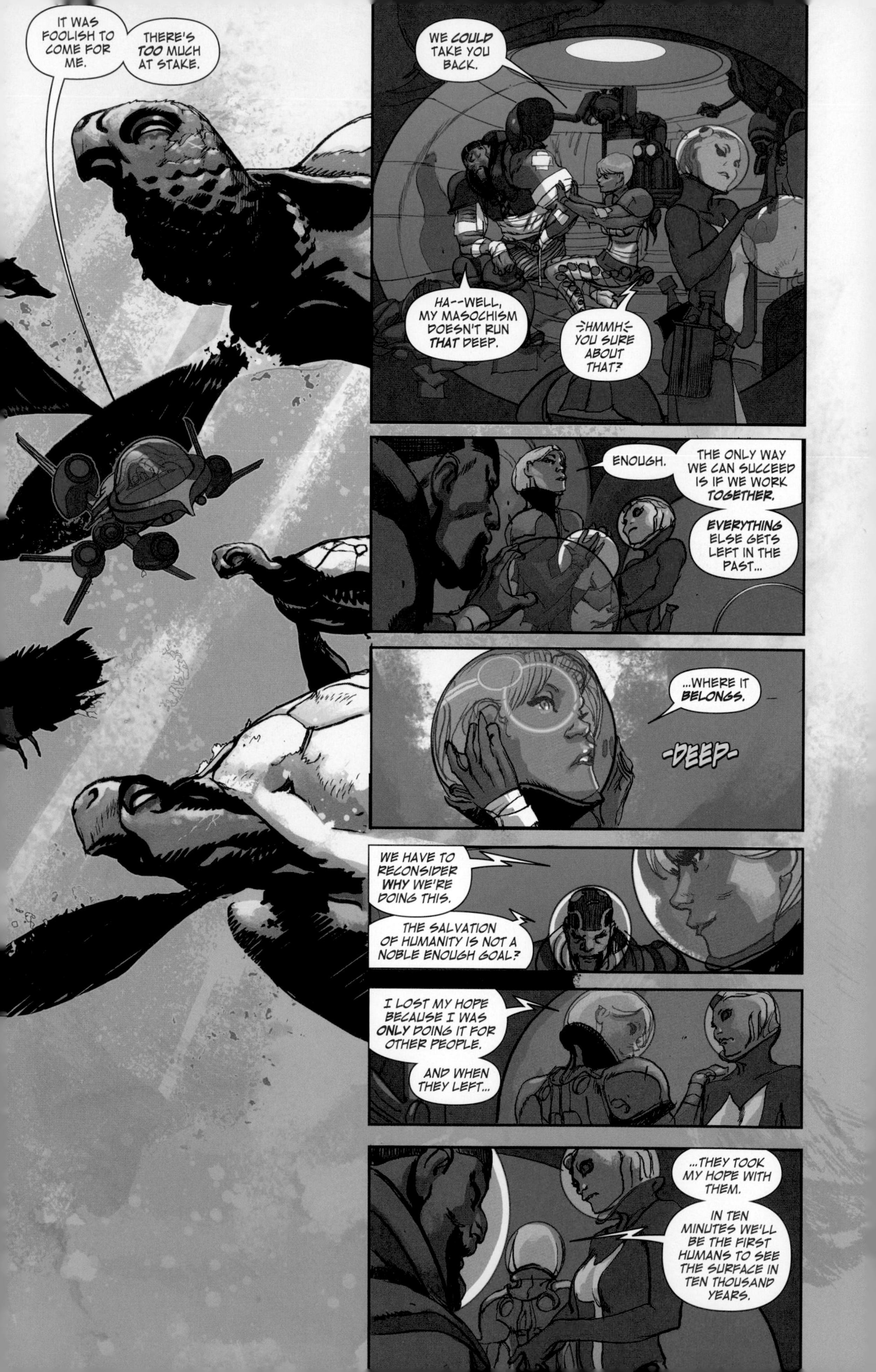

IT WAS FOOLISH TO COME FOR ME.
THERE'S TOO MUCH AT STAKE.
WE COULD TAKE YOU BACK.
HA--WELL, MY MASOCHISM DOESN'T RUN THAT DEEP.
-HMMH- YOU SURE ABOUT THAT?
ENOUGH.
THE ONLY WAY WE CAN SUCCEED IS IF WE WORK TOGETHER.
EVERYTHING ELSE GETS LEFT IN THE PAST...
...WHERE IT BELONGS.
-DEEP-
WE HAVE TO RECONSIDER WHY WE'RE DOING THIS.
THE SALVATION OF HUMANITY IS NOT A NOBLE ENOUGH GOAL?
I LOST MY HOPE BECAUSE I WAS ONLY DOING IT FOR OTHER PEOPLE.
AND WHEN THEY LEFT...
...THEY TOOK MY HOPE WITH THEM.
IN TEN MINUTES WE'LL BE THE FIRST HUMANS TO SEE THE SURFACE IN TEN THOUSAND YEARS.

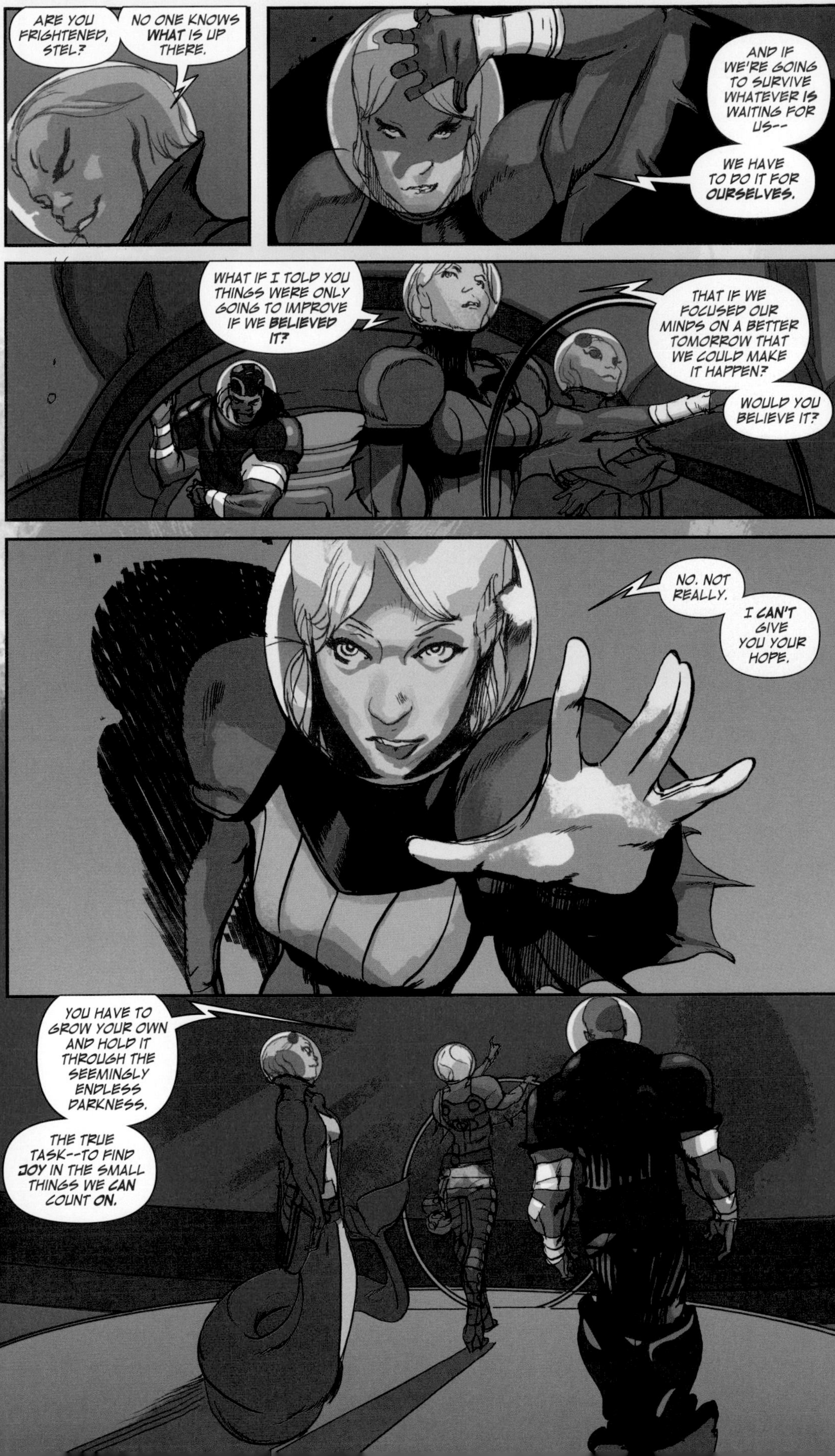
ARE YOU FRIGHTENED, STEL?
NO ONE KNOWS WHAT IS UP THERE.
AND IF WE'RE GOING TO SURVIVE WHATEVER IS WAITING FOR US--
WE HAVE TO DO IT FOR OURSELVES.
WHAT IF I TOLD YOU THINGS WERE ONLY GOING TO IMPROVE IF WE BELIEVED IT?
THAT IF WE FOCUSED OUR MINDS ON A BETTER TOMORROW THAT WE COULD MAKE IT HAPPEN?
WOULD YOU BELIEVE IT?
NO. NOT REALLY.
I CAN'T GIVE YOU YOUR HOPE.
YOU HAVE TO GROW YOUR OWN AND HOLD IT THROUGH THE SEEMINGLY ENDLESS DARKNESS.
THE TRUE TASK--TO FIND JOY IN THE SMALL THINGS WE CAN COUNT ON.

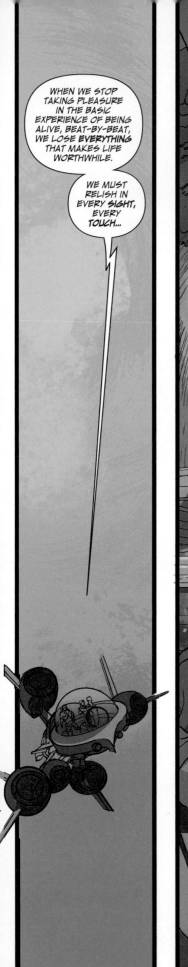

WHEN WE STOP TAKING PLEASURE IN THE BASIC EXPERIENCE OF BEING ALIVE, BEAT-BY-BEAT, WE LOSE *EVERYTHING* THAT MAKES LIFE WORTHWHILE.

WE MUST RELISH IN EVERY *SIGHT,* EVERY *TOUCH...*

"...EVERY *MEMORY.*"

"MY DAUGHTERS PLAYING IN THE GARDEN.

"JOHL KISSING MY NECK.

"MARIK'S ELATION AT A NEW INVENTION."

THESE MEMORIES ARE LUMINOUS ENOUGH TO LIGHT MY DARKEST HOUR.

TO FACE *WHATEVER* AWAITS US ABOVE.

WE ALL OF US CARRY BURDENS THAT SEEM TOO HEAVY...

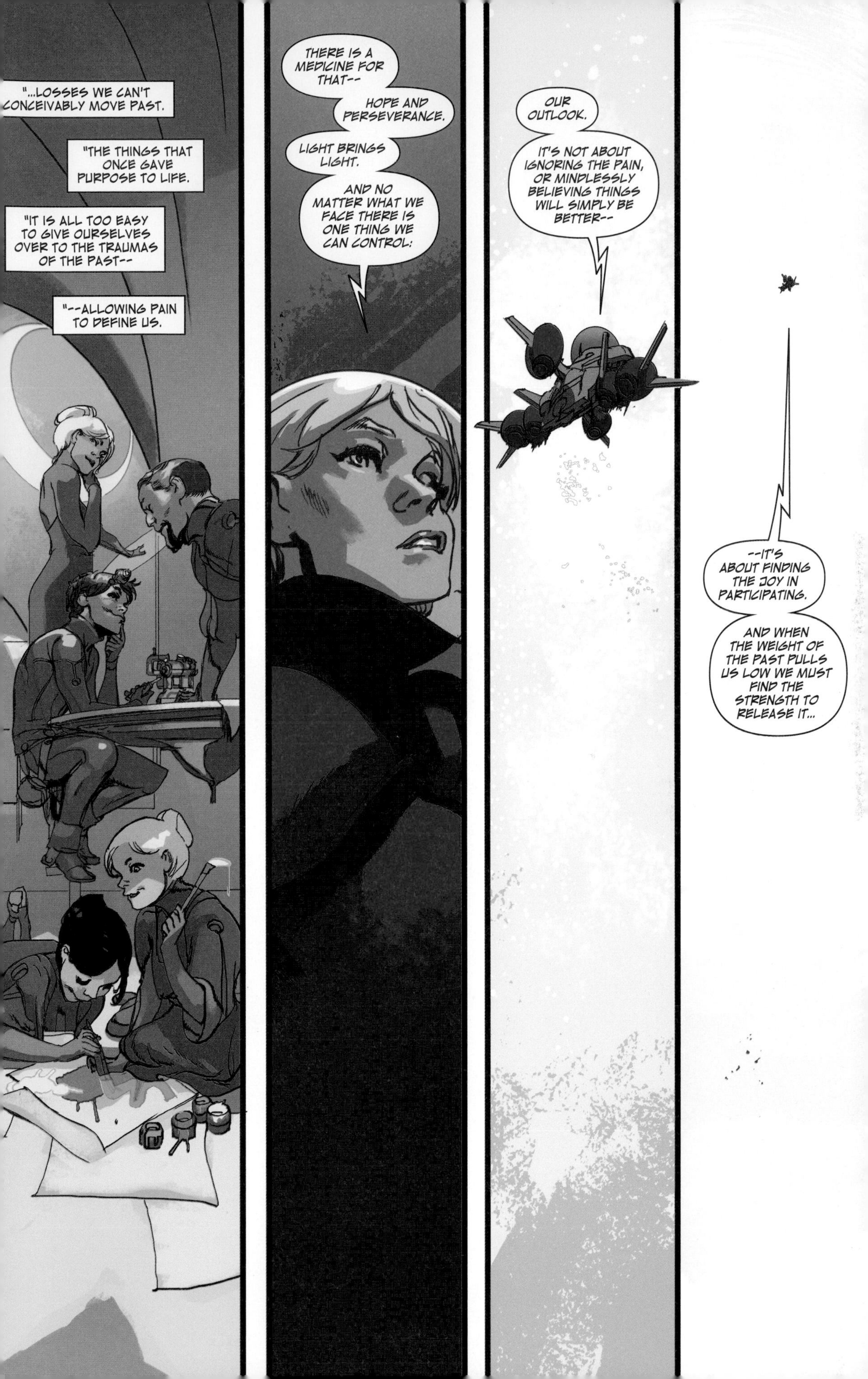
"...LOSSES WE CAN'T CONCEIVABLY MOVE PAST.
"THE THINGS THAT ONCE GAVE PURPOSE TO LIFE.
"IT IS ALL TOO EASY TO GIVE OURSELVES OVER TO THE TRAUMAS OF THE PAST--
"--ALLOWING PAIN TO DEFINE US.
THERE IS A MEDICINE FOR THAT--
HOPE AND PERSEVERANCE.
LIGHT BRINGS LIGHT.
AND NO MATTER WHAT WE FACE THERE IS ONE THING WE CAN CONTROL:
OUR OUTLOOK.
IT'S NOT ABOUT IGNORING THE PAIN, OR MINDLESSLY BELIEVING THINGS WILL SIMPLY BE BETTER--
--IT'S ABOUT FINDING THE JOY IN PARTICIPATING.
AND WHEN THE WEIGHT OF THE PAST PULLS US LOW WE MUST FIND THE STRENGTH TO RELEASE IT...

"...AND FINALLY GIVE
OURSELVES PERMISSION
TO START OVER."

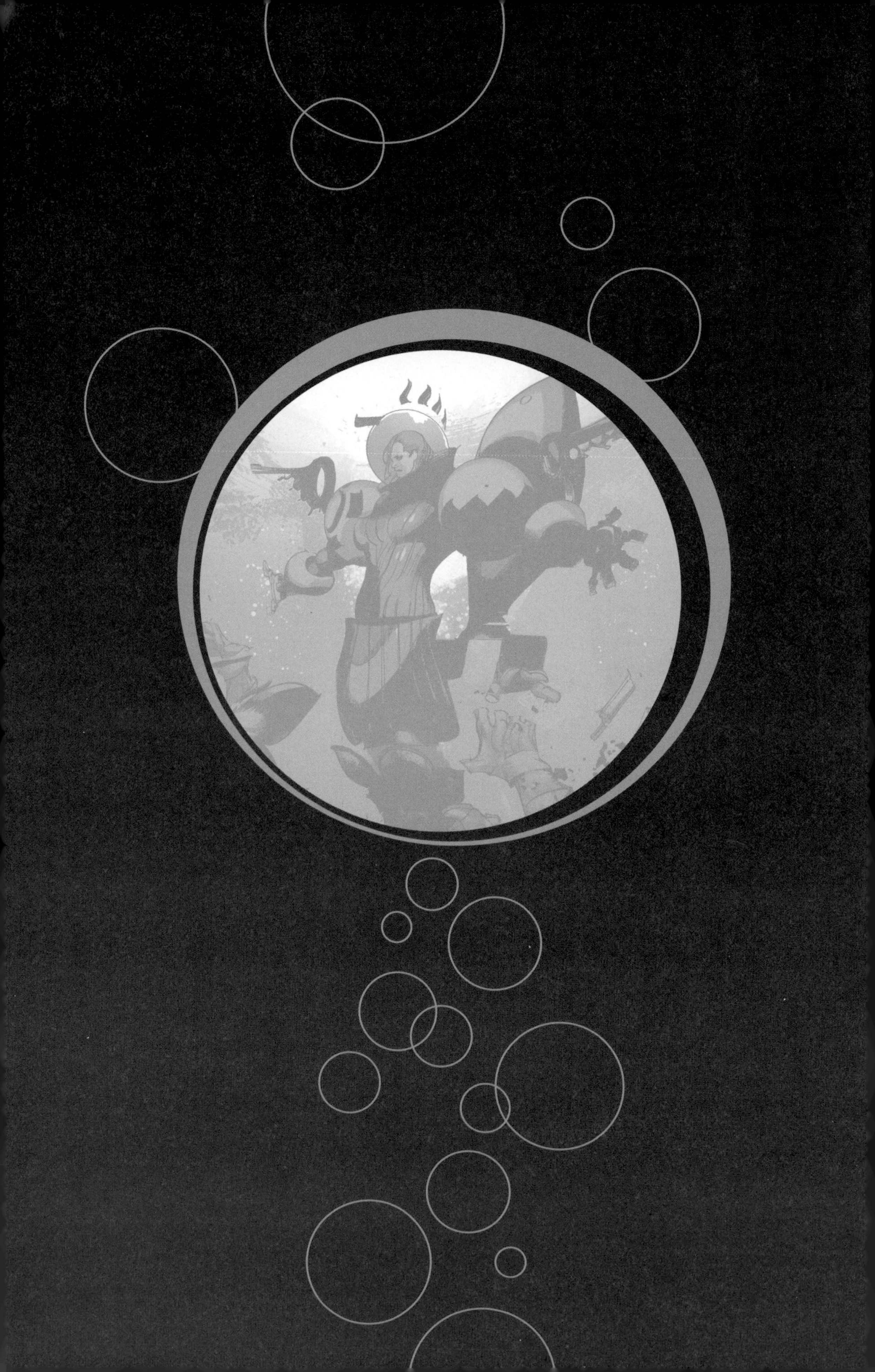

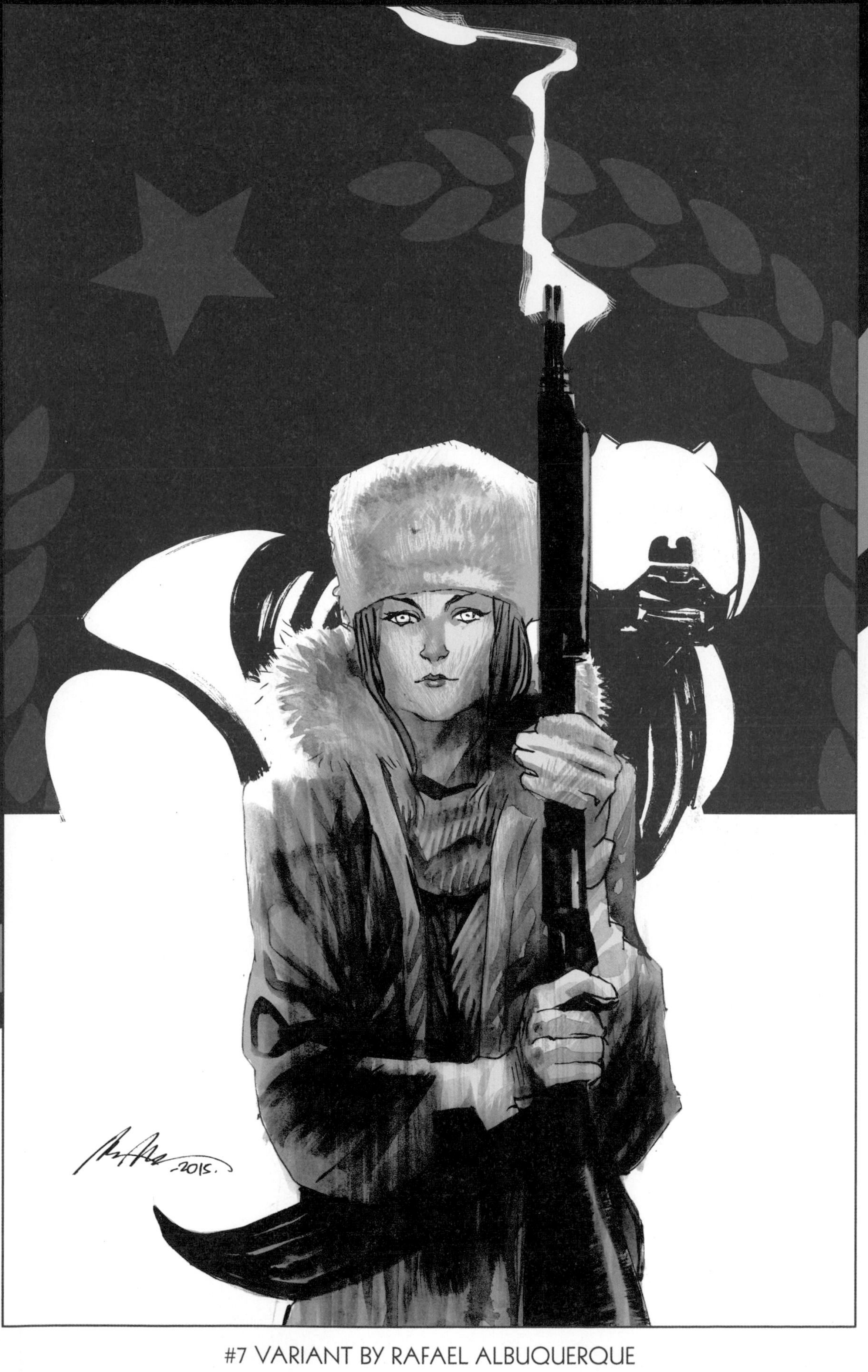
-2015.

#7 VARIANT BY RAFAEL ALBUQUERQUE

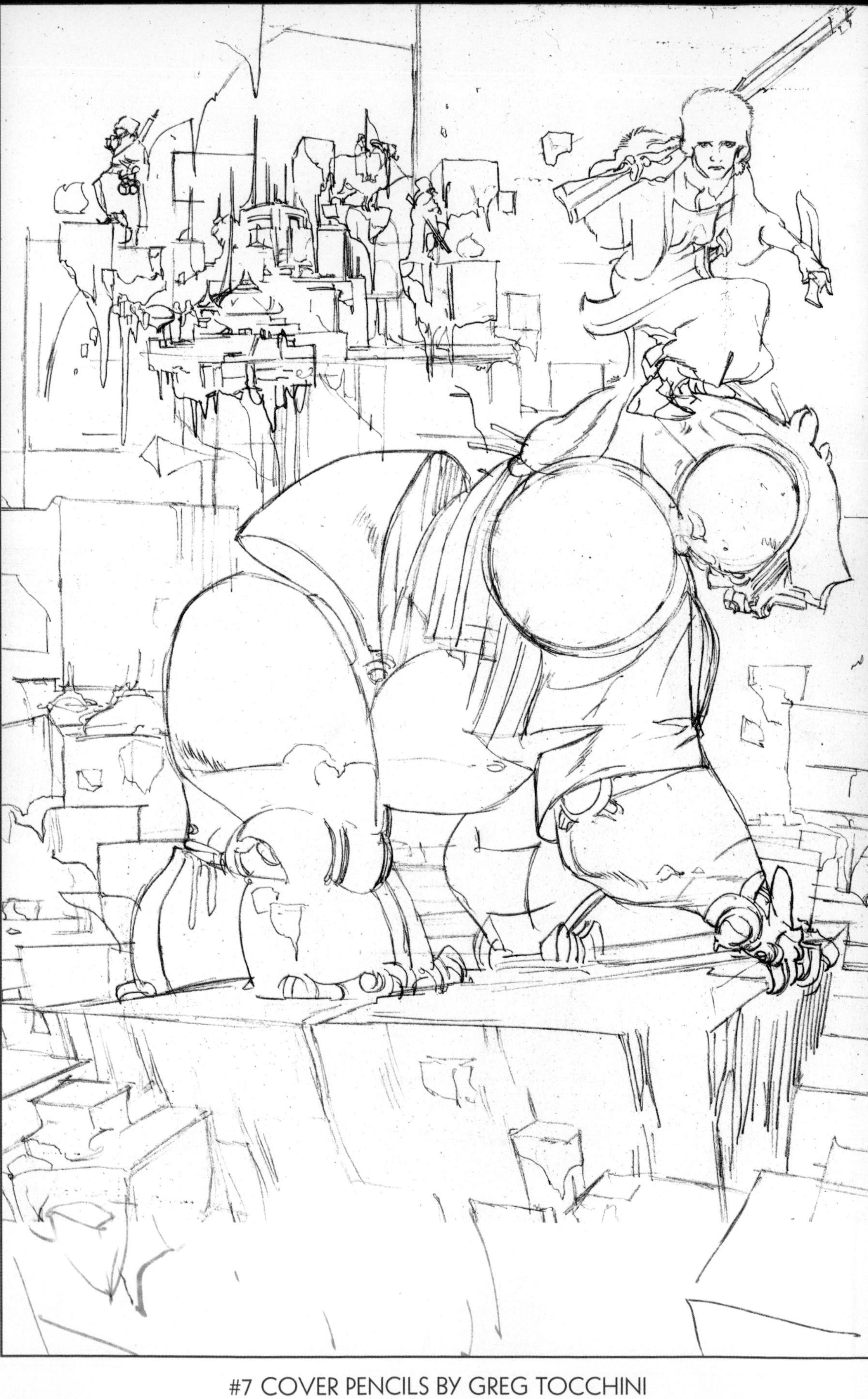

#7 COVER PENCILS BY GREG TOCCHINI

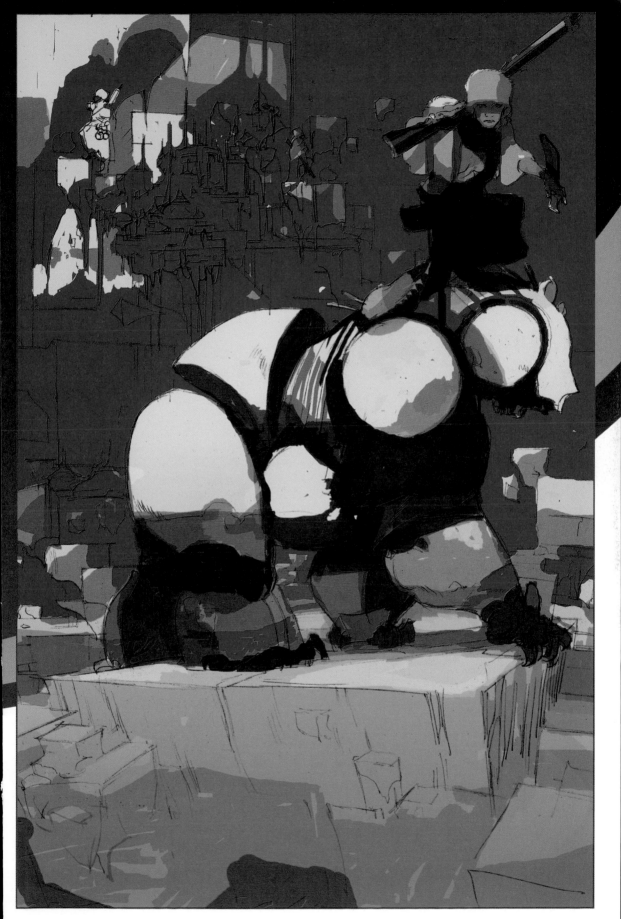

#7 COVER TEST COLORS BY GREG TOCCHINI

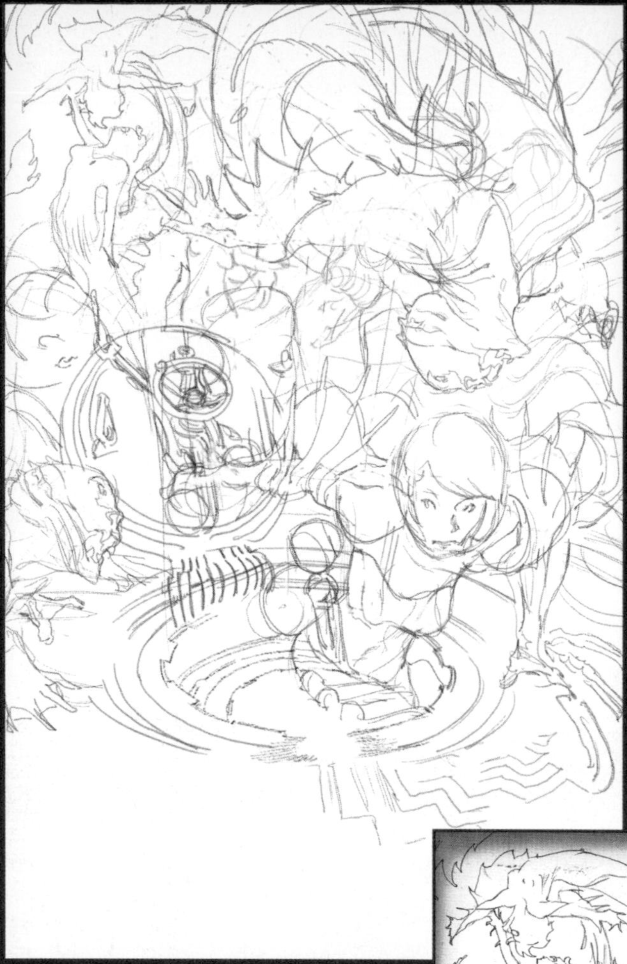

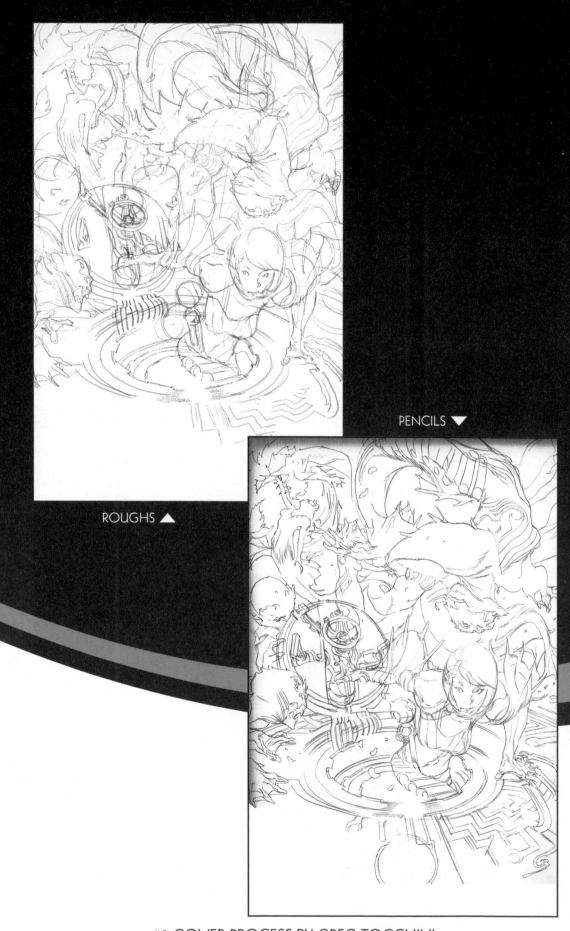

ROUGHS ▲

PENCILS ▼

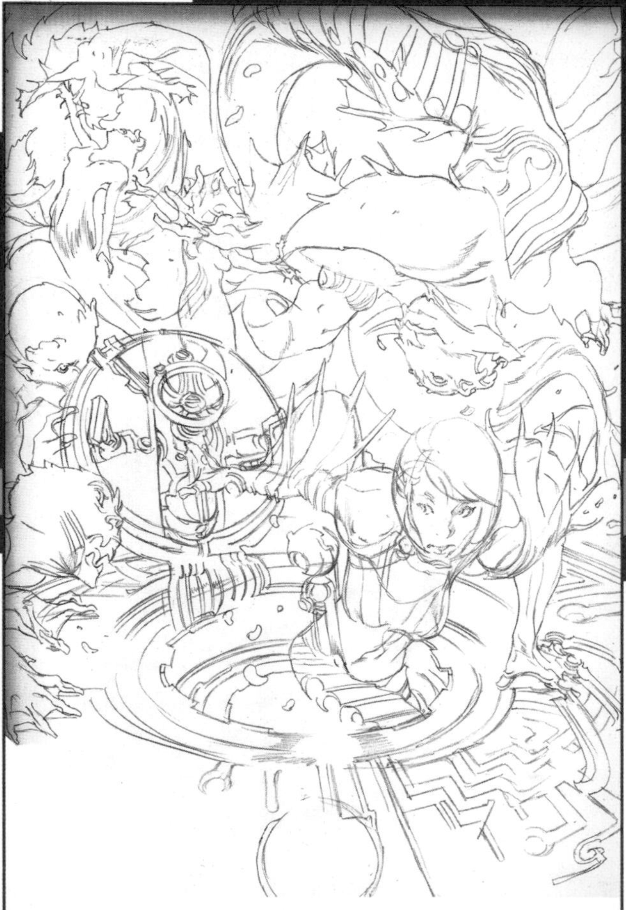

#8 COVER PROCESS BY GREG TOCCHINI

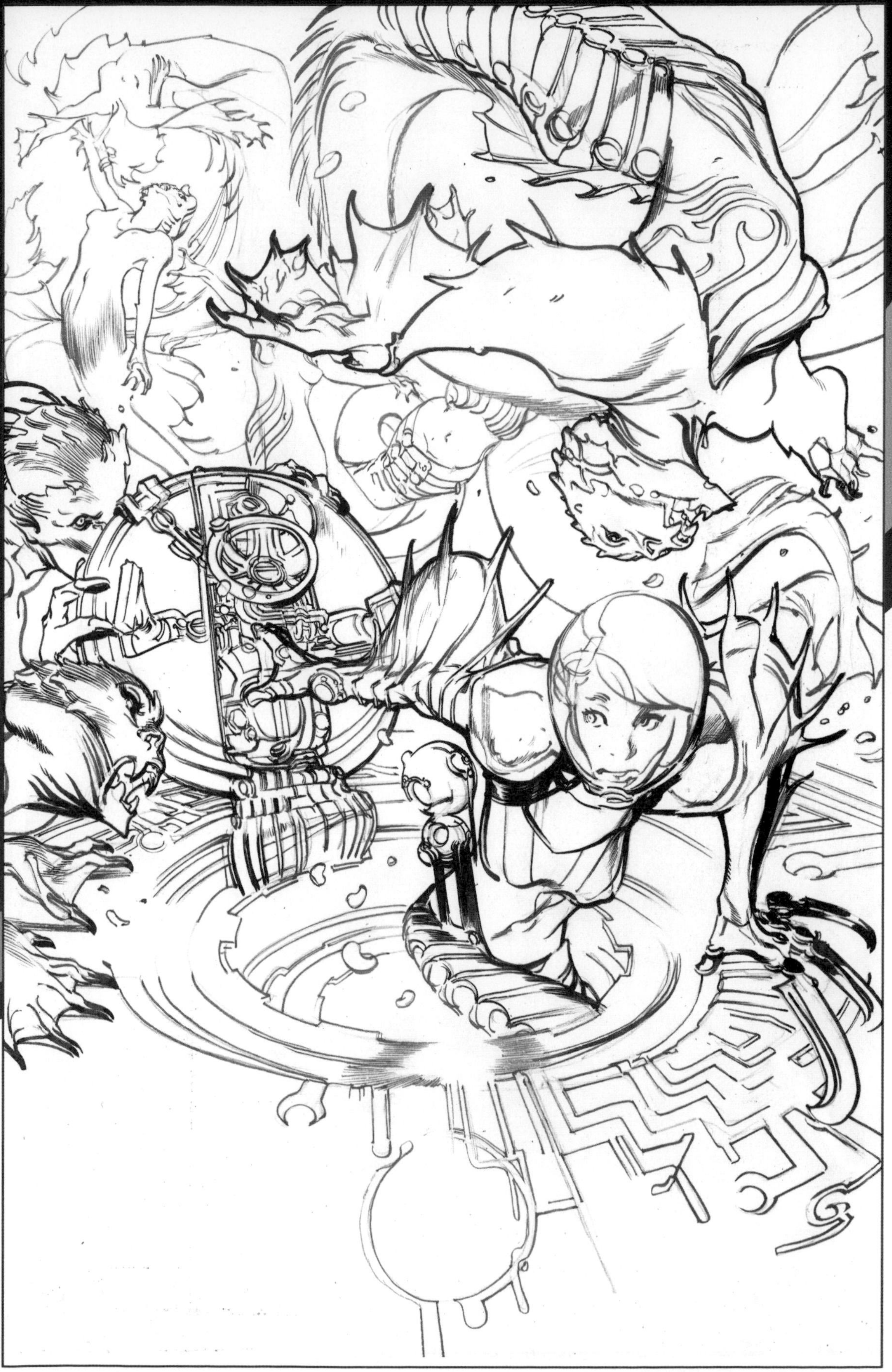

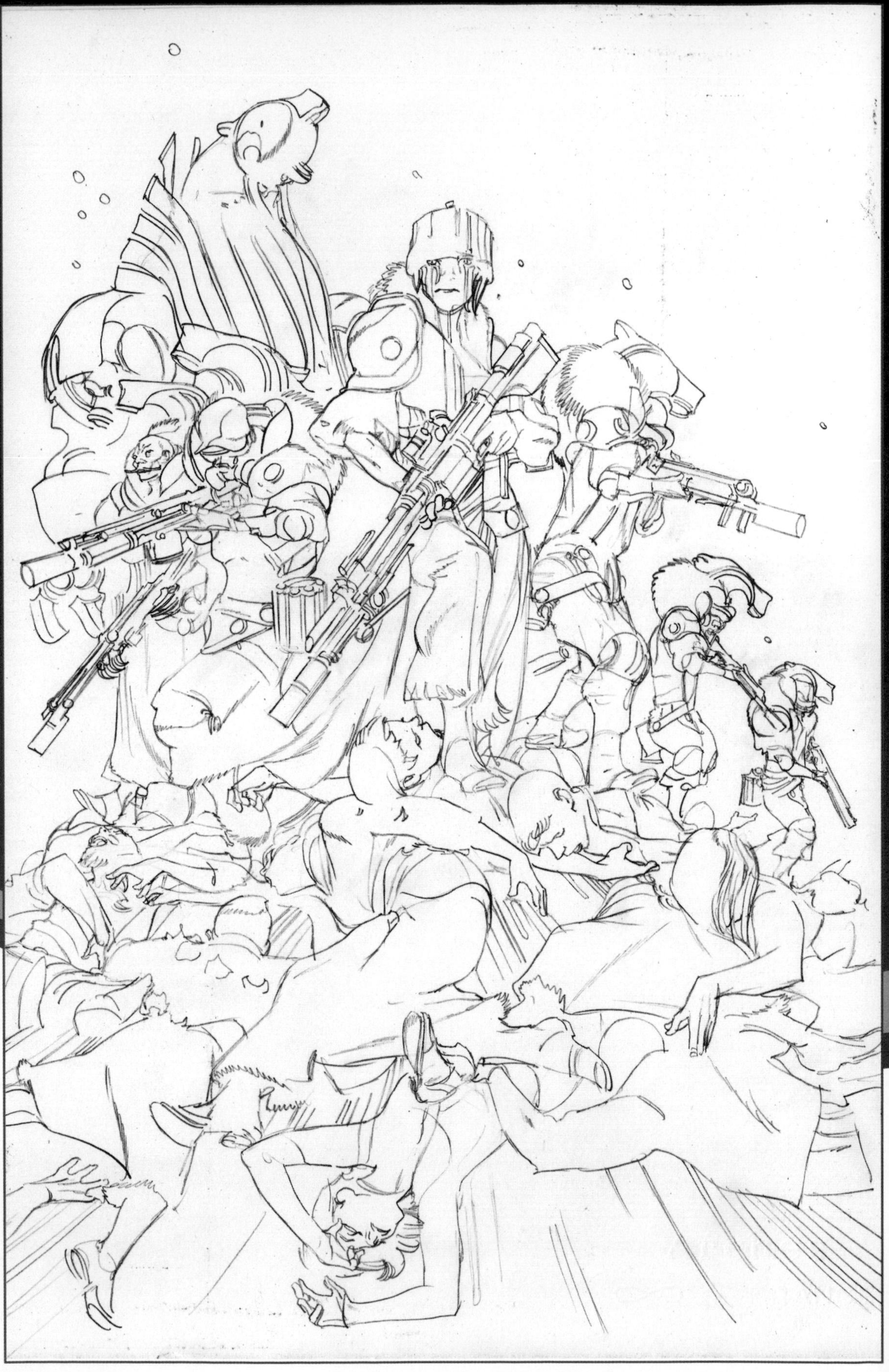

#9 COVER PENCILS BY GREG TOCCHINI

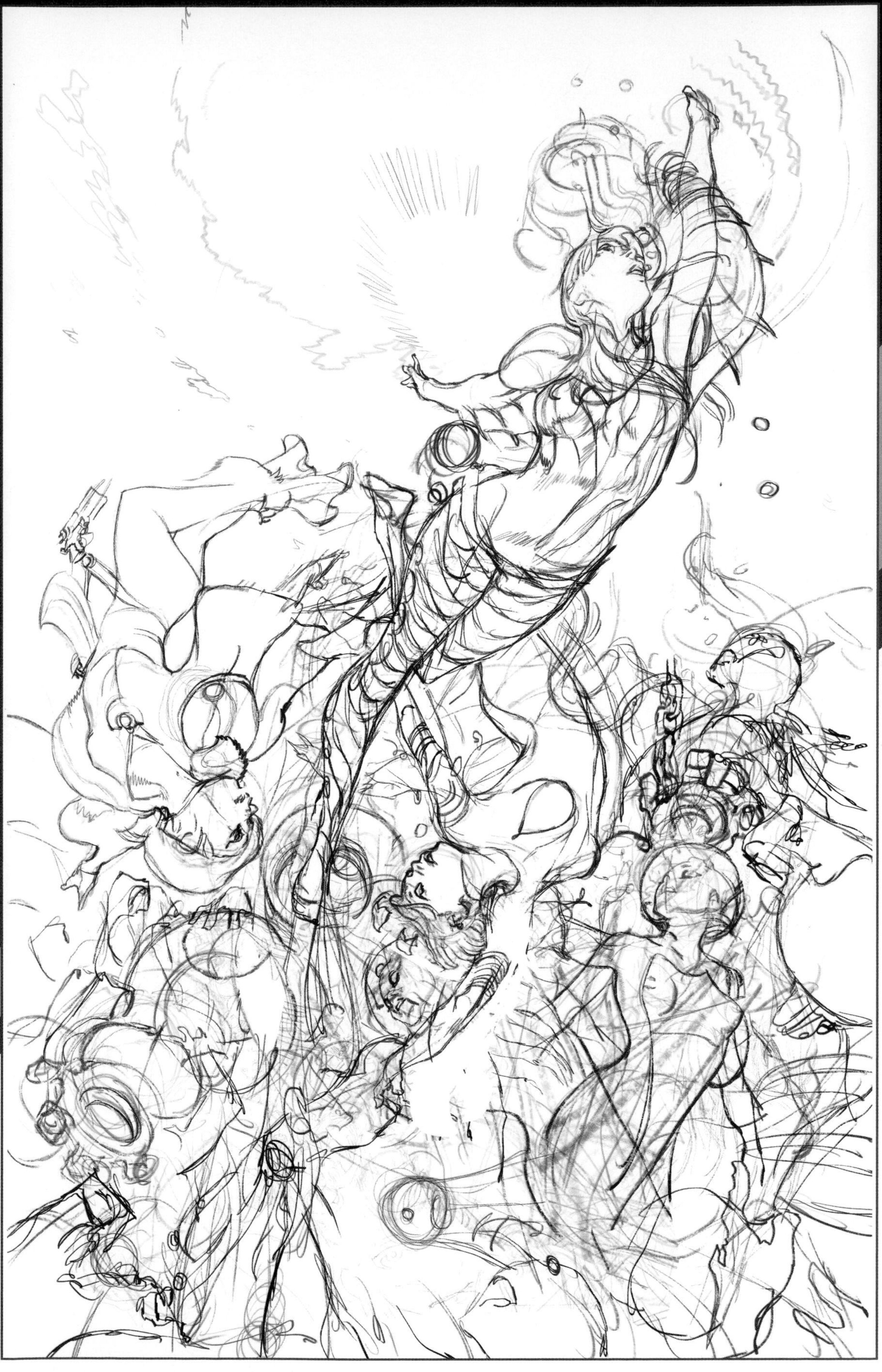

#10 COVER PENCILS BY GREG TOCCHINI